"King Moarte," Wolfsbane said, daughter in marriage to save l_____ _____, his, but really to save himself."

"Liar!" the black-haired mortal screamed through the bars where her wrists were bound on either side of her. "My father would *never* agree to such a deal. You're despicable, all of you vile, dead things!"

Her dark eyes shot a fiery malevolence towards Wolfsbane, and her teeth gnashed together twice as if she would bite through the wooden doweling and disembowel him. But Wolfsbane was not watching her. He, like everyone else in the room, was watching the King of the Vampirii.

Moarte rose dangerously slowly, like the predator he knew himself to be. A predator fixated on prey. His eyes were glued to the all-too-familiar face of the Sapiens Princess Valada.

Despite all the torture her father had ordered, *she* was the one who tried to murder Moarte. Ironically, her violence provided him with the intense motivation necessary to find a means to escape that realm and make his way home. It took nearly a moon's cycle to walk over the high mountain because he could not fly and his body was severely damaged. With little food but for the blood of the small earth-bound creatures he could catch, starvation kept him from recovering. He finally reached the vampirii stronghold near death, a state requiring many months to reverse.

And now, before him, was one of his two enemies; it was a dream come true.

Acknowledgments

The author wishes to thank early readers
Caro Soles and Sara Burrows
for their overwhelming encouragement.
Thanks to David Dodd for the cover concept
and to Istvan Kadar for the cover design.
She appreciates the feedback on the details of the various covers from:
M. Werier; E. Kauppinen; H. Leblanc; U. Sommerlad;
C. Soles; S. Burrows; S. Giron; E. Primack; K. Kamaras
Special thanks to Dave Wilson and his crew at
Crossroad Press for their faith in her work.

Macabre Ink is an imprint of Crossroad Press Publishing

First Edition

Revenge of the Vampir King

VOLUME 1 OF THE THRONES OF BLOOD

NANCY KILPATRICK

CHAPTER ONE

M oarte sat on the black marble throne impatiently watching the parade of his warriors as they entered the cavernous grey-stone throne room in sixes through the massive Oak doors. Directing this procession was Wolfsbane, his second-in-command. His most trusted warrior dressed like all the other tall and lean vampirii streaming in: sleeveless black metallic banded shirt and kilt, knee-high black leather boots laced through forty holes—battle gear. The vampirii style favored long hair pulled severely back on the head through a metal cone that contrasted in color to the hair, the strands dangling down the back like the tail of a horse. Even after nearly 200 years as King of the vampirii, Moarte still felt a welling of pride as he watched this assembly of his strongest and bravest.

On display was booty garnered from their raid on the Sapiens realm. There were ruby red, sapphire blue and aventurine green jewels of varying shapes and sizes; hammered copper and gold bracelets; luxurious black and white furs; multi-hued cloth woven to a fine, soft texture; delicately filigreed hardwood furniture inlaid with ivory and ebony; aromatic spices used by the slaves for cooking; small animals of every sort kept as pets... it went on and on, mostly useless items in Moarte's view, for what did his realm of Deathbringers need with such goods? His warriors, all of his subjects but for the slaves, they were vampirii, living on blood, and these items might be interesting entertainment now and again, but were completely unnecessary to existence. And secretly he thought luxuries encouraged weakness in those of his kind. Whether birthed as he had been—an exceptional event!—or turned as every other vampir in his realm, all were innately hunters, predators, and their skills relied on honing hungers to motivate them, not the acquisition of looted objects.

But there were many types of hunger and blood was but one of them.

Revenge was another, and Moarte was filled with that, a lust he had begun to hone half a year ago and that appetite proved to be an all-pervasive driving force.

"The land of the Sapiens is rich with goods," Wolfsbane noted. He was a handsome vampir, with wavy dark brown hair and penetrating eyes the color of jade. Strong. Powerful. And Moarte relied on him.

"We swarmed and ravaged the mortals as revenge for what they did to you, our King," Wolfsbane continued. "These are your prizes which we offer to you in adoration."

Moarte nodded, uncomfortable that his troops had been gone almost half a moon's cycle without him leading them. But he had been in no shape to return to the realm of the Sapiens after the physical, mental and emotional torture his enemies had inflicted upon him. His body had recovered sufficiently, and nearly so his mind, but he did not feel whole. A passion for vengeance sliced through him at the oddest moments, and he knew he had been changed forever by what he had endured as a prisoner.

He felt required by custom to accept the spoils of war from his faithful as an indirect revenge, but it rankled. He would have preferred to be in the forefront of battle, rending and tearing his enemy limb from limb, the Sapiens ruler at the top of his list.

The row upon row of items brought into his throne room were symbolic, he knew, which is why he let this lavish show proceed. His subjects needed to affirm in his presence that they had been victorious against the mortals, and they needed to see that their efforts pleased him. But *he* needed something more, and hoped this glut of goods would culminate in the knowledge he craved: that Wolfsbane had either secured the Sapiens King and brought him to the land of the vampirii, or had killed him. Moarte would prefer the former, of course—revenge is sweetest when executed directly—but he would settle for the demise of his enemy at the hand of another. Bringing down the Sapiens King from the far side of the mountains would ensure peace and stability and danger-free hunting, at least for a time, and he wanted that for his Kingdom. He owed it to his subjects.

Incense, flora, leather, some exotic blue and green birds that he had never seen… It was an endless parade, including captive Sapiens by the dozen, male and female, all young enough to be pleasing to look at, but he knew that most of his followers were not examining their faces and bodies but rather smelling the blood coursing beneath skin slick with acidic sweat produced by terror.

"I selected only the strongest, my lord, as I knew you would prefer. You have often said: There is no point in taking the weak. Their blood is thin and prone to disease and that does not satisfy."

"I've said many things, my most trusted warrior, and you have a good memory," Moarte said, his features unable, like all vampirii, to reflect the smile he felt. "If I had not known you for centuries, I would accuse you of flattering me unduly with some hidden agenda."

"I am not my sister!" Wolfsbane said with a touch of annoyance in his voice, referring to Hemlock, his twin, who, on more than one occasion had tried to charm Moarte in order to be granted power. Hemlock would have liked nothing better than to be chosen by Moarte as his mate. Fortunately, as King by birth and not by transformation, Moarte had inherited a type of rational second sight from his blonde haired, blue-eyed mother Belladonna, and a searing intellect and physical strength from his late father, Morpheus, who had platinum hair and paler eyes. They bestowed fortitude and attractiveness as well and Moarte, even had he not been King, would have had his pick of females. Hemlock had not gotten far with such duplicitous endeavors. When, or *if*, he ever mated— and with the passing of time, that seemed improbable to him—, it would be with a guileless female; he possessed enough guile in his character for two beings.

"And where is Hemlock?" Moarte inquired, realizing he had not seen her in some time and she was not in the throng of warriors crowding the hall. "Did she venture on the hunt with you?"

"No, she did not. Her battle skills are not lacking but I felt we did not require her presence in this campaign. I suspect she has retreated to her chamber in a prolonged pout."

Moarte felt some amusement at this. It was well known that Wolfsbane and Hemlock were adversaries in many ways and that given his position as second in command of vampir warriors, Wolfsbane frequently deprived his sister of positions she would otherwise have automatically assumed. Partly this was out of spite, Moarte suspected, but also out of expediency. Hemlock was unpredictable and not given to following orders, dangerous traits in battle.

Larger animals were brought into the hall, their strong odor annoying to the vampir olfactory, and Moarte said tensely, "Wolfsbane, when may I expect this exhibition to end? I have more pressing matters to attend to than watching my subjects entertain themselves with these dubious treasures."

"Calmness, my son," Belladonna, seated to his right, said. "Your warriors need to see your enthusiasm. It's part of the vanquishing of a long-time enemy."

"I have not vanquished him yet, Mother, unless Wolfsbane knows more than he is saying about the raid. Is the Sapiens King Zador part of this circus?"

The question was directed to Wolfsbane, who answered truthfully, as always, because he knew Moarte could read him very well and there was no use in avoidance. "No, my King, he is not."

"Then you did not find him in the city."

Wolfsbane hesitated. "We did find him."

"And?"

"He managed to elude us. He distracted us and must have escaped through a secret passageway into the mountain's haunted caves."

Moarte felt the small amount of blood in his veins heat to boiling. They had lost him! The one who had tortured Moarte for weeks. The entire raid was a waste! He *knew* he should have led the hunt! He should not have remained behind, broken though he was. If he had gone, and waited until he was strong again, the Sapiens King would not have evaded his fate. The mortal's blood would now be swelling Moarte's veins and his head would be staked and hanging from the highest tower, a trophy of war, a final victory over the persecutors of the vampirii. His soul would be—

"But King Moarte, I have brought you something almost as good."

Moarte wondered what that could be, since nothing would equate with the capture of the Sapiens' King. He waited. And then his eyes fell upon the last item that was being brought into the throne room—a large cage covered by purple velvet, carried on horizontal poles on the shoulders of four of his sturdiest bloodsuckers.

"What is this? Another animal?" he snapped, his tone a warning that everyone in the room understood and, because of the danger inherent in their King's temper, fell silent.

"This is a gift to you from the Sapiens King. One he offered as a token of his desire for peace. It was during this exchange that he vanished, which I deeply regret. My King, it was my fault entirely, and I throw myself upon your mercy now."

Wolfsbane knelt before Moarte, head back, exposing his throat for the fangs.

Aggravated, Moarte snapped, "Stand!" and waved a hand dismissively, indicating that he had no intention of punishing Wolfsbane. Wolfsbane was an excellent warrior, a friend even, one of the few Moarte trusted implicitly. And in a way he was glad the Zador had escaped. It meant he still lived and that would allow Moarte to hunt down his enemy himself, and that thought gave him no small amount of pleasure.

The warriors parted to let the bearers bring the cage—tall enough to house a newborn giraffe—almost to the bottom of the three grey-marble steps that led to the throne. At Wolfsbane's order, they lowered it onto the slate floor.

"You say this is an offering?" Belladonna asked. As the former Queen of the realm, she held a place of honor by Moarte's side. Upon the death of her husband Morpheus, Moarte's father, she assumed the reign, but only for a short time before relinquishing her right to rule, clearing the throne for her son, the only known half breed, born when she was still Sapiens. At times, though, she did not remember that she no longer held real power.

"Yes, Dowager," Wolfsbane said. "The Sapiens King offered this to effect a truce. We did, of course, not agree to a truce, but as I mentioned, the offer left us startled and confused and this afforded the Sapiens ruler a means of escape, which we now see as having been planned."

"Indeed. A rather poor excuse for your error in judgment. Or was it simply incompetence?" Belladonna said.

Wolfsbane bowed in her direction. If she were still in charge and he had bared his neck, her teeth would have been in his jugular by now, and he knew it.

Moarte said, "Mistakes occur, Mother. I have made them myself, as you well know. As have you."

She nodded slightly and surreptitiously brushed her son's bare arm to validate his remark, careful not to let the vampirii see this intimate motherly act.

Moarte did not acknowledge this touch of flesh as cold as his own. Instead, he said, "Alright, Wolfsbane, you have whetted my curiosity, and I wish to see an end to this pageantry. What is this wondrous gift the Sapiens' King sent my way to make up for a month of torture in his dungeon?"

Wolfsbane inclined his head slightly towards Moarte and then walked to the cage. Quickly he pulled back the purple fabric and as it lifted, wooden bars were revealed, like a prison holding something feral. What came into view *was* feral. The silence in the cavernous hall echoed like a piercing shriek.

Moarte stared, struck dumb, unable to believe what he was seeing.

"My lord, the Sapiens King offered you his daughter in marriage, to save his Kingdom, to bind our realm to his, but really to save himself."

"Liar!" the black-haired mortal screamed through the bars where her wrists were bound on either side of her. "My father would *never* agree to such a deal. You're despicable, all of you vile, dead things!" Her slim, tense body was clothed from the top of her neck to her ankles in a crimson dress of silk. Her dark eyes shot a fiery malevolence towards Wolfsbane, and her teeth gnashed together twice as if she would bite through the wooden doweling and disembowel him. But Wolfsbane was not watching her. He, like everyone else in the room, was watching Moarte.

Moarte rose dangerously slowly, like the predator he knew himself to be. A predator fixated on prey. His mother attempted to secretly touch his arm again, to temper him, but he ignored her. His eyes were glued to the girl, the Sapiens Princess Valada, only child of the Sapiens King. And Moarte's newest enemy.

Despite all that the Sapiens King had ordered done to him by his chief torturer, *she* was the one who had tried to maim him which, ironically, provided him with the intense motivation necessary to find a means to escape that realm and make his way home. It took nearly a full moon's cycle to walk over the high mountain because he could not fly and his body was so damaged. There was almost no food but for the blood of the small earth-bound creatures he could catch; starvation kept him from recovering. He finally reached the vampirii stronghold barely alive, a state that required many more months for convalescence.

And now, before him, was one of his two tormentors; it was a dream come true.

His movement had brought the girl's attention his way. He remembered her clearly, very clearly, and knew she remembered him—how could she not? She had whipped him often enough, as had the other in the Sapiens King's dungeon, but it had been her hand which snapped the fine bones in his wings so that he could not escape through flight. Despite the vampirii ability to heal rapidly, some injuries were fatal and others nearly so and took much time to heal, if ever they *did* fully heal. The broken wing bones had required nearly one month to knit together, partially because of his enfeebled state and partially because they had melded wrong and, when he reached home, had to be re-broken, which only added to the excruciating pain.

His mother's ministrations with the salves and drugs made of herbs she had learned to recognize as a girl when she was still mortal helped. But much of the healing time involved him lying in agony, drinking as much blood as he could keep down, building his strength back one night at a time by sheer will, as the bones slowly wove together properly. And all the while he nurtured a white-hot hatred for this girl as the scalding desire for revenge festered within him. It was Wolfsbane who could not bear his suffering and insisted that Moarte allow the warriors to attack the Sapiens city and hunt down their King.

Moarte moved slowly down the three steps, his body tense, never taking his eyes off her. She was proud and haughty still, not accepting that she was a prisoner, and one given freely to him by her treacherous father.

"Bloodsucker!" she snarled as he neared the cage, her dark eyes flashing hatred and defiance, and she spit at him. He paced slowly in front of her in one direction, then the other, many times, back and forth, silent. His fangs extended, his eyes which he knew had turned the color of blood, radiating fury, never leaving her face, her eyes following him, the tension palatable to all in the throne room.

"I should have torn them off!" the girl shrieked loudly in the quiet hall, referring to his wings.

He stopped before her and stared down at the Sapiens Princess with hair and eyes the color of a raven's feathers and skin nearly as pale as his own. The blood-red dress, the black hair and eyes, all of it made for a startling contrast with her calcimine flesh and she looked like a corpse to him, one more than twenty but not yet thirty of the Sapiens years. It was rumored by the slaves that she was truly her father's daughter, his only offspring, who he may or may not have been grooming to inherit his throne. Rumor also had it that his new young wife had conceived with the hope of a boy, but may have died in childbirth, the life in her womb dying with her. Wolfsbane would unearth the facts in detail from the newest Sapiens slaves he had brought back with him.

It was said this girl Valada was still a virgin, refusing to marry, and only in that regard going against her father's wishes. The father, no doubt, wanted a grandson to hand his crown to, since the Sapiens preferred male rulers. It was known that otherwise she was devoted to him, wholeheartedly so, even when his subjects were not so enamored of their treacherous, brutal ruler.

But her blindness to the reality of the Sapiens King's cruelty did not alter Moarte's feelings towards her. His rage was so close to erupting that he felt on the verge of cracking the bars and snapping her head off her shoulders, gorging on her blood. He had enough control at his disposal to realize that such an action would give him immense pleasure, but only momentarily. The calculating reason that his father bequeathed him kicked in; if he was smart, he would use her in a way that would lead him directly to the Sapiens King. And then he could destroy both father and daughter at the same time.

His voice hummed perilously low, the result of holding himself in check. "Take the cage to my chamber!"

Moarte was excited, rattled, brimming with violence and anger, logic in shockingly short supply. He would need time to summon thought to aid him. This was a rare opportunity. He had at hand one of his two enemies, the one he had spent months dreaming about, his fantasies of exacting revenge for her cruel and callous act towards him delicious and all-consuming. And she had been delivered into his hands by her own father! This was a precious gift that he must use carefully. Yes, it required much thought.

"You did well, Wolfsbane," he said, his voice still low, betraying the control he fought hard to retain.

As if coming out of a trance he woke to the hall and knew that direction was expected of him. "Secure one quarter of the riches for the crown, and half that again for yourself. The rest is to be divided between the warriors, starting with these," he said, his hand sweeping across the front line, indicating the males and females who were the oldest and strongest, his premier warriors who made up the bulk of his war council and had proven their bravery and loyalty time and time again. "They will choose first, then the rest."

Wolfsbane knelt, as did the first line of warriors, and behind them the others fell to their knees as one body, throats exposed before their ruler as a sign of deference.

Moarte stalked out of the throne room through the side exit, the heat within him rising again to match the emotional fury he could no longer keep at bay. He needed time in solitude and headed for the locked gardens at the back of the fortress, his private world where none, not even his mother, were permitted to enter; he would meditate on this 'gift' and what he could do with it and he would not be disturbed as he entertained strategies. But the thinking part of him was nearly obliterated by emotions and if the Sapiens King had been killed in the raid, Moarte knew he would have torn the girl limb from limb quickly, publically, glutting himself on her blood, just for the sheer pleasure of it. And that image brought a smile to his lips. He could always do that once her father had been killed. And would.

CHAPTER TWO

Valada, encaged, had been transported to the private chamber of the King of the vampirii and there she waited, knowing that whatever he did to her, it would be brutal. The Bloodsuckers were cruel, violent, and liars—her father had proclaimed that often enough, and every Sapiens knew it. If these undead things thought they could somehow wear her down by saying her father handed her over to them like some prize so that he could escape…! No, that was something she would *never* believe! Her sire was a good ruler, a fair man, one who needed her help to control a Kingdom of rebels; the throne had been his destiny and, by inheritance, would be hers. The bloodsuckers were just trying to torment her…before the real torture began.

Moarte would show her no mercy. She could see that in his red eyes, the hatred for the beatings she'd inflicted, and especially for clipping his wings. He would take revenge on her because her father was not available for revenge. She had to steel herself for whatever he threw at her until her father could reform his army and rescue her from these night creatures that only wanted the blood of the living like her to fill their veins. She was a prisoner, at the mercy of beings who were merciless. Creatures that had preyed upon Sapiens since the beginning of time. Undead, inhuman, cold, soulless entities that should not exist, and yet they did. The nightmare of the living.

She was strong and would have to remain strong, but she felt both exhausted and agitated. Partly, it was the fear generated by imagining what horrors would come her way. Partly it was what she had already undergone. She had been bound for two full nights as they traveled over the mountain and into the land of the vampirii with slaves and animals and goods, then tied in this way inside this cage for the last hour of the long journey. Her arms throbbed, her hands were red and numb from the ropes tight around her wrists, her legs ached and she knew if the rough hemp wasn't holding her up she would collapse. Added to that and the lack of sleep, they had not fed her and she had only received enough water throughout the trip to keep her alive—the one called Wolfsbane told her that. He also said, "King Moarte will be happy to have you, and all the better if you are in good enough shape for his purposes. Prepare yourself for the worst!"

There were no windows in this large and desolate room made of grey stone, only a vast open space with little furniture, a walk-in fireplace, and not much more. The stone room opened onto a stone balcony with a three foot ledge surrounding it. She could tell from the trees in the distance that she was high up in this fortress but not in a tower. High enough that perhaps she could not escape but she might be able to fling herself over the balcony and die from the fall if it came to that. Anything but to be in the hands of this monster who had killed her mother.

All her life Valada had wanted revenge for her mother's murder and her father had assured everyone that one day it would happen. One day the King of the Vampirii would be in their hands. And her father had been right! She'd had an opportunity to avenge her mother. The Bloodsucker King was snared in a mesh trap made of metal when he flew over the border between their lands and above their castle. The minute she knew he had been captured, she raced down to the dungeon where her father kept him, just to see for herself this demon that had drained her mother's blood. And thanks to her quick thinking, she had a guard bring her pruning shears and snapped the bones of his wings with her own hands so that he could not escape by flight. She had been so excited by the act that she could not speak. The securely-bound vampir King had not uttered one sound but had glared at her with red-eyed hatred as she snapped as many bones as she could and laughed in his face, feeling ecstatic and insane.

She whipped him with her own hand almost daily but could not understand why her father had not destroyed the Bloodsucker outright; had she been ruler of the Sapiens she would have. Even the pleasure of torture would have been relinquished just to watch him writhe and burn in the sunlight where she would have chained him. He and he alone was responsible for her mother's death. And she knew that because her father had witnessed it with his own eyes, helpless to aid her mother, and had often told the story when he held court...

One night, when Valada was three years old, the creature had swooped in, gliding through the air on those same enormous black wings, like a giant bat, right into their rooms. Her father had fought him, of course, but had been asleep, taken by surprise, no match for the superhuman strength of the undead. He was knocked to the ground, hit his head, and only awoke in time to see the Bloodsucker tear into the flesh of her mother and steal all the blood from her veins, leaving just an empty shell.

Valada had apparently been in the room with them, but she was so young she remembered nothing. No, that wasn't true. She remembered the stench of blood. An overwhelming odor that had filled her with horror and to this day she could not bear the rank smell.

And now she would choke on the smell of blood again, when the vampir King took hers. She only hoped he would be quick about it because she had no idea how long her father would be in rescuing her. And if she was completely honest with herself, Valada realized that forming an army of what soldiers had been left alive and intact in the city would be difficult and time-consuming, and realistically she could not expect rescue soon. And likely not soon enough. She would probably not be alive long, ravaged by this slayer of Sapiens.

She vowed to find a way to antagonize him so that he would lose control and kill her quickly, putting her out of the misery she knew would come. Above all, she wanted to die proudly, the daughter of a proud ruler, bringing glory to her father's name and to all Sapiens. She refused to die a victim.

But her mind kept returning to one thing: how had he escaped, this undead King of the vampirii? He had been under Sapiens control, securely chained to a wall and locked in the dungeon cell. It was inconceivable. He must have had help, but who—

Amidst these thoughts he entered the chamber, his pale eyes fixed on her dark eyes. She felt like prey. How else could she feel? He was a predator.

The vampirii spoke a language of their own but they also spoke the same language as the Sapiens. In the language she knew, he told the four guards who had brought her here, "Go! Guard the door. No one enters, and I mean *no one*, on pain of draining."

And all the while, his eyes did not leave hers. She forced herself to hide the trembling in her limbs by tensing muscles so that she would appear strong, far stronger than she felt.

When the others had left and the door was securely closed, he remained standing where he was, silent as death, staring at her from across the room as if to hypnotize her, like a pale snake mesmerizing a small animal it was about to devour.

Suddenly he moved, as slowly as when he had come down from the throne, almost gliding across the floor like a mist, which unnerved her. It was all too slow, too tense. She wanted fast movements. Let him come and break her neck so she could avoid torture! She held her breath.

He reached the cage and at close range stood staring down at her, his bloodless face hard, unmoving, his pale blue eyes with pin-point pupils piercing and hypnotic. More than anything she wanted to look away but any sign of weakness would be used against her.

Suddenly he reached out and grabbed the bars in front of her face and pulled them out. The cage rocked while the wood snapped and splintered as if he had broken twigs, not thick wooden poles. Then, quickly, he broke the others until all of the poles at the front had shattered and he'd dislodged the dowels from the grooves they were set in and there was nothing between him and her but air.

His eyes never left hers as he reached to the horizontal sheath he wore at his waist and slid out a gold-handled dagger, the blade long enough that if he plunged it into her chest it would easily pierce her heart.

"You want revenge, vampir!" she snarled, trying to bait him, "so take it! If our positions were reversed, I would. I did a good job of clipping your wings and maybe you're no longer virile enough. If you ever were!"

Her words didn't affect him as she had hoped. She saw no shift in his features or his body.

Silently and quickly he sliced the rope at her left wrist with one cut, then the rope at her right. Despite not wanting to show weakness, her trembling legs gave way and she grasped the side poles to hold herself up.

He held the knife point poised at her throat but she did not break eye contact. *Do it!* she thought, sending a mental message through her eyes that she hoped would sway him, that she hoped would end this before it began.

But instead of slashing her throat, he sheathed the knife. Then in a movement too quick for her eye to follow, he reached in and grasped the hair at the top of her head and yanked her out of the cage. Now her legs did give under her and he dragged her body through the room and out onto the stone balcony, close to the ledge. Her heart beat wildly; he was going to throw her over!

But there he stopped.

Instantly a roar came from below. He held her back just far enough that she couldn't see over the edge, still grasping her by the hair which he had twisted tightly in his fist. Her scalp hurt so much that she almost cried out, but she wouldn't show him that he was affecting her, not if she could help it.

Suddenly he pulled her closer so she was forced to look over the low ledge. Below, she saw an enormous crowd of vampirii. They filled the courtyard and the grounds beyond that, dark wings unfurled or half unfurled, flapping, creating a loud snap-sound and a breeze that reached the balcony. *There must be thousands of them!* she thought, horrified by so many in one place. The din from their roars and screams deafened her and they went on and on, growing wilder when they saw her.

A chant built, rising up, in their mutual language; they wanted her to understand. Over and over they shouted until others took up the call and the voices of this mob of blood-consuming beings became one, a wall of sound rushing at her: "Drain the Sapiens bitch!"

Moarte let them chant. He also let her dangle, only her toes touching the balcony floor as he pulled her hair up and almost out of her head. Her hands couldn't aid her; she tried but couldn't loosen his grip which was too close to her scalp.

He looked out over his subjects with obvious pleasure. And then suddenly his head snapped around towards her, his face leaving that pleasure behind as his eyes narrowed and hardened and his teeth parted enough that she could see the tips of two enormous white fangs. He looked like a rabid animal about to attack.

He yanked her to him until her face was just below his, only a few inches separating them. His breath smelled of blood and her stomach lurched.

"Princess Valada," he said evenly, and she heard his voice distinctly amidst the screams and shouts. "My soon-to-be bride."

"Never!" she managed to hiss, which brought a very nasty smile to his face, if she read the minimal expression correctly. With a further twist of his fist it felt as if her burning scalp would leave her skull.

The pressure on her head almost made her cry but she hardened herself and instead glared with red-rimmed eyes that she hoped belied her fear of him. If she feared him, he would torture her for the sheer pleasure of it. If she was fearless, he would be enraged and she could soon manipulate him into attacking her fatally.

Suddenly he leapt onto the three foot high ledge which was only a few inches wide, then hauled her up by the hair so that she was forced to climb the rough stones or have her roots torn out.

The crowd roared.

He yanked her head back so she would look at him. "On your knees!" he hissed.

She did not move.

He pulled her close by the hair and leaned down to whisper in her ear to be certain she heard him amidst the cacophony. "I said, get on your knees, Sapiens Princess, and bow before your new King, unless you want me to whip you to within an inch of your life!"

Now he pulled her hair down instead of up and she was forced by the narrow width of the ledge to do what he wanted or fall over into the pool of bloodsuckers below who were eager to rip her apart. Despite resolving to suicide if she had the chance, that was not how she wanted to die.

Carefully she bent her knees until they touched the stone ledge, her eyes level with his crotch. She could reach up and grab the knife at his waist, stab him in the stomach, or cut her own throat…

As if reading her mind, and before she could actualize that or any other plan, he turned the belt that held the sheath until it was behind him, out of her reach.

She watched his free hand separate the kilt-like metallic fabric he wore and hook first one edge of the separated material then the other to studs in the belt, exposing his pale erect penis to the air. On seeing this, the roar from the crowd swelled.

He pulled her head forward and guided his flesh to her lips, which she clamped shut.

From above her she heard, "Worship me! And if you try to bite me, I'll whip you before my subjects until your blood splatters them and they lap up the drops."

His grip on her hair tightened even more until her vision began to alter, blurred by tears, and it was as if there were sparks flying before her eyes. She had always feared being whipped and knew it was something he would happily do to her. She tried to find a place within her that could accept that treatment, but could not.

"Open your mouth, Sapiens Princess! Taste me, your King, your new master!" The last words were spoken with such vitriol, such evil intent, her breath caught in her throat.

He waited only a few seconds, then said, "So, you prefer my whip!" and was about to leap down from the ledge.

In a split second, her fear won out and she parted her lips and took his flesh between them.

His skin was not as cold as she had imagined it would be but slightly warm, yet felt unreal to her, as if he was made of something skin-like but not Sapiens skin. He thrust deeply into her mouth, hitting the back of her throat, and she almost gagged but sensed if she reacted that way he would hurt her. She focused on what she was doing to avoid vomiting and, she hoped, to dull the sound of the crowd below going wild, their shrieking stabbing her eardrums. He was thick, too long, filling her mouth, and she was forced to breathe in short sniffs through her nose.

His hand, still clutching her hair, guided her head so that she was moving along his shaft in a rhythm he wanted. It didn't take long before she felt a slight quiver as he thrust hard and deep into her.

Her mouth filled with the liquid flowing in that had a vaguely metallic taste and she wanted to spit it out and opened her jaw as wide as she could so it would seep out of her but he yanked her head back sharply and roared, "Swallow my gift, Sapiens Princess, or you will suffer my lash!"

If she did not swallow, she would choke to death. The liquid tasted salty and she wanted to vomit. She hardened her mind and swallowed, somehow managing to keep it down, this coppery tasting juice from his body, knowing he would beat her if she didn't, but afraid he would beat her anyway.

The crowd had gone insane with yelling, screaming, cheering. It was madness, so loud it seemed to create a tangible, physical vibration as if the earth was quaking, and her eardrums reverberated painfully.

Suddenly, his enormous stygian wings unfurled, a mighty and terrifying sight. They were black as onyx, the feathers shimmery, and he flapped them several times creating a powerful gust that threatened to blow her off the narrow ledge.

The crowd roared.

His pale eyes emitted evil, letting her and everyone else know that he dominated her. He wanted to make her feel weak and submissive, but she had prepared herself for humiliation. He could intimidate her but he would never break her will.

Suddenly he snarled and she saw those enormous eye teeth—long, thick and needle-sharp—and remembered them from when he had been her prisoner. He had snarled at her then too, and she had threatened to yank those canines from his gums. She had a sense that he remembered that threat at the same moment as she did. Involuntarily, she trembled in the face of this monster that had come to life from her worst nightmares.

His wings furled close to his body as he crouched down, one foot braced on the narrow ledge, the knee of his other leg also on the ledge, and quickly pulled her backwards so that she lost her balance, limbs flailing, and would have fallen over and into the crowd if he had not been unnaturally strong and held her hair so tightly. He bent her backwards over his raised thigh and with his free hand pushed the rest of her inky hair behind her shoulder, still gripping the hairs at the top of her head tightly to control her.

The sense of falling was strong and her hands grabbed for anything to keep her from pitching over, one gripping a jutting stone underneath her, the other flailing for something, anything, finally clutching his booted calf until she realized what it was and let go.

Suddenly, he tore away the top of her red velvet dress on the side facing his audience, exposing her throat, revealing a shoulder and a breast as well, and the crowd roared wildly again. Her feet were barely on the ledge, she was unbalanced, only one hand grasping something, and that was not secure. She panted, small sounds of distress coming from her despite her desire to silence herself. She was totally at his mercy, and he showed her none.

She felt him, still hard and erect, pressed against her arm, a symbol of his power over her, no doubt, a symbol whose meaning was aimed both at her and at his followers.

Then, in horror, she watched his irises turn from cyanotic to bloody. Like a viper striking, his head reared back, snapped forward, and his enormous incisors sank deep into her throat and finally she screamed, her cry lost in the roiling waves of sound from the crowd that stabbed her brain.

The bite burned, as if her throat had caught fire, then throbbed in dull pain when he extracted his sharp canines from the wounds. His lips clamped onto her flesh and he sucked hard. She felt blood flowing out of her rapidly as he greedily stole her vitae. As he had with her mother, he was going to drain her to death!

He drank leisurely, long, deep pulls, swallowing in gulps, and weakness seeped into her body. Her heart fluttered and her vision began to blur then darken. She felt cold and trembled uncontrollably and heard herself gasping in air.

Finally, he lifted his head, his eyes on fire, and drops of her blood dripped from his fangs onto her face as he showed his world what these undead vampirii do best: the blood warming him was stolen from the living. His followers cheered their King with a frenzied madness.

She was nearly unconscious and only became alert, if she could call it that, when he finished his game of dominance and threw her back into the room. She hit the floor with a thud and slid a little until she stopped then lay still, stunned. The din from outside died down enough in the room that she heard a ringing in her ears.

But too soon she was aware of him standing over her, fists on hips, straddling her body. Her eyes were slit open and she watched him crouch down above her chest and she could only see his hard flesh hovering near her face, and his eyes—emotionless as cool blue agates—his teeth and lips stained violent red with her blood.

"Welcome to my home, Sapiens Princess. It's your first night, but not your last. I regret I cannot offer you my full attention at the moment, as you so well deserve, and sadly I've been forced to go easy on you. But tomorrow has twelve hours of darkness and I can assure you I will provide you with the same level of hospitality that you bestowed on me in your dungeon."

That was all she remembered before plummeting into unconsciousness.

CHAPTER THREE

"That was quite a performance, my son. A real crowd pleaser." Belladonna relaxed against the back of a blue and red brocaded chair taken in the raid of the Sapiens castle. It fit well with the extravagant and intricate decor of her chamber that blended both Sapiens and vampirii artwork and craftsmanship. She smiled across the polished walnut table at Moarte, the smile she, unlike most vampirii, had retained the ability to actualize to a limited degree. He had seen this small smile all of his existence and still did not fully comprehend it; it could mean anything.

He raised an eyebrow. "What did you expect, Mother? She beat me, and broke my wings, nearly killed me. Murdering her outright wouldn't have been satisfying."

"Yes, I know, my son. If you recall, I saw you after your return. I tended to your wounds. None would have done less than you did tonight, many would have done more. I'm impressed you did not hurt her beyond what you did. It shows some maturity and restraint."

"There are many nights to come," he said, feeling even more angry and bitter than he had before he took the Sapiens Princess' blood. His desire to destroy her had become all consuming, an obsession. Despite hours of reflection in the dark night as he tried to think of the best way to get her to lead him to her father, he found he had little control over his more violent passions.

Belladonna, always so perceptive, said casually, "I don't think you will win her over this way."

Moarte jumped to his feet, the fury in him breaking through. "I'm not trying to *win her over*. I intend to break her will and force her to tell me where he is. And when I have the information I need, I'll break her in two physically."

"You cannot break her will this way. Your violence feeds her violence."

His mother's calm voice infuriated him further, causing him to pace the cluttered room. But he had learned to heed her words because she had insight as well as a psychic ability to understand situations he could not see until much later. "How do you know that?" he asked sharply.

"I saw it in her face when you took her on the ledge."

He paused in his pacing.

"My son, her eyes betrayed what lives deep within her. For some reason she hates you, *you specifically*. That's why she broke your wings. Why you won't be able to get her to reveal exactly where her father hides. Why she won't believe he is anything but a perfect parent and a superior ruler. Your approach won't work."

He looked down at her, infuriated. "Then offer a suggestion, Mother," he said in a tense voice.

Belladonna, like the others in this realm, was slim, which came with the change. But she was unusually tall, as tall as her son, and graceful. She had been beautiful as a mortal when his father first found her, or so his father told him, and was even more so after he turned her. She wore her hair through a cone, but curled the strands into ringlets, and decorated her attire with intense-smelling herbs and brilliantly-colored flowers, something almost unheard of in this world of darkness, though a few of the females emulated her. But her golden hair, blue eyes and creative ways were not the main source of her allure. More, it was something inside which flowed out of her and stunned everyone who had ever had contact with her—mortal and immortal alike. She possessed a wisdom that had frequently amazed Moarte—and just as frequently drove him insane—but it was why he sought her advice now.

"What do you suggest?" he asked with less hostility when she did not answer.

Finally, she, who against all odds had, as a Sapiens impregnated by his father birthed a hybrid son, one-of-a-kind, the first ever cross-species, this Sapiens female who had nurtured him until he was six, and then the Blooddrinker who reared him beyond those years after his father changed her, who had raised Moarte until he became independent, this female he trusted beyond all other vampirii said, "Love her."

He exploded in rage. "How can you *dare* suggest that? She is a demon, vicious, violent, and she nearly killed me. And she is Sapiens, our mortal enemy, as you well know. Blood sacs who have relentlessly hunted our kind for centuries, who have blamed us for every ill that befalls them. They hunted down my father, your husband, which you should remember—"

"Do not lecture me on the past, Moarte. You were only a child. I was there. I can vividly recall every moment that occurred without a nudge from you."

He took a seat and glared across the table at her. She was right, she had been there. And she, more than he, understood the violence of the Sapiens because she had been one and lived most of her mortal existence in that world. He had not. At best he was a half breed, but his father's seed was strong in him and he had always felt vampir, and never Sapiens.

It wasn't in him to apologize to her and she understood that so she bestowed on him that small, inscrutable smile, letting him know they could proceed. Then she said, "I suggest this because it is a way of disarming her. She expected you to be brutal and you met her expectations. She expects more brutality and if you fulfill that expectation it will be *her* plan, not yours. She wants nothing more than to push you over the edge so that you kill her quickly in a rage."

That made him think and they were silent for some time until finally he admitted, "Mother, you may be onto something."

"I am," she said, never having been coy about her self confidence. "The girl is the daughter of a corrupt King who does not love her."

"How do you know this?"

"Well, for one thing, he gave his daughter to you in order to protect himself and escape our warriors. For another, your father and I encountered Zadors several times, including before you were born, and you know the stories. And you have met this Sapiens King yourself, as his prisoner. You will recall him well, no doubt, as you have always had a sharp memory, which, I should add, you inherited from me. He is incapable of love. But she does not know this because he has deceived her; I do not know how, and I don't understand why, but I am sure of this. And she will only understand that deception if she is loved. Then she will have a comparison against that false love which she cannot, *will not* give up. I'd say it is all that anchors her."

"All good in theory," Moarte said, "but how am I suppose to love my enemy, who I loathe."

"You need a combination of tools to do this."

"Such as?"

"I suggest combining enthrallment and beguilement with sweetness."

"Sweetness?" he sneered, and he felt like pounding his mother's prized table until the wood turned to sawdust.

"Yes. She will not expect that. If you mesmerize her first, planting the seeds in her mind, she will see everything you do as sweet and loving, whatever that is."

He laughed. "So I can whip the flesh off her back and she'll see it as love."

"Perhaps. But to go that far your enthrallment skills might need honing. And I fear such a vicious act would ultimately turn her against you." She smiled and he could not be angry with her, although he wanted to be, because he could not be certain that she was completely supporting him.

"We have seen this before, Moarte. Your father did this once to a Sapiens from the East, a dealer headed to the West to sell arms to another of our enemies, to be used against us. Instead of murdering him outright, your father mesmerized him and altered his way of thinking. And he treated him cordially, as if he were a guest."

"And what happened?"

"The arms salesman was released by your father and went West and sold arms."

"Then it meant nothing, what my father did. He failed."

"On the contrary. The dealer sold our enemies the wrong type of arms, weapons which cannot harm vampirii."

Again, her enigmatic smile.

Belladonna stood suddenly and said, "I think you should meditate further on your goal. You want to get to her father. She loves him and will protect him with her life. She will only betray him if she loves someone more and perceives her father as a threat to that greater love. You, my son, can be that greater love, but you may need to find storage for your hatred. At least temporary storage." She turned away from him, occupying herself with mixing herbs she had told him were for a sick Sapiens slave.

Alone with his thoughts, Moarte did not know if he could do this, even by mesmerization, a skill which he, like all vampirii, possessed. Could he control the Sapiens Princess' mind enough for her to believe he loved her? Could he *not* fatally harm her when every cell in his body wanted to inflict retribution for what she had done to him? For what her people had done to his realm over millennia? For all that the Sapiens

King had done to him personally?

His mother's plan made sense, but he didn't know if he was capable of enacting it. Yet about one thing he knew his mother was correct: there was nothing he could do to the girl physically that would force her to betray her father. The Sapiens Princess would die first. Even he had seen that in her eyes, and it had made him more furious.

He walked in the garden for many hours, until the sun was only sixty minutes from rising, but finally he returned to his quarters with an idea that might satisfy both his long and short term desires.

Chapter Four

Valada lay curled into a ball on the floor beside the bed where the vampir King had chained her. She felt incredibly weak, exhausted, blood drained, humiliated, only half conscious, but no longer worried about what would happen to her. She understood now that she could not predict events and therefore could not prepare herself for the brutalization to come. All she could do was accept her fate and struggle to hasten her demise.

She worried what the effect on her would be of him drinking her blood, and of his blood entering her body, and she knew it was blood, at least partially so, that had come from his penis, what she had been forced to swallow. What was the process for turning into a vampire? She did not know.

The world of the undead was so secretive, little was known about their ways, other than that they were killers of the living. Rumors abounded and she had no idea what was true and what wasn't, but surely when human beings were drained, not everyone died and returned to life in an undead state. Her father assured his subjects that her mother had not risen from the grave. But the blood she swallowed was more of a concern. She didn't know what swallowing vampire blood meant. *With some luck*, she thought grimly, *I'll be dead before I find out.*

She heard Moarte return and instantly closed her eyes, pretending to be asleep, and she wondered if this Deathbringer, with all his supernatural powers, could hear her heart pounding in fear.

He walked towards the balcony where the darkness in the sky was receding and there pulled a heavy curtain across the opening that separated the balcony from the room, then another heavy curtain in front of that one—both from ceiling to floor—blocking rays of light that might try to enter. She could tell from the position of the mountains when she had been on the balcony that this room was on the North side of the fortress, not East where the sun rises, or West where it sets. There were lit candles on stands and in sconces around the vacuous chamber and he did not hurry as he moved to them with a snuffer, suffocating the flame of each, one by one, until only a tall thick taper on a high stand by the bed remained lit.

When he reached her he straddled her body as he had before and crouched down. "Open your eyes, Sapiens Princess!" he commanded.

There was no use pretending; he knew she was not sleeping.

She opened her eyes, her vision hazy. When the haziness cleared, his face came into focus, almost sculpted, features perfectly symmetrical, flesh like alabaster and hair pulled back from his chiseled face and through a cone, so long it hung below his shoulders, more than blonde, silver-white. Although he was tall and slim, every muscle appeared toned. Behind him she could just make out the stark contrast of those inky-black wings, pulled tight to his pale body. The face and physique of a death angel.

Unlike the warriors, he wore nothing on his chest but two crossed bands and just the short kilt-like outfit on the lower half of his body plus boots to his knees, all of it such a dark grey it could easily be called pale black. The vampirii she'd seen so far, both males and females, had worn battle gear, also metallic, but deep black, a style similar to his but more of it on their colorless bodies. She imagined there might be a variety of hues available to this horrifying species, but all of them dark, like the night, not the bright shades of daylight favored by the Sapiens.

His pale eyes held a bare hint of blue in the irises with black dots in the center, far smaller than a Sapiens' pupils. Those otherworldly orbs had looked different earlier and now seemed darker by the illumination of this lonely candle. Staring at his eyes made her queasy and she wanted to look away but knew she had to be strong. Strong enough that he would destroy her.

He bent forward, his face close to hers, closer, until only a few inches separated them, and she again felt the cold blood-stink breath of death on her skin, riddling her with terror.

She braced for an attack, but none came, just his words. As he stared into her eyes, she became fascinated by those contracted pupils, like pinpoints of dancing darkness leading to another place, another time—if only she could see inside them to see where they led! "You belong to me now, Princess. I *own* you. You are mine."

She opened her mouth to deny this but he placed a taloned finger over her lips. The next words he said shocked her. "I *will* marry you. You *will* be my wife, the mother of my children. I will take you in whatever ways I want whenever I want you, and I will want you *often*. You will obey me and love me and because you do so, I will love you. Do not argue with me, do not resist me. I am your ruler. You need a master, one stronger than you, who will absorb your violence and anger and transform it…"

He continued to talk and she lost track of the words, feeling drowsy, too sleepy to block them out. Whenever her eyes threatened to close, he ordered her to open them. In this light, his irises seemed to change color and became fiery red coals with cool black coals at the centers, burning through her, searing her brain. And while she told herself she was immune to these lies, to these wrong meanings, the sleepiness from the weakness of having so much of her blood drawn from her and from all that she had endured crashed over her in heavy waves. She could barely keep her eyes open, but his repetitive command for them to remain open whenever they began to close, she felt compelled to obey.

Finally he stood, leaving the one feeble candle lit and the room in almost complete darkness. He lay down on the chevron-shaped bed beside her, and she felt relieved. He was ready to sleep and there would be no more torture tonight, at least. She could rest and rebuild her strength.

Suddenly, she felt movement. He reached down, his hand patting the top of her head where her scalp still ached as if she was a dog, and she tensed. Then his hand moved over her face slowly, along her neck to where the bite marks were, two fingers stopping at the wounds, pressing against them, causing them to burn, then his hand sloped further down and along her shoulder, very slowly, feeling her skin, and despite her ragged, fearful breathing, she pretended to sleep as his hand slid onto the half of her chest where he had torn her dress away, moved around her exposed flesh and captured her breast in his grip. He held her breast for a long moment but soon ran his fingers with the claw-like nails over her breast, cupping it, squeezing, and she tensed even more, expecting to feel the sharp pain of incision.

But no pain came. His fingers moved in slow circles and she felt her nipple tightening. He zeroed in on the aureole, circling many times before reaching her nipple, which he went round and round with a nail tip, making it firmer still. He used his long nail to flick the nipple back and forth until it hardened more, sending small currents of terror through her with some other feelings she couldn't identify mixed in. Suddenly he grasped her nipple between his finger and thumb and began to pull and twist it, creating sharp heat in her flesh that bordered on pain and pleasure, forcing intense sensations through her, despite her desire to block the feelings that rode this cusp. She believed it would all turn to pure pain soon and tried to prepare herself.

But as the last minutes of night faded, before he slept, he continued to toy with her nipple, pulling it up, squeezing, pinching the hard fleshy bead, and she could only lie panting, struggling unsuccessfully to stifle moans, feeling her body quiver with both terror and an excitement she did not understand, that straddled a line between opposites that verged on unbearable.

He did not stop until he dropped into sleep and when he did, her nipple securely locked between his now rigid finger and thumb, she was forced to lie on her back that way through the long hours of daylight, feeling trapped, and as if her body was no longer her own.

She had never felt so exposed. Even on the balcony when he had forced her to take him into her mouth before the vampirii, when he had ripped open her dress and let the crowd see her breast, then sank his teeth into her throat so they could see that too. The way he held her nipple, with the confidence of dominion, as if he *owned* her...

These unfamiliar thoughts were inspired by sensations new to her, a Princess who, because of her status, had avoided fleshy contact and refused to marry. She, who never imagined being owned by another, and felt no love for any but her father. She had avoided the caress of any man and now she was forced to accept the touch of a male who was not even a man but a vampir.

He would have his way with her when night broke. She knew that. The knowledge both terrified and thrilled her. And secretly she thought: *I may die soon but I will surely not die a virgin*, and she was ashamed of such thinking.

When his hand came alive again, she knew it was night. He fondling her nipple as if he had paused only a moment, not having yielded to vampir death sleep.

She could not feign unconsciousness. She moaned softly and her body trembled with sensations rippling through it as he worked her sensitive flesh to further arousal, making it sear, causing intense shivers to run down to her genitals again and again, surprising her, and she endured an electricity in her body that forced her back to arch involuntarily in almost a spasm, thrusting her chest towards his hand wantonly for more instead of pulling away.

In the near darkness of a room lit only by the remnants of one candle, he reached down to pull her up by the waist. The chains holding her were just long enough that he could lay her on her stomach across the width of the bed, her head and arms dangling over the side. Quickly he raised her dress up from the hem and his hands roamed over the backs of her legs, rounded her buttocks, slid along her waist and up her back, and then down again, and she trembled.

He spread her wet thighs so that she was wide open then his fingers found the fleshy button where her femaleness began. She was slick with burning juices and he spread the moisture over the button causing new sensations that rocked her and made her body jerk as she lay naked before him in the faint light, fully exposed, embarrassed, knowing he could clearly see her in this near darkness as all the cat-eyed vampirii could see with little or no light, but even if she had been on her back she would not have been able to see him.

She felt him move into the space between her thighs and she quaked with both longing and terror. With her head down and her wrists chained to the leg of the bed, she was nearly immobile and completely helpless. She felt his penis press against her between her legs, not at her woman opening but the other, further back, and small cries came from her lips because she was confused and frightened, but he stroked her with his hand as if he was soothing a terrified pet.

His fingers spread her cheeks apart and the head of his penis found her opening and nudged in only a little but it felt enormous; he couldn't possibly enter her there where nothing was supposed to enter, only exit! She cried out "No!" and instead of comforting her, he pushed his flesh inside her. She gasped and cried, startled by this burning penetration. He felt too big, monstrous, and this orifice too small to hold him; he would surely tear her in two!

She could not utter words begging him to stop; no words were available to her, only incoherent sounds. But she knew there was nothing she could say anyway to make him stop. And despite feeling about to be split apart, he pushed in deep then deeper and it hurt so much she was amazed that her body could hold him and all she could do was cry out.

Then he went deeper still, until she thought there would be no end to this pain, this filling. Then suddenly he stopped.

Still panting and trembling, unable to comprehend what was happening, how she could be so filled, she felt staked by him, and suddenly recognized that in this act he was again claiming her.

He began to move, pulling out, slowing, then back in, and each time he re-entered it was as if he pierced her anew, over and over, out and in, and she could only moan and make small animal-like crying sounds, her face slick with unstoppable tears, sobbing from the pain, from being startled as he took her with imperious ownership, she who had no desire to be owned.

It went on and on. She wanted to beg him to stop, yet a part of her wanted him to never stop, and then he began to move faster and her buttocks, her legs, all of her lower parts swelled with a scorching heat, a steaming nearly unbearable pleasure that sent fiery sensation racing through her like waves of flame and she was sure she would ignite.

Finally he moved rapidly and she felt totally out of control and could only moan in sync with the thrusting, lost in the movement, so aware that he was taking what now belonged to him and she felt owned and, instead of being repulsed, experienced this as desirable, oddly, both safe and secure. Even at her awareness of this, it made no sense, but she was well beyond rational thinking now.

She felt him quiver slightly—as she had experienced on the balcony—and he thrust one last time, very deep, then lay still, embedded in her.

He stayed this way in silence for some time, his body pressing hers, and she wanted so much to be held and shocked herself with this desire.

Almost as she thought this, he reached down and gathered her long hair, catching it in his fist to raise her upper body until her head was far back, her throat exposed. His teeth found the holes he had made in her neck and re-pierced her, reopening the wounds, cutting deep again, as deep as the teeth could get, as deep as his flesh still inside her. He pulled the teeth out and the cut vein, muscle and skin burned and throbbed with stinging pain, but instantly his lips latched onto the openings and the pain dissipated and he was sucking the blood from her vein through the two wounds.

His free hand reached under her and ripped the rest of the bodice of her dress away to pull at the virgin nipple that he had not touched before. She felt out of her mind! Ecstatic! She wanted to give herself to him, and moaned. He could do whatever he wanted to her, and she knew he would take his pleasure with her at his will, just as he had promised to do. She shivered in anticipation of submitting to him again and again. As long as he wanted her, she would give him anything. And she could not understand or accept that she felt this way, but she did.

When Moarte finished with her, he removed the chains from her wrists and turned her over. He pulled the one lit candle close so that he could see her eyes with light; he wanted to examine in detail what was there. He was surprised that the thoughts he had fed her had taken such deep root so quickly. Her eyes looked glazed, very round, the pupils dilated from the darkness but also because she was seeing through a lens of submission, one she would not have imagined herself capable of with him. She gazed at him with desire, a softness he wouldn't have expected in her.

His kind had always had the ability to manipulate the minds of Sapiens, but it worked much better when there had been an exchange of blood. What he had done spontaneously, drinking hers, forcing her to drink his fluids on the balcony, that had set up this enthrallment to achieve the effect he wanted.

He fed her words now that he could see she longed to hear even though she didn't yet know she wanted to hear them, and especially not from him. And if asked, she would have denied wanting to be possessed by him.

But it was the truth. He did own her now. Body, mind and soul. All that he had said was accurate but for one thing: he might wed her, if that step was required to turn her towards him and away from her father, but she would never be the mother of his children. She would be long dead before that could come to pass. Once she had led him to the Sapiens King, he wouldn't need her anymore. And then he could open the flood gates of his hatred and destroy her.

In the meantime, he would use her as he liked, taking his pleasure, whatever that entailed, including hurting her. He adjusted his features as much as was possible, enough that she could interpret this as a smile. She smiled back. But the reason he smiled was not what she thought. He would do what he wanted to her and she would believe what he told her to believe. Pain is pleasure. Hate is love. He could play with her, fucking her mind while he fucked her body, and eventually when he brought her out of the mesmerized state, she would, to her horror, remember it all. Until then, whatever he did to her, she would believe that he loved her. Whatever he told her she would believe as truth. He could see that she wanted to obey him, submit to him, and soon he would reprogram her to the point where her thinking about her vile father would be altered.

He had taken her in this way because he knew that for her it would be the ultimate abasement, and the ultimate humiliation. He was dominant, she submissive to his will. This penetration required her to hand over control to him, and she did. Now, she felt owned, and she wanted to feel owned because he told her she belonged to him and despite everything, his mother was right—the Princess needed to be loved because she never had been. She belonged to him now, and he would make sure she gave him what he wanted both tonight and in the future. And then he would drink a cup of very sweet revenge.

CHAPTER FIVE

The third night of her capture at the vampirii stronghold, Valada awoke to Moarte's voice saying, "Feed, wash and prepare her."

She was faced away from his voice but soon felt the chains that bound her to the leg of the bed being unlocked by a cool hand.

Within seconds she heard, "Princess Valada, I am Serene. King Moarte has instructed me to take care of you."

Reluctantly, Valada turned over to find a young woman, between eight to ten years her junior, with red-gold hair, green eyes and a sweet smile, wearing a white dress and gold bangles on her wrists. A girl who was human.

"You're Sapiens. Are you a slave?"

"I am. And I was."

"Then you wish to escape. Help me escape and we will leave this realm of blood-thieves together."

The girl looked pained. She turned and walked across the room to a table, picked up a plate of food and brought it to Valada. "Princess, you must eat to restore your strength."

The food smelled good and looked appetizing. It was Sapiens food, what she had grown up with, a blend of meat in a sauce with potatoes and carrots and other vegetables, and the scent reached her nostrils making her mouth water; she hadn't eaten in several days.

The girl crouched down and offered the plate and Valada took it, knowing she had only two choices: either renew her strength or wilt into immobilizing weakness. But now that she had an ally for an escape plan, she would need her strength. The food was good and, ravenous, she ate it.

The girl also brought her red wine to drink, and a slice of dark bread, and like the starved person she was, Valada tried to eat everything quickly.

"Princess, please, take care! There will be more meals."

"Come, we have to escape now," Valada said, standing on shaky legs, "while I'm free and the vampirii are somewhere else."

"I can't escape," the girl said.

"Don't be ridiculous! There must be a way out of this fortress. We'll go together. I'll rescue you. Tell me how to get out of here."

"I do not wish to leave, Princess Valada."

Valada looked closely at the girl. "You've been hypnotized by the vampirii."

"No, I have not. I stay here willingly."

Bile rose in Valada. "Then you're a traitor!"

The girl looked pained again. "I'm sorry, Princess Valada, but you don't understand. Many of us brought here as slaves prefer to live with the vampirii."

Valada felt annoyed. "As I said, you're mesmerized. Girl, these are killers, Blooddrinkers. They'll drain you and steal your soul. You're already under their power."

The girl moved away and went to the door. She spoke softly to one of the two vampir guards outside the room and within a short while there were more Sapiens—females, a veritable procession—bringing in pitchers of steaming water, which they poured into a short tub in the corner that Valada had not noticed before.

At some point the girl named Serene said, "Princess Valada, your bath is ready. May I help you?"

She reached out and Valada shook her off. "I don't intend to bathe. I will not ready myself for *him!*"

The girl, in fact all of the Sapiens girls, looked frightened. Finally, Serene said, "As you like, Princess Valada. But please know that King Moarte will be displeased both with you and with us."

Valada did not want to turn Moarte's wrath on these girls who, clearly, were so victimized, so downtrodden that they did not even know what the word *slavery* meant. Finally, she said, "Alright, to keep you from being martyrs, lead me to the bath," and all the girls smiled as one unit and some clapped or did little dances and Valada worried that they were so enthralled by the vampirii that she could not count on help from these seemingly simple-minded Sapiens.

Still, the bath water felt warm and soothing, washing away not just the dirt of days but some of her aches and pains. The girl, Serene, washed her body and her hair with a lilac-scented soap and tossed lilac petals into the water as well. Some of the stress that Valada had acquired over the last week vanished in the heat of the waters and the pleasant ministrations of the girl.

"Why do you feel you want to remain here?" she asked the girl in a soft mumble.

"Because the vampirii treat me well."

Valada's eyes opened to slits and she stared at the girl. "And yet you're afraid of the wrath of King Moarte. That doesn't speak of being treated well. You sound as entrapped as I am."

"May I speak freely?" the girl said.

"Please do. I value candor."

"The vampirii can be cruel. Disobedience is punished. But in my short life, I experienced more cruelty, far more extreme, at the hands of Sapiens."

Valada's eyes snapped fully open. "I don't believe that!"

"I'm sorry if I have offended you, Princess Valada. I speak only of what I know."

Clearly, the girl did not know anything much if she believed this. Valada realized that she could not rely on Serene to help her escape. She was on her own. But she would look for a way. That, or die trying.

The girl helped her out of the tub and gave her a simple floor-length, sleeveless white dress to wear with slits in the front about breast and crotch level, and one slit in the back, all hidden by pleats. "King Moarte would be pleased if you wear this in his presence."

"Why not?" Valada said. "I wouldn't like to see you beaten because of a dress I refused to wear."

Again, the girl looked pained as she slipped the dress over Valada's head.

They stood on the balcony near the ledge and Serene brushed Valada's long black hair which reached to her waist. "You have lovely hair, Princess Valada," she said. "Thick and shiny. And now you look refreshed. King Moarte will be happy to see you tonight."

"King Moarte will be happy to pull the hairs from my head and then rip my scalp from my skull. I'm his prisoner and he'll torture me but I will never submit my will to his as you have handed over yours to the vampirii."

The girl said nothing, just continued to brush her hair.

Valada stared at the nightscape before her. The mountains were so dark in this nearly moonless sky and the stars provided little illumination. Beyond one mountain lay her home and her father, who must surely be planning her rescue. Yet even as she thought about rescue, she knew the chances were slim that he would arrive in time.

The most reasonable course of action would be to hurl herself off the balcony. They were close enough that she could see over the edge and she estimated the length of the fall to be four stories above ground level. She wondered if such a plummet would kill her instantly or only leave her paralyzed, which would be much worse. Paralyzed, she would be subjected to Moarte's fury without the possibilities of fighting back, escape or death. A grim thought.

Suddenly, she heard a male voice and her body tensed. The girl named Serene backed away from her, leaving her alone on the balcony contemplating whether or not to jump in the short moments she suspected she had for this decision.

Then, cool hands were on her bare arms, sliding down them to her wrists then back up. His hands moved inside the dress slits to her breasts and began kneading them. From behind her, he leaned in close to her ear and whispered, "Princess Valada, did you miss my caress?"

She pulled away from him and jumped back so that she was up against the ledge, spinning to face him with all the fury she felt. "Amuse yourself, Bloodsucker, while you can, because you'll pay for the evil you've perpetrated. My father will soon be on your doorstep and all your undead warriors combined won't be able to withstand his wrath. Prepare yourself for the stake! Your nights are numbered."

Moarte laughed in her face as she had laughed in his. Then he stared at her for several seconds, his features fixed in what she would have described as serious.

"Tell me, Sapiens Princess, what punishment would equal what you did to me? What can I inflict on you? You have no wings for me to clip, no fangs to pull from your mouth. How can I repay you for your hospitality? Should I banish you to my dungeon where you can wither and die slowly? I can flail your skin until there's none left. Do you think that would equal the agony you brought to my flesh?"

"You brought it on yourself with your evil and despicable acts, loathsome Bloodguzzler!" More than anything she hoped to inflame him until he lost control. He just had to shove her and she would go over the balcony, her neck would break and then she would be dead and this would be over!

"Your tone is that of an equal, which you are not. You may be royalty in your own land but here you're nothing but my prisoner, as I was yours. Remember that!"

"You're right, walking corpse, we're not equals. I'm alive and you're dead. You are mold, decomposition, old, stinking, rotting soil beneath my feet! Loathsome and degenerate."

Suddenly he snarled and reached out for her. But instead of pushing her over the ledge as she had hoped, he grabbed her arm and threw her into the room. She stumbled, barely able to keep from falling. He came in right after her. "Lie on your belly, Princess. You're going to bleed!"

She spun around to face him, defiant, and cursed him. "Monster! Unclean thing from Hell! Death is far too good for you! Breaking your bones wasn't nearly enough!"

But suddenly he stopped moving and became rigid as a statue, staring at her.

"Do you know, vampir, what I intended to do to you next when you were my prisoner? I planned to chain you in the sunlight! I so longed to hear you scream and watch you fry! Just a little each day every day, upping the dose, until you were beyond repair. I was looking forward to smelling your undead flesh smolder, eventually sending you back to the fiery Hell that spawned you, and where you belong! Demon!" she screamed.

It only took him three strides to reach her and she tried to back away, but there was nowhere to go and not enough time. He grabbed her by the throat, cutting off her air, his eyes turning red and his incisors in her full view. For a moment she floundered. Then she lashed out at him with her left hand, slashing his cheek. He grabbed her wrist, but she was scratching his face with the nails of her right hand, struggling to gouge out his eyes as she fought for air, punching him with her fist, kicking him, trying to bite him and crash a knee into his groin. But he soon overpowered her, snagging the other wrist as well, and she gasped air into her lungs. He shoved her against the wall face-first, capturing both wrists in one hand above her head, his body pressing hers into the stones while he pulled her head back hard by the hair.

His teeth were in her throat before she could do anything more but curse him. "Rot in hell, filthy beast of darkness!"

She struggled and railed at him but he bit viciously, deeply, sucking the life blood out of her body fast.

"This is your death game, vampir, the *only* game you know how to play. And you can't even do it well! If *I* were vampir, I would have the guts to take revenge and siphon all your blood in seconds, but you, you're incapable of that. What a pathetic and insignificant lifeform you are!"

She felt her strength ebb and her will to taunt him sap further each time he swallowed. She hoped she had enraged him enough and that this would be the end, that all her blood would soon be gone and she could die in peace.

But suddenly, he pulled away from the burning wounds and flipped her around, his face close to hers, letting her inhale the sharp scent that turned her stomach as she viewed her blood on his fangs and lips, running down his chin. And those blood-red ferocious, inhuman eyes!

"You would be wise to learn to behave yourself, Princess, because you have yet to taste my wrath."

She stared with contempt into his eyes as those orbs paled rapidly, reminding her of glacial waters in the high mountains. "And you, disgusting cadaver, have yet to taste mine!"

Quickly the water receded, going in seconds from pale to muddy, then again to red-tinged, and soon to red as a harvest sun on the horizon. And against her will, Valada felt entranced by this brilliant color surrounding the dots in the centers like flames erupting from black suns, as if in some way the black and red called to her and she wanted to see more clearly, examine more closely, and needed to understand what this vermillion and ebony pairing symbolized.

She heard his words but their meaning felt obscure, as if this was a lost language, one she did not understand, but felt she comprehended on some pre-cognitive level.

"Sapiens Princess, stop resisting. Give yourself to me. I will take you anyway, whenever I like. Submit to me and instead of suffering, you will experience pleasures beyond your wildest dreams. It is a small thing to give yourself over to me to receive pleasure in abundance. Submit to me, your master, who owns you, and knows what's best for you, Princess Valada."

He talked and talked, and a calmness fell over her. Soon, he moved her to the bed and lay her face down. She felt him enter her as he had the night before. This time, though, it did not hurt so much, and to her surprise, partly she welcomed the penetration. There was a release that came to her with the submitting, allowing him to do as he wanted. She wanted him to overpower her so her body would be a vessel for his pleasure. When he took that pleasure she experienced her own. But she was confused and could not understand or justify her conflicting responses.

In the quiet room she heard, as if from far away, a woman panting in time with his thrusts, and moaning, "Yes, yes, Oh YES!"

Moarte could have laughed. It was too easy. She was a willing victim, though she would have never viewed herself in that light.

He could do whatever he wanted with her and she would submit to him. He saw it in her eyes again, that eager surrendering of her will to his. Soon he would quash all the rebellion in her and have her more than eager to please him and with that, he would find out where her loathsome father was hiding and murder him. He just had to keep control of the violence he longed to inflict on her, violence she tried to trigger, and tonight he had almost lost control. He needed to remain alert because she wanted him unhinged. But he would not play her game, he would play *his*—until he won. Then, Princess Valada, the Sapiens Princess, would taste his passions in a way that she would have no desire to submit to, and he was eager to exact his revenge.

CHAPTER SIX

On her seventh night with Moarte, King of the Vampirii, who she now called Master and to whom she readily submitted, he led her to a small room with wooden furnishings and shelves with papers on them, some bound. In the room was a man whose skin was not inordinately pale and she could see in his mouth when he spoke that he had no fang-like teeth. His face was severe, though, full of lines and creases, a down-turned mouth and two piercing and judgmental eyes.

Moarte said to her in that voice she now heard as melodious and which she loved to listen to, "Princess, this is Blander, who you will recognize as being Sapiens. He is from the land of your birth and has chosen to live with us."

She turned to Blander. "You chose to come here?"

He nodded.

"Why?"

"Because the King Zador is a bad ruler, one who uses and abuses his people. He is evil."

"Traitor! You're talking about my father!" she snapped, and felt about to attack him when suddenly Moarte's hand slid down her back along the simple white cotton dress he insisted she wear. The dress had folds and within the folds were disguised slits in the material. His hand stopped at her buttocks and slid into the opening of the dress where he cupped one of her cheeks. Inexplicably, that act calmed her and she felt her head fall back slightly, and was aware of her hardening nipples, and sighed.

Over the last nights he had taken her blood and taken her sexually so many times that she had become living, breathing passion, her body electrified by his touch.

"You are here," Moarte said from behind her, "in order that Blander can teach you the history of your people, the Sapiens. Pay attention. Learn your lessons well. I'm certain that you do not want to disappoint me."

He moved his hand away from her flesh and she felt abandoned. Her voice trembled with the fear she felt at the loss and she said, "No, Master, I do not, I *will* not disappoint you. I promise."

"I expect nothing less," he said, then left her alone with the severe-looking man.

Blander held a short, flat stick in his hand and tapped the seat of a low stool opposite his higher one, indicating that she should be seated.

Sitting opened the fold below her waist and it was her flesh that perched on the wooden stool. She liked this dress; not only were there areas that could expose all her pleasure zones, but the dress made her feel special, as it allowed her Master to open any part he desired while she sat at his feet in the throne room watching him rule his Kingdom. She marveled at how thoughtful he had been to have such a dress created for her. She could not believe her good fortune to be his slave. Her desire for him brought her flesh alive as if she was a needy animal that longed for continuous petting.

He loved to play with her breasts and she loved this too. He loved to penetrate her, and this she also loved. She wondered if he would enter her womanly orifice but he had not so far and she could not bring herself to ask him. He entered her where he wanted, when he wanted, and she was happy to submit to his desires which thrilled her and filled her with passion. Making him happy made her happy and—.

"Pay attention!" Blander said, smacking the flat stick against a nearby pillar where it cracked loudly.

The sharp and dangerous sound focused her thoughts away from her lover and onto this man who wanted her to learn something, but she did not know what.

He began with ancient history.

"The Sapiens go back in recorded time to at least 2500 BC because that is their first written record. In *The Epic of Gilgamesh*, the tale of a Sapiens King, Deathbringers, what are now known as vampirii, are mentioned. From the start, Sapiens did not understand the role of the Deathbringers and did not trust them because they were the opposite of the Sapiens, night instead of day. The Sapiens treated them as adversaries when in fact the Deathbringers tried to befriend the Sapiens by easing the passage of their souls through Death as they reached the end of their mortal lives—even though the Deathbringers had no need to do this. Sapiens are in many ways their inferiors. Sapiens do not *value* death despite the fact that it is inevitable for them, rather, they *fear* death, which is why the Deathbringers began to offer some of them life after death.

"It was the Sapiens who started the long cycle of wars that have ebbed and flowed over millennia and, because of the animosity, at first the Deathbringers became more aggressive towards Sapiens and took them indiscriminately, not just at the approach of their demise.

"As time has passed, vampirii, as they are currently known, have learned to temper their hunger so they do not need much blood to survive and will use Sapiens for nourishment without harm coming to the donors. However, on a rare occasion, they will transform a Sapiens into a vampir. But the Sapiens, through constant war-like interaction, have forced the vampirii to form armies to protect themselves and their realm."

He paused, staring at her intently. "Why did Sapiens treat the Deathbringers as adversaries?"

She blinked.

He waited for an answer, but she did not have any idea why the Sapiens and vampirii were adversaries.

"You are not paying attention," Blander said.

"I am. I just don't know why."

"Stand up!"

She stood, as did he.

"Come here," he said.

Reluctantly she moved towards him.

"Put out your hand."

When she didn't move, he snatched her wrist and turned her hand, opening her fingers up. Suddenly he smacked her palm smartly with the flat stick and she yelped.

"Why were they treated like adversaries?"

She tried to think of a reason and couldn't and the stick smacked her palm again, creating flames across her flesh.

Instead of answering the question, she yelled, "My master, King Moarte, will be angry with you, traitor, when he learns what you've done to my body, which belongs to him!" she said bravely.

"It is King Moarte who requested me to instruct you by Sapiens methods of instructing children, using whatever incentives are necessary for you to learn these lessons. That is his desire. If you do not pay attention, you will be punished. Open your hand!" And he brought the stick down onto her palm again to emphasize the point he was making, bringing tears to her eyes and a sob to her throat.

Then he said, "Go back and sit on your stool and this time, Sapiens Princess, pay attention!"

She sat down on the hard stool, her palm smarting, tears sliding down her cheeks. Blander repeated the lesson and this time she got the answer right: "The Sapiens didn't trust them because the Deathbringers were opposites."

"Good. You've saved yourself some pain."

Over the course of the night he instructed her on how the war-like Sapiens—when they weren't destroying one another—had hounded and hunted the vampirii for millennia, almost to extinction. Sapiens learned that vampirii are vulnerable to sunlight. That they can be killed with a stake through the heart, by decapitation, by incineration, and began tailoring their weapons to those ends. Clipping vampirii wings causes agony and recovery is protracted and exhausting and sometimes results in fatality. Sapiens have used every method to trap, torture and murder vampirii, leading to an escalation of the wars as their weaponry became more sophisticated and the vampirii, which are not prone to grouping, have been forced to band together in order to fight for their existence. Being propelled into warfare with the Sapiens on a regular basis, the vampirii needed to become warriors, which resulted in a necessary hierarchy of a military nature in order to precipitate survival.

"Over the last 1,000 years, Moarte is only the third King, the fourth ruler of this realm.

"The first vampir King—also named Moarte—died in battle, and Morpheus, his second, was elected ruler by the war council. Morpheus named his son Moarte, after the powerful and honorable King he had served under for several centuries. When Morpheus died, the title went automatically to his wife, Queen Belladonna, who ruled only a short time then chose to abdicate in favor of her son, the current King Moarte."

"What happened to Moarte's father?" Valada asked.

Blander ignored her question and instead drilled into her facts of battles and broken truces, dates of conquests, details of the vampirii fighting back and winning on occasion, but more often than not being driven further into the wilderness by the Sapiens. It was a lot to memorize and twice more she received a series of smacks with the flat stick on her palms, nine altogether, and the scorching pain left her face and the bodice of her dress soaked with tears.

Towards the end of the night, when her brain was filled with more information than it could retain and her hands blazed, Moarte came for her.

"Did she learn well, Blander?"

"She has learned everything to the 6th century. I've had to punish her three time but she should remember now."

"Good." Then to Valada he said, "Come," and she followed him eagerly through the dimly-lit fortress, up curving steps and finally into his chamber.

Her body trembled with desire and she hoped he would fuck her for the rest of the night, giving her pleasure to take away the pain. But instead of going to the bed, he sat on an armless, backless chair he placed in the middle of the room, his folded dark wings on either side of him glistening so beautifully in the flickering light from the fireplace, and told her to stand before him. "Undress."

She slid the simple dress down her body. Her nipples were firm already, her genitals hot and moist, the heat from her stinging hands not so bothersome as before.

"Turn around."

She did, and she felt him studying the back of her as if his eyes emitted hot flames licking her skin.

"Turn back."

She did.

"You were punished three times. Why?" he asked.

"I...I didn't remember information."

"What information?"

She struggled to remember now; her brain felt stuffed with facts and figures, dates and names. "The first time I didn't remember what Blander said about why the Sapiens distrusted the Deathbringers."

"And why did they?"

She knew the answer and felt proud when she said, "Because they were opposites, day and night. The Sapiens didn't understand the vampirii and their role in the larger scheme of things; they feared them."

He did not give her any indication that she was right or wrong, or that he was pleased or displeased.

"And the second punishment?"

She had a harder time remembering but then said, "It was in the year 1, between BC and AD, the time of the Christ. He said 'Take eat, this is my body, drink, this is my blood,' and the Sapiens thought he was vampir and killed him by crucifixion because they believed the bars of the cross would ward off vampirii."

"And the third?"

She thought a long time but her brain felt frozen and she could not recall why her palms had been smacked the last time. She tried to force logic and did a quick mental scan of the centuries. It must have been a time between 1 and 6, because they had stopped at the 6th century, but she could not recall what she had stumbled over in any of those six hundred years.

Finally, she admitted, "I don't remember." She hung her head and her teeth caught her lower lip. She felt she had disappointed her Master in some vital way; she had displeased him, even failed him, failed to meet his expectations. She felt miserable.

"Come here," he said, his voice cold to her ears.

In trepidation, she went to him.

"Kneel down."

She did.

"Come close."

She moved forward on her knees until she was against his shins. He leaned towards her a little and took both her nipples in his fingers.

Instantly, moans escaped her lips as he played with her flesh, bringing the sensitive tips up firm, rocking her body with sensation that wet her labia and sent ripples zipping through her. And all the while he said, "Look at my eyes, Princess, because I want you to understand me."

She stared into his lovely, pale eyes and saw them change to the color of garnets; that shift so fascinated her.

"I'm going to spank you because you are a spoiled Sapiens child and Blander informs me that Sapiens are known to punish their children in this way, children who only seem to learn through pain. I want you to remember your lessons so I am giving you this additional incentive to help you with the ones you will learn tomorrow night, when you will pay more attention. Do you understand me?"

"Yes, Master," she gasped. All the while he talked he toyed with her nipples, pulling them out, away from her body, pinching, twisting, rubbing until they burned and the current between her breasts and genitals ran continuously back and forth. As he talked, she stared into the two crimson pools with black islands of safety at the center, and felt herself falling into those eyes, living in them.

"Tonight, I will not pleasure you because you have disappointed me."

A gasp of shock escaped her lips.

"The spanking is your reward for failing me. Tomorrow night you will do better so I won't need to spank you. And if I do not need to punish you, I can pleasure you. Do you understand me?"

"Yes," she said, not able to stop the large tears from rolling down her cheeks.

"Yes what?"

"Yes, Master. I understand."

"Tonight you will receive pain. Pay attention tomorrow night and if you are not punished by Blander, you will receive pleasure. You will be fucked by me, which I know you like. Do you like this?"

"Yes, Master," she said, "very much," aware now only of the pleasure he was providing her nipples.

Suddenly he stopped fondling her breasts and moved his hands away. Her hard nipples burned and throbbed, alive as they had never been, and she panted with desire and an acute sense of loss. Her inner thighs were slick with her juices, the scent permeating the air, washing through her nostrils. She felt her body pulsing.

He said, "Over my lap, Princess of the Sapiens," and when she hesitated, he lifted her by the waist and lay her across his thighs on her stomach so that her bottom was high, exposed, vulnerable.

"You have nine stripes from the stick. I will give you nine as well. Do you understand me?"

"Yes, Master."

"Nine on each cheek."

A little cry came out of her and she quivered in fear of the unknown; she had never been spanked and she did not know what to expect.

"Do you understand why?"

"Yes."

"Yes what?"

"Yes, Master, I understand. I have displeased you."

"You have. And the spanking will speak to you of my displeasure."

His palm smacked her right cheek hard, then again, the same cheek, creating a shocking pain, and one of her hands automatically flew up behind her to cover her flesh to protect it.

"Put your hand down!" he said coldly.

She did.

He smacked her a third time and she squirmed, sobbing uncontrollably by the fifth, the muscles of the cheek dancing in agony, struggling to avoid more pain, but he was relentless and laid on nine hard smacks.

She cried full out, loud racking sobs, clotted with despair.

"Do you know why I'm spanking you, Princess?"

Between sobs she managed to cry out, "Because I have disappointed you, Master."

"Not only that. I'm spanking you because I love you. I am doing what's best for you. Do you understand me?"

She cried hard, gasping out the words between the wails coming from her, "Yes, Master, I understand. You love me. You want what's best for me. I deserve this and need this. I have disappointed you."

"You understand why you are suffering?" he said. But before she could respond, he applied his palm to her left cheek, hard, nonstop, nine times, laying it over increasingly seared flesh, and soon she was out of her mind with the biting pain, screaming, unable to avoid, only submit to the harshness on her raw skin, reminding her to pay attention tomorrow evening so that she would not disappoint him again.

When the night ended, he chained her to the cold stone floor and she felt miserable, alone, in burning pain, and she could not stop crying.

"I won't pleasure you when you disappoint me," he said, blowing out the last candle and lying on the bed. "How will you learn if I reward you for disobedience?"

In the chilly darkness she sobbed hard, inconsolable. "I'm sorry, Master. Please, forgive me. I won't do it again. I'll pay attention tomorrow night, I promise!"

But the next night proved to be almost a repeat. Instead of nine strikes on her palm, she only received three.

Moarte quizzed her, fondled her nipples and spanked her twice the number of mistakes because, he told her, "You did not learn your lesson well enough last night. I was too lenient with you. If I'm not harsh, how will you please me? Me, who loves you and only punishes you for your own good. Do you understand me?"

And she accepted the punishment that left her buttocks aflame throughout the day and brought continuous tears because he did not penetrate her again and would not even touch her as she lay on the floor, desolate. It made her resolute in her desire to get the answers right the following night. She would prove to him she was worthy of his love. And he *did* love her, she knew that now. Why else would he punish her so severely?

But her body was not only in pain. Imbedded in it was desire. She imagined him between her burning cheeks but that fantasy could only satisfy her for a short while and it did not bring her release; she knew she would do anything for that piercing, anything.

By the third night she was sharp, paying complete attention, and was not punished.

That night Moarte lay her naked over a lower part of the ledge at the corner of the balcony so that she looked down like a gargoyle onto the courtyard where his warriors walked by and stared up to watch her being penetrated, but she didn't care. Let them see. She belonged to him, proudly.

One of Moarte's feet was on the balcony floor as was the knee of his other leg, and he thrust slowly and deeply as the moon crossed the sky and her breasts bounced in the air and she moaned out the agony and ecstasy for what felt like hours.

Below, crowds gathered, their calls and yells animal-like, syncopated against the moans and cries she made, which were in sync with his thrusts.

Only afterwards, when he pulled her up by the hair, her bare breasts jutting into the night air like a carved figure at the prow of a ship, his teeth finding their way to the familiar wounds in her neck, did he reach around and play with her nipples and rub her clitoris while his hard flesh staked her.

Later, he took her to the bed. She didn't know how to say it or if she should say it, but when he told her to lie face down it slipped out of her mouth, "Please, Master Moarte, enter the woman part of me. Please, take my virginity."

His voice was strange as he said, "One day, Princess. One day, when you love me enough, I will breach and ravish you."

That night she slept sated, her body tingling, on fire, her vagina hot and wanting, so ready for him, whenever he wanted her there. Her flesh was alive with passion and she knew she would do anything to please him. Anything.

CHAPTER SEVEN

"Don't you think you're overdoing it?" Belladonna said. "Her ass is always red and by now her rectum must be like raw meat. How is this reaching your goal?"

"It's the best of every world, Mother. I get to drink her blood, fuck her body and mind and torture her, all at the same time. She's learned the history of what the Sapiens have done to the vampirii. Now she moves on to her personal history."

"And you'll punish her until she loves you."

"She already loves me."

"Then why do more? Bring her out from under the spell and ask her now where the Sapiens King is hiding."

"Maybe I want to split the skin on her ass first."

Belladonna made a small motion with her mouth, not a smile but not unlike one, either. "You're smitten," she said.

Moarte felt shocked and before he could furiously deny it, his mother said, "Don't bother to deny it. Your defense is testament to your desire. You want her. There's no shame in this. Vampirii have always taken Sapiens. Some begin as slaves and progress to lovers. A few are even elevated to spouse."

She was speaking of her own progression. His father had captured her in a raid and had fallen in love with her, his slave, waiting until she gave birth before turning her. He brought her over six years after Moarte was born.

He'd always been curious about his mother's path, and asked her now, half expecting she wouldn't tell him. He had to phrase it delicately. "Did my father treat you well when you were a slave?"

Belladonna, never one to mince words, said, "Your father liked to fuck me and did, nightly. And when I displeased him, which I suppose I did often enough, he whipped me, as is the Deathbringer way with slaves. At least he whipped me at the beginning. But soon he grew to love me and when I became pregnant with you, he changed. He treated me as an equal—well, as much of an equal as is possible for a vampir with a Sapiens—then after your birth he married me, then altered me. You know the rest. But you're avoiding my question."

"What question? I thought I answered them all."

"You've become enamored with the Sapiens Princess."

He said nothing.

"When are you going to take possession of her vagina?"

"Why do you want to know?"

"Because what you're doing now, beating her, fucking her in the ass, this is fine if revenge is your goal, but it isn't progression. Why hold out the one thing that will bind her to you forever?"

"Because it is the one thing she desires. It's a carrot I will keep from her until the moment is right to use it to get what I want."

"How did I raise a son so manipulative?"

He felt hurt by this.

As always, her insight into him was astute. "You may feel hurt by my words, but they are true. There is no need for further manipulation, if in fact your goal is to find the Sapiens King."

He did not have a response.

"You're bent on revenge with this girl. Why?"

"She broke my—"

"I *know*! It was vicious. You were in pain. You almost died the final death. But your wings have healed, and the pain you have inflicted on her is ten times what she caused you. She has been paid back. Get beyond that, Moarte. You've got to wake her from this stupor in order to get the information you want and once you do that, she'll remember everything you have done to her and she will not view these acts as love. And unless you manage to truly love her, she will not betray her father and align with you. Right now, if you wake her tonight, she will turn against you. She'll view what you've done to her as brutality, not the blood drinking, which is the least of it, but the rest, the dominance, she'll see you as a brute and nothing more. She longs to truly belong to you but you won't take her. Why? If it's revenge, bitterness, anger, you are defeating yourself and wasting your time. If there is another reason, you had better be honest with yourself and find out what it is so that you can deal with it."

He was silent a long while, fighting the rage within him, justifying to himself why he still abused the Sapiens Princess, but knowing there was more to it than revenge.

Soon he came to the conclusion that his mother was right; there was no point to this. It had ceased being amusing for him. Now he acted by rote. When he stared into the eyes of the Sapiens Princess, eyes without a flicker of awareness, it was like playing with an inanimate object that could not play back because it held no spark. And yet the game he played with her allowed him to justify being with her. If he was anything, he was honest with himself, always. He wanted to be with her. He wanted to know her. And he would never know her this way. It occurred to him that he was afraid to love her because he knew she could never love him. He was born of a Sapiens mother and a vampir father but to her he would always be an enemy.

Finally he said, "What do you suggest I do?"

"Marry her. Shatter her maidenhead. Take her as a woman, as your wife, it's what she wants. If you do this she will believe you love her. Perhaps it's possible that you can impregnate her with your sons and daughters. With conception, she will give you anything and everything, regardless of what you've done to her in the past."

"How do you know?"

"I know because I did."

Chapter Eight

The following night Moarte announced to Valada's dread that she would again be seeing Blander for a further lesson. She did not look forward to making mistakes and exposing her tender palms to the stick and her bottom to another spanking, not to mention the fear of displeasing Moarte again and suffering a night when he did not penetrate her. She could not bear the thought of a night without him inside her. Sex with him was all she thought about day and night.

Moarte had become her obsession. Each night when he took her she rode waves of sensation. Sometimes it was his cock inside her, other times she pleasured him with her mouth and by doing that she pleasured herself, swallowing his gift, as he called it. She loved either way, and felt herself submit eagerly to his will—so much so that her worries and insecurities were washed away by this total giving over of herself to her master.

His teeth at her throat sent chills of pleasure through her body, knowing she was nourishing him. Often he now fucked her and drank from her at the same time, which thrilled her beyond any pleasure she could ever have conceived of before. In fact, she could hardly remember anything that had occurred before Moarte, only a feeling, that her life had been empty, hollow, as if there had been *no* life and whatever had been behind this black wall that blocked memory had left her unfulfilled.

What would make everything perfect is if he took her virginity. She had begged him twice. The second time he became enraged and reddened her behind until she could not sit the following night, and he did not fuck her. She did not beg again because she knew it displeased him. She tried to content herself with believing he would take her that way when he was ready. She just needed to wait patiently and submit to his will. But despite telling herself this, she experienced a yearning and an emptiness, as if something important was missing.

She arrived at Blander's and Moarte stayed with her this night.

Blander began before her birth. He talked about her father and his position as King in the Sapiens realm, how he took the throne from his own father by a violent act that resulted in her grandfather's death under mysterious circumstances. Her mother was from some other land— Blander didn't know which one, since despite living in the Sapiens castle, he had never seen her mother— but he knew that her father had not married her. This upset Valada and her body began to tremble.

Moarte moved close behind her, his hand entering the slit and sliding around her waist, pulling her body back against his, and a wave of lust spread through her, heating her, and then she calmed.

Blander continued. "Three years after you were born your mother died, but not by the hands or teeth of any vampir, which is what the Sapiens population was told."

"How do you know this?" she managed to say.

"I was there. I lived in your father's castle at the time, his advisor on many matters, including education. He did not want you educated beyond the ability to talk. He told me he demanded obedience from you and nothing more. You were to remain ignorant."

He let that sink in and Valada tried to reconcile that information with what she knew—or felt she knew—but could not remember details, only feelings. She could not make sense of this. If only she could clearly remember the past; if only her memories would somehow spread apart like clouds in a windy sky.

Finally, she asked, "Were you in the room when my mother died?"

"No. I told you, I never saw your mother."

"Then how do you know it wasn't a vampir who killed her?"

"No vampirii had been anywhere near the Sapiens lands when the alleged murder took place."

"How do you know that?"

"Everyone in the Sapiens land knew that. There were guards at the highest location, searching the sky and the ground for vampirii. You are aware of the Sapiens defenses, Princess Valada."

She did know that, or thought she did, but she had no clear mental picture of Sapiens defenses.

Finally she asked tentatively, "But vampirii have broken through Sapiens defenses before?"

Blander said, "Yes, there have been times—"

Moarte held up a hand. "Much of the time vampirii have not encroached on Sapiens land. Sapiens have disrespected truces, and captured vampirii on our own land. Such was the case with me recently." His tone was harsh and she felt his fingers against the skin of her waist tense.

Valada had not thought about Moarte being on Sapiens land but now that he said it, she had a vague memory of that, the details extremely hazy.

Moarte gave a signal to continue and Blander said, "Returning to your childhood, Princess Valada, you were not educated by the King's orders, and yet I was able to surreptitiously teach you some simple words and rudimentary mathematics before I left. And Reena, one of the female servants, secretly taught you to read."

Did she remember Reena? She thought she did... And suddenly out of the blue a realization struck her: The first vampir she had seen must have been the one her father had watched drain her mother. But the childhood knowledge of this vampir was so ephemeral that she could not grasp it or hold onto the memory. And more, she could not compare any image from the past that her father must have conveyed to any vampirii she had seen here, especially the being to whom she now belonged. Moarte loved her. He could not be the one who drained her mother! After all, he had not drained Valada. It must have been another King of the vampirii because it couldn't have been Moarte.

Blander's information was confusing and hard to listen to and integrate and Valada found herself almost hyperventilating. Only Moarte's fingers stroking her skin kept her from losing control. She did not remember any of this. She did not remember Blander, though he said he taught her when she was a young child, before he left the land of the Sapiens by choice, as did others.

"Many Sapiens turned against your father, rebelling at his unjust rule. We suffered great shortages of food and fuel while he and the wealthy grew richer. He insisted resources must be used for defense of the city because the vampirii could attack at any moment, but in my years with the Sapiens I had only seen the vampirii attack three times, each in retaliation for Sapiens acts of aggression. Under your father's rule, citizens were acutely aware of the watchful eye of the military, and especially their spies, fearful that anything we said or did would be used to imprison us, and worse. Many Sapiens rebels were abducted by the military and never seen again."

She had difficulty repeating back the lesson and found her face coated with tears as she struggled to remember what Blander told her which did not align at all with the emotional reality that existed in her brain though she could not remember the details to match the feelings. She missed some of the information and it was not Blander who punished her but Moarte. He lay her over the tall stool and opened the slit at the back, then used Blander's flat stick to whip her until she screamed.

That night in his chamber she lay sobbing on the floor, her body in an agony that would not dim. Moarte ignored her completely and the pain of abandonment was the sharpest punishment by far. A different and unknown agony tore at her heart that caused her to cry until sunset.

When he finally awoke, he pulled her to her feet and stared into her wet, red-rimmed eyes, her eyes still leaking tears, his eyes changing color, and said, "You must do better with your lessons. You will make me believe you prefer punishment to pleasure. "

"No, no Master, it's you—"

He placed a finger on her lips and said, "Tonight is your final lesson and you must remember what you learn. Only if you retain this knowledge will you be my wife."

He would marry her! She could not believe he said this! Joy spread through her and she felt light and free and hopeful and the pain disappeared. She stared up at his beautiful face and knew hers reflected the love for him she felt, the need, the desire. "I will be perfect for you tonight, Master. For you!"

She did not know whether he meant marry as in a ceremony or marry as in breaching her hymen only, because she did not know what the vampirii did, how they mated. But either way she wanted this, longed for it, and resolved to pay attention and learn everything tonight. No punishment would be needed and anyway her flesh was destroyed for the time being and could not be used as a way for him to express his disapproval. And that meant if he was displeased, he might not be able to show her and that would keep them even further apart. But it wouldn't come to that! She must learn all she could to please him!

Tonight when he took her to see Blander, Moarte remained again. An older woman with hair rivaling the sun and eyes the shape and same color but two hues darker than Moarte's joined them. She spoke with Moarte in the language of the vampirii so Valada could not understand.

Blander began where he had left off—with her birth and the death of her mother.

Tonight he spoke of her father and presented him as underhanded, conniving, cruel and ruthless. A liar.

"He destroyed his own people and he tortured vampirii whenever he could capture one. He broke truces and raided the vampirii stronghold during the day, when they could not fight back, burning them alive in the sun. He told lies that blamed the vampirii for every ill in his city, but the Sapiens population knows the truth; they are just too frightened to rebel. The Sapiens King is a monstrous despot with no honor."

She had difficulty hearing this because it wasn't true—it couldn't be!—and memorizing what he told her was hard.

"Your father did not love you."

"That is false," she said proudly. "My father loved me. I'm his only child. How could he not?"

Blander paused and glanced at Moarte who nodded once. "Think back on your life, Princess Valada. Then calculate the number of times you recall your father being with you as a child, while you were growing up, when you became an adult."

She dug into her memory, which was difficult, because her brain felt as if it was stuffed with thick cotton and getting to the events of her life was an exhausting struggle. Her past seemed unreal, as if she had dreamed it and then mostly forgotten the dreams. She could not find more than five occasions when she saw her father for longer than just 'in passing.' No! That could not be! "I'm just forgetting," she said, her eyes moving fearfully to the flat stick. "My father is a loving man."

"How do you know that?" Blander asked.

She didn't know how she knew, and was afraid this would displease Moarte, but when she chanced a glance at him and the woman who looked like him, he seemed pleased.

"Relate the five incidents," Blander instructed.

She related each one slowly, Blander encouraging her to provide as much detail as she could remember, which she did, although she could not recall many of the particulars.

There was the one time—the only time!—they ate a meal alone together, and another when they happened to be in the garden at the same moment and walked together for half the length of the hedge until her father ordered her to her room for no reason that she could see, but she obeyed.

Another time, her father showed her the dungeon—and threatened to send her there if she did not obey him. But she always obeyed. Always.

Rather than feeling any of these to be full and pleasurable experiences with her father, the retelling of every one brought to her awareness that they had spent almost no time together, and none of it good, and that left her feeling alone and parentless. He had been brusque with her. She spoke and he ignored her, or quickly sent her elsewhere.

Her father had been perpetually impatient and annoyed with her and she had learned early to avoid him when she could. As she related the incidents, she felt more and more depressed and alone and recognized the terror she had experienced in his presence which she had skillfully managed to keep at bay.

Blander guided her through her life. As she related it, she could not recall one time in which her father had smiled at her, held her, said anything to her that conveyed love. Despite a growing foreboding that she had never felt loved and cherished by him, still, stubbornly, she insisted, "I *know* he loved me."

"How do you know?"

Forlornly, she shook her head. "I don't know how I know." Again, she feared this was the wrong answer and would gain her punishment, but on her Master's face she could see it was not wrong but right. And she felt even more confused. Lost.

Blander finally questioned her about the young wife her father took, who would have borne him the babies already in her womb had she not died suddenly. This was a time Blander had not been in the realm and which had occurred less than a year ago. Consequently, his questions became more general and intellectual, less specific and emotional, and when he pointedly asked, "How did your father feel about these unborn children?" suddenly a memory surfaced that she had suppressed and she stopped speaking in mid-sentence.

"Speak," Moarte ordered her, his tone serious, and she glanced at him fearfully.

"I overheard him talking with her. I was passing, not listening in, but I couldn't help it. He said that he wanted a son and if not this time, the next, and he would even settle for a daughter. Then he said, 'As long as that other doesn't get my crown!' Because...because of my mother..."

"What about your mother?" the woman asked.

Valada turned to stare at her knowing that the horror she felt must be reflected on her face. Awareness crashed down onto her as if the ceiling had caved in.

"Speak!" Moarte demanded.

She stared at him and his eyes held hers, providing a rock, an anchor in a sea of chaos so strong it was like an ocean storm, waves impossibly high, knocking her off balance, threatening to drown her.

Moarte came to her. He took hold of her trembling shoulders and pulled her close, staring into her eyes, his turning from paleness to a solid red within seconds. "Speak!" he demanded.

"My mother. My mother...my..."

Her body quaked in his grip, and she gasped as if the air had been sucked out of the room.

"Speak!" he commanded, and suddenly she knew she must obey or he would be lost to her forever.

"She was...*vampir!*"

The three in the room looked as shocked as she felt.

"That's not possible," Moarte said. "The female vampirii cannot—"

The woman in the room lifted a hand, which silenced him.

For Valada, the full weight of her life now swamped her and she let this wave of knowledge that had crashed over her wash out again with a huge groan of agony, so loud, coming from so deep within that it threatened to drown her in despair.

Pictures formed in her mind, images that showed her the past, and she fled the room she was in for this other room, the one she had slept in when she was three.

"My father murdered her. I saw it! He killed her because she was vampir. And he blamed Moarte, King of the *Vampirii*. He tolerated me because I was half Sapiens, and I stayed out of his way. But he had no intention of giving up his throne to a half breed, a half Sapiens, half vampir. He never loved me!"

Suddenly, as if a steel door slammed closed within her trapping her life energy, she went limp, her body failing as her mind blanked and her overloaded emotions shut down, everything blocked, stopped.

From far away she heard Moarte say over and over, his voice growing louder, "Look at me. Look at me! Open your eyes."

Finally she was able to comply but her vision was hazy, as dull as her brain, and she could barely see him.

He picked her up and carried her back to his chamber and placed her onto his bed. The woman came with them and lay a cool compress on her forehead and held her hand, rubbing it in a soothing way. Valada stared at the ceiling listening to them but not fully comprehending what they were saying. She felt dead. Had she died?

"You must pull her out now," the woman said, "before it's too late."

"It's not complete."

"It has to be now," the woman said again. "It's trauma. You'll lose her if you don't."

"I'll lose her if I do. She'll remember everything."

"My son, you must take that chance. Do it now."

Suddenly Moarte's face was above hers, his eyes pale sapphires in a paler sky. She watched his eyes change to blood red and his lips move and she heard words like 'undoing', 'returning ', waking'. Then: 'remember'!

The brilliant rubies with black onyx imbedded in them faded and then she was staring into his pale blue otherworldly eyes, the black dots contracted to near pin points.

She looked around as if she had been in a coma and was just waking. This room, she recognized it; she had seen it before. This is where she slept, on the floor, beside this bed, chained to this bed. This is where Moarte staked her body, where his teeth cut into her and he sucked out her blood. He whipped her and sent her to Blander to be hit with the flat stick because she could not remember what was being taught, a history of the Sapiens she had never known about. And then she remembered her own history that she had not let herself be aware of and gasped like the thought-to-be-dead grasping for the breath of life.

She saw it all, remembered it all, from the cage, to sucking his cock and being bled on the balcony before his warriors, to the nights of sex and the pleasure she felt abandoning herself to him. To the blood he stole from her, so painful that it flipped her into ecstasy. His horrifyingly beautiful pale-as-death face, angry, furious, filled with hatred and a lust for revenge for what she had done to him when he was her father's prisoner and she broke his wings. She remembered it all!

The face she saw above her now was not the one in her memory from when he had been her prisoner in the land of the Sapiens, nor the one she remembered when she had first arrived here as a prisoner. No, not a prisoner, a gift—from her father—to save himself, giving her to this vampir King to do with as he liked. And he had done what he liked to her and she remembered all of it.

She shifted to a seated position on the bed. And while she wanted to hate Moarte, she also wanted something else, but all she could articulate was a confrontation, one she found strange. "Why didn't you want me? Why?" And she wasn't sure who she was talking to.

He backed away from her slowly, his face blank, and the woman came into view.

"Tell her, or you'll lose her," she said.

It was difficult for him to speak, and clearly he had trouble forming the words. It was as if he could not bring himself to admit what he knew and finally, instead of saying it, she could see in his eyes that he hedged, opting for indirect words, and finally said to her a little gruffly, "I will take you when I wed you. I told you that. And that will be soon. And then, then I will hunt down your father."

She drew her knees to her chest and closed her eyes, tears gushing out as she sobbed. He had brutalized her, mesmerized her, tortured her, used her, and yet she did not feel only hate for him and she wondered if she was still under his spell. But no, she knew she was not. Then why?

This made no sense. But what he had done to her was only part of the agony she felt. Most of it was because she no longer loved her father. She now saw him for what he was, for what he had done to her mother, for what he had done to his Kingdom and to the vampirii, for the lies he told her and especially for never loving her, his only child. She hated herself; she had tricked herself into believing her entire life that he *did* love her because she could not bear the truth. But the truth was, no one had ever loved her. Not her father, not Moarte. She could see that now. And she knew that everything Moarte told her was suspect.

She opened her eyes and could hardly see through the blur of tears but she saw Moarte's face and cried out, "I despise you! You hate me, that's clear, but the loathing I feel for you is so much greater. I don't believe anything you say. You wanted revenge and have taken it out on me, punishing me far more than I hurt you. Just because I'm Sapiens. But despite it all, Blooddrinker, I'll help you find my father, because as much as I hate you, I hate him more! But, I'll only help you on one condition."

"You're still my prisoner, Sapiens Princess! You are not in a position to make demands!" he said sternly.

"Hear her out, my son."

Valada said, "I want you to teach me to fight with a sword."

"So you can slay me?"

"So I can kill my father."

"It is *I* who will kill the Sapiens King!"

"Let us both kill him," she said bitterly. "My father is an evil man. He deserves to die, and twice. The Blooddrinker half of me will help you destroy him, and the Sapiens half will cry tears of joy at his demise. I will only lead you to him if you promise to let me participate in his death. Do you agree to this?"

"Watch your attitude, Sapiens Princess!"

Suddenly she remembered that he was King, and she nothing in this realm, nothing to him. Her voice softened with desperation. "Please, Moarte, let me help you slay him."

He stared into her eyes a long time, as if trying to read what might be a hidden agenda.

The older woman said, "Answer her, my son. You need to decide."

And finally Moarte said, "All right, Princess. But know this: if you're trying to trick me, you will not live to see another sunrise or sunset, and I do not care if you believe your mother was vampir. You will neither die quickly at my hands nor painlessly. And you will be fully conscious of what I do to you. Do you understand me?"

"Yes," she said. "Yes, I understand."

Chapter Nine

O ver the following week, Valada did not see Moarte other than when he awoke and when he came in to sleep. He did not speak much with her and did not touch her physically. She was fed and bathed by the girl Serene, and other than that left alone with the excruciating awareness that had descended upon her and which she was having tremendous difficulty integrating.

One night when the full moon shone over the vampirii stronghold, Valada was brought to the throne room wearing a jewel-encrusted gold dress and matching boots. Her long raven hair had been braided along the sides of her face and the rest draped down her back like a waterfall and laced with white night bloomers.

The woman she had seen before, the one who looked like Moarte, stood before the throne at the bottom of the three steps and to the side. An enormous number of vampirii warriors, both male and female, filled the cavernous room and she saw Blander in the crowd, and the one named Wolfsbane, near the front, the Sapiens girl Serene—who smiled at her— and a female vampir who resembled Wolfsbane near him.

Earlier, Serene and another Sapiens girl named Portia had come into Moarte's chamber to bathe her. Serene had been caring for her since her arrival and Valada had grown comfortable with this girl.

She asked Serene questions but all the girl would say is, "We're preparing you for your wedding to King Moarte." Which caused Valada's heart to sink.

Tonight, she was given no food or water, but encouraged to drink a foul-tasting herbal brew that made her urinate several times, and defecate. As if that wasn't enough, they gave her an enema and once everything was out of her that would come out, they sat her in a steaming bath and washed her body and hair with a lavender-scented soap. She felt her insides had been emptied because Moarte intended to enter her from behind again, and that upset her. But, she had not needed to be emptied before when he took her that way, so she was confused as well as troubled. Serene had not given a complete answer when she had asked, "Why are you doing this?"

Serene had only said, "Purification, Princess."

"Kneel before your King!" the woman who she had discovered was Moarte's mother ordered.

Valada hesitated and felt the pressure of everyone in this vast hall. She wanted to run away, but there was nowhere to run, and she didn't want to be brutalized anymore and then still be forced to marry him. If she did not comply, it would go badly for her. She held onto the one thing that fueled her now, the desire to murder her father and for that reason alone, finally she knelt before Moarte.

Moarte was dressed in black metal and leather, the latter so tight it was like a second skin on his slim frame. He wore a black metallic kilt, black hide bands crisscrossed his chest, and black leather boots laced to his knees, the color darker black, purer than that worn by his warriors. His hair the color of the moon gleamed in the candlelight, pulled through an inky metal cone. His midnight wings were folded behind him. The effect of so much darkness on this pale-skinned, platinum-haired blue-eyed being made for a striking contrast. His golden sheath had been exchanged for a black leather one, and imbedded in it at his waist was the dagger which he always carried on his person.

He looked confident and attractive to her, and she could not understand why she saw him this way when she should hate and fear him, and find him both loathsome and repulsive.

When she had woken from the trance he'd put her under, she understood everything, including why he took her in the ways he had, why he beat her, why she was made to pay for what her father had done, as well as what she had done to him. None of it painted a pretty picture of him. He was callous, cruel, calculating. Every action had been designed to manipulate her.

But despite that, here she was, about to be married to him, and that did not gel with what he had done to her. She had already agreed to lead him to her father so there was no need for this pretense. She thought that he might want the sanctity of matrimony, if vampirii believed in the sanctity of marriage, as a way to justify brutalizing her further.

In the Sapiens Kingdom in which she had been born, a husband could do virtually as he pleased with his wife—that was the main reason she had kept her heart locked away from any who tried to win her hand. She realized her resistance had been instinctual, motivated by what she now recognized as her father's cruelty, which she had not allowed herself to be consciously aware of. The vampirii were probably the same demented patriarchs.

And thanks to her father, she, a Princess born, was betrothed to this demon. But what mystified her most was that although she did not love Moarte, she didn't hate him. How could that be? Maybe she was just emptied out of all emotion.

"We are here," Belladonna began, "to witness an unusual ceremony, the joining of this one to our ruler, as is King Moarte's wish. Half Sapiens, and half vampir she claims to be, possibly one of our own, but definitely one of our enemy."

Valada heard grumbling in the ranks—the vampirii did not believe her lineage, but she knew it was true.

Belladonna said to Valada, "Our King demands this joining. You will go to him now, on your knees, baring your throat, to signify that you bow to his authority."

Valada clutched the skirt of the dress and moved forward slowly on her knees, climbing the three steps until she reached him, stopping just at his feet. She looked up and he was staring down at her, his face beautiful and cold as a winter's night, not alive, but not dead, his ice-blue eyes penetrating. And she knew her eyes were sad.

She felt deep despair. Life as she knew it had unraveled and was undone forever. All that she believed, or thought she believed, had evaporated like a mist at daybreak, replaced by a knowledge that felt too stark to live with. A cutting awareness of lovelessness and cruelty that did not encourage her to continue. The only desire she felt strongly was to murder her father to avenge her mother, and herself. Beyond that, all else seemed unimportant, including this event.

As she stared up at him, head back, and he stared down at her, she knew he could see this grief in her eyes. He had caused it in so many ways but mostly by forcing her awareness. She could not unlearn what she had learned. It would stay with her and permeate every aspect of her life until she died.

If he wanted to marry her to torture her, there was nothing she could do about that. If he married her to force the demand that she give him the location of her father, well, she would comply again, provided he agreed to her demand. He indicated that he would but she did not trust him. She no longer trusted anyone.

Words were said by the woman Belladonna, Moarte's mother, and Valada did not pay attention. Whatever the words, they had little to do with her. She was a prisoner, forced into a marriage to a being that had brutalized her, that had hated her and probably hated her still, by a father who at best never cared for her and at worst hated her also, and who had murdered her mother before her eyes. Nothing would lift the veil of grief laced with aloneness that clung to her like a shroud. This ceremony was a farce and unimportant.

But the speech only lasted a short time. And when Belladonna finished, Moarte gestured with his fingers for Valada to stand. He turned her to face the others in the room, then reached around and opened the front of her dress, pulling the fabric apart to expose her breasts to the crowd.

A Sapiens girl, naked, came up beside them on one side, head bowed, holding a black velvet cushion with two gold rings sitting on top. On the other side a bearer, a young vampir, also naked, approached, head back in the vampirii submissive posture, carrying a small black cauldron with three metal rods in it; steam rose from the pot as if it had just been taken from a fire.

Moarte removed one of the skewers which had been shaved to an extremely fine point at the end, like a needle. The metal glowed red hot. He stood behind Valada and slightly to her right side. His free hand reached around her torso on the left and grabbed her left breast. He squeezed it until the protruding fleshy nipple firmed like a ripe cherry.

The needle moved toward her nipple and, panicked, her hands started to come up.

"Do not resist!" he commanded.

There was nothing her hands could have done anyway because before she knew what was happening, he stabbed her nipple from the right to the left with the searing needle.

Her body convulsed and she fell back against him screaming, her face coated with tears, barely able to catch her breath. The iron was blindingly hot and she smelled her flesh cooking.

He held her breast tightly and firmly until the needle was completely through to the other side, and all the while she shrieked and her body buckled but her breast stayed rigid in his hand and his arm pressed her chest tightly against him so she could not move that part of her body easily. He pulled out the needle but even when it was removed, the searing pain remained.

Someone handed him a wet cloth that smelled of savory herbs and he pressed the cool fabric against her breast, dimming the burning. He then lifted one of the rings from the pillow and slipped it through the new hole in her nipple while she gasped air and her body trembled as if she would shake apart. She felt on the verge of fainting.

He finished by closing the ring with a strange locking mechanism imbedded in it that let her know she would not be able to remove it. Ever.

Fearfully, she watched him pick up another hot needle-like skewer from the small cauldron. He took her hand and placed it onto the handle of this rod and his hand over hers. This time he pierced his own nipple, the one on the right. He did not flinch, did not tremble, and as with her own burning flesh, she could see smoke as the blazing iron melted a hole in his pale nipple.

He did not use a cooling cloth and she wondered if vampirii did not feel pain as Sapiens did. That led her to wondering if she was more Sapiens and less vampir. He took the other ring from the cushion, handed it to her and moved her hand to his chest. She slid the ring through the hole in his nipple, but he closed it in the same, permanent way.

The piercings and the rings were symbolic, she knew; her left, his right. Sapiens used rings as well, on the fingers, but there was no pain.

A peculiar feeling came over her. She did belong to him now. In the Sapiens world, a marriage was usually permanent until one died or divorced. With the vampirii, Serene had told her that they, too, mated for life, or what they called life, which might be eternity. The enormity of this was not lost on her, that she was bound to the King of the Vampirii forever. The vampir King who had used and abused her and probably would again, and might still kill her. She held no illusions; he was marrying her to control her and to force her to lead him to her father on his terms.

The older woman said something and she only heard the last part, about "...final symbol of this mating."

Suddenly Moarte picked her up around the waist and placed her over his shoulder so that she faced behind him, her cheek against one of his soft, feathery wings. She felt him lift the skirt of the golden dress and push it up above her waist so that it fell behind and over her head, exposing more of her naked body to the crowd. The skirt cut off her view of everything.

She lifted the fabric up enough so that she could see and turned her head. The bearer of the cauldron, whose throat was still bared, moved the pot around so that the third iron rod became available and Moarte took it. This one was shorter and her brief glimpse before it was out of sight let her see that the tip was not fine and pointed but was some sort of shape; it looked like the branding irons used by farmers to distinguish ownership of one herd of cattle from another. She couldn't see the image on the brand clearly but it might have been the letter 'V'. It didn't matter what the image was, he was going to brand her flesh with a scalding iron!

Suddenly, Belladonna said from behind her head, "The symbol of the vampir throne."

Moarte gripped her thighs tight by wrapping his strong arm around them, and the older woman locked her arms around Valada and leaned against her so that she could not move her torso. With the skirt well over her head now she could not see at all. She knew what was coming but had no time to prepare herself, if she *could* have prepared herself.

Scorching metal tore through the skin of her buttock, into the muscle below and she screamed and thrashed to the extent she could, hyperventilating from the pain. Water gushed from her eyes and her throat was soon raw from shrieking. If she'd had food in her stomach, she would have vomited it. If she'd had urine in her bladder or feces in her rectum, those would have come out as well.

Pain engulfed her and she became just pain, throbbing, unable to stop screaming even if she had wanted to. Lightheaded, feeling as if she was on the verge of losing consciousness, she hoped she would pass out. Despite being held rigid, her body spasmed. Her buttocks quivered from the fiery rod, as if flames had exploded on her skin, blistering her flesh as it cooked.

She heard metal clang against metal as the iron was dropped back into the cauldron yet it felt like it still burned through her and she could not stop screaming, out of her mind with pain.

Suddenly, a cooling cloth gave her some relief so that the sounds coming from her died down until she was left whimpering and her body trembling.

Belladonna released her and Valada's body went limp, dangling over his shoulder like a rag doll until he pulled her up and lowered her feet to the ground, saying, "On your knees!"

Her legs trembled uncontrollably and she could not stop shaking and moaning but somehow, almost falling, she managed to kneel before him.

"Bare your throat!"

She lifted her face to him, her head back, what he had inflicted on her twisting her features into a mask of misery.

And then he gave a speech in the language of the vampirii while she knelt, head back, racked with the residue of pain, her trembling body beyond her ability to control, and she did not understand a word of what he said until his strong and powerful voice ordered her, "Stand before me, Wife. I am your husband, but I am also your ruler, your King."

She stood on shaky legs, her face wet with the tears still leaking from her eyes, and he half turned her to face the crowd, his arm around her waist pulling her close to him.

And then, in a moment she could not track, his head reared and his teeth sank deep into the familiar wounds in her throat. He pulled them out and clamped his lips onto her wounds. The room was reverently silent, the only sound her sobs and gasps and panting as her body trembled, victim of a primal reaction.

Finally he finished and lifted his head. Out of the corner of her eye she glimpsed his scarlet eyes, his red mouth and chin, his teeth coated with the vibrant crimson of her blood.

He slit his chest near the pierced nipple with one of his talon-like nails and at the same time his other hand behind her neck pulled her face to him. She knew she was expected to drink his blood and while the idea was repellent, part of her saw no reason not to do this now. It was all too late.

She opened her mouth and swallowed down the red gore, her mind going even more blank than it had been so far, and she only stopped when the grasp on the back of her neck pulled her back.

She tasted the cool blood on her lips—her blood, likely, recycled through his body—and felt it dripping down her chin, coating the inside of her mouth. And although blood had always repelled her, especially the scent, oddly this did not bother her and she wondered if she was now dead inside, feeling little but physical pain, beyond jaded, her emotions pulverized.

Maybe it was the vampir part of her that was not repulsed. Maybe this act was already turning her into what he was. It was all out of her control and she dismissed the thoughts as irrelevant. *Everything* was irrelevant.

He turned her and they both faced the room with blood stained lips. For long moments, the crowd was silent. Valada had the thought that this silence was akin to the grumbling earlier, that they did not accept this marriage. They did not accept her.

Suddenly, Wolfsbane cried, "King Moarte! We honor you!" The crowd went wild.

The insane cheers and calls throughout the throne room echoed, bouncing around the high ceiling and the jagged stone walls, the sound intensifying. Instantly, music began, and tables were brought in as well as crystal goblets. Everyone, it seemed, expressed joy and happiness at the marriage of their King.

But Valada could not feel happy. She felt alone, apart, alien. The life had been sucked out of her and it had little to do with the pain of being pierced, branded or having her blood nearly drained.

Moarte sat on the throne again and Belladonna directed her to sit at his feet on a cushion. Crystal decanters of blood were being brought into the room. Naked slaves had been stationed at convenient locations, living winepresses.

Sapiens slaves danced to the music while vampirii watched and laughed and fondled them. She observed it all with no feeling, no sense of being here and part of this. She felt Moarte's hand run through her hair at the back but it gave her no real sensation, no feeling of connection. Her nipple ached. Her buttocks burned. But mostly, her soul felt gouged from her body and the hollow space left behind was achingly raw.

He pulled her head back and bent to pierce her throat again where the holes had already closed after leaving trails of blood drying on her neck and chest.

He cut deep and quick and then was drawing blood from her and into him until he was sated, and she became lightheaded and felt weak and nauseous, though there was nothing inside her but his blood.

The party, if that's what this could be called, lasted most of the night. Towards dawn, Moarte stood and said to her, "Come, Wife!"

She got to her feet on wobbly legs and followed him passively to his chamber where he pulled the curtains closed and then snuffed all but a few candles near the bed.

He turned and motioned with his fingers moving in waves, beckoning her towards him, the talon-like nails resembling nothing less than daggers.

CHAPTER TEN

For the first time he wondered what she saw when she looked at him. If she was to be believed, they were both half breed children—although he could not fathom how a female vampir could possibly conceive. Valada's mother had probably turned after her birth. He looked entirely vampir while she could be mistaken for nothing but Sapiens. With her upbringing, her life with her insidious father, she could only fear vampirii and must see him as something both unnatural and terrifying, and yet she had been good at disguising those fears.

She had been through a lot tonight. The agony of the piercing and branding had exhausted her, that was clear. He took her blood because it was expected of him—his mistrustful and rebellious warriors needed symbols of his potency and mastery, especially during such an important ceremony, and he understood that. But he had not taken as much as he could have, aware that her body was barely able to sustain what she had to have perceived as a violent assault.

He stared at her face, studying her eyes, intensely aware of the sadness, the desolation imbedded in her. He felt helpless to alter those feelings.

She came to him obediently, passionlessly, and when she was near enough, he slipped an arm around her waist and pulled her close. Her hands stayed at her sides and she would not meet his gaze. He lifted her chin and her eyes still avoided his, as if he would again mesmerize her, and that bothered him. He leaned down to kiss her lips, the first time he had done this. She kept her mouth closed, and he pulled back at this rebuff.

"Do not close off to me, Valada!" he said, a bit more gruffly than he had intended. "You are my wife now. For we vampirii, this means you are with me, you belong to me, and I am responsible for you." He did not say that he belonged to her as well. "We are together. Do you understand me?"

"I understand you, Husband" she said, and both of them were keenly aware of the deadness in her tone.

He searched her face, her eyes, for some spark, but couldn't find one. His mother had been right: she remembered everything and held his actions against him for what he had done to her. No one could fault him for his fury and the desire to take revenge for the callous way she treated him in the Sapiens dungeon. And he had punished her for her father's acts as well. But who could understand—and even he could not—why he had wanted to keep torturing, using and abusing her. What pleasure had he derived from that game? He could not remember what he'd had in mind, what feelings had propelled him, but he now saw the result of acting out the sinister elements of his nature. What he saw before him reflected his cruelty.

Not all of it was from his actions, of course. Much of her bleakness had to do with her father, her life before she came here. But he had a part in it and did not know what to do to nullify that.

Suddenly she lifted a hand to reach out to him and he thought she would touch his waist, a gentle gesture, one he needed from her. Instead, she grabbed the dagger from the sheath and jumped back and away from him.

Her dark eyes flashed with fury and fear in equal parts. "Stay away from me, Blooddrinker! Keep back!"

He felt hurt that she would do this, but not afraid. She could not wound him physically. He could move fast, faster than her, and he would anticipate her intent.

He held out his hand. "Wife, give me the weapon and I will forgive this. You're skittish on your wedding night. I understand."

She shook her head and continued pointing it in his direction.

"Are you afraid of being penetrated as a woman?"

Her face shifted and he thought she might cry. "I'm not afraid of you, Moarte," she said, her voice high and laced with fear.

"Then what?"

Her features shifted again, creased with a hopelessness that he could barely comprehend. Suddenly and quickly she was raising the dagger, the blade's razor edge headed towards her neck.

He moved blindingly fast, grabbing her hand to keep her from slashing her throat. Still, she managed to slice the skin and muscle beneath, but not the artery she was aiming for, and he quickly wrestled the weapon from her grasp.

She doubled over with deep, forlorn, racking sobs that spoke of isolation and abandonment, of despair and an eternity of hopelessness.

He pulled her to him and wrapped his arms around her, holding her tight as she fought him, containing her, and she finally gave up fighting and wailed like a mourner for the dead.

He moved a hand behind her head and her cheek pressed against his chest, hot tears coating his cool skin, and that desolation melted him in some way he could not have anticipated and could not comprehend.

He sensed the night fading, pressing on him, and moved her to the bed and undressed her, and she did not stop crying.

It was as if all the tears in the universe came out of her, everyone's, an inconsolable wretchedness that would never end.

Instead of talk, he removed his clothing and when they were both naked he laid her down and positioned himself between her legs and pressed his cock against her hymen and broke it quickly.

She gasped and then instantly ceased sobbing.

He took her slowly, penetrating deep, wanting her to feel him as he kissed her lips and fondled her breasts. The rims of her eyes were red as cherries, the whites bloodshot, glistening from tears, but her lips parted and she sighed and moaned a little.

He made love to her continuously during the darkness, wanting her more than he could have imagined, his enemy, who had injured him almost fatally, who he had hated so recently and wanted to murder. He knew his passion must be rubbing her nearly raw but he needed her to remember him inside her during the daylight hours while he slept. He wanted her to think of him. He wanted her to feel that she belonged to him, not as a mesmerized prisoner, or a slave, but as his mate. He wanted her to want him. To need him. To love him. Finally he could admit this to himself.

"You belong to me," he whispered over and over softly, "but now it is different," hoping that the words he feared sounded inadequate to the task would act as a balm on a deep soul wound, and she stilled.

And then something changed. Her body began responding. Her arms circled his neck, her hips lifted to meet his thrusts, her legs wrapped around his waist to pull him in deeper. He heard her breath quicken and felt the warm air from her panting against his neck. Her vagina turned slick and heated.

From the pit of despair she lost control and as her body spasmed she cried out, first just sounds, then erotic moans. He felt her climax like the earth at the start of a quake, and when she called his name he became strong and virile and released his blood/sperm into her at that moment.

Before he fell asleep, he chained her wrists as before, but higher up on the bed so that she could lie with him.

"I won't run away," she whispered into the candlelit room.

"And I am making sure of that," he told her, and fell into a deep sleep, his hand between her legs, stroking her clitoris until he stopped moving, only to wake and find her beside him, hot and wet between the legs, waiting for him, wanting him, her hymen blood staining the sheet.

He rose from the bed to her questioning eyes, pulled the sheet out from beneath her, and went to the balcony naked to drape the fabric so that his warriors could cheer as they passed, as was tradition, but also so that they would accept her as their queen, if not tonight, one night. Eventually.

Chapter Eleven

Moarte unlocked the chains holding Valada and left the room as soon the Sapiens girl Serene entered. "Come, my Queen," the girl said, "please, sit and eat and drink to renew your strength. Your husband needs you."

Valada ate the food and drank the wine with herbs that Serene said fortified the blood. All the while she watched the girl as she directed the other servants who brought water to fill the bath.

Once Valada's hunger was sated, Serene led her to the tub, the water only tepid because of her new wounds, and as she had many times, bathed her, washing her body and hair with a sweet-scented soap that smelled of roses, as did the oil in the bath.

Valada felt good. She did not really understand why. A night ago she had entered a state of deep despair for many reasons, two of which involved being married to Moarte, her enemy, who had abused her, and for being forced to see her father for what he really was. Her entire world had crumbled and left her floundering with nothing stable to hold onto, nothing in the universe she could call good. And yet, despite how he had treated her, something in Moarte *was* good. She believed he loved her a little, that he had changed. And as if reading her mind, Serene said, "My Queen, the vampirii are different than the Sapiens; I've seen this. I've been with Wolfsbane for several years, since I was a child."

Valada was shocked. "You came here as a child?"

"Yes, I was brought here a slave, as I told you, at the age of sixteen. But Wolfsbane loved me and soon he took me as his lover. One day he'll marry me. And I'm not the only one. There are many like me, both females and males, Sapiens who have abandoned their former life to live with a vampir. The vampirii are capable of great shifts in emotion. Our kind has seen this, and you must see it. King Moarte loves you."

"How do you know?"

"He married you."

"To control me."

The girl shook her head. "That's not a reason to marry. The vampirii marry forever. It's not a commitment to be taken lightly as their existence is very long and ultimately they must turn the Sapiens; that's part of the marriage contract."

"What contract? I don't recall signing one."

The girl looked surprised, then smiled. "But my Queen, you agreed in the ceremony. I was there, and witnessed this. You acquiesced to the will of our King by kneeling before him and baring your throat and in doing that agreed to belong to him as he belongs to you."

Valada thought about that. "He belongs to me?"

"Yes, of course! Did you not hear that in the words spoken by Belladonna?"

As she stood from the hot and scented water, Serene toweled her dry and gave her a midnight dress of thin material that draped over her body in soft folds. "Come," Serene said, and led her from the room, down a corridor, and to a chamber where there were a lot of Sapiens, both males and females, most naked, lounging, eating, talking, brushing one another's hair or painting nails. In this harem-like space were mirrors, long, short, wide, and Serene led her to a full-length one. A number of the young Sapiens crowded around them. "Look at yourself, my Queen. You're beautiful!"

Valada stared at the image in the mirror. Her body was slim, her posture erect, her hair lustrous and dark as her eyes, her lips red naturally, not stained by blood. She had never been interested in her appearance but now gazed at her own features as if looking at a stranger and for the first time in her life saw herself as beautiful. And as if reading her mind, Serene said, "This is what King Moarte sees. How could he not love you?"

The young Sapiens surrounding them enthusiastically agreed with this.

"He might care for what she pretends is her vampir side, and I doubt there is one, but never for the Sapiens," came a female voice, and Valada turned. The Sapiens slaves, though, did not turn, and their heads were bowed in a way that looked more fearful than respectful.

She saw the female vampir who resembled Wolfsbane, and remembered seeing her at the wedding. This undead strode into the room, her silver-black boots and skirt shimmering in the candlelight. She wore a thin shirt like all the warriors with straps crossed between her firm naked breasts of a pale color that Valada could not identify. A short sword hung from her waist.

"So," she said aggressively, "you are Valada. The Sapiens that Moarte has made his queen."

The tone of voice of this vampir evoked wariness in Valada. The coldness was both in her words and in her eyes and Valada believed that something else entirely resided in her heart.

Instead of a direct response she merely said, "I am Valada."

Instead of responding to Valada, the vampir snapped at Serene, "You've been filling her head with nonsense, as you fill your own! My brother can no more love you than Moarte can love her, and you will never be his wife." Now she spoke as if Valada was not in the room. "True vampirii are incapable of loving Warmbloods. It's our nature. You're nothing but prey to us!"

Serene kept her head bowed and did not respond.

Valada felt she should say or do something. "I suspect that some vampirii are capable of love, others not."

The air in the room chilled as Hemlock turned her eyes on Valada, who felt their tremendous hypnotic draw. To save herself, she glanced elsewhere. "An intriguing room," she said in a general way. "Why are all these Sapiens here?"

"Because they're slaves. Our playthings. All Sapiens are our playthings, and it might be good for you to remember that, Valada." She did not call her Queen, as Serene did, and Valada knew from being Highborn that it was a slur, but ignored it. She would find out the scope of her status eventually, but already sensed this vampir was an enemy-in-the-making, for some unknown reason.

She said to Serene using an imperious tone, "Escort me to Moarte's chamber!"

The girl looked up and Valada saw relief in her eyes.

"We will meet again," the vampir said, "under different circumstances."

Valada didn't know what to say to that so she said nothing, just left the room. As she did, she heard this: "I will have you and you tonight. To my chamber now, and bring the long whip!"

Once they had returned to Moarte's room, Valada said, "Serene, who was that and why is she so antagonistic towards me?"

"My Queen, please, I should not be saying this."

"Speak freely, Serene. I won't repeat what you tell me nor reveal the source if the subject comes up. Your words are safe with me."

The girl looked relieved again and her voice lowered as she said, "Hemlock is the twin sister of Wolfsbane. They were turned centuries ago. She's long desired to be Moarte's wife. She resents you now, and you must be careful. She's vicious. Before Wolfsbane elevated me to his consort, Hemlock took me to her rooms. She will play with both female and male Sapiens through the night, using them for sex and whipping them severely."

Serene lowered the shoulder of her dress to reveal scars on her back.

"Hemlock did this?" Valada said.

"Yes. It was her cruelty that caused Wolfsbane to take me for his lover, to save me. I became his personal slave so that no other could have me. He's a good vampir. His twin sister is not. Please, my Queen, do not trust her."

"Thank you for the warning, Serene. I will heed your words."

"My Queen, the hour grows late. May I massage you with oils so that you will be relaxed for our King when he returns?"

Valada agreed and Serene went to the door and asked the guards in the mutual language of the vampirii and Sapiens to send for a table. It arrived quickly and Valada lay on the padded surface on her stomach.

Soon, small but strong fingers were working the muscles of her neck, back, arms, legs and buttocks with rose oil, kneading, sliding over her skin sensuously so that she felt dreamy and sleepy and fell into a semi-sleep state like an erotic daydream.

She awoke to the sense that the touch had changed and the hands were different and felt her body slowly pulled until her legs draped over the end of the table.

Familiar hands spread her cheeks and her body grew warm and soft and wanting as Moarte slid into her vagina and she moaned. He fucked her until her temperature rose and she felt she could not bear the intensity of this heat and then suddenly exploded into a fiery wave of passion that left her moaning helplessly and quivering as he thrust deep into her one final time.

Moarte stayed inside her for long moments before pulling out.

Finally, he lifted her up and carried her in his arms to the bed where he made love to his new wife until the sun rose and she went from warm to hot, over and over again, from dead to alive, despair to hope, emptiness to a swelling love for him that left him feeling more whole than he had ever felt in his many centuries of existence. And he was astonished.

Chapter Twelve

They were just outside the locked gate to his private gardens at the back of the fortress, and Moarte handed her the broadsword, which she had requested. The second he released it into her hands, it dropped to the ground; she couldn't lift it, the metal was far too heavy. She looked up at him.

"As I warned, this isn't the right weapon for you," he said, and went to the long box his servants had carried out, rummaging through it until he found a very short weapon. He presented it to her, handle first.

Valada examined it for a moment then looked up at him. "Is this a sword? I've never seen a small one like this."

"It's a dagger."

"Like what you wear?"

"Yes, but because it's longer, the blade will sever a head."

Carefully she touched the edge of the blade with her fingertip. It was so sharp that even this gentle contact produced a line of blood. She looked up at Moarte again and his eyes went to red from the bloodlust brought on by the sight and scent of her sanguine fluids.

She held her hand out to him to drink and his eyes narrowed and hardened and the red faded.

"What?" she asked. "I thought you wanted this."

"If I want your blood, I will take it. I do not need you to feed me."

She didn't understand but withdrew her hand. Whatever pride he felt that involved restraint and control, she had stepped over the line. "I'm sorry," she said.

He walked to her and stood behind her, gripping her hand that held the dagger. "This is a weapon that should be hidden. At the same time, it is useless unless you have ready access to it. Once it's out in the open, once you bring *any* weapon into the open, do not hesitate to use it. The aggressor is usually the one who wins the fight."

He pushed her hand forward sharply and the dagger cut air, almost knocking her off balance. "Now, you will do it," he said. "Stand with your legs apart, for balance. Yes! Use your other hand also for balance. If the dagger goes up, your other hand goes down. And the opposite. If part of your body leans forward, another part must lean back. Part to the right, part to the left. These are natural movements. Always stay in balance. If you lose your balance, your enemy will take advantage of that weakness."

They spent hours with her thrusting the dagger and staying balanced. Moarte took a dagger himself, half the size of her blade, and sparred with her. Most of the time the tip of his dagger was at her throat before she could even move. "You leave yourself too open," he said. "Keep the narrowest angle of your body facing your enemy, not the widest part. Protect your vulnerable areas by the way you stand and hold your head. Don't be wide open to your enemy and offer him flesh to attack. And always look your enemy in the eye. That is the only way you will know what he intends to do."

At one point, Valada asked him, "Can we rest? I'm not a full vampir. My Sapiens side is tired."

"Sapiens are weak. And you did not learn defense."

They sat side by side on a bench, the waning moon with bats flying across its glow above them. "I wasn't taught *anything*," she admitted. "I must have been smart enough to learn more sophisticated language on my own with just a few lessons from my nursemaid, and I taught myself to read starting from the basics, and to play a stringed instrument. I didn't remember all this, until…"

She stared straight ahead and soon she felt his hand slide up the back of her neck and through her hair.

"Moarte, I can't tell you how my life seems to me now. It's as if I lived someone else's life and I don't know who that person is. She walked in a grey land of shadows like in a strange dream, believing things that were not true, not able to see the truth, not able to face what really happened."

"You were young, Valada. You could not remember what really happened to your mother."

"Maybe not, but I should have been able to recognize that my father was cold and callous towards me. Why did I hide this from myself?"

"How could you have seen this and continued? You did learn defense, an unusual defense, one that allowed you to survive an impossible situation."

She shook her head. "If I had let myself see, I could have done something."

"What could you have done? Where could you have gone? You had no options."

She shook her head again and he turned her head and kissed her, fondling the breast with the ring, and she fell into the kiss, her body warming and lifting slightly as she responded to him.

The kiss turned feral, lips moving, his tongue into her mouth as he opened the top of her dress, then his lips were on her ring-free nipple, her hand slipping under his kilt to stroke him there until he firmed. Within seconds he had her undressed and kneeling on the bench.

His penis found her vagina easily, naturally, and he went deep into her and she exhaled from the wonderful sensation of this. Her body felt the now-familiar heat spreading along her vaginal lips and burning her as he penetrated her, his thrusts steady as the pace picked up. Sensation soared through her and she moaned her pleasure into the dark night.

They came together, she crying out his name, what always came from her lips now when he brought her to this pinnacle. And afterwards he held her and she him, entwined, touching, kissing, in a warm and intimate embrace.

"Enough of a break," he finally said. "We leave in two nights and it's crucial that you be ready."

She stood and began to dress but he said, "No. Fight me naked. The King wishes to watch his wife's tits bob and to smell her cunt juices on the air."

She had no idea that such rough talk could arouse her, but it did.

They parried for another two hours until light crawled up the sky and her arm that held the dagger trembled from exhaustion, then they returned to their chamber and made love until he slept, facing each other, her leg over his, his erection inside her still, and she could not believe how happy she felt with him and did not understand it at all.

And then, in an instant, sadness engulfed her. Then rage. She thought about her father. No matter what Moarte said, she knew she would be the one who would kill him.

Chapter Thirteen

Two nights later, the second the sun set, Moarte was up quickly. He called Belladonna and Wolfsbane to the private room just off the throne room. With his mother and his most faithful warrior listening, Moarte outlined the plan he and Valada had hatched.

"We will fly to the haunted caves closest to the Sapiens city tonight. This is where the Sapiens King is hiding."

Wolfsbane said, "Moarte, you cannot enter."

"And are you telling me something I do not already know?"

Wolfsbane bowed his head slightly. "My King, I am only wondering how you will enter the caves."

"Valada will go in alone and bring him to me. She knows where he'll be."

From the looks on their faces, Belladonna and Wolfsbane both thought this was not a good idea. Belladonna spoke first, since she could get away with it.

"My son, your wife might still align with her father."

"I don't think so, Mother. I see no signs of that."

"Perhaps. But there is another risk. She might kill him herself."

Moarte had thought this, but he also had Valada's promise. They had pledged to destroy the Sapiens King together. "You were there the night she made her wishes known," he said.

"Yes, I was. And this is why I'm concerned. She wants revenge, perhaps more than you do. Being alone with her father might prove irresistible."

"I'll have to take that chance," he said. It was a scenario he had entertained already, but didn't know what he could do about it. "Unless, of course, you see another option."

"I do not," his mother acknowledged. "Perhaps Wolfsbane..."

"My King," Wolfsbane said, "I suggest that your warriors can surround the caves. We can send in captives, those now loyal to us. They can set fires and whoever is within will be smoked out into the open."

"A good plan, Wolfsbane, and perhaps if my strategy doesn't work, I'll adopt yours. But there are problems with this. As you well know, each of the four mountains contains caves, all of them haunted but for one area on the mountain closest to our stronghold. Valada tells me that the mountain on which the Sapiens city is built has many dozens of entrances, some of which do not exit to the outside but lead directly into the castle of the Sapiens King, and others lead by underground tunnels to caves in the other mountains. Should the Sapiens flee to the caves in the mountains to the west, they would be safe and we do not have enough warriors and Sapiens slaves combined to attack all entrances at once. Also, there would undoubtedly be a loss of vampirii as well as our slaves; the losses might be great. At present I do not wish to risk this. This battle is between me and the Sapiens King and if Valada can lead him to me, I can kill him without losing one warrior."

"A noble ideal," his mother said. "You are your father's son."

He took that as her blessing.

"Mother, you will assume the throne in the short spans of my absence, and if, for some reason, I do not return..." he did not need to say it.

She acquiesced with a nod.

"I will fly close to the cave entrance with Valada tonight, and return here alone before sunrise. She will enter the caves when the sun rises. Tomorrow night I'll return to kill the Sapiens King when she lures him to me."

"I have a concern, my king," Wolfsbane said.

"And I," said Belladonna. To Wolfsbane, she said, "I believe we share this."

"What is it?" Moarte asked, staring from one to the other.

"In all likelihood," Wolfsbane said, "the Sapiens King will murder his daughter. He expects her to be your prisoner. That she would come to him will make him suspicious that her allegiance has been swayed. He'll see it as a trap."

Moarte nodded, his heart heavy. "Yes, I know. We have created a plausible story she'll tell him, persuading him that she escaped."

"There are always options, my son," Belladonna said.

"Such as?"

"Wait."

"For what?"

"Everything changes. The Sapiens King will not want to live out his life in a dank cave with little food and no sunlight, where he rules his unruly citizens from afar. He must emerge eventually. Perhaps former Sapiens who now have turned can be returned to the Sapiens city with instructions to keep a view of the various entrances and exits, who can alert you to his presence—"

"I will not wait!" Moarte said. "This travesty has continued long enough. He will die now and the vampirii will have peace for a time."

"Your mind is set," Belladonna said, and gave him that enigmatic smile. "I wish you well." And while Wolfsbane bared his throat in submission to his ruler, Belladonna surreptitiously brushed Moarte's arm.

Moarte turned away, troubled. He knew he should wait for the Sapiens King to emerge from the caves. Time was meaningless to the vampirii. If it took one year or one decade, it would make no difference. And their King would only live one lifetime—he could wait for him to die. But impatience gnawed at him. He longed for an end in order to reach a new beginning. For his people. For himself. With Valada. Even eternal time would not be enough for her grief and fury to abate. She would never fully belong to him with her heart crowded by such emotions. He needed to do something *now* and while it was not the best plan, it was *a* plan, and it might work, but he had doubts. Many.

He left Belladonna and Wolfsbane to return to his chamber and found Valada practicing with the dagger. She had become adept in a short time, which pleased him.

They needed only minimal weapons at this point, and some food and a little water for her. The cave entrance they had chosen together as they perused a map of the area was located just across the border, within Sapiens territory. A stream ran through the woods in the area but she required some water until they reached it because it would be a long flight and being buffeted by the air currents would be both dehydrating and exhausting for her.

Once they landed in vampirii territory, there would be a natural copse of trees to block the view of any guards at the mountain's highest elevations. Whatever guards the Sapiens King assigned to the border areas would not be fearful of vampirii trying to enter the caves, and Valada said there wouldn't be many guards, if any; she believed that the

Sapiens army had been gutted in the last raid, from what she had seen before she was removed from the city.

"Put that away," he told her, and she slid the dagger into the hidden sheath strapped across her chest through the fake pocket of the blousy shirt she wore. The shirt disguised both the blade and the hilt. The soiled and torn shirt had come from one of the Sapiens slaves. She wore a skirt in the same rough condition made of the bottom of the red dress his warriors had captured her in, which might hinder her if she needed to fight, but at the same time, her father expected this type of clothing and if she were to wear anything from the vampirii realm, he would be even more suspicious than Moarte anticipated him to be.

They had discussed the Sapiens King's paranoid nature, and Valada had convinced Moarte that she knew how to react so that her father would believe she was as she had always been.

Together, they created her story: she had escaped after being a prisoner for half a moon's cycle and returned home on foot over the mountain between their two lands and came searching for her father in the one place she knew he would seek safety. Moarte had made her go through the lie a number of times until it flowed smoothly from her lips.

When they had finally gathered everything, the small bag of food and a gourd for water slung across her chest, her dagger, the dagger he usually wore and the one he had used to parry with her in the garden, he said, "Come, Wife," and she followed him to the edge of the balcony.

"Keep your arms tight around my neck. Once we're airborne, you must wrap your legs about my waist, no lower, no higher, and do it quickly. Do you understand me?"

"Yes, I do, Moarte."

"Good. Let us go."

CHAPTER FOURTEEN

He leapt onto the ledge and reached down to pull her up. Valada wrapped her arms around his neck so that their faces were close together for several moments. He stretched his arms out and his dark wings unfurled behind him with a snap, the sleek feathery wings taking her breath away.

The span was enormous, at least six feet, the color an electrifying iridescent black that shimmered beneath the moonlight.

Suddenly he jumped off the ledge and they plummeted towards the ground, and a short scream came from her lips. She tucked her head beneath his chin and squeezed her eyes shut as the velocity of the fall increased.

But within what must have been only fragments of seconds, she felt and heard those huge wings flap, once, twice, and on the third time it was as if a current of air caught beneath them and instead of descending, she and Moarte floated and then soared as if a giant hand lifted them upward.

She remembered that she needed to curl her legs around him and did. His wings grew from his back between the shoulder blades and stopped before his waist, so there was room for her to clasp onto him with her legs.

It did not take long until they were high above the fortress, circling it, then flying through the mysterious night, buffeted as they cut through the cool air. She turned her head and looked down, amazed at the landscape beneath them. Everything appeared small, the dark forests textured, the paler rivers curving serpentine through them, the high snow-capped mountains erupting multi-dimensional on the horizon, all of it aglow under the brilliant moonlight. There were paler curving lines that cut between the four mountains and between vampirii and Sapiens land and she realized these were valleys. She wondered if those dots of fire were vampirii on the ground. It was as though the world had become a miniature of colors and patterns and only she and Moarte were normal size.

The haunted caves were more than a day's walk from the vampirii stronghold—the warriors who brought her, the slaves and the stolen goods here had passed it as they departed the city of the Sapiens and came over the mountain that separated territories. But the speed at which Moarte flew brought them to the place they had selected within two hours, amazing her. She wondered why she, as a half vampir, did not have wings, but she saw no sign of them. She wanted to ask Moarte if he knew, but not now, not when his concentration and strength were needed for the flight.

They had not spoken since taking to the air; Moarte had warned her that he needed to conserve his energy because the extra weight of her body put pressure on damaged wings only recently healed. They descended a mile from the place where they would eventually reach, where they would be hidden, but here was a good spot to land, in a large clearing at the back of the Sapiens mountain but far enough away from the caves, yet still within the territory of the vampirii so that any guards positioned high on the mountain would not be alerted unduly. They would have to walk the rest of the way.

Moarte alit in the grassy clearing, and the landing was not jarring, and that too impressed her. She unwrapped her legs and arms and stretched them—two hours in the same position had been difficult. If not for the spectacular view, her stiff limbs might have been a problem. She was also thirsty from the air constantly buffeting her face and drank deeply from the gourd.

Moarte seemed unaffected by the flight. With barely a pause, he began walking into the nearby trees which stretched many miles and led to the spot they had chosen. This was a dense forest of tall, thin Birch growing close together, the better to hide them until they arrived at the natural cove they were headed to. Where they would stop was near both the border and a particular cave entrance which she knew could be approached from three different directions, and that gave her the best options for presenting herself as a runaway from the vampirii lair.

The trek through the forest was tiring. His legs were long and he walked rapidly and she had a hard time keeping up with him. She wanted to stop but knew Moarte would not. He was tense, she could feel that. She sensed his vulnerability out here, alone with just her, none of his warriors nearby. The woods could be infested with Sapiens, he had told her—that was how he was captured six months ago, when Sapiens infiltrated vampirii territory—and he wanted to get to their destination quickly.

But she did not think there were Sapiens in the forest now. Her father's army had been decimated. There were not enough veteran Sapiens warriors available to both watch for vampirii from the castle's high towers and the mountain's apex and also to swarm the forest on the chance that a lone vampir would be close to the border. More, they would watch the skies, and Moarte knew this, but she sensed he needed the reassurance of her knowledge of how the Sapiens army worked. It only occurred to her now how unprotected he must feel so close to Sapiens territory where he had been a prisoner and suffered brutalization, some of which had happened at her hands. It made her run to catch up to him as they entered another much smaller clearing.

She touched his bare arm and he paused to look down at her, a question in his eyes. On impulse, she reached up and kissed his lips gently.

He was a warrior, not accustomed to a mission being infected with a dose of caring. He turned away without a word and started walking again.

Eventually they reached the cove, a clearing of middle size surrounded by woods on three sides and the sheer curved rock face that made up the back of the mountain, with no cave entrances or exits in view. He led her to the rock face and then moved along it until they were in the forest again, hidden by the trees.

A small brook cut a path through the forest, the water flowing down from the nearby mountain. Valada bent to the stream and drank, then washed her face. She would have to leave the gourd and food here to present herself as a refugee.

When she stood, Moarte was leaning against a tree staring at the mountain. She approached and looked up at him. His eyes were fixed to the concave wall that almost glowed in the moonlight as if he was seeing something. "What is it?" she asked.

At first he did not react, as if he hadn't heard her. She touched his arm and only then did he drag his view from the grey-white stone wall to her face. His eyes looked haunted.

"Come, my Husband, sit with me," she said, gently holding his arm and leading him deeper into the forest where they found a fallen tree and sat on the trunk.

She knew that the vampirii could not enter the haunted caves within the mountain, but she did not know why. For millennia Sapiens had hidden there when vampirii attacks occurred. There were many rooms in her father's castle that led to secret passages that went directly to the caves in this mountain, where her father had obviously gone once he had handed her over to the vampirii. The mountain was filled with tunnels and caverns and some led to more tunnels underground that went to the caves in the other mountains. Growing up, she had found many entrances on her own and wended her way through the tunnels, just to see how far some of them went and where they led. Maybe it was her half vampir blood, but entering the caves had always had a strange effect on her, making her feel the presence of the ghosts they said haunted the mountains. But who were these ghosts and why did they haunt just the vampirii and not the Sapiens?

She turned to face Moarte and said again, "What did you see?"

He did not look at her but stared straight ahead. "I saw nothing. It's what I heard. Voices. Of the dead."

The fact that by Sapiens standards vampirii were dead made that statement ominous. "Which dead?" she asked.

Now he looked at her and his eyes showed something she had never seen in him before, even when he had been her prisoner and she had wounded him almost mortally. "I don't know," he said, and he looked confused.

She touched his cheek, hoping to reassure him, but he caught her hand and held it instead. "Valada, you must be careful. If you *are* half vampir, the caves will affect you. You may be disoriented. Your father will be suspicious."

"He of all Sapiens knows full well that I'm half vampir," she said bitterly.

"Yes, but the mental confusion… I can't explain it, but it may lead you to drop your guard at a crucial moment."

She could feel his concern for her and it was touching. She lay her cheek facing back, against his cheek, and said softly in his ear, "Moarte, please, don't worry about me. You've taught me well. I have the dagger. I'm not afraid to use it."

He reached up and placed his hand against her other cheek, keeping her face pressed against his. It was a tender moment, one she savored. She wondered if she would ever experience another.

Suddenly Moarte stood. "I must leave. You have half a mile to travel, at least, and it would put both of us at risk for me to go with you into Sapiens territory."

"I know," she said. "And you must return before sunrise," she reminded him uselessly—he knew that better than she did.

"There's enough time," he told her. "You must lead him from the caves to me. Tomorrow night I'll be here two hours after sunset until two hours before sunrise. And every night until you return. Return soon, Wife."

What he didn't say was that if she did not return he could not rescue her. There would be no way he or any vampirii could enter the haunted caves and survive. They would be driven mad and even standing so close to the mountain, being this near the caves, Moarte was exhibiting the signs. He thought he heard voices. If he stayed longer, he might be seeing things that were not there.

"Go, my Husband. I'll be safe. We'll be safe for each other so that we can be together again."

He pulled her up and into his arms and kissed her lips as if he needed to drink her in. But he was a warrior. Practical and single-minded in battle. He did not dawdle but soon left her standing by the log.

She watched him walk away, trying to memorize the sight of him, his tall, strong, perfect pale body, his exquisite face, his glistening plutonian wings, remembering how his skin felt, the scent of him, his intense eyes that changed color with emotions his face could not easily express. She watched until the forest swallowed him and she lost track of this being who had enticed such an extreme range of emotions from her depths, feelings she did not even know dwelled within her. She listened and thought she heard in the distance his wings flap three times as he took off.

"Goodbye, Moarte," she whispered. Despite the mild night she felt cold and alone. Hot tears formed in her eyes. She sat down on the log, wrapped her arms around her body, bent her head and sobbed quietly; she would never see him again.

CHAPTER FIFTEEN

Just after sunrise, Valada entered the mountain to find no guard on duty, no one at all for the first quarter mile she traveled through the narrow tunnel of rock. She had explored this tunnel often as a girl, exiting where she just entered, excited to find this and other paths that took her out of her father's palace, out of the city, into the woods which always brought her peace. And now she understood why she had needed that peace.

Back then, she had felt the caverns and tunnels to be a strange world, dark, moist, fossils imbedded in the sandstone walls, limestone stalactites hanging from the ceiling like sharp teeth and equally sharp stalagmites reaching up from the floor in places. This had been a fascinating environment to investigate but, at the same time, claustrophobia-inducing, and back then she had been a little frightened by the feeling of pressure in her head. The revelation that she was half vampir explained why the atmosphere had troubled her in the past because it troubled her more now.

The air was dank, the walls damp to the touch, and they smelled a little like vinegar. She heard the echo of her footfall and the crunch beneath her feet of crumbled rocks and pebbles and stopped periodically, wondering why there were no sounds but what she created. Surely there should be Sapiens near this major entrance/exit protecting it, since they as well as she knew that it opened very close to the border of the vampirii territory. But, of course, all Sapiens felt safe in the mountains where vampirii could not enter, so their guard would be down.

The daylight from the outside faded when the tunnel curved and she proceeded along a darker area that, with another turn, surrounded her in blackness. She felt her heart pounding and could hear her breathing and stopped again and held her breath so she wouldn't miss other sounds. But there was nothing, just increasing pressure in her head.

Eventually she saw a dim light in the distance and knew it for what she remembered—an area of unusual rock contained in each of the mountains she had ventured into as a girl. These rocks shimmered and glowed in the darkness with a crystalline light of their own, reminding her of ocean waves she had once seen when she wandered half a day from the Sapiens city. Because she had been here before, when she stepped into a cavern composed of this rock that surrounded her on all sides, she was prepared to have her perception altered.

She stopped to catch her breath, glad to be released from the narrow tunnel and the darkness, but then held her breath because suddenly the waves of glittering light disoriented her and were accompanied by vague sounds, a kind of colorful noise that pulsated in time with the light waves, leaving her slightly dizzy.

She did not recall this intensity from when she had entered here as a girl. She stood clutching herself in the middle of the chamber, engulfed by the rocks of moving white light and the odd, discordant sounds, unable to think.

She shook her head to clear it. There were six openings that went off this cave-room at an angle that reminded her of the legs of an insect, which meant she was in its belly, and that unnerved her. One was the tunnel by which she'd entered. The other five branched out and she had difficulty assessing which way to go. All led to more blackness, and she remembered that some tunnels were dead ends. She should remember which way led to her destination, but she did not, and went down the closest with no real reason for selecting it.

Being physically smaller in the past had made the tunnels seem larger. Now, Valada experienced them as narrow and low, escalating the closed-in feeling she experienced the second she'd entered the mountain. In this curving, lightless tunnel, she touched the wet walls to guide herself, soon discovering this route went nowhere when she walked right into a wall at the dead end.

She turned and made her way back to the lit room where the light and sound seemed to vibrate and increase as if in response to her approach. Quickly, she took the next tunnel to her left, this time with only one hand on the wall, the other in front of her.

She did not walk long through this zigzagging canal of stone before she saw yellow light emanating from the far end. She made her way there cautiously because what had been lower-level noise quickly increased in volume and resembled moaning that at points turned into agonized cries and even screams, growing louder, as if the sounds were chasing her. These were not Sapiens sounds, nothing that came from the living. And if the vampirii made noises like this, she had yet to hear them. What assaulted her ear was eerie and reminded her of a bad dream. The noise grew so piercing that she had trouble concentrating on where she was going.

She reached the end of this tunnel and stepped into another cavern, lighted with torches, and in it she found a Sapiens, one she had not expected and who she dreaded meeting.

He turned as her feet crunched gravel at the entrance, sword lifted, though there was no need for this, since only Sapiens could enter the mountains.

The second he saw who was before him, he lowered the sword and a leer spread across his face. "The Sapiens Princess returns to us. Your father will be surprised," Varmik said, though amidst the noise in her head she could no longer block out she still discerned an undertone from him, and knew precisely what it involved. She had felt his lust before, directed her way, and now she was alone with him and feared he would attack her as he had tried to do twice in the past.

Before, she had been a virgin and the fear was all pervasive about actions unknown. Now, she knew what to expect and that frightened her in a more concrete way.

She steeled herself, pushed back her shoulders, raised her head and assumed an imperial posture and tone, one that told him she was still royalty and he must submit to her. "Tell my father I've escaped from the lair of the vampirii and I wish to see him."

"Tell him yourself, Princess!" Varmik said, moving towards her.

If only she could block out the noise, so much like voices gone insane through agony, distracting her from what she had to do to get past this vermin. "And where can I find him, Varmik? Or do you not know the answer to this simple question, as you so often don't know the answers to simple questions?"

He had reached her, towering, as tall as Moarte, but not as slim. His breath stank of the meat Sapiens consumed several times a day.

Valada moved her hand to her waist casually so that she could slip it inside her shirt and grab the dagger if she needed to.

"Our King is in his hidden throne room. Don't you remember where that is?"

She turned from him and said, "Of course. But I wish you to lead me there. Surely you would like my father to infer that you aided in my rescue."

Varmik thought about this for a long moment. He had never been adverse to gaining favor with her father and this situation was not an exception. "Come Princess. I will take you to him," he said, reaching for her arm, which she pulled away.

"Then let's go now. I'm hungry and tired. It was a long journey from the vampirii fortress from which I escaped."

They stared at one another for a moment. "Follow me, Princess Valada. Place your trust in me."

And with that statement, she feared he would trap her in one of the tunnels and take advantage of her. On the two occasions in the past when he had tried, she managed to rebuff him. But there were Sapiens within screaming distance. And now, with the noise growing louder and louder in her head, she did not want to be alone with Varmik when she was at such a disadvantage. She kept her hand at her waist, ready to retrieve the dagger.

He led her down yet another narrow corridor that twisted and curved slightly and had darkened branches going off to the left and right where she feared he might drag her and rape her, and she tried to keep several yards behind him. But this tunnel was lit at both ends, which helped orient her. Soon, she was standing before a small throne of white marble on which sat her father, Zador, the Sapiens King, dressed in tanned animal hides and silver battle armor, his dark beard on robust cheeks flecked with white, his soil-brown eyes hard and unforgiving under judgmental brows, and she nearly gasped. Suddenly she became aware that she had seen this cruel, hateful look all of her life yet had not allowed herself to feel the terror she now experienced in his presence.

He was not a tall man but his powerful body was sturdy and muscular, and she knew him to be fast, recalling the one time he chased and slapped her for being in the same room with him and not leaving quickly enough. The memory of that instant violence frightened her now and with it she understood why she had spent so much of her life repressing memories, and avoiding being alone with him.

He did not seem pleased by her presence. "You were a gift to the vampirii!" he said by way of greeting. "How and why did you escape?"

Not the slightest concern for her well being, this monster who had handed her over to his enemies to save himself, and she was appalled. "Greetings Father," she said in as even yet submissive tone as she could muster, the calls in her head and the rage in her heart nearly overwhelming her. "It's good to see you again."

"I asked questions!" he snapped. "You will answer me!"

She and Moarte had formed a story and she repeated it now. "The vampirii warriors brought us to the great hall of the vampir King, Moarte. There were many slaves and much goods they had stolen from our people. The vampirii celebrated their victory over the Sapiens and drank long and deep from the slaves. Before they reached me, and while they were drunk on Sapiens blood, I managed to undo the ropes they bound me with and get away. I travelled over the mountain between our lands on foot and have been walking for days, possibly a week, not knowing where I was going. But when I saw the Sapiens mountain, I knew I was home and hoped I would find you here, where it's safe."

"Did you? And how do you know of the caves?"

She smiled a little. "I explored them as a child."

This did not please him at all. "And you're not troubled being here?"

She was indeed troubled, having a difficult time concentrating on what he said, but managed to reply, "No, Father, I'm not troubled. I'm Sapiens. Why should I be troubled?"

Her father grunted and stared at her and Valada felt uncomfortable under that dissecting gaze. He must know about the voices in her head. Surely he could see she wasn't herself. She struggled to assume an obsequious face that he would recognize, one of the love and devotion that she had felt for him before, laced with subservience. She lifted the corners of her mouth to a smile and made her eyes round and for a moment she thought of Moarte and felt calm and relaxed and adoring.

Her father must have bought this charade because he acted in the way he always had, which she had never noticed before. He turned away from her and waved a dismissive hand. "Go wash. You stink of vampirii!"

"I'll escort her to the castle, if your majesty wishes," Varmik said.

"I need no escort!" she said, not wanting anything to do with Varmik. What she wanted was to be alone with her father so she could kill him!

"Yes, take her. Quickly. Remove the stench."

Varmik came close and grasped her arm and she pulled away. "I can find my way but if you insist on accompanying me, keep your hands to yourself."

Her father seemed disinterested in this exchange. She turned, distracted anew by the voices in her head, staring at eight tunnels, seven of them new avenues, wondering which way to go.

Varmik stood hands on hips watching her.

"Well, lead on!" she snapped at him.

Suddenly he grabbed her upper arm and pulled her towards one of the tunnels. She struggled and pulled down and back. His grip loosened but his hand grabbed the fabric of her shirt near her shoulder. As she turned sharply away from him, the high collar of the shirt she wore tore and the fabric ripped at her neck.

Quickly, she pulled the cloth up to her throat and held it there, hoping to cover what she did not want him to see. "How dare you, imbecile! Lead on!" she snapped.

But Varmik just stood there, frozen to the spot. "M'lord!" he called.

"Yes, Varmik, what is it?" her father said, his tone impatient and dangerous as always.

"I think you need to see this."

The sounds in her head were overwhelming now and she sensed that her quickened pulse escalated the volume but she could not do anything about that.

She pulled the dagger from her shirt and jabbed it in Varmik's direction. But she was not fast and he was a seasoned warrior, much quicker defending himself than she was at attacking. He blocked her arm, then knocked it with his fist, sending the weapon flying.

Varmik pulled her arms behind her back and shoved her towards her father. The flap of fabric hung down and the Sapiens King could see, as Varmik had, the marks of the vampir that Moarte had made in her throat.

Her father's eyes widened before they narrowed and then turned vicious. "Traitor!" he screamed, and used his fist to hit her in the face. Her head snapped back and she reeled but she heard him order Varmik, "Throw this trash in the dungeon! She's no spawn of mine!"

There was no use in pretending now and as Varmik dragged her backwards through the room, her wrists still gripped in one of his massive hands, she shouted at her father, "I was *never* your daughter. And you were never my father! You murdered my mother!"

And she screamed this through the dark, damp tunnel, her voice echoing as it bounced around the walls, louder than the voices of the ghosts that crowded her now.

Varmik pulled her along backwards and she could not resist his strength and knew he would no longer bow to her position. She had no position with the Sapiens anymore.

The minute they left the mountain's interior, the voices in her head died and she could think again, but it was too late for thinking. No plan would work against brute strength.

Sapiens guards stood awe-struck, watching Varmik dragging Valada backwards, staring at her bloody split lip. She tried to gain their allegiance and cried, "Help me! Sapiens warriors, I command you to help your Princess!"

"By order of the Sapiens King!" Varmik's voice boomed. "I am to take his treacherous daughter with the marks of the vampir to the dungeon."

As he rushed her along the city streets, small crowds gathered to watch and while there were some looks of sympathy, none dared intervene.

Once they reached the back alley where the dungeon entrance lay, he shoved her ahead of him through a wooden door and down steep stone steps, then, when she stumbled, shoved her down the rest of the high flight of stairs and she tumbled to the dirt floor.

This was the dank and cold world she remembered her father promising her. A windowless world, formed of a massively high ceiling, and stone pillars and walls adorned with torture equipment. The stink of sweat and blood saturated the air, mingling with the cries and moans of prisoners and the vibrations of fear.

Bile caught in her throat; she remembered seeing and sensing all this before, when her father gave her a tour for her tenth birthday, threatening to imprison her here and have her whipped if she ever disobeyed him.

The Dungeon Master met them and Varmik told him what had happened, what the King ordered.

Many prisoners—all males—were chained to the pillars and she thought she would be as well, until the Dungeon Master said, "She's Highborn, flawed royalty to be sure, but even so she deserves special treatment."

The Dungeon Master hauled her to her feet and pulled her to a door, opened it, and shoved her into the only room in this desolate place, the one prison cell.

Once the wooden door was slammed closed and bolted, a small window in the door opened, letting in dim light which surrounded Varmik's face and she could see only the sides of his thick, bushy brows and his beard.

She knew Varmik must be grinning, his foul mouth filled with rotting teeth and rank breath. "I'll visit you soon, Princess, then we can finally get to know one another." He slammed the little window closed leaving her trembling in the cold darkness, overcome by terror.

She tried to grip onto any bits of sanity, telling herself that she could survive this. She just had to think about what happened and see where this might lead.

The cell was small, unlit, infested with insects and spiders she could hear scurrying. There was nowhere to sit but the floor, nothing but dirt under her feet, and only the chilly, weeping stone walls surrounding her but for the wooden door.

They hadn't searched her and she now thought that if she had not acted so impulsively with Varmik, had not pulled out the dagger, she would still have it in her possession. If she had stabbed him in the room of lights, en route to the tunnel, and found her father herself, she could have killed both of them. She might not even be in this cell if she had used her head. If she *could* have used her head. But the voices had thundered and she hadn't been able to properly gather her thoughts. She had used the dagger at the wrong time, when the voices of the dead haunting her peaked, and now everything had gone wrong!

It suddenly dawned on her what Serene had been trying to tell her. Whatever she had grown up believing about the vampirii was a lie. It was the Sapiens who bred guilt, fear and loathing into their offspring, who kindled wars and famines to control the population. She did not delude herself that the vampirii world was perfect but already she could see that even though they, too, had a very brutal streak, the undead were far more humane than the living human beings on this earth. But that knowledge would do her little good now.

She wrapped her arms around her body, partly for comfort, partly for warmth, and she thought of Moarte. What would he do when she did not appear tonight? Tomorrow night? Ever? He could not come for her, as much as she knew he would want to, because he would think she was in the haunted caves, not in the city where he *could* rescue her.

She had not told him everything because she knew he wouldn't have let her back into the realm of her father if she had. The baby inside her had been conceived on their wedding night. She felt that conception and did not know how she knew, but she did. She carried their child, a child that would likely die with her at the hands of the people she had lived with the vast majority of her existence. The people she had called her own until recently.

Through a torturous and circuitous route she had found love, and now lost it. Fate seemed grim and cruel to her. "Oh, Moarte," she said softly. "I'm sorry. I should have told you about the child. I should have told you that despite all that happened, all that you did to me, I've grown to care for you. I should have told you that I love you."

Chapter Sixteen

Moarte returned to the vampirii stronghold for the third night, arriving so late the sky had turned pink in the east. He alit on the balcony and folded his wings behind him, then quickly entered his chamber, rapidly closing the heavy curtains against the impending light.

"You're back late, my son," Belladonna said, and he was surprised to see her here in his room, where normally she did not dare to venture without an invitation.

"Mother," he said wearily. He felt racked with worry and fear for Valada. Helplessness had settled on him like a thick fog, choking hope.

"No sign of your wife?"

He did not bother to answer the obvious.

"Do you think she has aligned with our enemy? Perhaps even now giving the Sapiens King information about how to infiltrate our defenses and destroy us?"

Moarte had thought this himself, when he wasn't thinking that Valada was dead. Finally he said to his mother, "No," and sat on the long bench at the foot of the bed. The bed where he and Valada had slept and loved and...

He couldn't let his mind go there. It would destroy him completely.

Moarte was grateful that his mother did not contest his denial; the hour was very late and also he was in no mood for a battle of wits. In some ways he felt defeated; he was helpless to rescue his wife.

Belladonna came and sat next to him, her movements sluggish as she too felt day breaking. Her cold hand touched his lower arm and he placed his over hers. "My son, this does not bode well. If she has not betrayed us, she is dead. You must accept this."

He shook his head no.

They were silent for a time, both feeling the brutal pull downward that the rising sun created in the vampirii.

Finally, Belladonna stood slowly, the lethargy a heavy weight on her body, her voice tired, causing her words to slur. "There is only one way to find out the truth. As Wolfsbane suggested; send in Sapiens loyal to us. Some of them might live to return with news."

She turned and was out the door, gently closing it behind her, and he was left alone in the darkness with his misery and a dilemma.

How could he ask his warriors to turn over slaves or lovers who were now aligned with the vampirii? Sapiens that some of his warriors might have come to care about, even to love? This was too great a sacrifice to demand. And yet even as he dragged himself to his lonely bed, he knew he would demand it. His mother, as always, was right. There was no other way.

CHAPTER SEVENTEEN

Moarte sat rigidly on his throne. Before him stood his elite, a dozen of his most trusted warriors. Also in the room were Wolfsbane, Belladonna and a few Sapiens who were close to the warriors who were closest to him. He felt uncomfortable requesting a favor from his war council. Normally, he made decisions, gave orders, his realm being his priority, what he focused on, and providing for his followers. Now, he had something else in mind.

Valada had not met him, with or without the Sapiens King, on this, the fourth evening since he had left her by the haunted caves. Tonight he returned early to call this meeting of the council and present the strategy that Wolfsbane had suggested and his mother had affirmed as the only option.

"I seek volunteers," Moarte said, "for a dangerous mission into Sapiens territory."

Immediately, every warrior in the room knelt before him, head back, throat exposed, indicating they were ready and willing to support their King.

Moarte felt touched. He knew these would always rally behind him. But now he had to ask them for something besides their own lives. "You, my most trusted warriors, are not the volunteers I require," Moarte said.

He could see the confusion registering on faces and quickly added, "I seek Sapiens loyal to us to return to their former land and infiltrate the haunted caves."

Moarte felt embarrassed that he needed such a personal favor from his warriors. Always, his actions had been directed towards the common good. And in one sense, this, too, was for the good of all. The destruction of the evil Sapiens King would benefit his followers. But the main reason he had resorted to this path was to rescue Valada. If she could be rescued. If she still lived. He felt vulnerable expressing this need, even indirectly.

Wolfsbane—always his friend and confidant—sensed this and interjected. "My King, if I may speak."

"Yes, of course."

He turned to the warriors. "Our Queen is missing. She is half vampir."

"If she is—which I question—then the other half is Sapiens!" Hemlock called out from the back of the group.

"As is your King," Belladonna said.

"Our King is vampir and has always been loyal to us, Dowager," Hemlock said with a slight nod of the head.

Wolfsbane continued as if Hemlock had not spoken. "Queen Valada has put her life on the line to bring the Sapiens ruler to King Moarte so that he may put an end to the constant hostilities between our nations. And now our Queen is missing. She entered the haunted caves four nights ago and has not been heard from since."

"She could be dead," one of the warriors said.

"It's possible," another added.

Moarte felt dejected, until Wolfsbane said, "That is unlikely. Our Queen, if captured by her father, would be kept alive. She possesses valuable information about our realm, our defenses, which the Sapiens King would want and he would do all in his power to extract that information from her."

"Unless she gives it willingly," Hemlock said. "In which case, she's aligned with them."

The room remained silent. Moarte did not feel this was going well.

His mother said, "We do not know the reality of the situation which is why those who can enter the caves would prove invaluable."

"You are asking us," one warrior said, "to volunteer our personal slaves for this task."

"Our lovers," another added.

"And they might be killed instantly," a third contributed.

"My King," said the first, "I would offer my own life willingly."

"I also," another said.

"Are we to ask for volunteers or order our slaves to volunteer?"

Wolfsbane held up a hand for silence. Before he could speak,

Serene's soft and melodious voice rang through the room. "King Moarte. Wolfsbane. I happily volunteer. I've come to know Queen Valada and believe she is aligned with the vampirii, as am I. I will go to the caves and see if I can find out what's happened to her. With the permission of my King and of Wolfsbane." She bowed slightly, knelt, and put her head back, moving her hair to offer her throat.

Moarte looked at Wolfsbane, who seemed caught for several moments. He knew his trusted second loved this girl and hoped to impregnate her if possible, then marry her when the offspring was born, and would, eventually, alter her. He saw Wolfsbane torn by this offer.

"Go ahead, Brother," Hemlock said. "You believe in this cause. Here's your first volunteer."

Wolfsbane turned to Moarte and said, "My King, if it pleases you, I will allow Serene to return to the Sapiens land."

A few others spoke up, volunteering their slaves or lovers, and soon a handful of Sapiens loyal to the vampirii were designated to return tomorrow evening.

And then Hemlock spoke. "My King, we cannot permit these Sapiens slaves to return to their land without supervision. I volunteer my services to escort them to the edge of our territory and wait until one returns with news, which I will, of course, bring to you immediately."

Moarte would not have chosen Hemlock for this task, but he could not humiliate her, Wolfsbane's sister, before her peers, especially given the delicacy of the task and also the limited number of volunteers. There could be little or no harm in this and someone had to be present to receive the information and bring it to him. "Indeed, Hemlock, you are well qualified for such a mission and I am grateful to you for your offer."

Wolfsbane turned his head to look at Moarte, as if he would say something, but Moarte lifted a hand. He did not want to be bogged down by a brother/sister squabble, which he could envision erupting and diverting him from this delicate task—to organize this project so that it could begin at sunset tomorrow evening.

Still, Wolfsbane said, "King Moarte, I believe I should accompany the Sapiens."

"Unwise," Hemlock said. "You have a vested interest in your slave. Besides, you are our King's second and he may need you for strategies, depending on the information gleaned."

Wolfsbane could not respond and Moarte held up his hand again and said, "Thank you for volunteering the Sapiens you own," he told his warriors. "I cannot say this is a risk-free maneuver. You all know too well the dangers of the Sapiens mind and actions. Send the volunteers here now and the rest of you are dismissed. Time is of the essence and I wish to proceed with a briefing immediately."

The warriors left the room and within minutes the five Sapiens which, including Serene plus the warrior Hemlock, stood before him, as did Wolfsbane. Belladonna was by Moarte's side. "It is crucial," she said to the Sapiens, "that you embark on this project of your own free will. If any of you cannot commit to this wholeheartedly, you must speak now. There is no shame in this. I ask you because of the danger and also because if you meet resistance, you must be strong enough in yourself to not break under torture and reveal vampirii secrets." She paused. "Are there any who cannot commit wholeheartedly?"

A fragile-looking boy timidly raised his hand. "Forgive me, Dowager," he said. "I cannot guarantee I would not break."

Belladonna nodded to him. "There is no shame. You are dismissed. Are there any others?"

A thin waif-like girl raised her hand and said virtually the same thing and Belladonna dismissed her as well. This left Serene and two others. "Of you three," Belladonna said, "do you each feel secure in your ability to perform this task for your King?"

All three nodded ascent.

Wolfsbane outlined the plan. "We will take you to the forest at the edge of the vampirii territory, near the caves. There are several entrances nearby and you can present yourselves as three of a small rebellion against the vampirii. During the rising up, the other Sapiens were recaptured but you three were able to escape. You seek refuge and to return to your people.

"Once you are inside the caves, you must be careful to not reveal your hand. Do not ask direct questions about Valada but do keep your eyes and ears open. There will, undoubtedly, be Sapiens you know and if you find any you believe are trustworthy, you can venture a question or two, presented in a general manner, stating that you knew Valada had escaped and wondered if she had made it home. Hopefully the information will then be forthcoming.

"We are also extremely interested in locating the exact whereabouts of the Sapiens King Zador.

"Once you have learned anything you believe is pertinent to either finding out if Valada is alive or dead or what has happened to her, or information about the location of either Valada or the Sapiens King, you will need to find a way back to vampirii territory, to the place where we left you, and report to Hemlock, who will be waiting where you will have last seen her. Once you've passed Hemlock the information you've gleaned, at that point, you must return to the caves to avoid suspicion. Are there questions?"

"When can we return to the vampirii?" one male asked.

Wolfsbane hesitated but the other two Sapiens volunteers noticed. The questioner said, "We cannot return, can we?"

Moarte spoke for the first time. "Once we discover where either Valada is located, or the Sapiens King, we will form a plan to rescue our Queen. Meanwhile, find your way back to Hemlock and you can return with her. Failing that, make your way into the city if you are not already situated within the city's walls."

Wolfsbane interjected, "Go to the derelict cemetery on the west side of the city. We will find you there."

Moarte added, "There is a good chance we can help you escape. This may not happen immediately, but once an attack takes place, you will be brought back home to your loved ones."

Even Moarte did not see this as a viable option for these Sapiens. In all likelihood, the vampirii would not be able to rescue them. He anticipated that the Sapiens elite would hold up in the caves permanently so raiding the city again would be fruitless and cause the unnecessary deaths of vampirii. And the most likely scenario would be that these three would be killed as spies. He could see in Wolfsbane's eyes that his assessment of the prognosis was similar.

The male who had asked the question looked troubled.

Belladonna addressed him, "You are free to go." He left the chamber.

Only two, Moarte thought. A very small army of infiltrators. He hoped they would find a way.

Once Hemlock as well as the Sapiens Serene and Portia had been dismissed to ready themselves for this assault, Moarte glanced at Wolfsbane and his second looked unhappy.

"I will do everything in my power to return Serene to you," Moarte said.

Wolfsbane began to kneel but Moarte gestured that he remain standing. "I know you will, my King," Wolfsbane said. And Moarte had never heard him sound so uncertain nor known him to look so forlorn.

CHAPTER EIGHTEEN

Despite vowing not to, Valada had taken to sitting on the dirt floor her first day in the dungeon, her back against the cold stone wall. Her legs just could not handle the stress of standing for so many hours.

All around her were the insects that inhabited such dark and earthy places, and the warm-blooded vermin that scurried through chinks in the stone walls searching for food. Moarte had told her that when he was a prisoner here, he only survived because he drained the rats and mice that he caught of their blood, but she did not believe she could do that. Her flesh crawled and she had even stopped brushing off spiders and other things she could not see. What was the point? There were just more and more of them and when she disturbed them, they bit and stung her skin.

She had no idea how long she'd been imprisoned. A cup of rank water and a dish of food came sometimes, if she could call it food. At first she wouldn't eat but again, her body protested and she consumed the gruel that she knew every prisoner was fed, a thin, watery mixture of some sort of grain that smelled half rotten, which more often than not she vomited out later. If they fed her once a day, she had been here nearly a week. But it was always dark and there was no accurate way to calculate time amidst the depression of her spirit.

This was the cell where her father had housed Moarte. Where she had tortured him. Being here made her feel oddly close to him, as if the air still held his essence. Thinking about him was all that kept her sane. But at the same time, thoughts of him led her down a slippery slope to despair; he could not rescue her.

She dozed now and then and felt her way to a corner and used that as a toilet, causing the air in the small cell to reek. The situation was impossible but she had to make it possible. She had to survive. She couldn't give up hope. A fetus lived and grew within her and she must protect that future child in every way, and some of that involved holding onto hope.

The one thing she did not understand was why her father had not interrogated her. She was convinced that he would do that immediately, to find out what she knew of the vampirii defenses. If she ruled the Sapiens and he had returned with the marks of the vampir on his body, she would have interrogated him. At least in the past, when she had been aligned with the Sapiens. Now, she was not. It didn't help her at all to be aligned with the vampirii. Her world had eroded and she knew she would probably rot in this pitch-black cell, parched, starving, battling diseases brought on by unsanitary conditions and infections from insect bites, fighting the night chill and the fetid air until she succumbed to illness and death. And with her would die the baby in her womb. That horrifying thought made her sob aloud. She could not protect her unborn child, and she should have been able to. She should never have come here. Revenge is only enticing when there is no one else in jeopardy and she had put her child, Moarte's child, in jeopardy through her stubborn desire to murder her father herself.

Suddenly the door opened, the hinges screaming, and lantern light blinded her after so long in darkness. She squeezed her eyes shut automatically but forced herself to try to see who was holding the lantern, and then wished she hadn't looked.

"The King wants answers," Varmik said, "and has authorized me to get them by any means."

She did not bother replying. What was there to say? He held the power now. But a chill raced up her backbone. Varmik was known for extreme brutality. That was why her father kept him around, to force others to obey him.

"Bring her!" he ordered, and two guards came into the cell, one on each side of her, and lifted her to her feet.

She was weak from lack of movement, even though she had tried to walk around to keep up her strength. But not eating decent food and only being given the little bit of dirty water they provided that went straight through her system did not leave her enough energy to build on.

They brought her into the main dungeon and there she saw the men she had heard screaming, men chained to pillars, the skin flayed off their backs or chests, pools of blood at their feet, a few sobbing or moaning, most unconscious. Or dead. She expected to be chained up herself and beaten until dead, or nearly so.

But Varmik clearly had other plans. He climbed the steps and the guards dragged her up after him until they reached the level of the door that led to the street. Instead of going outside, they turned down a hallway at the end of which was another door that opened into a nearly empty room. The guards brought her in as far as the mat on the floor and Varmik snapped, "Leave us!"

Once they were gone, he stared at her, his beady rodent-eyes piercing. "You are a Princess and therefore you deserve special treatment." He found a key on the large ring he wore attached to his belt and locked the door from the inside, trapping her with him. She felt the stone walls closing in and her heart raced.

"What did you tell the vampirii about the Sapiens?"

"Nothing."

He strode to her and slapped her, so hard her ears rang.

"What did you tell them?"

"I told them nothing. I escaped."

He slapped her again.

She could see on his face what was in store for her.

"Always the snotty Princess!" he snarled. "Thinking you're too good for me. And then you give yourself to the fucking vampir King. Slut!" He hit her again. "So now you'll have me, who is Sapiens, better than that undead Bloodsucker! Now you'll find out what a living man is like, something you should have discovered long ago."

He tore the shirt and skirt from her body, seeing right away the ring in her nipple. "Remove it!" he demanded.

"I can't."

"Then I will!"

He pulled on the ring, forcing her close to him. He held her wrists together and pushed back her body as he yanked at the metal and she screamed in agony. "It will come off or I'll cut off your tit!" he yelled, pulling, twisting until she thought she would pass out from the violent pain.

After an endless time of this torture, her screams grating her throat raw, he tore her skin until the nipple was severed in two and the ring slipped out through the blood.

While he wiped her bloody ring on his pants and then pocketed the treasure, she doubled over in blinding, sobbing agony, blood soaking her skin, dripping to the floor. She could not stop screaming.

"Shut up!" he ordered.

But she couldn't stop herself and he slapped her half a dozen times, knocking her back against the stone wall where she hit her head and then fell onto her face.

Now, he saw the brand on her backside and became enraged.

"Their mark! You piece of shit! Whore!" He kicked her again and again, grabbing her up and pummeling her with his fists in the chest and the head. She doubled over to protect her stomach, but she could not and he knocked her to the ground again, kicking her in the gut several times. When she was nearly unconscious, he dragged her to her feet and made her suck his cock. After he ejaculated in her mouth and onto her face and then peed in her face, he hardly paused, the violence in him expanding. He threw her to the ground and over the next hours raped her repeatedly in every orifice, and she felt her body tearing. When she resisted he beat her with his fists until her eyes swelled shut and she spit out bits of broken teeth, tasting blood in her mouth. She was sure she was also bleeding from her vagina.

It went on and on, and whenever she let herself hope for unconsciousness, he tossed icy water into her face to keep her awake. Finally, after what seemed many hours, he was sated and had the guards drag her limp and broken body back to the small room where the door slammed shut, leaving her in darkness, naked, bruised and beaten, her body raped repeatedly, the only sound her labored breathing and low moans of pain.

The physical agony left her gasping for air, but she knew she was in shock and that anesthetized her, at least temporarily. She thought one or more of her ribs were broken, and likely her forearm. Worse than that, she knew she had lost the unborn which now would never be born, and with that awareness, Valada lost hope.

CHAPTER NINETEEN

Hemlock carried the slave Portia while Wolfsbane insisted on flying Serene to the site they had selected. They flew through the darkness landing in the place Moarte had directed them to, which Serene agreed gave them good access to the caves and was still within vampirii territory, although during a Sapiens raid, borders did not much matter.

Once they were safely hidden in the woods, Wolfsbane took Serene aside. "You do not have to do this. I will love you if you change your mind," he said.

"And I will love you always," she told him with a smile that was his alone.

He pulled her to him and kissed her lips, tasting her saltiness, instantly wondering if he would ever kiss her again.

"We have no time for this," Hemlock said. "There are few enough hours of night and our King needs a report. You two slaves, one of you will return when you have news, any news. Do you understand?"

Both Sapiens girls nodded, but Serene thought, *of course we understand! This is why we're here and we are not stupid*; she so resenting Hemlock. She knew Hemlock would never treat her as an equal but when she and Wolfsbane married, his sister would no longer have the power over her that she held over all Sapiens slaves. Then, when Wolfsbane turned her, it would be another story completely. Serene had already moved up a notch from slave to lover, but it was a thin line where Hemlock was concerned, and she knew she still had to be wary of this vicious vampir. She had often thought that King Moarte did not know what Hemlock did with the slaves. For that matter, Wolfsbane had only the vaguest of ideas. He knew what Hemlock had done to her but Serene expected that he viewed this as an isolated incident, Serene tortured because Hemlock knew that Wolfsbane loved her. He did not know the depths of his sister's depravity.

All of the slaves were fearful of telling anyone and Hemlock had threatened them with death if they did, so Serene too had kept her mouth shut, if only to protect the others. But once she was married and safe in that status, she would tell Wolfsbane the atrocities his sister committed.

"Come, Portia," Serene said, holding her friend by the hand, blowing a kiss at Wolfsbane, who looked very sobered. She had no fear that she would not return to him. She had to. He was her life now.

When they had walked for half an hour, she said to Portia, "I know a way in through the caves which will lead us directly to the city so that we can find out where Queen Valada is, and where the Sapiens King is hiding."

"But King Moarte wanted us to go into the caves!"

"We will, but I believe Valada is not there. She has been gone a week now. If she could have returned, she would have. I suspect she is being held prisoner and that's in the dungeon."

"But we should not disobey the King!"

"King Moarte put Wolfsbane in charge of our mission. I talked with him about it and he approved my plan." This was only partially true. She had brought up her theory to him but he had neither approved nor disapproved it. His focus was exclusively on her safety and he was preoccupied with instructing her where to go in the city if she could not escape once the information was handed over to Hemlock, all so that he could find her and bring her home.

Serene led Portia to a low cave entrance at ground level and once they were inside, the tunnel immediately sloped upward at a steep angle. They walked and walked in the darkness, bending over slightly because of the low ceiling and intense incline, stopping periodically to catch their breath. Finally, at the far end, they saw the light of daybreak and Serene whispered, "Follow close behind me and do not speak. At all. You must pretend that you were so frightened that you lost your voice completely in the vampirii raid. Do you understand?"

Portia said, "Yes, but—"

"Shush! You must be mute now."

What Serene didn't want to tell Portia was that the cave would exit by the large well at the center of the city. It was not-quite-dawn and few people would be out and about. With luck they could wander unnoticed and unidentified until she found her brother, Rivard, who would help them. Serene was counting on the city being devastated in the last retaliatory raid by the vampirii. People would be missing or dead. Her sudden reappearance, and Portia's, would not be so unusual, and Serene would say they had been hiding in the caves. Of course, Portia had been gone for less than six months only but Serene had not been to the place where she was born in years. Hopefully, they would not be recognized.

Serene had another reason for not revealing her plan in full. Portia was known for being unable to keep secrets and the other Sapiens slaves had learned to not trust her with any. The less Portia knew, the better. In fact, that was why she wanted Portia to play dumb, as if she could no longer speak. Serene would only convey a minimum of information to her, which would be all that Portia could blab if she were caught.

They appeared at the cave exit, which was well disguised as a boarded-up building, and found few people by the well or in the square. Most had a shell-shocked look on their face, as if the raid had left them vulnerable and bereaved. Serene was aware that besides those captured and brought to the vampirii stronghold, many Sapiens must have died, either in battle, or by being drained by the vampir warriors. She also knew that several vampirii had been killed in that battle. It was the one thing she hated most in all the world—the enmity between the Sapiens and the vampirii. It didn't have to be. But she had no power to change things. At least not until she altered.

Serene pulled Portia along and they were only stopped once by a friend of Serene's from childhood who asked where she had been for so long and she lied and said living in the caves for a few years, serving food to the King's warriors who guarded the city from the top of the mountain.

The friend said she was in a hurry and had to find inexpensive medicine for her grandfather who had been injured when a vampir talon raked his back and the deep gouge had become infected.

"Crush apple leaves," Serene said, "and apply them directly to the wound. They have a natural antibiotic."

Her friend was grateful for the suggestion and promised to visit soon before hurrying away.

Finally they reached Serene's home, or what had been her home. The door of the cottage was locked—so unlike the realm of the vampirii where doors were never locked—and she entered by a back window she knew could be forced, and then opened the door from within for Portia.

The interior of the house was composed of a kitchen and three rooms, all small. One had been her bedroom when she reached the age of ten years, one her brother's that they had shared through her earlier childhood. Her parents slept in another room, and her grandmother in the final bedroom until she died, the room Serene had inherited. She and Portia stood in the kitchen amidst the clutter and disarray.

There were signs that Rivard had been here recently—dishes in the sink held bits of food not long hardened.

"Sit," she said to Portia, moving papers and tools to make space for her on the bench. She gave her some water to drink. It had been a long walk to the cave and another long and hard walk up and through the steep tunnel, but they were safe here.

She found pears, dark bread and some goat cheese and they ate, and drank a bit of the tart wine her brother made each quarter. It was enough to revive them so that when Rivard entered the room, Serene had the energy to jump to her feet and hug him.

"I cannot believe you're alive!" he said, picking his little sister up and twirling her around.

He kissed her cheeks and she hugged him, and they both laughed and cried for several minutes. Finally, she said, "This is Portia, my friend. She can't speak. Portia, Rivard, my brother."

"But where have you been these past three years?" he asked as they sat at the table and Serene brought him wine and bread and cheese.

"Eat," she instructed him. "and I'll talk while you do."

She told him about being captured during a raid and how she had been taken by Wolfsbane, who treated her well and wanted to marry her. As she talked, she watched a myriad of emotions flicker across her brother's face. "It's not like they told us, Rivard. The vampirii are kind, unlike Sapiens."

He stopped eating and looked at her. "You've been hypnotized. They're killers who steal our blood. I've fought them. I know what they are capable of."

She took his hand. "I'm not under a spell. They can be cruel, of course, mainly to their enemies. But Rivard, there's much you do not know. Much that has been hidden from us. There are many Sapiens who live with the vampirii by choice. I'm one of them."

He shook his head.

"I know I can't convince you right now, but please, hear me out, and be on my side. I need your help. Do you still work at the dungeon as a guard?"

"Yes," he said, biting into the slab of cheese. "Some things never change."

"I need information. Queen Valada was captured in the last vampirii raid of this land."

"*Queen* Valada? You mean *Princess*."

"No, she married King Moarte and is Queen of the vampirii."

Her brother's mouth hung open in mid chew, and he looked stunned. Serene hurried on. "She returned here to confront her father and was to return to the vampirii land but hasn't been seen in over a week. Do you know if she's being held prisoner?"

He nodded and swallowed wine. "She is. Varmik brought her in nearly seven days ago. She's been alone in a cell but for last night when he interrogated her."

Serene paused and cold snaked up her spine. "Is she alive?"

Rivard also paused before answering. "Barely. When Varmik was through with her…" He left it unsaid and Serene could imagine the worst. Every female and male in the Sapiens city avoided Varmik when they could. He was brutal, noted for being irrational and violent, and it was well known that he had lusted after Valada for many years.

"Brother, I need your help."

He drank more wine then looked at her. "I know what you want and I can't help you free her."

"Sneak me in so that I can speak with her."

He shook his head.

"Please, Rivard. I can bring in food to the prisoners. I only need a few minutes with Valada. Let me talk with her so I can send word back to King Moarte. He's so worried about her safety."

He shook his head again, not quite as forcefully as before.

She sat back. "I know you helped King Moarte escape."

Rivard looked stunned. "How?—"

"I overheard him describe the Sapiens who aided him and I knew it was you. I knew also because you're my brother. You're kind and caring and sensitive. Our parents raised us properly. You likely couldn't bear seeing Moarte brutalized, even if he is vampir and the enemy of the Sapiens. You've heard the stories I've heard, that he's a good King, fair and just. And we know about the Sapiens King from first-hand experience. Truth is not what the Sapiens King wants his people to hear, but you could see this first hand when you met Moarte. I know you, and I know you could see the truth. You helped him escape."

Rivard stared at her and turned his head slightly to glance at Portia who was listening avidly.

"She won't betray you. As I told you, she can't speak," Serene said, giving Portia an intense look to keep her from opening her mouth.

It took more discussion but Rivard was finally persuaded to allow Serene access to Valada by bringing in food to her and the other prisoners. They would do this late afternoon before the sun set, when the meal was served. Normally it was his job, but they formed a plausible reason for Serene's presence.

Two hours before dusk, the three returned to the well and Portia was left there, sitting hunched over like a beggar, her face half covered, so that she would not draw suspicion. Serene warned her again about not speaking. She wanted Portia near the tunnel entrance so that when she passed along whatever news there was, Portia could immediately go down the tunnel and back into the vampirii land and give that information to Hemlock, then return here before sunrise.

Rivard took Serene with him to the home of the grim and terse woman who was paid to cook the food he usually fed the prisoners and explained that tonight Serene would undertake this onerous task.

Once they entered the dungeon, Serene approached the ten prisoners one by one, all of them tied to pillars or stretched on racks or hanging upside down on crucifixion-style poles. Some she believed were already dead, others might as well have been. Only two took food from her and she had to feed them. Her heart broke at such brutal treatment and once again she realized that she had never seen a Sapiens murdered by a vampir except in battle, and yet look what her people did to one another!

The Dungeon Master wanted to know who she was and why she was here and Serene let Rivard answer. "She's my second cousin. My aunt needed her looked after tonight because of all the looting and molestations in the city and I brought her here so I could keep an eye on this naive girl." This seemed to satisfy the keeper of the dungeon, who gave Serene a lustful once over, and grunted before he walked away.

Soon they reached the cell where Valada was kept. Rivard searched for the key with nervous fingers and whispered to his sister, "You cannot stay long. The Dungeon Master will notice. Be quick."

She slipped inside the door, and he left it cracked and also opened the small slat in the door that acted as a window so that there was some light within.

Serene saw Valada collapsed on the floor and hurried to her. The Queen was naked and her body in the dim light appeared to be black and blue and swollen in places. She had been beaten severely and Serene knew it was the work of Varmik.

She grasped Valada by the shoulders and shook her hard to get her to consciousness, whispering, "Queen Valada, it's me, Serene. King Moarte sent me and I must send him news of you. Speak to me quickly for I have only seconds."

Valada opened the one eye not swollen completely shut. "Are you a dream?"

"No, my Queen. I'm grateful you're still live. Are you alright?"

Of course she was not alright, and Serene had to say again, "Please, answer me quickly."

"I've been raped and beaten. My baby killed."

"Your baby?" Serene realized in an instant that much blood was around Valada's thighs. She had been pregnant. "Oh no!" she cried.

"Finish!" Rivard hissed through the opening.

Serene whispered, "Do not despair, my Queen. King Moarte will rescue you. You're not inside the mountain, so he can. Is your father still hiding in the caves?"

"Yes," Valada said, and suddenly Serene heard the Dungeon Master's gruff voice.

"What's taking her so long?"

Serene jumped to her feet and raced to the door, exiting the cell as the Dungeon Master reached it.

"I—I'm sorry," Serene stuttered, bowing her head like the timid girl and humble servant she was expected to be. "I had to feed her. She couldn't lift the spoon."

"That's not your job!" the Dungeon Master snapped.

"She's young and stupid," Rivard said. "I'll set her straight about this task." He turned to Serene and spoke harshly. "She's a prisoner, like all the rest! Keep your gentle feelings in check, girl. Valada is a traitor to our people."

"Forgive me, cousin, and Master," Serene said. "I'm sorry."

"She won't do it again," Rivard said, and the Dungeon Master grunted and walked away.

Rivard stayed at work and Serene hurried up to the street level, finding Portia where she had left her. She sat down beside her at the well, leaned close and whispered, "Tell this to Hemlock so that she may give the information to King Moarte: The Sapiens King is in the caves. Queen Valada is in the city, in the dungeon. She's been raped and beaten severely and has lost her baby."

Portia looked up sharply. "She was pregnant?"

"Shush! I told you not to speak here!" Serene hissed, glancing around. Then, "You must leave right away. Follow the tunnel all the way to the ground. Can you find the path back to Hemlock from there?"

Portia nodded.

"Good. Let me leave first, then wait a few moments before you go. Check that you're alone in the square before you move towards the hidden entrance. I'll watch and make certain you're not followed. Come back as soon as you can, before sunrise, so there will be less people on the streets. Can you find your way to my brother's house?"

Portia nodded again.

Serene left the square but stayed in a doorway in the shadows. Eventually, when only an old woman talking to herself sat on the other side of the well not facing her, Portia stood and moved towards the wall with the obscured entrance to the tunnel. She glanced around and saw that but for the crazy woman by the well, the square was empty; she disappeared into the darkness.

Serene watched but no one followed and she let out a sigh of relief. She hurried back to her brother's home and there sat by the blazing fireplace feeling a coldness creep into her bones. Queen Valada was not in good shape physically. Her baby was dead, killed by Varmik. But more that all this, Serene had sensed that something had vanished from Valada's spirit. She prayed that King Moarte would come soon, before it was too late.

Chapter Twenty

It was well after sunset when Portia reached Hemlock, who said immediately, "You have returned, Sapiens slave. Where is the other one?"

Portia bowed her head and clasped her hands in front of her, her body expressing the hesitation and fear she felt by being in the presence of Hemlock. "Back in the city, Mistress Hemlock. She is endeavoring to get further information with the help of her brother."

Hemlock considered this for a moment. "And what have you found out so far? Where is the Sapiens King?"

"He's hiding in the haunted caves."

"So, he doesn't even have the courage to face his people!" Hemlock paused. "Is there more?"

"Not about the Sapiens King, no. But about Queen Valada."

"Queen!" Hemlock snapped, pacing in a circle, infuriated at hearing that word attached to Valada's name. "And what have you learned?"

"Queen Valada is in the dungeon, alive."

"Did you see her?"

"No, mistress, but Serene did. Her brother Rivard works in the dungeon and helped his sister sneak in. Valada has been raped and beaten. And she lost King Moarte's child."

Hemlock stopped dead. "She was pregnant?"

"Apparently so, Mistress."

Hemlock's lips parted slightly. "I see. This changes things."

She glanced at Portia and noticed the girl look away, as if she'd been watching Hemlock.

The vampir said in a soft voice, "You have done well, Portia. You will be rewarded, as will Serene. Come here."

In trepidation, Portia moved slowly to Hemlock, saying nervously, "Serene expects me back in the city right away, so I'm not missed."

"Don't worry about time," Hemlock said, pulling the girl close, pushing back her long blond hair, exposing her throat. "Time for immortals ceases to exist. You would like to be immortal, would you not?"

"Yes, Mistress Hemlock," Portia said, her breathing rapid, her words quivering. "Azazel has told me that she'll turn me when—"

"Do not be afraid," Hemlock said as she pulled the girl's arms behind her and reared her head back. Her teeth sank fast and deep and Portia screamed. Hemlock nearly drained her within a minute, taking every last drop of blood she dared take before accomplishing her goal. She used one of her talons to sever a vein in her wrist and let drops of blood fill Portia's open mouth, which the nearly-dead girl swallowed automatically, and Hemlock resented giving this. And then Hemlock sucked the remainder of the blood from the girl's neck, leaving an undead shell that would revive at the next full moon if it were properly preserved until then.

But the body would not be preserved at all. Using her talons, Hemlock dug deep into Portia's chest, gouging out her still-beating heart.

The organ dripped blood and pulsed weakly three times, then stopped, and Hemlock licked blood from the muscle, savoring it, then spontaneously bit into it.

She tossed the remains of the heart into the clearing where the sun would scorch it and then lifted the undead body and hurled it into the clearing as well, knowing it too would burn in the sunlight and whatever remained would decompose with the forest debris.

Refreshed, revived, full of information she could relay to a grateful King, she unfurled her wings and soon soared above the forest, heading back to the vampirii stronghold at as fast a speed as she could manage, the hint of a smile of satisfaction playing on her vampir lips.

Yes, everything had changed!

It was the second night of the new plan and Hemlock was still in the forest but would return before sunrise with, Moarte hoped, information.

He sat briefly, then stood and paced the throne room, alternating, what he had been doing for hours, his tension palpable to those around him.

"Moarte, you cannot make things happen faster than they can occur. If our Sapiens spies have found out anything, Hemlock will bring the information to you."

"I am as aware of this as you are, Mother!"

He sat again then said to Wolfsbane, "I am not certain this was a good idea. My instincts tell me our warriors should have raided the Sapiens city again, me leading them, taken our chances that way to rescue Valada."

"And would they follow you so willingly to rescue Valada? She is Sapiens," Belladonna reminded him. "I am not convinced you would have the backing you need, and you would risk an insurrection, possibly risk your rule."

"I don't care about my rule!" Moarte said, his ire rising. "I care about my wife."

"Your *Sapiens* wife."

Before they could travel further down this dangerous path, Wolfsbane said, "It is unlikely that the Sapiens King, and our Queen, are there."

"Perhaps." Moarte stood again to pace more. "But sending in the females was wrong. I see that now. I should not have allowed myself to be talked into this. Any of it!"

He thought back to discussions with Valada and realized that she had very subtly persuaded him. And that he had been willing to give her anything to atone for what he had done to her. And in his blindness, he had allowed her to put herself in harm's way. He could not forgive himself for this.

"Valada was your best hope," his mother said.

He turned on her. "You're the one who said *wait*! I should have listened to you."

"Perhaps. Perhaps not. It is difficult to say in retrospect what should or should not have happened. And what's done is done."

A sound like a growl came from Moarte. He had never felt so helpless, even when he was a prisoner of the Sapiens. With every torture, they reinforced his will to survive. But now, he had languished in ignorance for more than a week, and the inability to act left his will teetering on the edge of collapse. What if there was *no* news? What if Valada had vanished, murdered secretly by her father in the caves? Who would know? How would the two Sapiens slaves find this out? How would he ever find out what happened to her?

The caves! The ghostly voices that eroded his mind, left him incapable of rescuing her and of killing the Sapiens King! He slammed his fist down onto the arm of the stone throne, nearly breaking the bone in his hand. This did nothing for the tension pressing within him like steam about to erupt its containment. He needed an outlet through action and could not see one.

"King Moarte, Hemlock has returned!" a warrior shouted from the back of the room, his voice excited, and Moarte jumped to his feet.

Hemlock strode through the large main doors and into the chamber with the rest of the war council streaming in behind her.

Moarte leapt down the three steps as one and met her halfway across the hall. "What news do you bring?"

"I have seen one of the slaves, King Moarte," Hemlock said, staring into his eyes.

"Which one?" Wolfsbane asked.

"The other," Hemlock told him without glancing at her brother.

"And Queen Valada?" Moarte asked impatiently. "What have you learned?"

Hemlock took her time, relishing this. She felt powerful, in control of him at last. She sensed Moarte's tension and wanted to turn it to her advantage now, and in the future. "The Sapiens King is hiding in the caves, afraid to face his people."

"As we expected," Wolfsbane said.

"Answer me!" Moarte shouted, the force of his tone at an explosive pitch. "Is there news of Valada?"

"Yes, my King, and it is not good news. I regret to report that she is dead. She was imprisoned in the dungeon, raped and beaten to death."

Moarte stood like a statue, and Hemlock enjoyed this moment too. He would not be happy for a while, but eventually, when he had grieved long enough...

She said, "I am so sorry, my King," staring into his eyes, eyes stunned, shocked, vacant, not seeing her; he was paralyzed. She knelt before him, baring her throat, but Moarte only stared at her as if transfixed.

Wolfsbane came to him on one side, Belladonna on the other.

"My King," Wolfsbane said gently, within an inch of touching his arm.

"Come, my son." Belladonna did take his other arm.

They turned him and he became passive, letting them lead him away. But suddenly he spun back to Hemlock, "Who did this to her? Did you find out?"

Hemlock, still kneeling, lifted her head. "A jailer, my King. His name is Rivard, the brother of Serene."

"That cannot be!" Wolfsbane said.

And Hemlock hid the smile in her eyes. She had injured both with one blow.

Black rage overwhelmed Moarte, all the better to suffocate the intense grief ready to fragment him.

He allowed his mother and Wolfsbane to guide him away from the throne room, knowing his warriors present saw this as weakness and would relay it to others, destabilizing his rule, and not caring that it would. He had lost everything. No, all but one thing. He still possessed a scalding desire for revenge.

Once the three had reached Moarte's chamber, he announced, "I will go to the caves to kill the Sapiens King!"

"That is not a wise plan," Belladonna told him.

"I don't care about wise or foolish now, Mother. I don't care if I die the true death. I have lost everything. Everything. I exist now for revenge."

For once, she had nothing to add.

Wolfsbane said, "My King, allow me to accompany you, at least as far as the Sapiens land. I must rescue Serene. And perhaps there is a way I can aid you in entering the caves, if you will permit me."

"Come then, Wolfsbane. I will not stop you. But whether you accompany me or not, I will leave now. There is no point to waiting."

"There is one point," his mother said. "The sun will rise even before you are half way to the caves and you will be forced to find shelter. It is unwise for you to sleep so near and also to find shelter in the light. It will weaken you when you need strength. Wait for tomorrow's first darkness. Leave here nourished and powerful. My son, you will need all the strength you can gather for the caves."

"I agree with this," Wolfsbane said. "My King, please heed your mother's advice and let us depart as the sun sets tomorrow evening."

Moarte could not bear to wait and yet he saw the logic of what they said. He would need every ounce of fortitude to face the ghosts in the caves and entering in weakness would lead to automatic defeat. "Alright," he finally said. Then, "Send Hemlock to me. I wish to question her further."

Wolfsbane left to fetch his sister. Moarte's mother said, "I advise you against seeking further details."

"Why is that, Mother? Are you fearful I'll fall apart?"

"Yes, I am. You are punishing yourself unjustly."

"Not unjustly. I alone am responsible for this. I allowed myself to be swayed by Valada."

"In love, one is swayed by a lover."

He turned on her, for the first time hating his mother. "She is dead because of your son and his inability to control his emotions. I am weak, a failure as a ruler, as a male. I let her be trapped, unable to see what was happening until it was too late. If I die at the hands of the Sapiens King, I deserve to."

Belladonna looked shocked. She had never seen him like this before, he knew, but he had not felt this before, this utter desolation, a complete abandonment to self-loathing.

But instead of retreating, she stepped towards him and grasped him in her arms. "No!" he shouted, trying to push her away, but she held him firm in a surprisingly strong grip, and in truth, he did not have the strength of will to resist her.

Within moments, against the little self-control he still possessed, Moarte found himself sobbing in his mother's arms, as if he were a child.

"I've killed her!" he said over and over, and his mother held the grieving child he was during those moments as his blood tears coated her shoulder.

Finally they sat side by side on the bench at the foot of the bed, she holding his hand, his shoulders slumped, feeling as if his very life had been drained from his body. He wanted to fold in half and disappear.

A knock came on the door and his mother said, "Enter."

Hemlock strode into the room and he had forgotten that he wanted to speak with her.

His mother stood quickly, letting go of his hand so that he would not be embarrassed before a warrior, but he noticed that she stayed in the room and it didn't matter to him.

"You wanted to see me, King Moarte?"

"Yes. You may sit, Hemlock. I wish to thank you for bringing me the information."

She remained standing. "*My* wish is that it had been good news. I am so sorry, my King."

He exhaled, like a sigh. "Tell me again what the Sapiens slave Portia told you."

Hemlock went over what she had conveyed before, almost word for word.

"Do you know when Valada's death occurred?"

"I do not. I was not informed of this."

"Was there any indication of where Valada's body is located?" he asked.

She hesitated. "I do not know, my King, but from the story as told to me, I suspect it was buried immediately, as is the Sapiens way."

Moarte could think of nothing more to ask and yet he did not wish her to leave. Hemlock was the only link he had with Valada now, the only one who had been close to her through Portia who had heard all this from Serene.

He sat for a long time saying nothing. Finally his mother said, "I think you may leave now, Hemlock."

Hemlock turned to go but then suddenly walked to Moarte and knelt at his feet. "My King, I deeply regret bringing you this news. I know you loved her dearly. If I could wish for anything it is that you can love again."

He looked in her eyes and said, "Hemlock, you are kind and caring. I thank you for your service to me. I do not think I have appreciated you in the past as you deserve."

"I am here but to serve you, King Moarte. I would be honored if you would nourish yourself through me tonight," she said, bending her head back to expose her throat.

Moarte had not fed. The vein in her neck stood out, blue and plumb, filled with Sapiens vitae, and he would need strength for what was to come.

He leaned towards her, about to partake, when his mother's voice intervened. "My son, I suggest you need blood directly from Sapiens. Allow me to send in two slaves to feed you tonight, and two more tomorrow night when you go in search of the Sapiens King. Their blood is stronger, more nourishing, and you will need all the strength you can get."

He knew she was right and said, "Thank you for your offer, Hemlock."

She bowed her head, then said, "My King, if you are headed back to the land of the Sapiens, I volunteer my services to go with and assist you. I am fast on my feet and some have called me ruthless in battle. I would be honored to aid you again."

"We three shall fly together," he told her, "your brother and you accompanying me. Between the three of us, one may survive the ghosts in the caves and bring down the menace of the Sapiens King."

"Thank you, my King. I am thrilled to be of further service to you and would face the true death for one of your caliber."

When she was gone, Belladonna asked the guard outside the door to bring two slaves, a male and a female, ones who had not given blood recently. While they waited, she said to Moarte, "My son, I am concerned about your plan but now that it has altered I am more concerned."

"Why?" he asked, feeling that he did not really care about her concerns.

"Hemlock is not trustworthy."

He looked at his mother, who had never much liked Hemlock. "She volunteered for the mission. She brought me back information speedily and was not afraid as some of my warriors might have been to convey the worst news. Now she offers to fight by my side after offering her blood. I see nothing to be suspicious about."

"Then let me tell you this, Moarte: Hemlock has her own agenda, always. You are in a state of grief and that means you are not seeing clearly. I implore you to be careful."

Moarte sighed heavily. "At this point in time, I don't much care for existence so being careful is not at the top of my priorities."

"My concern exactly. Hemlock is unscrupulous. Do not fall prey to her hidden agendas."

Just then another knock came on the door and again Belladonna said, "Enter."

A young male and female Sapiens walked tentatively into Moarte's chamber. "The King needs nourishment," Belladonna said. "Go to him. Do not be afraid. He will not harm you, only take some blood."

The two walked to Moarte who motioned for the boy to sit at his feet and for the girl to come to him.

"I bid you a good evening, my son. I will see you tomorrow just after sunset, before you depart."

"Sleep well, Mother," he said, already pulling the girl to his lap and moving her brown hair behind her shoulders, tilting her head, opening his mouth so that his incisors could soon find their way to the vein.

As he pierced this Sapiens girl and began to swallow her pure and clean blood, he thought that his mother was right, as always, at least about one thing: the blood *is* better directly from a Sapiens. It always had been that way and always would be.

Chapter Twenty-One

Belladonna was troubled about Hemlock. She sensed something was not right but couldn't put her finger on what. But she knew she did not trust Hemlock, not one bit. And she also knew Moarte was extremely vulnerable right now. That he had seemingly forgotten Hemlock's duplicitous nature alarmed her.

She feared for his safety. Headed into the haunted caves, with or without Wolfsbane and Hemlock by his side, he would be disoriented and at an extreme disadvantage against the Sapiens King.

Moarte was a hybrid, the only one she knew of, birthed by her when she was mortal, fathered by an immortal. As such, he was different in some ways than those who had been turned, including herself. It had taken the vampirii some decades to accept him as ruler, but his natural leadership savvy combined with having his mother by his side, they had finally given him their complete allegiance. Most of them, anyway. But after tonight, she was worried. They had seen too much vulnerability in him. Hemlock and those like her would use it against him, Belladonna had no doubt.

Moarte's genes should allow him to access his Sapiens nature as well as his vampiric, which might help him out in the caves. She had not entered the caves since her husband, Morpheus, had captured her in a raid, and she had been Sapiens then. She had no idea what it was like for vampirii to enter, but she had heard stories, many from her husband. Moarte accessing his Sapiens side was possible, but she was far from certain it could be done or that he could do it on such short notice or under such emotional duress. Still, it made sense that he should try.

She would talk with him before he left tomorrow night. It wasn't the best time but his spirit had been crushed this evening and there would be no other chance to offer this suggestion, and he would need something to help him in the caves and there seemed to be nothing else. She was unsure he could survive the ghosts, and if he couldn't, he would be helpless in the hands of the Sapiens. Again. This made her heart heavy.

As she walked down the long hallway that led past the place where the slaves lived, she stopped to listen to a familiar voice.

"I'll want four of you tonight, for the blood, and for my pleasure in other ways. Four with unmarked flesh so that I may leave my mark on you before any others have the chance. Who volunteers?"

After a long pause, Hemlock said, "None? Well, then I take you, you, and you two. Bring whips and switches to my room. I have been burdened tonight, thwarted, and want to relax."

Belladonna quietly stepped back several paces and began walking as though she were just passing the door the moment Hemlock stepped through it. Hemlock's surprise at seeing Moarte's mother was evident in the warrior's eyes, and in the way she halted so abruptly.

"Dowager!" she said, her tone startled, but she bowed slightly and recovered quickly.

"Hemlock. Are you looking for a particular slave?"

"No, Dowager, any will do." Behind her, four young slaves, naked, with gloomy faces, followed, each carrying something to be flogged with.

Hemlock noted Belladonna's mouth turn down in disapproval. "I need relaxation after my arduous task of bringing somber news to our King."

"Understandable," Belladonna replied. "And yet I see four slaves. It seems excessive."

"My appetites are strong in general, perhaps stronger than your own."

"Perhaps."

"Possibly as strong as your son's."

Belladonna became wary. "Moarte has good control of his appetites."

"I understand that was not so with Valada."

"An exception. You, of course, recall the circumstances."

"Yes, naturally. She was a slave, the daughter of our enemy, an enemy herself, and one who had harmed our King. He had every right to inflict pain on her, as much as he wished. She deserved nothing less. Had it been me whose wings she clipped, she would have died instantly at my hand. Your son, our King, showed great restraint. But Valada is gone now, and possibly his appetite for love will rekindle."

"In time, perhaps. But not soon. I would encourage none to hope for a speedy recovery of the emotion of love."

"Love is overrated," Hemlock said, motioning the slaves to follow as she turned to walk away. "You may not recall but there are other appetites which are just as strong, and I'm certain King Moarte will be indulging in those sooner than you might imagine. I bid you a pleasant evening, Dowager. Rest well."

Belladonna watched her head down the hallway, the four slaves of the evening following like miserable ducklings who, by sunrise, would be bleeding from many wounds to sate Hemlock's self-proclaimed strong appetites.

This vampir was dangerous and Belladonna must warn her son again. Hemlock had an intention and it involved Moarte, that was clear. If left unchecked, she would insinuate herself through Moarte's grief and soon be his new bride. This would neither be good for Moarte nor the realm. Something must be done, and Belladonna would need to think long and hard about what and how to actualize that something before he left tomorrow evening.

CHAPTER TWENTY-TWO

Serene worried when the sun rose and Portia still had not returned. She did not know what to do. At dawn, her brother had come home from work and was now fast asleep, but Serene lay wide awake, tossing in her bed, feeling helpless.

Finally, she decided to go to the well and wait, but more waiting there left her even more frustrated. The old, crazy woman who had been at the well the night before still perched in the same spot, rocking, mumbling to herself, and Serene decided to sit beside her.

"Grandmother," she said, addressing the woman respectfully as the well-brought-up young did with the old, "have you been here all night?"

The old woman nodded.

Serene took a piece of bread from her pocket and handed it to the elder, who chewed the dense grain slowly and Serene saw she had no teeth left in her mouth.

Finally, Serene took a chance and asked, "Did you see another by the well last night?"

The old lady said nothing.

"Do not be afraid, Grandmother. This is only between you and me and will go no further." Everyone in the city had been paranoid even before Serene left because information too frequently was relayed to the authorities, ending up in the wrong hands, and coming back to harm the source.

"She sat on the other side. Slim, with a white shawl over her head. She's like a sister and she hasn't returned home."

Again, the old woman said nothing.

"Have you seen her?" Serene pushed.

A croaky sound came from the elder's mouth that sounded like "Yes."

"When?"

"Last night. She went there and was swallowed." And she pointed behind her, towards the wall with the hidden opening to the tunnel.

"Did you see her return?"

The old woman shook her head.

"Thank you, Grandmother. I'll bring you more food later today."

As she began to walk away, the old lady said, "Take care, child! There are dark forces you do not know about at work. Your sister is gone."

The hairs at the back of Serene's neck suddenly tingled. She stopped and turned, but the old lady was focused on the bread she gummed so laboriously.

Serene made an instant decision. She headed to the wall, ducking into the tunnel entrance when none of the early morning risers passing would notice.

She hurried down the sloped tunnel reaching the bottom quickly, then ran through the forest with sprays of sunlight streaming amidst the thick stands of trees. The woods were alive with birdsong and small scurrying animals like the black squirrels and striped woodchucks she saw, the scent of sweet flowers and verdant plant growth saturating the warm air, and the thought flashed through her mind that she might never experience this again when Wolfsbane turned her. And she wondered why there could not be vampirii who had once been Sapiens who could walk in daylight.

She reached the largest clearing, the spot where Hemlock would have been waiting last night, and combed the area, but there was no sign of Portia. Of course not! She had probably headed back to the city and become lost hunting for Rivard's home.

Serene was about to turn and go back when she noticed sunlight bathing the clearing awash with buttercups whose yellow lit up in the golden rays and she decided to take a few moments to go there to lie in the grass and feel the sun warm her and give her skin a little color. It might also cheer her since she felt stressed and needed her mood lifted.

As she entered the tall grass, a dozen dark-winged birds took flight from the ground. Crows. A murder of them. They perched on the limbs of a tree at the edge of the clearing, squawking loudly at her as if she had interrupted something. *They were probably enjoying a meal of carrion,* she thought, and headed to where they had been to see what poor dead creature's flesh was in the process of being devoured.

She stopped abruptly. What lay in the grass was familiar but not. She bent low to examine it yet something troubled her deeply about this flesh. It did not appear to be an animal at all but more a part of an animal. A large animal. And despite the bits pecked out by the crows, she finally let herself recognize this for what it was: a heart. A *large* heart.

She inhaled sharply and looked around the clearing. Where was the rest of this beast?

By walking in a small circle that she extended wider with each pass, she had just about reached the point where the clearing met the surrounding trees when she found it.

The body was nearly unrecognizable. The flesh had turned black as if charred by fire. But the clothes told her everything. This was the remains of Portia. The throat showed clear bite marks in the seared flesh. A large hole had been opened in the chest and Serene knew that what she had found earlier was Portia's heart. She knelt beside the girl, sobbing.

The evil and vindictive Hemlock had done this! There was no doubt in Serene's mind. And with that awareness came another: Portia would have passed the information but likely it would not reach King Moarte, or not as it had been presented. Suddenly she sensed that she was in danger, and not just her but more importantly, Queen Valada.

Serene jumped to her feet. She retrieved the heart and lay it next to the body, covering both with as many leaves and as much dirt as she could scoop with her hands, sensing that further exposure to sunlight and hungry animals would destroy what remained of the girl, and she didn't know whether or not those remains would be needed at some point. And if not, at least she could bury Portia, even if this was a poor interment.

She raced back through the forest to the tunnel and up into the city. The old lady was no longer at the well as she passed it, and the streets were crowded with shoppers and people going about their daily business.

Serene burst into her brother's home, waking him with a shout. "Rivard, wake up! We have to help Valada now! Her life is in danger, as is mine."

CHAPTER TWENTY-THREE

"This isn't a good idea," Rivard whispered as they sat at the kitchen table, dust motes visible as the mid-day sun drifted through the one window.

"It *is* a good idea," Serene insisted. "Trust me, Brother. We can do this."

Serene was at a counter, preparing a mixture of herbs she knew would induce sleep. Their mother had been a healer and passed this knowledge on to her daughter. Serene remembered many of the recipes and this one in particular her mother had taught her at the age of fifteen, when she was old enough to memorize a complicated potion.

She recalled that it had been mid-fall when she and her mother had harvested the herbs that grew wild at the western part of the city in one of the old abandoned cemeteries. They dried them in bunches, hanging them from the rafters in the ceiling, their aromatic fragrance filling the house, causing her father to sneeze but her mother just made him a tea to deal with that allergy.

This was the last recipe her mother taught her. By winter, both parents would be dead in a revolt by the populous that the Sapiens King crushed in its infancy. The next year Serene was captured by Wolfsbane when the vampirii raided the city.

"Are you sure you have all the ingredients?" Rivard asked. "Without a recipe being written down—"

"Don't worry, big Brother. I know that such concoctions aren't something you've ever found interesting, but I did. And I know what I'm doing."

"I hope so," he said bleakly.

It had taken her much time and patience to convince him about the danger to Valada and to herself, but finally Serene persuaded him this would be a safe way to free the Queen. She spent the late morning and early afternoon measuring and crushing herbs like Valerian root with poppy seeds, boiling them, straining the liquid then cooking that to a reduction to which she added a little sugar which turned it to a thick syrup. Finally, she added this to the cast of wine Rivard had made.

"The beauty of this recipe is that the herbs cannot be detected by taste or smell. No one will even know they were poisoned."

Rivard frowned.

"Of course, 'poisoned' is just a term; naturally, they won't be harmed. And they'll wake. Eventually."

They had agreed on a plan. The Dungeon Master would be furious when he discovered Valada missing, but hopefully he wouldn't notice for a day—or several—Rivard said he never checked on her. It was only if Varmik returned would they be found out; with luck, he had tortured Valada enough.

When it was discovered that Valada had escaped, everyone would assume that someone had come in and freed her. Suspicion would likely not turn towards Serene but even if it did—because she had provided the wine—Rivard had a backup story: his cousin had gone missing.

Whether or not Serene was suspected, she and the Queen would be long gone, hopefully returned to the safety of the vampirii fortress.

Rivard felt this story made sense and he would be above suspicion, because he had worked so long for the Dungeon Master, but Serene was not as certain, though she did not tell him that. Still, it was their only plan and she knew they had to hurry.

Once they were inside the prison, Serene loaded down with gourds of drink, she fed the still living prisoners wine. There were only two guards on duty besides Rivard and she flirted with them in the enthusiastic yet embarrassed way of a virgin and made comments like, "What a shame to waste good wine on ones such as these."

"Then hand it over to us, pretty!" the stocky, red-headed one said, and she poured two tin cups of wine and took one to each of the guards. They drank it down quickly and wanted more.

"If I give you more, there won't be enough for Princess Valada."

"She deserves none!" the one with grey hair and brown eyes assured her, his gaze riveted to her breasts. "She's a traitor. Here, give me her share!"

Serene poured more in each cup. By the time she and Rivard reached Valada's cell, the two guards were fast asleep. Everyone in the dungeon slept—everyone who was alive.

"Where's the Dungeon Master?" Serene asked.

"He went to see the King today to find out what he wants done with Valada."

"Then it's fortuitous that we're acting now," she said, "because that does not bode well for the Queen. Open the door."

Rivard unlocked the door and pulled it wide for the light and they entered the cell together. Valada lay in a heap as before, as if she had not moved in a day, and Serene checked the temperature of her skin, opened her eyes, and brushed away insects feeding on the dried blood at her nose and mouth and held her hand at the nostrils to make sure she was breathing. The Queen was breathing, but she was not responding.

"Hurry! We have to get her out of here quickly," Rivard said.

Together they lifted Valada but hers was a dead weight and Rivard ended up picking her up in his arms to expedite the rescue. Serene poked her head out the door to make sure the guards were still asleep—they were. Rivard locked the cell then they hurried through the dungeon room and up the many stone steps to street level.

It was the end of the afternoon rest period and there were a few people on the streets, but not many. Still, they clung to the shadows and doorways until they reached the square with the well.

The old lady sat there, as before, and when they passed, she looked up to watch them. Serene had suspected that the woman might be waiting, since more food had been promised, and she had brought along bread and cheese and a few nuts, which she handed to the wrinkled woman to distract her while Rivard hurried to the hidden tunnel entrance.

"I said I would return, Grandmother. Eat well."

As Serene turned to join Rivard, suddenly the beggar woman reached out and snagged her wrist in a surprisingly strong grip.

"You must hurry, child! The wind will pick up this night and it is best to be indoors when that occurs. Darkness hides many secrets that a strong wind will unearth and you may not wish to know them all. Sometimes it is best to hide from what is hidden."

This riddle confused Serene for a moment and at the same time left her unsettled, but she said, "I'll remember your words, Grandmother. I must go now," and the old woman released her.

They hurried down the tunnel and reached the ground exit while light still clung to the sky. Serene had a strong sense that they should not be near the area where Hemlock would wait when darkness fell, yet it was the shortest route back to the vampirii stronghold.

For a moment, she was indecisive, but finally said, "I think we need to move through the forest but close to the mountain." This decision was based purely on instinct and she trusted her instincts. The route was longer because rather than walking a straight line from the tunnel exit, they moved around the winding shape of the mountain that jutted into the forest and back out, weaving their way in wide and narrow 'S' patterns close to the rocky wall.

They were still on Sapiens land when the sun threatened to set but close to the border, too near where Hemlock would be when she arrived in two hours, or much less if she had slept nearby. Serene didn't like being this close, but Rivard showed signs of fatigue and finally she said, "Put the Queen down over here on this patch of soft grass."

A stream ran beside where Valada lay and Rivard drank long and deep of the fresh water. Serene washed Valada's face, neck and hands and poured some cold water into her mouth. Some of the water spilled out but she saw the Queen's throat move and knew at least a little was swallowed.

"Serene, I must return now. If I hurry, and go the direct route to the tunnel entrance, I can get back to the dungeon as the others are waking and pretend to wake myself."

Serene jumped to her feet and clutched his arm. "Please, Rivard, rethink this. Come with me! You will be welcome in the land of the vampirii. You will have a good life."

"As a slave?"

"Perhaps one of the vampir females will take you as a lover. No, I'm sure of it. You're not too ugly!" she teased, because they both knew he was handsome. She hoped to bring up his spirits, which had sunk. She knew he was skeptical of all this.

"I can't produce children as a female Sapiens can. What would one of the vampir females want with me?"

She gave him a look.

"Besides that!" he laughed.

She laughed too. But suddenly, as his face turned serious, hers did as well. "Rivard, I'm afraid you'll be in danger if you go back."

He hugged his younger sister. "I'll be fine. I'm a trusted guard, and have worked in the dungeon since I came of age. No one will believe I had anything to do with Valada's escape, nor that I aided you in any way. But, I've got to go. It's already night. Be well, Sister. I hope we see one another again, but I don't know when or how that can be."

She didn't want to let him go but knew she had to. Every minute he remained was one where he was not in the dungeon, so she released him and said, "Be well, Brother. And know your baby sister adores you!"

His smile was both sweet and sad as he turned and ran through the forest along a different path than what they had used, the more direct route back to the tunnel that led to the city.

Serene suddenly felt alone and unprotected. She shook off that feeling as best she could. Valada needed her to be strong and she could not fail her.

She tried to wake her. "My Queen, can you hear me? Please, give me a sign. You need to be awake, and hopeful. We're near the border, just inside vampir territory. You're safe now."

That was an exaggeration. Even though they had crossed the border, Sapiens frequently infringed on vampir land. But the greater danger was Hemlock, and Serene did not know where she could hide Valada now that the sun had set. It would take Hemlock less than two hours to reach the spot where she had agreed to wait, less if she had found a place en route to hide from the sun. And in flying over the trees, with the sharp night eyes of the vampirii, Hemlock would surely spot them.

The walk to the vampir stronghold would take a robust Sapiens one full day. Alone, it might take Serene two days. With Valada helpless, Serene did not know how long their return would be. And in truth, she did not know how dire Valada's condition was.

An idea suddenly occurred to her and she realized that intuitively this is why she had wanted to stay near the mountain. Through the dark hours, when Hemlock would be near, she and Valada could hide just inside a cave entrance. Hemlock would not know they were there and had no reason to venture in; besides, she would not want to risk encountering the ghosts.

Serene knew of one entrance back across the border that led nowhere.

It was not too far away, a short lateral tunnel with a low entrance, but long enough and with a curve that they would be hidden from anyone venturing past the opening. All Sapiens knew this tunnel was a dead end and it was extremely unlikely anyone would bother entering, especially after dark. Hiding throughout the night would give them time to rest and Serene needed that. She also needed to think of how to proceed.

Hemlock must return to the stronghold about two hours before sunrise, at least an hour to find shelter in the woods, and Serene and Queen Valada could start fresh just prior to daybreak.

Serene had brought a gourd with her packed with herbs to help revitalize Valada. She filled it with water from the stream to make an infusion. She had food in her pockets, enough for two days, if she was careful. Valada would not likely eat much, but she must ensure her Queen did eat to build her strength.

She tried to help Valada to her feet, but the Queen's battered body was heavy and awkward and finally Serene simply took the Queen's hands and, walking backwards, dragged her along the ground. Valada moaned and Serene suspected her arm might be broken so she lifted the Queen under the arms instead, making the job much more difficult and tiring. By the time she had pulled the dead weight to the cave entrance, Serene was sweaty and exhausted and full darkness had descended.

Once she had Valada inside the tunnel, she stopped to rest. The tunnel was not long and when a second wind came to her, she dragged the monarch down the tunnel and around its curve to the dead end where they could hide and rest for the night.

"My Queen? Queen Valada?"

There was no response.

Now that darkness had fallen outside, the tunnel was very dark. By feel, Serene moved Valada's head back and fed her more herbed water slowly, making certain it went into her mouth. Then she drank some herself. She had worn a large shawl tied around her hips and wrapped Valada in that.

Normally a positive person, Serene found her spirits wilted. Dragging Valada only a short distance had worn her out. It had also been slow. She could envision twelve hours of daylight where they moved through the forest at the pace of a turtle. This would not get them to the vampirii stronghold for many days, if not weeks. And meanwhile, every night, Hemlock would be flying over these woods. Too near.

"Oh my Queen!" she cried, feeling despair. "If only you could awaken, it would be so much better."

But the body she held in her arms did not stir.

CHAPTER TWENTY-FOUR

Moarte summoned Wolfsbane and Hemlock to his chamber the minute the sun had set. Before they arrived, his mother did, bringing with her two slaves and insisting that he feed.

While he fed, she talked with him in the vampiric tongue so that only he could understand, and he listened with half an ear. Not since he had been recovering from the breaks to his wing bones had he drunk so much in such a short space of time. He did not want to feel bloated. The blood would increase his strength, yes, but would also leave him heavy for the flight. He took just enough so that he would be almost sated. Besides, he wanted to leave room for the Sapiens King's blood!

"Moarte, I've been thinking quite a bit about how you can survive the haunted caves. It seems to me that because you're half Sapiens, you stand the best chance of survival, as opposed to Wolfsbane and Hemlock—those brought over do not seem to retain Sapiens cells. I know that from experience. But you have the genes of both your father and me within you."

He paused long enough to say, "I do, but I have been alive for hundreds of years. And vampir genes are dominant, as we know. Whatever Sapiens genes are left would not matter and have probably shriveled by now."

"I disagree."

"Of course you do, Mother!" He set the boy aside and pulled the girl to him, positioning her so that he could take from her neck—the best spot. The blood was freshly pumped here, up the carotid artery and through the brain and returning via the jugular. She was passive and acquiesced to his needs, which made her blood calm and all the more desirable.

"I believe you have the ability to tap into the Sapiens genes at will. It won't be easy to do, and of course you have not done it before, but the option is there. The more you can access your mortal genes, the better you will survive the caves. And you must survive in order to reach the Sapiens King."

He did not take much from the girl, still wanting to keep his appetite honed. He moved her aside and said to the two Sapiens, "Thank you for your service. You may go."

Once they were out the door, as he wiped his mouth he said to his mother, "How do you envision me reconnecting to these genes?"

"Let me mesmerize you."

"What? Have you gone over the edge mentally?" he shouted.

"No, Moarte, I have not. But I do see that this might be a way to allow you to access parts of yourself you have not touched on before and at a time when it might be crucial."

"What makes you think you can help by mesmerizing me?"

"I believe it's worth a try, since you have no other plan but to plunge yourself into the haunted caves and search for the Sapiens King. He won't be easy to find. He will be secured away, heavily guarded, and quite likely at or near the central part of the caves for better security against attacks. In order for you to get to him you must withstand the ghosts, who will automatically enchant you until you're bound by their spell. Anything that can help you withstand the ghosts must be tried."

He thought for a moment. The idea of his mother mesmerizing him felt repugnant and he was reluctant to give himself over to this. Vampirii did not mesmerize one another! It was dangerous to hand over control to another predator, be they Sapiens or vampirii. And yet… "You do have a point," he finally admitted.

"Of course I do," she said, walking towards him, which made him tense and wary.

"Don't be fearful, Moarte," she said, she who had always known him so well. "I am your mother. I have only your best interests at heart. I would do nothing to harm you. Have I ever?"

"No," he admitted.

"You are a strong male and do not wish to be either dominated or dependent. I understand that. I promise you I will not step out of bounds."

He shook his head and sighed but permitted her to approach him and to look into his eyes.

He watched Belladonna's eyes change color. The pale blue shifting to the blue of a twilight sky in summer melded with what at first appeared to be the color of soil then slowly blossomed to what he could easily identify as blood red, and that calmed him. He had not realized the extent to which he'd been stressed.

Amidst this new tranquility was a pain so deep he sensed it might destroy him and fear welled but then he heard her voice, soothing, familiar, reassuring as she began telling him that he could do anything, reminding him that he came from her as well as from his father, that he was strong, honorable, brave, and so many other words he had not heard in a long, long time, since he was a child.

Then she began talking to him about being Sapiens as well as vampirii and while he could not feel what she said, he did understand her, and the words made sense to him on some level and seemed extremely reasonable.

She talked more and he listened and agreed with all she told him, feeling her energy as a balm swirling within him, strengthening him, hardening him for what was to come.

And then he heard the words, "Return, and remember."

And he did.

Amazingly, Moarte felt refreshed, as if he had had a good and trouble-free day's sleep, which he had not had. He felt full, virile, master of his fate, determined to reach his goal, ready to brave anything. He felt driven.

He looked at his mother and smiled with his eyes and she smiled back with her eyes and lips, that same smile that he knew but didn't know, but tonight it did not matter to him. He leaned forward and kissed her cheek. "Thank you, Mother."

"Moarte," she said, "I could have told you this while using enchantment, but I gave you my word. So now I must tell you something else because my heart is heavy."

He felt his lips turn downward in a frown. "You do not believe I can enter the caves?"

"Of *course* you can enter the caves, and survive."

"You fear the Sapiens King is stronger than I am, that he will kill me?"

"No. I know you are the strongest. I feel that."

"Then what, Mother?"

Just then a knock came on the door and it opened. Wolfsbane and Hemlock entered the chamber uninvited, dressed for battle.

"Good! You're here!" Moarte stood. He saw that his second was relieved to find him in such good condition. "We leave immediately." He turned to his mother. "You will assume the throne until my return. And if I do not return—"

"Yes, my son, I know what to do." She leaned in to kiss his cheek, despite the fact that both Wolfsbane and Hemlock were in the room. But instead of a kiss, she whispered in his ear. "Watch your back. Sapiens *and* vampirii."

He felt startled but did not want to interrogate her in front of these two, and not now. Not when he was eager to go. When the blood still boiled in his veins for revenge.

"We depart!" he said, striding to the balcony and leaping into the air. He felt his wings expand and tonight he was strong and potent and lifted upward immediately, the wind he created helping him soar. Within seconds he sensed the two behind him.

The Sapiens land was two hours away but tonight they would arrive sooner. His energy was high and the air currents from behind would aid them.

Finally, he was resolved to kill the Sapiens King and he would succeed or die trying. His only weapon was the dagger he usually carried at his waist. But he did not want to use the metal if he could help it; he longed to strangle his enemy with his bare hands. He wanted to press on the windpipe and cut off air until blood seeped from the mortal's mouth. He wanted to stab his canines into the face vein, the neck vein, into the leg, then into the artery near the heart, to first suck slowly then strike quickly, taking nearly all the blood, leaving him near death, and then, when the Sapiens King was not dead but at the edge, Moarte would rip the still-beating heart from his chest and devour it!

But this was only part of his goal. This Rivard, the one who had murdered his wife, would also die this night!

These thoughts helped him fly fast and the two behind could barely keep up. Tonight he would be glutted on blood, and on revenge. For his warriors, for himself, but mostly for Valada.

Chapter Twenty-Five

When the light had faded completely, Serene's hopes dimmed, but after hours of total darkness they had sunk.

Two worries tormented her. The first was how to get the comatose Queen Valada walking so that they could make it over the tall mountain that stood between where they were and the vampirii stronghold. Despite thinking about it for hours, she had no clue how to accomplish this. Valada had sighed once or twice, but her body remained limp. Still, Serene made sure to give her herbed water regularly, but there was no way to get food into Valada.

Her second worry had also expanded with the darkness. As she thought over Rivard's story, she saw many holes in it and she did not believe he was safe. She should have insisted he stay with them, get them to the vampirii fortress. Once they were there, he would have seen how it is and he would have wanted to stay as she did, and she wouldn't have had to talk him into anything. It would have been easier that way. And even if in the end he wanted to return to the Sapiens world, he could say he had been caught in a raid when the vampirii stormed the dungeon and freed Valada. They took him as a prisoner to their land but he managed to escape. Even that would sound better. Anything but what he was doing.

She had faith in the herbed wine, but there was no way to know how long it would keep the guards asleep. Worse, there was no way of knowing when the Dungeon Master would return. And if Varmik came in… If either of them was there when Rivard walked through the door…

Serene felt that she needed Rivard for another reason as well: she could not get Valada standing let alone walking. And she could not carry her. They would not make it over the snow-capped mountain without him and one or both would die en route and she did not want Valada's death on her conscience.

Despite knowing that night had entrenched itself and that Hemlock was probably out there waiting and could either see her or sense her, Serene realized she needed to go back into the Sapiens city, back into the dungeon. Rivard *had* to come with her! And she had to know that he was not a prisoner now himself. Queen Valada would be safe here. Serene knew that Hemlock would not enter the mountain of her own volition, and Valada apparently could not leave it. Leaving it herself would pose a problem for Serene, but she was still in Sapiens territory and Hemlock was unlikely to breach the border, at least she hoped that was so.

At some point she grew tired of worrying and knew she had to act. She would go home where her brother should be sleeping and get Rivard and return here with him. In the morning they would take Valada across the mountain, as far as they could go, then find shelter at dusk from Hemlock, who would be searching the ground from the sky like a bird of prey—Serene felt sure of that. The vampir would not want Queen Valada to return and she could not risk Serene returning to tell what Hemlock had done to Portia.

"I'll come back for you, my Queen," she said to Valada. "Please, try to pull yourself together. King Moarte needs you. And you need him." *And I need you to help me help you,* she thought.

She stood and walked to the cave exit, peering carefully around, seeing no one, neither vampir nor Sapiens. That didn't mean they weren't there but still, she would have to risk it. A half moon lit the sky, making it too bright for her purposes but there wasn't anything she could do about the moon.

Instead of moving along the high outside mountain wall, she headed in a direct line towards the tunnel entrance that led to the city. It was not the safest route but it was the fastest way and she felt time pressing on her. And at the back of her mind, always, was Wolfsbane, and how forlorn he appeared when she'd last seen him, as if he was looking at her for the last time. The image cut into her heart. She would survive, for both of them. She had to.

Chapter Twenty-Six

Moarte had planned to alight where he had taken Valada but Hemlock assured him that there was a better spot, not so out in the open as the large clearing, which she suggested they bypass. This new clearing would allow them to land closer to the border and from what she had seen, no Sapiens guards had been on duty there either night.

He could see that Wolfsbane wasn't completely behind this idea, landing so near the border, risking being spotted by the Sapiens and having to fight even before they reached the caves or the city, but at the same time Moarte knew that his second was eager to find Serene and the closer to her he could be, the better.

Moarte agreed to this landing site readily. He felt he owed Wolfsbane and did not want him to suffer the same fate he had, losing the one he loved so dearly. The three would go into the city together, to the dungeon, find this Rivard who had destroyed Valada in the most vile way, and Moarte would end his existence and force him to endure as much pain as had been inflicted on his beloved. Then they would rescue Serene. And finally, Moarte would enter the haunted mountain alone and finish it once and for all with the Sapiens King. He expected that he would die somewhere along the way in the process, but at least if he murdered the beast who had beat his beautiful wife to death, he would have some satisfaction, and her soul could rest in peace. That might be all he could hope for.

As they flew north, Hemlock had been watching the sky east of the mountain onto which the Sapiens city had been built, and Wolfsbane watched the sky with the two mountains to the west, all part of the range that included the southern-most mountain which they had flown over. All of these four mountains contained haunted caves and the Sapiens could be hiding in any of them, but Moarte believed the Sapiens King wouldn't go far from his city and his eyes were straight ahead, fixed due North, on the city with its castle atop the mountain.

Finally, Hemlock gestured and they descended to a mid-size clearing close to the grey wall where there was a narrow path between the mountain and the forest that led to the city.

Moarte looked at both Wolfsbane and Hemlock. This close to the mountain, both showed signs of mild distraction. He felt it himself, but his mother's words rang in his head—*You are part Sapiens. You can withstand the ghosts.*

Ahead stood the Sapiens fortress, a structure high up on one portion of this mountain, the city walled, built of the indigenous rock but not within the mountain, otherwise the citizens would have had no sunlight and they and the Sapiens King's army would have had no ability to come and go other than through the caves which would have proved incredibly inconvenient. The construction was fortunate in another way: it allowed the vampirii to enter the city.

They moved quickly, sticking to the forest's shadows until ahead, high above, the main gates came into view. Moarte motioned for them to hang back.

He said softly, "There is an entrance to a tunnel that leads directly into the city. It's not a long tunnel and ascends sharply. Do you think you can tolerate the ghosts during this passage?"

Wolfsbane, who had tried once before to enter the haunted mountain and had not succeeded, nodded grimly. Hemlock, who had never entered to Moarte's knowledge, put on a brave face and said, "I will not be effected," although clearly she already was.

This was the tunnel he had been told about by the guard who helped him escape by unbinding his chains and leaving the door unlocked. He had slipped through the city late at night and found the well with the hidden entrance nearby, just as the guard said, then hurried down through the steeply declining tunnel, the ghosts shrieking loudly in his ears because of his weakened condition. He managed to stumble out of the exit without being seen. There had been no time to ask why the Sapiens was helping him but Moarte had been grateful. If it had not been for that guard, Moarte knew he would be dead by now. As dead as his wife. Thoughts of her demise depressed him and he tore his mind away from a mental picture he imagined of her broken body.

The second the three entered the tunnel, Moarte began to hear the voices. They sounded as if they called to him personally but from far away, otherworldly sounds, not mortal or immortal, like something else that was not of this earthly realm at all. And yet he knew Sapiens were not affected. One night, he would like to discover the source of these ghosts and why only vampirii heard them and not Sapiens as well. No vampir, to his knowledge, had ever discovered what this was about and it was one of the true mysteries.

Directly behind him was Hemlock, her breathing labored, and he knew the voices were haunting her. Wolfsbane, at the rear, would be likewise effected. Moarte picked up his pace, forcing them to nearly run up the tunnel.

Once they reached the top, he motioned for the two to stop while he peered out the hidden doorway. An old woman sat at the well, but no other Sapiens were in the courtyard. If need be, they would immobilize her so that she did not cry for help.

He motioned the vampirii behind him to come and he headed right for the old lady.

Hemlock raised an arm, talons ready to rake the jugular of the Sapiens, but Moarte held up a hand.

He stared into the rummy eyes of the old Sapiens who was munching on a piece of cheese that to his nostrils reeked. She looked up and stopped chewing. He leaned in, wondering if she could see enough through the cataracts so that he could mesmerize her. He had no qualms about killing Sapiens but drew the line at harming the helpless of any species.

"The one you seek is here," she said, and Moarte drew back.

"Let me destroy her!" Hemlock hissed.

"No," Moarte said softly. The woman clearly couldn't see him and was probably half mad. He said to his second and third, "Come, we have little time and much to do."

He knew the way to the dungeon, the route gouged into his memory, and they encountered no one else on the streets. The last vampirii raid must have left the populous sparse, and paranoid about venturing out at night when the vampirii might come.

They moved quickly down stone steps, encountering a guard right away that Hemlock slaughtered with one blow to the throat, her talon severing the carotid which sent the rich blood spurting into the air while the guard made a gurgling noise and held his neck for only seconds, struggling in vain to stem the flow of his life's blood pulsing from his artery. Hemlock stopped to drink but Wolfsbane shoved her forward and away from the nourishment.

Moarte took the steps three at a time and reached the bottom of the stairs quickly, battling two more Sapiens guards along the way. When Hemlock reached the bottom she took on one and, following her, Wolfsbane the other. Moarte was left with just the Dungeon Master, who he remembered from when he had been a prisoner, the one who had carried out some of the torture.

The Sapiens looked astonished to see him but acted quickly. The Dungeon Master reached for a long club with nails hammered into it leaning against a pillar and raised it, saying, "You came back to us, vampir. We've been hoping for your return. Now, we can treat you properly and finish the job."

He charged. But Moarte was no longer a bound, weakened prisoner. He was at full strength and not only avoided the blow but moved so quickly the Sapiens did not see him and only knew about it when Moarte had him on the ground, the Sapiens back pressured by a knee, his arm twisted behind him. "Where is the one called Rivard?"

"Why do you want to know, Bloodsucking filth?"

Moarte pulled his arm back hard. The joint popped and the Sapiens howled.

"Where is he!" Moarte shouted.

"The cell," the Dungeon Master grunted.

The two guards lay on the ground, either dead or unconscious, and Wolfsbane raced to the cell door and yanked it off its hinges. Hemlock rushed inside and dragged the screaming man out into the main room.

The Dungeon Master managed to twist and kick and knock Moarte off him. He spun around, a knife in his hand, and slashed it in the direction of the vampir King.

Moarte leapt back in time. He snagged the wrist holding the knife and snapped it backwards, shattering the bone.

The Dungeon Master howled in pain and Moarte grabbed him up by the shoulders and threw him into the far wall where he crashed against the jagged stones and was knocked out.

In a fragment of a second, Moarte spun around to face the Sapiens who had destroyed his love. And froze. How could this be? Here was the guard who had helped *him* escape!

"Come, swine!" Hemlock said. "My King wishes to repay you for what you did to his wife."

"I did nothing to his wife!" Rivard said.

Hemlock slashed out, her nails ripping into his face which was already puffy, bruised and bleeding from a beating he'd received before their arrival.

She and Wolfsbane each caught an arm and dragged the struggling Sapiens to Moarte and threw him to the ground at the feet of their King, who could only stare at this man in confusion, caught in a complex braid of emotions.

Finally, he said, "You raped Queen Valada, my wife, and beat her to death."

Rivard looked up at him, looked Moarte right in the eye, his eyes confused. "No. It wasn't me."

"Liar!" Hemlock said, kicking him in the groin.

Rivard doubled over and groaned.

"You helped me escape," Moarte said, "and then you murdered my wife? I do not understand your motives but I do not need to understand. You will die for what you did to her!" He grabbed Rivard by the throat and lifted him, about to destroy him.

"No!" came a voice like a bell from above, and all heads snapped towards the stairs.

"Serene!" Wolfsbane said, starting towards her.

"Please, King Moarte," she cried, "it was not my brother who beat and raped Queen Valada. It was Varmik, who is second to the Sapiens King. My brother helped me—"

"Liar!" Hemlock screamed, and she turned on Rivard, her talon slicing his artery, her mouth at the wound.

"No!" Serene screamed again, racing down the steps.

Wolfsbane caught her near the bottom while shouting at his sister. "What are you doing?"

Moarte yelled, "Stop! I command it!"

Hemlock pulled away slowly and reluctantly. She had been quick and much of the blood had left Rivard. She let go of the body and it dropped to the dirt. He lay pale and still, at the edge of lifelessness as the pulsing of his blood slowed.

Serene struggled to get to her brother but Wolfsbane held her back. Her eyes were clotted with tears. "You've killed him! Murderer!" she screamed at Hemlock, who only laughed.

"You can deny his guilt all you like, Sapiens slave, but he killed Valada."

Moarte stared at this scene in horror. He was confused. What was going on? Suddenly, Serene turned to him, speaking in a rush. "Queen Valada is not dead, my King. Rivard helped me rescue her, as he helped you escape. He is a good man. Please, do not let him die!"

"Valada is alive?" Moarte said, astonished.

"Yes. We took her from here into the woods, but she is injured and I could not bring her home myself. I came back to get my brother. And I was afraid for him," she sobbed. "I feared that he would be blamed for her disappearance and killed."

"Wolfsbane," Moarte said, "bring him over!" It was all that could be done because Rivard's artery pulsed so weakly that in seconds he would be on the other side of death.

"I will do it, my King," Hemlock said. "It is I who caused this."

"No! Not *you*!" Serene cried, lunging, but Wolfsbane held her back. And Hemlock already had her wrist slit and her blood dripping into Rivard's mouth.

"Murderer!" Serene cried.

Hemlock turned slowly, her face a mask of menace. "He is not dead, Sapiens slave. I will revive him, then he will belong to me. I will treat him well, since he is your brother, and since you are almost family and families must stick together."

She locked eyes with Serene, who felt stunned. Rivard would be Hemlock's slave! But she had something over Hemlock now. She could tell Wolfsbane and the King what the vampir did to Portia. In exchange for her silence, Hemlock was offering to treat Rivard well. Suddenly Serene said to Hemlock, "I *know* you will treat him well," her voice laced with a iciness not heard from her before.

"Calm yourself," Wolfsbane said to Serene. "Your brother will be all right." He pulled her close and she allowed herself to be held, touching his arm to let him know it was not him she felt cold towards.

"Lead me to Valada," Moarte said to Serene. "Now!"

Serene was reluctant to leave her brother and Moarte saw this. "Bring him!" he ordered Hemlock, who immediately picked Rivard up in her arms.

They left the dungeon quickly and Serene led them past the well which was empty of Sapiens now, including the old woman, and into the tunnel and down to the ground level exit.

She ran as quickly as she could, worried about her brother, worried about Valada, but maybe, just maybe, everything would be alright. Once they found Valada, they could all go back to the vampirii stronghold. If Valada was still alive. She had been anxious all through the night. She had no idea what would happen if Moarte found his wife dead after believing she had survived.

She entered the short tunnel with the dead end and there was no light so Serene could not see but she knew that Moarte, who followed close on her heels, could see in darkness.

"Where is she?" he said.

Serene felt around. It was a small space, at the end of this tunnel, and her fingers touched the shawl and the gourd of herbed water. "I left her here, King Moarte, not one hour ago!"

She heard him pace a few steps, his back to her, and she thought he was feeling the walls. "Is there another route out?"

"No. Only the way we came in."

She heard him racing back along the tunnel to where they entered and she followed quickly.

Wolfsbane held out an arm, and she moved into his embrace where he gathered her against his body. From this safety, she watched in horror as Hemlock drained the last drops of blood from her brother's body, blood she had just fed him as he neared death.

"Where is Portia?" Wolfsbane asked.

Hemlock's eyes lifted to Serene's and they told the girl everything. But her brother's welfare was most important now and she shook her head and kept quiet but held tight to Wolfsbane.

Moarte paced, staring at the ground. "Where would Valada go?" he asked.

"I do not know," Serene said. "She was not in good condition and even before we took her from the dungeon she did not speak or even seem to be awake."

"She might have tried to return to our territory," Wolfsbane said.

"No," Moarte assured him. "She went into the mountain. She is searching for her father. And the beast named Varmik. She has no weapon, and she is alone." It was as if Moarte spoke to himself aloud.

"I can lead you to the Sapiens King," Serene said. "I think I might know where his throne room is located within these caves. There will be guards along the way. And I would not be surprised if you find Varmik there as well."

"I want to find Varmik and the Sapiens King and kill both. Lead!"

Wolfsbane said, "My King, let me go with you."

"And I," Hemlock said. She nodded to Rivard. "He will not wake until near dawn."

Moarte said, "I do not know if either of you can withstand the ghosts, or if I can. But I must rescue Valada. Come," he said to Serene. "Which is the entrance that will take us quickest to the Sapiens King?"

She turned to lead them along the wall, but paused to watch Hemlock move Rivard off the path and into the trees to hide him. She did not trust Hemlock, but there was nothing much she could do about it. At least not right now.

The entrance she selected was the one Wolfsbane had told her that Queen Valada planned to enter through when Moarte had brought her here. It was the most logical place and the most direct route to the Sapiens King. Serene didn't know how any of the three vampirii would fare in the caves but she knew it would be difficult if not impossible for them.

Protecting Wolfsbane was her priority. She led the way, Moarte followed, then Wolfsbane, then Hemlock to the rear. It was a small army, three of its soldiers handicapped by a disease she barely understood which made them susceptible to a spirit world she could neither see nor hear. But even now as they neared the room of lights, when she glanced back their eyes looked far away, glazed, as if they were seeing or hearing *something,* but she had no idea what.

Soon they entered the chamber with the strange, unnatural rocks that shimmered as if a full moon glowed and this room was underwater. It had always been a peculiar place, one even she felt uncomfortable in.

But here enemies awaited them, not spiritual but physical beings. Two Sapiens guarded the room, one of whom was Varmik, and he held Queen Valada in his grasp, a sharp dagger at her throat.

(HAPTER TWENTY-SEVEN)

Moarte stopped just inside this oddly-lit chamber, and the others behind him were forced to halt. He heard the strange siren call of the ghosts but they were as flies buzzing to him now. Before him was Valada, naked, barely conscious, her body bruised, her one eye swollen closed, the other barely open but enough that she saw him. Her cut and swollen lips were moving as if she was trying to form words. Weakly, she lifted a hand towards him.

She was battered, her beautiful face nearly destroyed from recent wounds and bruises. It looked as if some of her bones might be broken. Her body was red with dried blood, her own, most of it around her face and thighs.

Seeing her injured made Moarte furious and if the dagger's blade hadn't been held so close to her, he would have attacked Varmik and torn him apart. But as it stood, even his speed would not be enough to prevent the blade from severing her artery.

"The vampirii come to visit," Varmik snarled. "You're the King—I remember you from when I beat you in the cell. You were weak then and not so powerful now, are you? And surely the ghosts are talking to you and your feeble army!" He laughed, a bitter sound, and Moarte remembered the voice of this Sapiens from whom he took a severe beating, fists pounding relentlessly for what felt like an hour or more, and his blood boiled for revenge.

"Sapiens dog!" Hemlock yelled, starting forward, but Moarte blocked her by holding up his arm and motioned for her to get behind him again. This was his game to play out. And Hemlock's aggression could get Valada killed.

"Tell me," he said to Varmik, his voice reasonable, as if they were friends and not mortal enemies, "why would a Sapiens like you, clearly powerful, need a female as a shield?"

"I do not need her as a shield, I am using her as a weapon against you."

"Really?" Moarte said, his tone cynical, his lips struggling to form the hint of a downturned smile. "It doesn't appear that way. It looks to me that you're afraid. That you believe without chains holding me, I'm stronger, and you need to protect yourself in the manner of a weak Sapiens."

Varmik was sinister, Moarte could see that. But he was also an egoist, and the implication that he could not win a fair fight rankled.

"Come," Moarte offered reasonably. "We two only. My warriors will not attack. You have a slight advantage as you are not affected by the ghosts, and that should counter my superior strength."

"Superior strength!" Varmik said snidely and spit. But Moarte could see he was interested.

He shoved Valada into the arms of the other guard, who aimed his knife at her throat.

"She is the prize," Moarte said, matter-of-factly. "The winner takes her."

"She's not worth a fight," Varmik said. "I've had her, many times, in every hole, and you can bet I would neither win nor lose for this bitch."

Serene stopped herself from gasping at this cutting remark, fearing Moarte would simply attack, putting Valada's life in jeopardy. But he said nothing. Then, finally he spoke.

"The prize is incidental, then. The victor determines the outcome of a greater battle. If you win, you have killed the King of the vampirii. If I win, I will kill the Sapiens King, whom you protect. If I can trust a Sapiens to make and abide by such a deal."

"*I* can be trusted," Varmik snarled, "but you are the undead. Drinker of Sapiens blood. You are not human and cannot agree to human conditions."

"Not so, Varmik," Moarte said, the other clearly startled that his name was known. "My mother was Sapiens. I have Sapiens cells in my body and I understand your values. Fight me and we will see who is stronger, a Sapiens warrior, or a half Sapiens half vampir warrior hampered by ghosts."

Varmik obviously wanted to fight, but he didn't trust Moarte, who saw this and said, "Wolfsbane and Hemlock, you will retreat."

"No, my King—" Hemlock began.

"Leave me!"

Wolfsbane motioned his sister back and tried to take Serene with them, but she ran to Valada and grasped her hand and the guard let this happen, likely because Serene was small and clearly posed no threat.

Moarte heard his second and third leaving the caves, Wolfsbane departing reluctantly. They would have been useless to him anyway. Already the ghosts were like bells clanging in his head, distracting him, and Wolfsbane and Hemlock must have been even more affected.

"I will use a weapon," Varmik said, "as you have one at your disposal."

Moarte removed the dagger from his belt and tossed it to the ground. "I will battle you without a weapon."

"Your claws are natural weapons."

"Fine. Keep the dagger if it helps you feel safe."

The slur had the intended effect on Varmik. Moarte knew this particular dagger well and its abilities and limitations; it was the one he had given Valada.

He glanced quickly at his wife, her body slumped against the guard who held her around the waist to prop her up, the blade of his knife not one inch from her throat. Her good eye was barely open and Serene touched her face gently in a spot where there was no discoloration, and he marveled at this brave and gentle Sapiens girl who had Wolfsbane's heart, and he could see why.

Varmik charged, assuming the lead, which Moarte wanted him to do. The Sapiens was power mad, and believed the ghosts would aid him, plus the dagger, giving him a strong advantage. He weighed more than Moarte, but the vampir King was mightier than he looked, and much faster, which the Sapiens should have remembered about vampirii, although clearly he thought the sounds in Moarte's head would slow him down.

The lunge was anticipated and unsuccessful. But Varmik spun around quicker than Moarte had envisioned he could, the Sapiens' dagger missing his chest by inches.

Let him tire himself, Moarte thought, planning on simply dodging until the Sapiens wore himself out. Moarte wanted to toy with him but ultimately he would have the advantage, even with the ghosts. And then he would release the full force of his rage on this monster.

But Varmik seemed to possess super human strength, his energy not flagging in the slightest, as if he were driven by some brew that reinforced him endlessly. Moarte knew that while he could defend himself eternally in normal conditions, the ghostly voices were escalating along with Varmik's aggression. For this to end, Moarte could not wait. He would have to go on the offensive, and soon.

Varmik charged yet again. This time Moarte started to lean to his left, only to get Varmik off balance. The Sapiens did go to that side, jabbing the dagger, which allowed Moarte to move blindingly fast to the right, and low. He kicked Varmik's knee. It buckled, the weakness sending Varmik further left but not down. Moarte slammed his foot into the back of the knee, and Varmik fell. At the same time the Sapiens was dropping, Moarte forced him hard to the floor face first.

It was an effort to hold this Sapiens down. Moarte pressed a knee into the small of his back. The Sapiens' weight was all muscle, more muscle than Moarte possessed, but the vampir King knew battle well, at least as well if not better than his opponent, and he did not hesitate to bring the Sapiens' leg up behind and twist. He twisted in two spots, snapping the foot joint and breaking both the ankle and knee, all in one move.

Varmik made a sound, but still he struggled and Moarte could barely hold him. He longed to use a talon to sever the carotid but feared the other guard would kill Valada. He might do that anyway. Moarte couldn't risk a glance there to see what was happening.

He leapt to his feet, jumped onto Varmik's back, then a quick bounce onto and off his arm, that hand holding the dagger. Another sound of bone—the tibia or fibula—snapping accompanied by a loud groan. This time Varmik did not rebound so fast.

Moarte kicked the dagger to the corner. He grabbed Varmik up by the back of his shirt and shoved him face-first against the wall. Close up behind him, Moarte felt the tension of holding the magnitude of his rage in check, even as the ghosts demanded his attention by their escalating screams. Together these two things kept him from speaking but not from bashing Varmik over and over against the jagged limestone.

Blood flew in every directions. The face of the Sapiens was soon nothing but crimson pulp. His body grew heavy but Moarte could not stop himself. He kept slamming the Sapiens into the jutting stones even though he was no longer moving or resisting. The increasing heaviness of the body said Varmik was unconscious, probably dead, but Moarte could not find a way to break his violence. He ripped off an arm and finally tore the head from the body. He wanted to destroy this being utterly until there was nothing remaining. Nothing!

But he did stop. And drank from the pumping neck artery, sucking in whatever blood still pulsed in his enemy until there was no more. And as he did, he realized that while he had been venting at the peak of his fury, the voices for those moments had been still. He only noticed because now they began anew.

He spun towards the guard and Valada and was shocked to see they were gone, and Serene too! While he had let himself explode with violent insanity, the women had been kidnapped!

He stared at the tunnels that led off from this lighted room. He had no idea which way the guard took them. The tunnel to the left of Varmik's bloody torso was where the vampirii had entered. He would have seen the three leave that way and via the tunnel to the right where Varmik's head lay. That left four more routes.

Suddenly, through the noise of the shrieking ghosts, he heard a sound and knew it was Serene, a small cry, like faked pain, a cry that he felt she had manufactured for his benefit to let him know which way to go.

He judged that the sound had come from one of the two tunnels directly across the room. It had to be one of those. But which one?

He reached down and snared his dagger and also took Valada's, then arbitrarily picked the tunnel on the right and raced into its blackness.

CHAPTER TWENTY-EIGHT

Everything looked hazy to Valada, the light sharpening and fading with each painful breath. She had some awareness that it was one of her father's guards dragging her down a tunnel, every step adding to the agony of broken bones and injured muscle and skin, the pain washing over her so wildly that she could not make a sound.

Her body felt like a bag of pain. She had no strength. Barely any will. And her mind had gone into a stupor that let her fantasize because she thought she had seen Moarte. And the girl Serene.

As if from far away, she heard a kind of low keening that blended with a high shriek and she recognized this sound from her past and vaguely thought: *these are the ghosts. The ones who demand that we listen to them.*

Now, she could only listen because she had no way to do anything else.

Suddenly, close to her, another sound, a loud cry.

"Shut up!" a gruff male voice ordered.

"I stubbed my toe. I was afraid," a voice she recognized said. The Sapiens girl Serene, who loved a vampir.

Every second was torture and Valada gasped at a sudden, sharp stab in her chest that was more acute than the pain in her arm. If only she could pass out again! But she had to kill her father. She had come here to do this. He was evil and must die.

Finally, finally, finally, they reached a lighted area and she heard the Sapiens who dragged her before her father's throne say, "Sire, Varmik is dead. The vampirii King killed him in the room of lights."

"How!" her father's angry voice demanded.

"There was a battle—"

"That's not what I asked, fool! How did the vampir withstand the ghosts?"

"I do not know, sire. He seemed troubled by them, but not enough to keep him from fighting."

"Who is this?"

"A girl who came with the vampirii."

"My name is Serene. I am Sapiens."

"I can see what you are. A traitor!"

"No, Sire. I was a prisoner for several years who escaped. The slave of Wolfsbane, King Moarte's second. The vampirii forced me to lead them to you on pain of murdering my brother. I know your daughter, Princess Valada, from when I was a prisoner of the vampirii. I knew she had been recently captured but I did not know she had escaped the vampirii."

"She did not escape, she came here on their behalf as you did, as a spy for the vampirii."

"No, my lord, I—"

Suddenly the warrior holding Valada smacked Serene across the face, "You do not speak unless our King asks you a question!"

Serene was silent for a few moment, then mumbled, "Forgive me, Sire," in a low and timid voice.

Valada's father ignored her and said to the warrior, "Where is the King of the vampirii now?"

"In the lighted room."

"Then he is coming here." A pause. "Call a dozen warriors immediately. And leave the women here. The vampir is after the half breed and after me. She will make excellent bait."

Valada was dropped to the floor, the broken rib stabbing her and making her gasp loudly.

She heard her father say, "Do you speak the language of the vampirii?"

This was apparently directed to Serene, who answered, "Yes, my lord, I have learned some. I do not speak well, but I understand."

"Then you will assist me and I will tell you how. If you prove yourself, you will live, and I will give you to one of my warriors. Otherwise, I will have you in my dungeon and you won't survive long. Am I clear?"

Valada understood that her father's hatred knew no bounds. She wanted to warn Serene not to trust him. The girl had said she was loyal to the Sapiens but either she had switched her allegiance and would betray Moarte, or she was planning on betraying the Sapiens King. Valada did not know the truth. Reality had turned on its head and everything said seemed convoluted and wrong, laced with the pain in her body and the siren call of the ghosts in her mind.

She closed her eyes, taking in small breaths, trying to will herself to slip into the pain, hoping in this way to lessen its intensity. She drifted, listening to the ghosts, struggling to understand them, and at last mumbled a desperate, "Who are you? What do you want?"

She was surprised when they answered her.

(HAPTER TWENTY-NINE

Moarte knew that the guard who had disappeared with Valada and Serene was taking them to the Sapiens King. Zador was no fool. He would have backup waiting, or coming. Moarte's only hope was that he could get to him fast enough to have a minute or two before the Sapiens warriors arrived.

This time, he did not intend to play with his prey. He would kill everyone but the women as quickly as he could, especially the evil ruler of this realm. It wasn't the death he had dreamed of for the Sapiens King, but Valada's life was far more important to him. Getting her to safety and treating her wounds was all that mattered to Moarte, and if he died the final death in the process, so be it.

The ghosts grew louder and his Sapiens genes were no longer aiding him. Their voices were chanting now, a mesmerizing sound, one that he fought with every ounce of will available to him. He would not succumb. Valada's life was on the line.

From behind, he heard a sound and at first mapped it onto the ghosts. But then he paused. Someone was coming. *Several* someone's.

He glanced behind and his night vision let him see Wolfsbane, Hemlock and, following them, a confused-looking Rivard, who Hemlock had obviously woken early. They caught up to Moarte, their faces reflecting the disorientation the ghosts bred. The spirits were wreaking havoc.

Moarte did not chastise his second and third for disobeying him. In fact, he said nothing, just turned and raced through the tunnel, the others following on his heels.

When he saw the light, he sprinted.

Moarte entered the chamber to find the Sapiens King on his makeshift throne looking smug. At that moment, Sapiens warriors entered from another corridor—thirteen of them—including the one who had kidnapped Valada and Serene, and he had already reached the women, this time with the point of his knife at Valada's chest, about heart level.

Moarte's wife lay on the floor and he could see she was alive, but not doing well. Serene sat beside her, head bowed, though she looked up at Wolfsbane when he entered, and the vampir could readily see that her lip was bleeding. Moarte motioned subtly to Wolfsbane to wait, in case he charged into battle over this.

It was a stalemate. Moarte, Wolfsbane and Hemlock might handle three each, if they could fight through the ghostly distraction. But Rivard was not strong enough yet. If he could fight *one*, it would be a miracle.

They were outnumbered. But fight they would, because there was nothing else to do.

Moarte rapidly assessed the Sapiens warriors. None looked afraid. Half were the strongest, and he would take three of those. He knew Wolfsbane would do the same with another three—they had been in so many battles together they could read one another well. Hemlock…he did not know what she would do. She was unpredictable. At least she was quick and vicious, both qualities that would come in handy here.

Moarte was about to leap when the Sapiens King said, "Vampir King, did you not appreciate the gift I sent you?"

He gestured to the floor and Valada, who looked broken.

Without taking his eyes off the warriors, Moarte said, "What sort of low creature sacrifices a daughter to save his own hide?"

"One who has no daughter. She is no longer Sapiens, if she ever was."

"And yet you fucked her mother. A vampir." Moarte used the harshest expression to let the other Sapiens in the room know what their King had done. But the Sapiens ruler only laughed.

"Yes, I fucked her. As we all fuck all the vampirii we capture. You should know that!"

Moarte had not been sexually assaulted when he was imprisoned. He knew the Sapiens King was implying this to demoralize the vampirii with him and to present him to the Sapiens troops as weak and a victim. "Perhaps your sources of information need refinement, Sapiens King. I came out of your dungeon as I came in. Unlike you, who will not leave this room alive."

"I will make you an offer," the Sapiens King said matter-of-factly. "I'll give you her and you leave. No blood will be shed."

"And why should I trust you?"

"Why not? I don't want this filth in my sight."

"Don't trust him. It's a trick!" Hemlock seethed, speaking in the language of the vampirii, the strain she felt from the ghost voices apparent in her tone.

"Translate!" the Sapiens King said to Serene, who looked at Wolfsbane apologetically.

"She said that you are not trustworthy, Sire. It's a trick."

"No new information," the Sapiens King said, waving a dismissive hand. "Warriors who repeat what is known are not the brightest, wouldn't you agree, Moarte?"

Moarte said nothing. Serene was either translating because she was afraid or something else had happened.

"I am willing to release Valada. She is near death anyway and it would save me from having to deal with a corpse. Take her and go. I can see you are all suffering from the ghosts. Yes, blood can be shed, but why? As I told your second, Valada was a gift towards peace."

Moarte stepped further into the room and the Sapiens warriors shifted for battle. But he stopped at the women and said to the one holding the dagger, "Move that from her throat or die!"

The warrior who was crouched down looked to his King, who nodded. He lowered the blade and Moarte reached down to pull Valada up and away, and she cried out in pain. He moved her behind him into the arms of Rivard, who was right now good for only this.

He didn't know if the warriors would attack. He didn't know if there were others hiding in the tunnel they had entered by or waiting outside. All he knew was that the voices in his head were screaming and as much as he fought them, that was the degree to which Wolfsbane and Hemlock could not fight them.

"Come!" Wolfsbane said to Serene, and held out a hand.

The girl sat looking forlorn and did not move. "Come!" Wolfsbane repeated.

Moarte saw tears forming in her eyes and she shook her head.

"She wants to stay," the Sapiens King said. "And she is Sapiens. She should be with her own."

"That will not happen!" Wolfsbane shouted.

"Leave her, Brother," Hemlock said.

In an instant, Moarte understood that Serene was sacrificing herself for Valada. She had made a deal with the Sapiens King, her life for Valada's. He felt boxed in by this. They could fight the Sapiens warriors, perhaps win, more likely suffer severe casualties, and likely Valada and/or Serene would be murdered during the fracas. Valada, he could see, needed immediate attention. She would not survive much longer without it. He made an instant decision that he knew would not go down well with Wolfsbane.

"Retreat!" he ordered the vampirii.

"No! I will not leave her to *him*!" Wolfsbane shouted, and moved to attack the Sapiens on the ground guarding Serene. Moarte shot out an arm to block his second.

"You will retreat. Now!"

"I see you cannot control your troops," the Sapiens King laughed.

Moarte's eye color moved from blue to red in a quick instant and Wolfsbane struggled under the hypnotic power.

"Come," Hemlock said, pulling her brother back by the black bands covering his chest. Even she knew that a fight with the Sapiens here, now, would be vampirii at their weakest and that would result in death at the hands of these mortal warriors.

Rivard had picked Valada up in his arms. Hemlock herded him and Wolfsbane from the room. Before Moarte backed out, he said to the Sapiens King. "This is not over. You have much to answer for."

"Perhaps," he said, "but then so do you, vampir, so do you."

CHAPTER THIRTY

Once they reached the outside, Moarte ordered them into vampirii territory and they made their way quickly, all but Wolfsbane, who left the mountain area reluctantly.

They reached the safety of the trees and Moarte stopped and turned to Wolfsbane, whose body had tensed with fury. It was an emotion Moarte had never seen in him before, but he saw it now. And he understood it, having felt this extreme emotion too often himself.

"Why?" Wolfsbane demanded.

Everything was in this one word, and Moarte walked to him until they were inches apart. "Because he would have killed her if we attacked. You need to see this for what it is, Wolfsbane. The Sapiens King choose her because Serene must have told him she belonged to you and he made a connection. If he could ignite one of us—you—the attack would not come from my command, which would undermine us to ourselves and to the Sapiens warriors. Serene would be the first murdered. She knew this and was clever enough to manipulate the Sapiens King so that he saw her as valuable to him. He'll let her live because she speaks our language and can translate for him, and that is a rare service, one he can use."

Wolfsbane did not look as if he believed this, but Hemlock jumped in to say, "Brother, it is as the King says. We were hampered by the ghosts. The warriors would have made short work of us."

"No! We would have taken them. All of them. And Serene would not be a prisoner!"

"You are wrong, Wolfsbane," Moarte said. "The ghosts had already effected you. I saw it in your eyes, in Hemlock's eyes. You could not think clearly and the internal battle was sapping your strength. I could only hold the voices off a little. Neither of you could do that much. We must wait to battle another night, on our terms."

"And what of Serene? You have Valada!" Wolfsbane said stubbornly.

Another time, another warrior, and Moarte would have been at his throat for the insinuation, for this impertinence.

Instead, he said softly, "I have given you my word before and I state it again. We will rescue her. But we must bide our time because tonight was not a good night for a fight with the Sapiens. Not there. Not with only three against so many. And the ghosts. This is not over," he said, as he had said it to the Sapiens King. "You have my word," he added again.

He watched Wolfsbane's lips tremble and then his second turned abruptly and walked deep into the forest, not wanting to exhibit more emotion before either of them.

"He'll get over her," Hemlock said.

Moarte faced her, this sister who had such a callous streak in her and he could not fathom from where it derived, nor how he had ignored it so recently. Wolfsbane said she had been this way even before the two of them came to the vampirii so many centuries ago, and this vein of pitilessness had always been glaring. "He will not get over her," Moarte said. "And I will not let this go. We will rescue Serene."

With that, he left her and walked to Valada, who lay on the grass beside Rivard, who looked pale and stunned as only the newly-turned did.

Moarte crouched beside his wife and touched her face. Her one eye opened slightly. Her lips were too dry for her to speak.

"Bring water," he said to Rivard, who got to his feet and went to the stream where he ripped fabric from his shirt, dipped it into the icy flow, and brought it to Moarte, who squeezed the water into her mouth.

"Hold on, Valada. I will have you home and safe and with me very soon."

He had to bend low to hear her. "Memento," she whispered, and he could see in her eyes that she was delirious.

He stood abruptly. "Come. We will return to the stronghold where we can rest and plot revenge."

Hemlock called Rivard to her and Moarte could see that her promise to treat him well had been diluted now that Serene was not with them. Wolfsbane was nowhere in sight, but Moarte knew he would follow. At least he hoped he would. That he might try to rescue Serene alone, that would be suicidal for him and such an act could precipitate her murder.

He picked Valada up in his arms and headed to the large clearing where his wings unfurled and he ascended without the luxury of free arms to guide him. But it was a straight-forward flight to the vampirii fortress and he would fly strong and quick and arrive soon.

He heard Hemlock, then watched her soar ahead of him, Rivard hanging onto her, her free arms giving her greater navigational ability. Behind he heard Wolfsbane and was relieved. His friend was suffering. He could not allow that. And he could not allow the brave Selene to be subjected to the violence of the Sapiens. There had to be a way to save her soon, and he would find it.

CHAPTER THIRTY-ONE

Valada lay in a stupor. Time passed but she did not know if it was a day, a week, a month. Sometimes she saw Moarte's face and heard his words as he spoke softly to her. Other times she saw Belladonna, who insisted she drink a thick concoction she could barely swallow.

"For the pain. I have reset your bones," Moarte's mother said, but Valada did not know when she said that. "You've been badly injured. Almost fatally."

She heard conversation, but only snatches. Words like "rescue her" "kill him" and "bring her over." None of it made sense but she didn't care. She wanted to drift, to dream. She wanted to die.

And then one night she opened her eyes and felt alive. "Moarte?" she said, and suddenly he was with her.

His face, his beautiful face, was creased with worry and she understood how frightened he'd been for her. "You were afraid I'd die," she said.

He did not reply but she could see in his eyes that this was so. "You're healing," he told her. "My mother has been treating you. She was a healer when she was Sapiens."

He was talking but she sensed he did not know what to say to her. Then, suddenly, as if it was an enormous struggle for him, he said, "Valada, please. Forgive me."

Tears filled her eyes. "It's you who should forgive me," she said, and he shook his head no.

"Help me to sit up." The movement caused pain in her chest and she inhaled sharply and moved gingerly as he supported her body and lifted her.

"Can we go to the balcony?" she asked. The night drew her. She needed to feel the warm breeze on her skin and watch the moon glide through the clouds and breathe deeply of the scent of trees and grass and the sweet perfume of flowers. She needed to reach the life around her.

"Of course," he said, picking her up carefully. He pulled a chair along with him and sat in it, her in his lap, and he held her gently, feeling her heart beat, wondering how she could be alive, grateful to whatever gods ruled the heavens that she was.

She gazed around her, at the mountains and the forests, touched by their beauty. "I loved to be outdoors when I was a girl," she said. "Maybe it was my vampir nature. Maybe the Sapiens. I liked to walk in the woods alone, where there was no one. No one to bother me. To harm me."

"I should not have taken you there!" he said, his voice gruff, but she knew he was angry with himself.

She turned to face him. The pain in his extraordinary eyes, eyes that rarely exhibited emotion, was nearly unbearable and she lifted her good arm which was not in a cast and touched his face. "I insisted," she said. "I thought I was strong. I persuaded you."

"I let myself be persuaded," he said. "I cannot forgive myself."

She did not know how to tell him but knew she had to. There had to be honesty between them. It was all that would hold them together now. "Moarte, I have something to tell you. It's unpleasant and I know I am fully responsible for this. You may not forgive me. I put myself in danger. And because I did this, another was in danger as well."

"We will find Serene. I've been in discussion with Wolfsbane and with my war council as to how we can rescue her."

"Rescue her?"

"She exchanged herself so that you could go free."

"Oh no!" Valada cried. Her eyes overflowed with tears, and he wiped them away with the backs of his fingers.

"It is not your fault, Wife. I could see what she did and why she did it. You were in danger of dying. She loves you and wanted you to survive. I made the decision. And now I must rectify this so that she can be saved and Wolfsbane can have peace."

"Moarte, I still must tell you something and I fear you will hate me but I have to say this. You have to know."

He said nothing, waiting.

"I lost our child."

He could not have looked more startled if she had staked him through the heart. On his usually immobile features she watched surprise, shock, awe, fury and grief flickering within fractions of seconds, as if these expressions had always been there but only now moved at a pace that could be discerned by her.

Finally he composed himself enough to say, "Tell me about this."

And she did. She told him that she knew she was impregnated the night they married. "And still, I wanted to go to the caves, to kill my father. To make everything right. I didn't think, and I put the baby in harm's way."

Then she took a long time, stumbling over words, holding her breath, trembling, telling him about meeting Varmik in the room of lights, about the ghosts, telling about how her father treated her and for the first time she allowed herself to feel his hatred towards her. She talked of her time in the filthy, insect-ridden cell. And the most difficult to talk about was when she told him about Varmik coming for her. How he raped her repeatedly and beat her to near unconsciousness and kept reviving her for more. How she tried to protect the child and could not.

By the time she was finished, her face was coated with tears and she was sobbing, barely able to catch her breath. "I cannot tell you how much I regret my actions! The loss crushed me. I wanted to die and nearly did. I know that Serene and her brother rescued me. It was only when she left me in the cave that I found the strength to re-enter the main corridor to hunt down Varmik and kill him. And then to murder my father. But I didn't get far. And after that, I don't remember…"

"Varmik is dead. I killed him."

"How?" she asked in a small voice.

"I beat him until the life left his body and then ripped off his head."

"Good!" And she burst into tears.

He held her, pulling her to him as much as he could without causing her more pain. He let her cry. Maybe the tears would cleanse her soul. And his.

Whatever he had done, whatever she had done, ultimately it was the Sapiens King who was responsible for everything. Moarte vowed to himself that he would kill her villainous father if it was the last thing he did.

Valada was nearly empty of tears when she said, "Moarte, can you ever forgive me? I'm responsible for the death of our baby!" The last words were so tortured he could barely listen to them.

"It was not you," he said. "Varmik murdered our child. Your father ordered this, I know it. Valada, do not torment yourself. You made a mistake, going there. I made a far greater mistake in agreeing to allow you to go. We have both learned from the grief of our errors and now we must focus on other things, one of which is that you need to heal. I need you to be whole again."

"Yes. To bear another child. I want to have your child," she said, "*our* child," her voice laced with a sweetness that cut through him, and he looked away.

"Don't you want that?" she asked, sounding fragile and frightened.

He turned back to face her. He had to tell her the truth. "My mother believes you've been damaged in a way which will not allow you to conceive."

The shock on her face said everything there was to say. She shook her head no, disbelieving.

"This does not matter, Valada. We are together. Always."

"How can she know?" she asked.

"She was Sapiens. She knows about Sapiens women. She suggested I bring you over, make you fully vampir so that you will heal quickly. You cannot get pregnant."

She started to rise, upset, still shaking her head.

"Valada, careful," he said, but she was angry. Still, he held her on his lap, not wanting her to reinjure herself.

"There is no way to know this, Moarte. I do not believe it. Your mother is wrong."

"My mother is never wrong."

"She is this time. I will heal. I *know* I will. Every part of me." And the ferocity in her eyes nearly convinced him that she would.

Chapter Thirty-Two

O ver the next while, while Valada's bruises faded and her bones knit together, Moarte met nightly with his war council, planning a strategy to seduce the Sapiens King from his hideout and to rescue Serene.

It had been weeks since their return and Wolfsbane was clearly agitated, needing action, leading Moarte to encourage his council to voice any and all ideas, even those that sounded ludicrous. He hoped that by throwing everything onto the table they might stumble upon something ingenious they hadn't thought of.

Every plan was vetted by Wolfsbane and it seemed to Moarte that he automatically discounted anything Hemlock suggested.

Hemlock, for her part, had been seen abusing her new slave several times in ways that Moarte felt he should put a stop to, if only in honor of Serene and her gift to him of Valada's life. In fact, he did say to Hemlock, "Rivard is not looking well. I suggest that he has not yet recovered from the trauma of the turning. You will recall yourself how it is. Sometimes gentleness is the best approach with new vampirii."

Her reply was stark. "He's recovered, my King. He's simply impertinent. This is not how a slave should act with his mistress."

"Well and good, Hemlock, but a demoralized slave cannot please a mistress either."

She said nothing just stared at him with a look in her eyes that he interpreted as scorn. Still, she had aided him when he needed aid, and he had not felt that he could order her to change her ways.

Finally the council reached a consensus: the best means of achieving their goal was to swarm the tunnel entrances, setting fires to drive every Sapiens within out and back into the city. Then they would attack.

It was a plan fraught with perils and imbedded with the strong possibility of failure. If Serene was in the caves, the Sapiens King might, out of vindictiveness, order her left behind and she would die from smoke inhalation. Or kill her outright. They did not know how many Sapiens warriors were in the mountain the city was built on, which was massive, and for victory this type of attack might require the participation of every vampir warrior. And more, there were exits that they did not know about, and might not find, and, as one warrior reminded them, "Remember, there are underground tunnels that connect this mountain with the other mountains, the caves of which are also haunted. If that's so, we'll never find them."

Despite all these possibilities of something going wrong, it was a scheme that with luck might work, and it seemed to be the only viable strategy. If they tried to send in Sapiens slaves again—as Hemlock suggested—they would surely be taken for spies and killed.

Moarte returned to his chamber exhausted from so much discussion. He had no more ideas and while this one wasn't perfect, he had to do something. Nearly a moon's cycle of watching Wolfsbane growing more and more inflamed had alerted him to the fact that his second might do something rash on his own, and that was definitely a bad idea. He felt he had no choice but to go with the only plan that made any sense and offered a hint of success.

They would leave in two week, when the moon was black, which would help disguise their flight into Sapiens territory. Wolfsbane had not wanted to wait that long, but he did grudgingly acknowledge that such timing made sense. Moarte just hoped that he would not do anything foolish in the meantime. His second's tension was high, his temper short, and his desire for action all pervasive.

But there was a further reason to wait—the war council needed time to persuade the warriors of the validity of such an attack. Attacking the Sapiens was never in question, but a raid that might result in a loss of vampiric life to rescue a Sapiens slave—Moarte hoped his council members could present the plan in a light that would inspire allegiance and not dissention.

Valada was walking and moving easier now. Her bones were nearly knitted together. Most of the swelling had subsided, and although bruising remained, the color altered to a ghastly shade somewhere between pale brown and yellow. Moarte was always astonished by the wounds Sapiens endured, and how long it took them to heal. He had forgotten their bodies were so fragile, but Valada was a stark reminder.

Tonight when he returned, she ran to him and he took her in his arms, grateful once again that he had her; that his existence felt near complete with her.

She looked up at him and said, "Kiss me, my King. I'm so hungry for your lips."

He smiled at her, as much as his features would allow, and at the same time wondered if she was well enough for where this kiss might lead. But he didn't wonder long.

Once his mouth found hers her tongue found his. He could tell what she wanted. And he wanted her. He knew he must be gentle. "Come, Wife," he said, and took her by the hand to the balcony, where she liked to spend part of each night.

There, he lifted her onto the ledge and she perched at the edge of it, close to him. She raised her skirt and he saw her severely bruised thighs. Thoughts of Varmik and what he had done to her brought up his rage and he struggled to push that feeling aside.

He stood between her legs, already firm, and she reached down to make him harder, her eyes so round and trusting and open to him.

His fingers played with her clitoris and the juices flowed from her as in the past. Slowly he slid into her warmth and watched her face for signs of pain, but saw none.

"I need you," she whispered, panting. "I live for you, Moarte."

His mouth found hers and that was his response. He knew he needed her too.

He made love to her slowly, gently, but there was passion enough to satisfy them both.

When the night faded and they lay in bed together entwined in each other's arms, her soft voice in the darkness next to his ear said, "Moarte, I love you. I should have told you before. When I was in the dungeon, I regretted not having let you know how my feelings for you had changed, and then I believed I would never have the chance to tell you. But I did. And now I can say it tonight, every night. You are my world."

He pulled her to him and held her close, inhaling the scent of her, soaking in the warmth of her skin, the silkiness of her hair. The beat of her heart. His feelings had also changed. She was his world now, too, and he vowed that he would not lose her again!

Chapter Thirty-Three

An army of vampirii amassed on the grounds and Valada looked over the balcony to see many hundreds of pale-skinned black-clad, winged warriors awaiting their King. She saw the normally calm Wolfsbane at the front talking with some of the elite warriors; he appeared agitated and she had never seen him this way.

His sister stood off to the side alone. As if sensing Valada on the balcony, Hemlock's head jerked up and even from here Valada could feel the hypnotic pull of those vindictive eyes and she turned away.

She knew that eventually she would be fully vampir. And then she would be invulnerable to other vampirii unless she allowed it, or so Moarte had indicated. But she had seen Hemlock and Rivard, and she wasn't so sure. She also wondered why Sapiens were so vulnerable to the mesmeric vampirii. Why didn't it work the other way around as well?

Moarte did not know, but he speculated, "We are in a state different than the Sapiens. We do not die in the way they do. All but me had been Sapiens at one point but the turning changed their cells. Sapiens call us dead, but we are not, but we can die. The change sets vampirii apart in some way that allows our spirit to speak with the Sapiens spirit through the eyes and for some reason they are drawn to us and submissive to this power we possess. It has always been so."

This left her with more questions than answers. She felt troubled and suspected the root of it was because she was half and half, although Moarte was also. But he had lived as a vampir for centuries and she had yet to see Sapiens traits in him. It was confusing and she wondered if she would ever know. On the other hand, she sensed no vampir traits in herself, other than being aware of the ghosts.

Now that Valada could move more easily, she managed to make her way around the fortress and became familiar with the layout beyond where she had been before. Some of that included the chambers of the elite warriors who lived within the main structure. Other warriors were housed in adjacent areas which to her resembled large stone crypts like those she had seen in one of the ancient abandoned cemeteries in the Sapiens city. The fortress itself appeared to be a gargantuan mausoleum carved out of the rock it was imbedded in and she had not noticed this before because as a prisoner she had not been permitted to wander around freely. Now that she was Queen, she had license to investigate and the realization struck that the vampirii lived like the dead.

She found this perplexing. The vampirii lived as if they were dead and yet they walked and talked just like the Sapiens. They were pale, their skin imitating the lividity of death, and their body temperature was cool. But their hearts beat, if slowly, and they breathed, though not as often as Sapiens. They were capable of speech, thought, movement, of taking nourishment, of making love and of fighting. If they were corpses, how could this be?

It was a paradox and she found no easy answers to her questions and even Moarte could not clearly answer her, insisting that, "What is, is. We have no way of knowing why vampirii are the way we are, not more than Sapiens can know why they are Sapiens. It's the mystery of existence."

She did not find any aspect of the vampirii repulsive, just odd. Nothing about these creatures repelled her now. Part of her was like them, and the part that was not had been so brutalized that she tended to write off the Sapiens beings she had spent most of her life with as nothing like her.

She knew that Moarte had to rescue Serene. It was more than a favor for Wolfsbane. He had told her that his reign depended on doing what was best for the vampirii and just as they had not been able to live with the knowledge that their King went missing when he in fact had been a prisoner, and they could also not exist with his grief when Valada had been sent to draw her father out but had not returned, now they could not cope with one of Wolfsbane's stature enduring the worry and stress he was under. As Moarte's second, Wolfsbane evoked fierce loyalty among the warriors, who shared that worry and stress that they were compelled to deal with as if it was their own. It made Valada think that vampirii were more like a colony, like birds, or bats, a flock, interconnected on many levels.

"I have to right this wrong," Moarte told her, "because we cannot continue as if this is not a problem. It is. It must be dealt with."

"But why must *you* go?" she asked, so afraid for him.

"Because I am their leader. They need me to feel strong. And I need their allegiance."

She did understand this, but worry for his safety clawed at her heart.

He knew this and tried to reassure her. "We will not be gone long. There are many of us. We have a plan and Serene knows where to hide if she has escaped and is not inside the mountain."

"I should go with you," Valada said, and his face turned stony.

"Absolutely not!"

"I can help you find her, I can—"

"No!"

"But I'm well enough—"

He grasped her shoulders firmly for emphasis and made her look at him. "Valada, I almost lost you. I cannot bear that again."

She was silent for a few moment, then said, "And I could not bear losing you."

"You won't," he said, kissing her gently. "We will find Serene and if we do not locate your father right away, we will return and fight him another time. I will not step into danger."

"Give me your word," she said.

"I promise you, my Wife."

He kissed her again then said, "I must go."

"Moarte, there's one thing I need to tell you that may help you, I don't know."

He turned back.

"When I was in the caves, just where you rescued me, I talked to the ghosts. I listened to them with both parts of me, the Sapiens and the vampir. Not just listened, but I asked them why they called to the vampirii. What did they want?"

He paused. "Did they answer your questions?"

"Yes. They said *Memento*. They said more, but this one word stayed with me."

"Yes, you said that word in the forest before we returned here. I thought you were hallucinating."

"I was. But I knew what they said. *Memento. Remember*! I don't know what it is they wanted me to remember, but I know there's something and I thought I should tell you because maybe you should remember too."

She could see he was not so esoterically inclined as she and that this information was not concrete enough for him to make sense of. She walked to him and touched his face, gazing into his eyes. "Just be open to them."

He looked skeptical but he took her hand and kissed it.

At that moment Belladonna entered the throne room. "Your troops await you, my son. Is there anything more you need?"

"Only that you take care of my wife," he said, and Belladonna aimed that enigmatic smile of hers at him, and then at Valada.

"Of course. She will be fine. You are nearly healed," she said to her daughter-in-law, "both body and spirit."

She held out her hand and Valada went to her and took the cool hand. She did not know why but she felt Belladonna liked her and had always viewed her favorably.

Moarte strode through the hall and left the two females standing together. Fear crept up Valada's chest, which Belladonna must have sensed because she said, "Do not be afraid, my new daughter. Moarte is strong and brave and he will be victorious. Have faith in him."

"I do," she said. "It's my father I fear. He's so treacherous that I worry Moarte might underestimate him."

"Impossible," Belladonna said with absolute certainty. "Come. Let us watch them depart."

She led Valada up a flight of narrow circular steps that climbed the stone tower and they had just reached the top when Moarte leapt into the air and took flight, Wolfsbane and Hemlock following close behind, then the elite. After them, the rank and file of warriors, many carrying Sapiens who would aid them in their assault of the caves. Other than the Sapiens slaves, all were pale beings, darkly garbed for battle, soaring into the moonless night sky like a cloud of black and white bats that circled the fortress twice then flew behind their leader in a chaotic formation toward the mountain that safely separated their land from that of the Sapiens. Valada and Belladonna stood and watched until they disappeared into the dark night. And then the night suddenly became quiet as a tomb to Valada's ears.

Eventually the two females made their way down the steps and back through the throne room and there they saw Rivard, looking broken of spirit and defeated.

Valada knew it was the heavy-handed treatment Hemlock inflicted on him that had beaten him down. She had talked to Moarte about this and he told her how it came about that her rescuer, and his, had become a slave to the cruel Hemlock.

"Isn't there something we can do to help him?" Valada asked.

"It's within my power to remove him physically from Hemlock's charge but I cannot sever the psychic link brought about by the blood exchange, which is strong between the one who *brings* over and the one *brought* over. Only death can fully release him—his death or hers."

This made Valada sad. It seemed so unfair that this Sapiens who had risked so much to help Moarte, and to help her, was now doomed to an existence of slavery to such a monstrous mistress.

"Rivard," she said gently, and he looked up at her with fearful eyes. "I wonder if you might sit with us in the garden tonight. I sense you need some companionship."

He looked cowed as he answered. "My mistress forbids me to associate with any of the other vampirii."

"Valada is not a full vampir," Belladonna said, "and she is your Queen now and you must obey her. And frankly, I doubt Hemlock would find out anyway. I must retire to my rooms, but you two go. The benches near Moarte's private garden are safe and secure and you will not be disturbed."

"Thank you, Mother," Valada said, realizing it was the first time she had called Belladonna that. The twisted lip smile was ambiguous and Valada chose to interpret it as fondness, believing she had used the correct address.

Valada led Rivard to the garden where Moarte had shown her how to use a weapon, and where they had spent several nights during her recovery. Nearby was the gate that she knew led to Moarte's private garden world, which he kept locked and she had never entered.

They sat on one of the stone benches under the moonless sky in a quiet so complete that it both comforted and unnerved her, but she tried to ignore this non-sound that felt like an omen portending an outcome that might be a success, or a tragedy.

She didn't know what to say to Rivard so she began with what was in her heart. "I know you and Serene saved me. And I know you saved Moarte when he was imprisoned. I can't tell you enough how grateful I am."

Rivard said nothing at first, just sat with stooped shoulders, his hands locked, his arms between his legs, head down, and he reminded her of a dog cowed through brutality. Finally he said, "My Queen, I did what I had to do."

She still did not know some of this story and asked him now. "When King Moarte was a prisoner and escaped the dungeon, I assumed he had help but had no idea who. You left the door unlocked and removed his chains. Why? Did he mesmerize you?"

"No, my Queen, he did not. He tried to, but I saw his eyes turning color and looked away."

"Then why did you put yourself at risk to help a vampir?"

He hesitated. "My sister and I, our parents were exceptional people. They held to the value that no earthly creature should suffer unnecessarily and that none should inflict suffering on another, be they Sapiens or vampir. This is not a widely-held value in the land of the Sapiens King."

"Yes, I know," she said, remembering the details of what she had forgotten about her cruel father.

"I watched King Moarte suffering with honor and his stoic bravery effected me. Never a word of complaint passed his lips. I had not witnessed such strength of character before. Rumors had always permeated the city that the King of the vampirii was honorable, honest and just, and this I saw with my own eyes and sensed it to be true. What was done to him…it was unjust. When an opportunity presented itself, I took a chance that if I freed him, with a hint of direction, he might manage to escape on his own, and he did. I could not witness what happened to him without intervening. I would have done the same for you, my Queen, but…"

"But what, Rivard. Please, tell me."

"But you could not have escaped on your own. What Varmik did to you…"

She sighed. "Yes, I was not able to escape. Moarte was. He's much stronger than me. But he is vampir."

She paused. "You know I lost my child?"

"Yes, my Queen, I know. Serene told me. She had planned to help you with that."

"Help me?" Valada said, turning to face him.

"Serene knows about herbs and potions."

"As does my mother-in-law, Belladonna, who believes I can no longer conceive."

"Serene did not feel that way."

A seed of excitement sprouted in Valada, the first true hope that she'd felt since Moarte had told her of Belladonna's pronouncement. "Why did she feel she could help me when Belladonna could not?"

"My sister learned from our mother, who was what the Sapiens call a Healer, but an extraordinary one. She helped many women who'd had no chance of conceiving."

"That's a different situation than mine," Valada said, staring off into the darkness again, bleakness about her state returning. "I'm damaged inside."

"Our mother helped many torture victims. Your father was not opposed to torturing females, and many suffered at the hands of Varmik."

Bile rose in Valada. "You mean they were abused in the way I was?"

"Yes. And some worse."

"And your mother was able to heal them, in all ways?"

"Yes."

"You believe Serene knows how to do this?"

"She does. Our mother taught her everything she knew, and Serene not only has our mother's knowledge but possesses knowledge and special powers of her own. She is intelligent and skilled and extremely intuitive."

"Yes, she is," Valada admitted. The girl had proven herself over and over. "I hope," she said, "they find her quickly and return. Not just for my sake but for all our sakes."

"I as well, my Queen," Rivard said, but his voice faltered and Valada glanced at him, knowing that their return would also bring Hemlock back.

"Rivard, my husband and I have talked about you. We want to help. There is a bond between vampirii who have shared blood in the turning process. I haven't experienced it as I'm not yet a full vampir, but King Moarte tells me that he cannot sever it."

"I know," he said, his voice grim, his posture deflated.

"He can, though, separate you physically, which is not everything, but it might help you at least a little."

Rivard nodded but said nothing. Then, "The bond creates a mental link. A pull like a presence that lives inside, one that can send messages to the brain, like the vampirii describe what the ghosts in the mountains do. It's that link that can't be broken. A kind of permanent torture in the mind," he said glumly.

"The mental link may be there and may be strong but at least physically you won't be tortured. I will not allow you to suffer if I can possibly help it. When the warriors return with Serene and Portia, I'll ask Moarte to take you from Hemlock immediately."

"Thank you," he said. "But my Queen, Portia will not return."

"How do you know that? Is she dead?"

He hesitated.

"Tell me, Rivard."

"I must not speak of this," he said, suddenly fearful and guarded.

Valada turned and stared at him and he looked as if something was eating at his brain and she wondered if whatever Hemlock had implanted in his thoughts acted as an instant torture when he ventured towards certain subjects. "You must tell me," she said. "I'm your Queen and I order it."

"I am forbidden," he said, looking horrified, terrified actually.

Valada did not know what to say or do to get him to tell her and ultimately she could only yield to his fear. "It's alright, Rivard. Please, don't stress yourself. All will be well."

Later that night she went to Belladonna's room and knocked on the large wooden door. "Enter," her mother-in-law called.

Valada had not been inside these rooms before and was surprised by how lavish they were, especially compared to Moarte's sparsely-furnished chamber. The fringed carpets were colorful and finely woven, furniture of exotic woods with inlays, chairs elaborately embroidered, paintings in gilded frames hung on the walls, and even a cupboard of walnut and glass crammed with gold-rimmed china cups and saucers. She stared at all this in wonder.

"Please, sit, my new daughter. I know you're surprised. I was once Sapiens and have a taste for these things which did not leave me with the change. My husband indulged me."

"This is beautiful," Valada said, glancing around her, touching a small onyx sculpture of a long black cat sitting upright.

"Yes. That feline came from another Sapiens land and was carved several thousand years ago. My husband gave it to me as a wedding present. I've always loved cats."

"How long have you been vampir?"

"More than two hundred years. I've lost count, though it is not three hundred."

Valada was silent for half a minute. "Did you know my mother?"

"No. I don't believe she was from here."

Valada was surprised. "Are you saying there are other vampirii in the world?"

"Absolutely. We are only one group. There are many others, as there are many Sapiens on this planet. I'm not certain how you would find out where your mother was from, short of asking your father."

"He'd never tell me, even if I had the luxury of conversing with him without being imprisoned and raped."

Belladonna reached out and touched her hand and though the vampir flesh was cool, Valada didn't mind; the gesture itself was important.

She sat in an elaborate chair with a carved back, and arms with animal heads sculpted into the ends, which she unconsciously gripped with her hands, only becoming aware of this when her mother-in-law said, "Something is troubling you, Valada?" and she was startled by Belladonna's acute perceptiveness.

"Yes. My conversation with Rivard in the garden."

"A tragic story, his. I would not wish any being a connection with Hemlock."

"Nor I," Valada said.

She related first what Rivard told her about Serene's medicinal skills.

Belladonna nodded. "Yes, I have some knowledge myself but I have seen that girl in action with the slaves. There was one who came to us who had also been brutalized by Varmik, in a similar way," she said, nodding towards Valada.

"Was she able to heal her."

"Yes. I was most impressed."

"Is the girl here now?"

"No, she died."

Valada's mouth opened and a small sound like a groan came out.

"Not from the treatment. She was cured. But she was still Sapiens and had a malignancy that had penetrated too deeply and spread through too much of her body. Nothing could save her and the tumor took her before her vampir lover returned from a raid to change her. We were in mourning over this for quite some time."

Valada paused, again aware of the group mentality of the vampirii. The idea of mourning was unknown in the Sapiens world, where everyone was encouraged to forget those who died as soon as possible.

"But, this girl," Valada said, "could she conceive?"

"Yes. And she did, before the tumor was discovered. The fetus was half Sapiens, half vampir."

"Is the child here?"

"No. When the mother died, so did the child in her belly."

"But do you think if she hadn't died she could have birthed the baby?"

Belladonna did not hesitate. "Yes, I believe so."

Somehow, this relieved Valada. "Serene has special powers. I need her help. It may be my only chance."

Belladonna nodded agreement.

After a silence that lasted several minutes, Valada's thoughts turned to the rest of her discussion with Rivard, and she related that to Belladonna too.

Belladonna said, "Hemlock has warned him against relaying what he knows on pain of death, or perhaps something worse. The mental bond can be torturous and clearly we're seeing the effects of that, as well as the physical brutalization she inflicts on him."

"He said very definitely that Portia is not coming back. He must know why. But what do you think it could be that he won't disclose?"

"I do not know, but I suspect. And I have a way to induce the truth from him."

Belladonna stood and walked to a fabric cord along the wall and pulled it. Within a few seconds they heard a soft knock on the door and she said, "Enter!"

A young Sapiens girl opened the door and came into the room. It was the same young girl who had attended with the rings at Valada's wedding.

"Go to Hemlock's quarters and tell Rivard I wish to see him immediately."

The girl bowed then left and Belladonna walked to a cabinet, opened it and removed two jars made of hematite, and a mortar and pestle. Valada watched her take two pinches of powder from one jar and one pinch of leaves from the other, then crush them together with the stone pestle in the bowl.

She then opened the china cupboard and took out a cup and saucer with purple and blue flowers painted around the outside and poured the powder into the cup. Then she opened a drawer and Valada gasped as Belladonna used a small knife to quickly slice her wrist, which she turned over the cup so that the blood would drip in.

"What are you doing?" she cried in alarmed.

But her mother-in-law said nothing, just squeezed the wound until what must have been enough blood to cover the mixture fell into the cup.

She licked the wound at her wrist as she used the knife to stir the mixture and then brought the cup to the table and set it down in front of an empty chair.

Within minutes they heard another knock at the door and Belladonna said, "Enter!"

Rivard opened the door and stepped tentatively into the room. "You wished to see me, Dowager?" he said, head bowed submissively.

"Yes. Please sit." She gestured to the chair with the cup before it.

Rivard glanced at Valada with a hint of betrayal in his eyes and she knew he was aware that she had relayed their conversation to Belladonna. Clearly he felt extremely uncomfortable.

"Rivard, you will drink this," Belladonna said.

He hesitated, staring at the cup.

"It is blood. Mine."

He looked startled. "My mistress forbids me to drink unless she authorizes it."

"And my station in this Kingdom is far higher than your mistresses', and she is not here. I command you to drink this blood which is from my body. You need nourishment. I will explain this to Hemlock on her return. Leave her to me."

Belladonna's voice carried the weight of authority. She had been vampir royalty for centuries and that was clear. The power of her command penetrated into Rivard's psyche as did the changing color of her eyes, and he could not disobey, though clearly he wanted to, out of fear of Hemlock.

He picked up the cup, stared at the contents, obviously lusting for the coppery-scented liquid, and Valada watched his eye color turn to red. Quickly he drank from the cup. The power of blood, this blood, any blood, was immediately apparent to Valada, and it was not something she could readily understand, though she'd seen the effects of blood drinking on Moarte many times. It was as if the crimson liquid imbued the drinker with a revitalization of body, mind and spirit, inflating them, taking him or her from being half dead to half alive. This is what she watched happening with Rivard now.

Once he had drunk the mixture, almost unaware of the two females in the room, he used his finger to capture what remained in the cup and didn't replace it onto the saucer until he had every smear of the blood in his mouth.

He sat back and if he had sighed, Valada would not have been surprised. His eyes looked clear, his posture had improved, and his general demeanor was one of strength rather than weakness. It was an astonishing change and she realized that he had been starved by Hemlock. Now, he could even look them in the eye.

Belladonna said, "I have invited you here because I wish to know what you know, and now that you have breeched your pact with your mistress you are in a position to tell me."

Rivard had not forgotten Hemlock and suddenly his face creased with worry. But that emotion faded as Belladonna snapped her fingers and his gaze returned to her face.

"You know something, Rivard. Tell me what you know about Portia."

His face said he wanted to tell her, yet he hesitated.

"I've laced my blood in the cup with a poison that will take effect quite soon. You will not have long and your mistress cannot save you in these minutes nor can she keep you from testifying to the facts as you know them. You have a brief time to clear your conscience and make things right. Do so now."

Valada was shocked. And she could see that Rivard was also. "Why have you poisoned him!" she demanded.

Belladonna did not take her eyes from Rivard's face. "Because he will not tell what he knows unless he is freed and I do believe he would prefer freedom to eternal bondage to a sadist. Am I correct in this?"

Before Valada's eyes, Rivard's face altered. He went from fear, to understanding, to a solidity she only remembered when he had been a guard in the dungeon and she a prisoner in her early days there.

"Dowager, you have assessed me correctly. I prefer death to existence with Hemlock and through the bond I cannot commit suicide. I will tell you what I know, which is what Serene told me. Portia was sent to Hemlock with news that Queen Valada still lived and was imprisoned in the dungeon, and that she had lost her child through the brutality inflicted on her by Varmik. When Portia did not return, Serene went to look for her and found her remains in a clearing, near the place where Hemlock was to wait each night. Portia's heart had been torn from her chest and her body had the mark of the vampir at her throat and had been blackened by the sun. She buried the body and came to find me."

"Is there more?"

"When King Moarte returned to the dungeon, he thought I had killed Queen Valada. My sister arrived in time to deny this but Hemlock changed me before the true story could be told. I have thought about this and believe my sister made an unspoken deal with Hemlock—she did not betray the vampir as the murderer of Portia because Hemlock promised to treat me well. But Serene is not here and that agreement could not be enforced."

"And is there more still?" Belladonna wanted to know.

"No, Dowager. This is all I know."

"You may retire then to your rooms and rest and find peace within yourself."

Rivard stood immediately, turned to the door, then turned back. "Thank you Dowager, for freeing me."

She nodded and he left.

The moment the door closed, Valada turned on Belladonna in a fury. "How could you poison him? There must have been another way to get the information from him. And now he'll die!"

"He will not die."

Valada stared at her mother-in-law. "You didn't poison him?"

"Of course not! Poison is only a word, and it does not always lead to death. I gave him a sleeping draught but needed him to think the worst. It allowed him to speak freely. He required blood and rest and now he will have both and awake refreshed."

"But what about when Hemlock returns."

Belladonna's face turned hard and became like a sculpture of a face, immobile, unreal. "Leave her to me. I think it's clear that she learned that you were alive and lied to my son. And I know her reasons."

"She wanted to be the new Queen," Valada said, suddenly aware of what was really going on. "And she took Rivard to keep him from telling Moarte and to keep Serene from telling what she knew."

"She has always been cagey with hidden agendas, but this time she's gone too far."

Suddenly, Valada felt frightened. "I must go to Moarte! I have to tell him this. He and Wolfsbane must be warned that they can't trust Hemlock; she might kill Serene. And also, if Serene dies, I will lose my one chance to be whole again and bear children."

"Wait!" Belladonna said. "You're correct, we must warn Moarte. And also Wolfsbane. Hemlock is treacherous and will do anything to protect herself. But you are not well enough to travel that distance."

"But I must!"

"I will go, Valada. And while I am gone, you are the reigning monarch."

"But…I cannot rule the vampirii! I'm not even fully vampir!"

"Few vampirii remain here, and few slaves. Until the return of Moarte or myself, do the best you can. And with some luck, you won't need to rule long." Belladonna stood.

She had spoken with the weight of ages behind her and Valada did not feel she could do otherwise. Yet at the same time she could not stay here. "There is one other thing you need to know," she said, making a last attempt to sway Belladonna. "I spoke with the ghosts."

Belladonna sat back down. "And?"

"Something Rivard said to me in the garden, about the voice in his head, the connection with his maker. I believe the ghosts are trying to tell the vampirii something, which is why they only speak to the vampirii and not the Sapiens. When I asked them what, they said to me, *Memento* and another word I've forgotten. That one means: *Remember.*"

Belladonna sat statue-still again for many long moments until Valada wondered if she was asleep or in a trance. But then suddenly she said, "*Memento Mori.*"

"Yes! That's what the voices said!"

"Remember, you will die."

"But why would they say that to the vampirii? Shouldn't they be telling that to the Sapiens who will die, not the vampirii who are, for all intents and purposes, at least by Sapiens standards, already dead, and yet continue to exist for hundreds if not thousands of years?"

Belladonna thought for many more moments then said cryptically, "I don't know why but believe we might be able to find out. Come, new daughter. We will both go to find Moarte. It's urgent that he know at least this much. And I believe it crucial that you be there when Serene is found."

Chapter Thirty-Four

Moarte led his warriors to the back of the mountain where he had taken Valada; there they could land in the largest clearing in relative safety. They then headed to a mid-size clearing near the tiny cave where Serene had hidden Valada, and there they regrouped. Finally, they moved into a clearing within Sapiens territory, close to the tunnel that he had used to escape the city, which he had entered by the well. This tunnel entrance was well located for what he and his elite had planned, but also more dangerous; besides being within enemy territory, there were other cave entrances in sight and, despite the foliage surrounding them, any Sapiens with good eyesight would spot a swarm of vampirii. Still, it was the best location and acting quickly was crucial.

Prior to leaving the stronghold, he had Wolfsbane assign a warrior to each of the Sapiens slaves with orders to guide them to a particular cave entrance identified on the map of the Sapiens territory, which all vampirii had committed to memory anyway. The plan was that the warriors would wait outside the mountain. The Sapiens slaves would enter the tunnels with the necessary materials to set fires and get as far in as they dared without being detected. Once the fires were blazing, they would return.

Despite having many hundreds of warriors at his disposal and hundreds more waiting as backup between this mountain and the stronghold, and close to half a hundred slaves, Moarte knew that the mountain with the haunted caves connecting to the Sapiens Kingdom had nearly as many entrances as he had troops, with other entrances inside the city, hidden, as was the one he had used to escape. There were also those tunnels leading to the two Western mountains to worry about, which he suspected the Sapiens King would head for when the fires began. They had discussed the idea of infiltrating some of those Western caves as well but there were not enough Sapiens slaves and Wolfsbane had vetoed the suggestion;

first and foremost, no harm should come to Serene. Better to allow the Sapiens King to escape than to have him kill her.

The plan was not foolproof by a mile and Moarte was aware that his second was also aware of the major flaws.

He and Wolfsbane stood together apart from the others while Hemlock went about making sure the warriors understood where they were headed, an unnecessary task as vampirii knew this terrain as well as their own. They should. They had raided it often enough over the centuries, always in retaliation for attacks on their fortress or the kidnapping of vampirii.

That the vampirii had not raided the city looking for Moarte was his own fault. They did not know he was a prisoner of the Sapiens King. He had talked with his mother and with Wolfsbane about flying West, towards another vampir realm, to visit King Thanatos, and he had, in fact, been seen heading West the night he left the stronghold. The vampirii did not suspect that he had been kidnapped.

He remembered that night. He had wanted adventure and did in fact head West but then changed his mind and flew North, towards the Sapiens city. He *thought* his flight path provided a reasonable berth around this very mountain. He intended to avoid a direct flight over the city and head to the ocean's shore beyond, and that's when he had been trapped.

While she nursed him back to health, his mother had, in her direct way, told him that he needed to trust more, to convey his thoughts and feelings to others. "As King, you cannot go off on your own. Your realm needs you, Moarte, and you have let us down."

This did not sit well with him; it made him angry, an emotion that seemed to aid his healing. He knew he was stubborn. And while he wouldn't admit it to his mother, he did to himself; he made a mistake. *You are King of the vampirii*, he had chided himself: *After two centuries of rule, you should know better!*

When Hemlock finished a briefing, each warrior took off with a Sapiens to their designated entrance. While they were all occupied, Wolfsbane said, "I need to go to the city."

Moarte had been afraid of this. "Wait," he said.

Wolfsbane looked as if he could do anything *but* wait. "Serene knows where to go. I need to find her."

"She may still be in the caves. We need to give the fires time to flush them out."

"If the Sapiens King has her still, then he will know of our plan and either kill her, or drag her to the mountains West of here and I can't get to her there. If she's in the city, I need to go to her now."

Moarte did not believe that Serene was in the city. He did not feel the Sapiens King would let her out of his sight—she was too valuable. If Wolfsbane entered the city alone, he would be vulnerable and Moarte knew he could not go with him. He had to lead his troops in battle—and it *would* come to a battle, eventually.

Wolfsbane knew this too and said, "You have Hemlock by your side." They both knew she was not the warrior Wolfsbane was. They also both realized that he had to go, and Moarte had to stay, and nothing could be done about this. As well, Moarte was the only vampir who had even a remote chance of entering the caves and surviving the ghosts, and there was very little chance of that.

"I know an entrance that has not been used in centuries, but I believe it's still viable and I can bypass most of the city and reach my destination."

"Alright, Wolfsbane. Go. Be safe. But you must return before morning. We're vulnerable here and unless we fly at least partway back to the fortress and seek shelter, we cannot do battle another night."

"I understand," he said. "I will go to the place Serene will be waiting and if she's not arrived, I'll return and go back tomorrow night."

He left immediately and, with a sense of foreboding, Moarte watched him rush through the woods.

Moarte went to Hemlock to check the map she held. She had crossed off the entrances that warriors had left for, or even reached by now, since Moarte could smell the acrid scent of smoke in the air and knew that some fires had already begun.

Three quarters of the entrances were marked and she efficiently spoke with each remaining warrior who took off at a trot with a Sapiens in tow. What troubled Moarte were the tunnels that led to the other mountains. If he were hiding within this mountain, he would not head for the city but take the tunnels leading to the mountains to the west. He was certain that King Zador would do likewise.

He thought about the tunnels and knew that if they could enter the mountain and find the tunnels leading to the other mountains, they could block them, keeping the Sapiens trapped in *this* mountain, forcing them to return to the city. But even one of those *ifs* was beyond vampiric abilities.

Finally, the last of the warriors with Sapiens were dispatched, and other vampirii had been sent to strategic locations, leaving less than half a dozen warriors remaining. Moarte knew it was risky waiting within Sapiens territory with so small a number, but already the first warriors and Sapiens slaves were returning, reporting that their assigned entrance was ablaze.

Moarte motioned Hemlock aside. He used the map to show her where he wanted her to go. "I want troops sent into the city. Wolfsbane is there alone; he needs backup."

"He shouldn't have gone in by himself. That is not a good strategy. Why put our warriors at risk for one who puts self-interest above the common good?"

He could only stare at her, once more marveling at her inability to empathize. Wolfsbane's hatred for his sister was suddenly apparent to Moarte. Her enmity was disguised behind a logic that undermined.

Instead of arguing with her, Moarte turned to his troops waiting for orders. "Hemlock will lead you into the Sapiens city, not by flight, but through the one tunnel we have not set on fire."

"How can we survive the haunted tunnel, my King," a warrior named Nightshade asked. Moarte knew Nightshade had made an attempt once before to enter this mountain and did not enjoy the failure he had experience.

"This tunnel is not long and the path leads straight up. It's a way to enter without alerting the Sapiens to our presence until we're in the city. Hemlock has familiarized herself with this tunnel and I have briefed her on the route to take within the city that will lead you directly to where Wolfsbane has gone, demolishing any resistance you encounter en route. There are probably dozens of hidden entrances to the mountain, perhaps even a hundred, all within the city which many of the Sapiens King's warriors will use to escape the smoky caves. Capture them as they enter the city. Hemlock will take over the Sapiens King's dungeon and secure all prisoners there temporarily. I want them alive. These are warriors and they will know how to find the Sapiens King, who I do not expect to return to the city.

"Keep your eyes open for Serene. If you find her, Hemlock will move her quickly to the place where Wolfsbane is waiting.

"Lastly, it's crucial that Wolfsbane lead all of you out of the city well before sunrise. We will assemble at the mountain peak closest to our stronghold, the usual meeting place, and there rest in darkness for the day. A lot will happen tonight but tomorrow night we will have much work to do."

"What of the Sapiens slaves? Shall we bring them with us towards dawn?" one asked.

"No," Hemlock answered. "They'll slow you down. Leave them here in the forest. They can fend for themselves one night."

Moarte would have said the same thing, but in a far gentler manner. Some of these slaves were precious to his warriors. He added, "They will be safe here and can withstand the daylight. Tomorrow evening you shall meet them again."

More warriors were returning, reporting that the caves were on fire and no Sapiens had tried to exit. This troubled Moarte anew. He did not believe that many Sapiens would head into the city. And he did not believe that Serene would be permitted to.

The newly arrived warriors joined the others following Hemlock to the access tunnel into the city.

Moarte instructed the rest of the Sapiens slaves who had returned to move to a particular location, the mid-size clearing between this one and the large one where they had landed. Being close to the back of the mountain, the high wall would protect them from view. This clearing was slightly further from the Sapiens border and they could set up a camp for the night, gathering water and firewood along the way.

He stationed one Sapiens and one vampir to direct new arrivals then left the others and went to the largest clearing directly behind the mountain, where he and Valada had gone.

He needed to think.

He didn't know what else he could do. No vampir could enter the mountain and sending in the Sapiens slaves to be slaughtered was both cruel and foolish. He had no way to draw out the Sapiens King and had no idea where Serene was. Fire in the cave's tunnels would likely send the Sapiens into the caves in the Western mountains and to his knowledge, no one had mapped the entrances to those caves. The Sapiens would enter through unknown tunnels—and who knew how many there were. They could hold up in the other mountains for years.

This was a foolish venture, one based on sentiment not logic, although he understood Wolfsbane through both sympathy and empathy. But he felt helpless because he could see no way ahead. Perhaps something would happen tonight. They might capture a Sapiens or two who would betray his people, who could identify where Zador had gone, where Serene was located. Maybe, with some luck—

He heard a sound and turned to look to the skies, seeing a lone female vampir flying towards the large clearing, a familiar one, carrying a Sapiens. A Sapiens he also recognized. He felt the tension of battle that he carried in him change direction, and escalate.

Even before she landed he had reached her and said in a fury, "Mother, what are you doing bringing Valada here!"

"I wanted to come, Husband," Valada said. "I need to tell you something about the ghosts."

He stared at her for only a fraction of a second then snapped his head back towards his mother, his anger building until his tone was over the top and Valada watched his eyes change color rapidly, which meant the emotions were high, too high. "This is a place of battle, a precarious situation! My wife is injured and you, Mother, are not accustomed to fighting and can defend neither yourself nor her. Must I quit my mission to protect two females who have stupidly left safety for danger?"

Valada watched Belladonna's eyes change color as well and she became afraid this argument would escalate to a dangerous level. Her mother-in-law said in an equally tense voice, "You might offer the benefit of the doubt, Moarte! Extenuating circumstances drove us here, otherwise we would not have come."

"Whatever these circumstances are, I hope they prove worth interfering with this delicate mission."

"Moarte, please," Valada said, rushing between the two, fearing they would come to blows.

His scarlet eyes with the black pinpoints focused on her and she gasped at the inhumanity she saw, remembering.

Suddenly, an explosion erupted behind them. Moarte spun around to face the cave's back wall. Red and yellow flames shot skyward from the top of the mountain, as if a volcano long dormant had come to life, spitting fire into the night sky.

He started towards the caves then turned and pointed a finger at his mother, saying to Belladonna, "Get her to safety!"

"Your wife has something—"

"Now!"

And Moarte moved so fast Valada could barely trace his path and he was gone.

She turned to Belladonna, feeling frustrated and helpless.

"Come, my daughter, we must return," her mother-in-law said.

"But if we return, Moarte may not find out in time to—" Valada paused in mid-sentence, then said, "Mother, give me your hand."

Belladonna hesitated.

"Please. Trust me," Valada said.

Belladonna grasped her hand and Valada led Moarte's mother into the woods heading east, away from the place the vampirii and Sapiens slaves gathered, in the opposite direction from where Moarte had headed.

Chapter Thirty-Five

Moarte raced back to the original location where warriors with Sapiens were quickly returning from the tunnel that led to the city. The second he arrived, Hemlock joined him.

"We were in the cave tunnel when the explosion occurred," she said in a rush. "I was at the rear, directing the troops in quickly, commanding them to run up the tunnel to the city end to outrun the ghosts. Suddenly, the walls of the tunnel collapsed on us. Warriors and Sapiens slaves at the head of the line are trapped. Those of us at the foot turned back, and we came here."

"Why were Sapiens in the tunnel with you?"

"I took a few with us. I felt we could use them to our advantage once we were in the city, perhaps as hostages, or for barter."

Moarte controlled his anger. Hemlock had made a unilateral decision, one he was certain had cost lives, and had disobeyed his order. He was not happy about it, but this was not the time to confront her.

"Did any vampirii make it through to the city?"

"I don't know. They may have. Or they may be buried under rock. The tunnel is impassable now, but I think we might rescue the vampirii near ground level anyway. They should still live, at least most of them."

Moarte knew that they would live, unless they had been decapitated, or their hearts pierced. The Sapiens, though, would be dead.

He had a new problem now, one which he hoped to fix quickly.

"Take these warriors back to dig out the debris and help with the rescue of their comrades. The Sapiens here will join the others in the small clearing and send those warriors waiting there back here as well to help with the rescue. All the Sapiens will wait for us in the clearing and we will fly them back with us tonight."

To make sure this order was carried out as he wanted, he ordered

the Sapiens to the middle clearing himself. Meanwhile, Hemlock began
organizing the warriors to return to the tunnel.

Moarte approached and grabbed her arm. Immediately she stopped
speaking and went rigid. Vampirii never touched one another in public
and this was an insult, but Moarte wanted his orders clear and this was
the way to do it. "Be cautious entering the tunnel, Hemlock," he said. "I
do not want more vampirii buried alive with the ghosts. Send in only a
handful of rescuers at first to make sure the tunnel walls have stabilized.
And change them frequently or the ghosts will immobilize them. Do you
understand me?"

She looked beyond annoyed. The instinct of every vampir was to
attack any who had breached this physical barrier who was not their
intimate. But she managed to say, "Yes, my King. We will proceed as
you wish."

He had snagged her arm to present this order to her in front of the
warriors because he wanted to make sure they *all* knew the plan and
would follow his wishes. Hemlock was incautious and would put lives
at risk without a direct command from him; dominating her publically
would help ensure his warriors would follow *his* wishes if hers diverged
from their King's.

The vampirii headed in one direction, the Sapiens slaves in the other,
and Moarte was left alone for a moment, hoping that Valada and his
mother were well on their way back to the stronghold. He was still angry
with his mother for bringing his wife here but would need to deal with
that later. Right now, he had two problems in addition to finding Serene
and the Sapiens King. One was discovering the cause of this explosion.
The other was getting to Wolfsbane and making certain he was out of the
city. As it stood, Wolfsbane would have no reinforcements meeting him
unless vampirii flew into the city, which would be suicidal. The Sapiens
were excellent marksmen and their variety of weapons seemed made for
killing vampirii by piercing hearts and severing heads from torsos, and
Moarte had no doubt that Sapiens warriors would be stationed at strategic
points to protect the city. Wolfsbane was extremely vulnerable. Moarte's
gut feeling told him Serene was not in the city. But he knew his second
well enough that he was certain Wolfsbane would remain there until he
found her, unless someone intervened.

Despite the danger of doing so, Moarte returned to the largest clearing
and launched himself into the air, wings flapping hard to lift him in

almost a direct vertical so that he would reach the top of the cliff back and then ascend above it. If there were Sapiens warriors defending the caves and further along the mountain where the city had been built high in its peaks, they would see him once he had risen high enough, and if they did, he would be in grave danger the longer he was in their view. But the tunnel being blown up left him no choice; he had to go high enough for an overview to assess the danger to his warriors.

The second he ascended higher than the mountain top, he quickly scanned all pivotal points. He saw no Sapiens, but what he did see was smoke coming from cave openings and crevices along the ridges at the top of the mountain, entrances that his warriors had not set fire to because there were not enough warriors for these highest exits.

The top of the mountain was the most vulnerable point. Vampirii ascending with Sapiens slaves in tow to the top as Moarte was doing now would be shot through the head or chest with any weapons that pierced those areas, dying a permanent death before they could descend to the apex. Likely the Sapiens slaves, too, would be killed. But what he saw meant that the fires they set below had sent smoke through the many tunnels and caves of this mountain. And since no Sapiens were here, that meant anyone inside the mountain had not headed to the peak. Good news at the moment, but bad in that it indicated they had left this mountain.

Even if Sapiens had climbed out of these openings, they could not live on top of the mountain where there was no food, exposed to the elements and, when darkness fell each evening, vulnerable to the vampirii. That there were none here now indicated that they had either re-entered the city or, more likely, headed through the tunnels to the caves in the Western mountains.

This smoke swirling into the darkness might be coming from the fires, but he did not believe the explosion was related to the fires. From this viewpoint, he could clearly see that the fires were one thing, the explosion another, and he wondered if the latter had originated in the city.

He swung left, away from the back side of the mountain, and soared towards the city, keeping a sharp eye out for Sapiens sharpshooters. He was able to fly close enough to see inside the city walls, to the well with the nearby hidden entrance to the tunnel. It was now obvious that the explosion that took out the tunnel had originated from inside the city, at the hidden entrance he had used to escape. Why would someone close off this entrance other than to keep vampirii from entering the city? And how did they know this was his plan?

He swung back to the large clearing, making sure he was below the mountain top, then went right. This side of the mountain had no entrances that he knew of. It, too, was a sheer rock face, but trees and shrubs clutched the rocks and grew on the ground right up against the mountain. This side would eventually become the Eastern wall of the Sapiens city. He wanted to do a quick fly-by just to make certain there were no Sapiens in the woods over here. If there were, he would send warriors to pick them off one by one.

Suddenly, below, he saw two figures moving through the trees. Valada and his mother! He could not believe his eyes. What were they doing here?

The sun-fed birches in this eastern forest were tall, taller even than on the western side and close together, and he found no place to land. Even swooping low, he was still too high above the females to catch their attention, though his mother did glance up at one point and he believed she saw him. Valada was in the lead, and they were close to the rock face, moving quickly, headed he did not know where.

He struggled to find a clear patch in which to land. Even if it was small, he could attempt a drop that was nearly vertical, but would need enough of an expanse that his wings wouldn't get caught in tree branches. He soared over the tree tops and finally found a clearing further from the rock face than he would have liked. He assured himself the clearing was large enough, but without much conviction. Still, he flew over and descended as slowly as he was able, furling his wings at a pace that let him descend steadily while at the same time missing the trees. At the last second he pulled his wings close to his body.

Moarte hit the ground with a thud, jarring him, but he was on his feet quickly, spinning in a circle until he located the rock face then raced that way through the forest.

(HAPTER THIRTY-SIX

Hemlock seethed. How *dare* Moarte touch her before the warriors—she had wanted to rip out his throat! And then he commanded her as if she were an idiot on how to proceed! He embarrassed her, humiliated her, and implied she was incompetent. He left no room for her creative handling of situations, the same as her brother. They were two of a kind, these vampirii, and she despised both of them.

The warriors she had led back to the tunnel entrance were as aware as she was that her position had been compromised. Still, she said, "Nightshade and Columbine, enter the tunnel and assess the strength of the walls."

"Do you think there are too many of us?" Nightshade asked a little sarcastically and Columbine laughed. Hemlock knew this was a direct confrontation of her leadership.

"If you are frightened of the task, tell me now and I will appoint a braver vampir to point."

Nightshade snorted but he and Columbine proceeded into the tunnel where the dust of rock debris still wafted out the entrance.

She waited with the rest of the vampirii for them to return and report, wondering why Moarte didn't just order an attack of the city, which is what she would have done, what she might still do, although would any of the others follow her now? Going through the tunnel was the long way around, one that put them in danger because of the ghosts. It was a ridiculous decision. If the objective was to enter the city and drag her lovesick brother out of there, this was not the fastest and best method of reaching that goal—flying into the city was.

Moarte was a poor leader. She could see that clearly now. The fact that he'd taken the Sapiens slut as a wife spoke volumes about his instincts and his loyalties, but what could you expect from a half breed. For a time, when Valada had first arrived, Hemlock had thought Moarte was on the right track. Rumors ran rampant about what he was doing to her, and she and all the other vampirii had seen for themselves several times on Moarte's balcony that he was giving the Sapiens princess all she deserved and more. They laughed about it and none believed that she would survive a week; they had even placed bets on how long she would last!

But Moarte was weak. He'd fallen in love with her and Hemlock still could not understand it. She could only think that the Sapiens part of him connected with this Sapiens princess and that he liked fucking her so much that he would betray the vampirii by aligning with her. And Hemlock wasn't the only one to think that, either; others had insinuated as much.

And then he had married the bitch! And risked his life, and the lives of her brother and her as well, for what? To rescue this feeble blood bag that should have died in the Sapiens dungeon. Valada couldn't even bear him a half-breed child now, so what was the point of keeping her around?

It was all beyond Hemlock's understanding. But she did not need to understand. She needed to make sure of two things: first, that Serene was never found, or if she was, that she was not found alive; and she also needed to find a way to turn Moarte away from Valada and towards *her* so *she* could take the throne. Her only hope for real power was to murder Valada and then partner with Moarte. Being Queen was the *only* way she could get close enough to him to kill him and take control of the realm. Then these warriors would know a true ruler. One who was smart enough and brave enough to lead the vampirii to a final victory over the Sapiens.

It had long been her dream to farm these blood bags and keep them for their blood and other physical gratifications, but nothing more. Once she ruled, she would outlaw marriage between the species. Vampirii were *created*, as she had been, not *birthed*! Clearly the birthing process produced genetic weaknesses and their mutant King was a prime example of an inferior strain.

This is why she had to take matters into her own hands as much as she could, otherwise all would be lost.

"We've found the walls solid enough, but we may need to brace them as we dig," Nightshade said.

"And there are voices," Columbine added.

"The ghosts?" Hemlock asked.

"No, vampirii."

"Good. Take as many as you need and get them out."

Hemlock sent several dozen warriors into the forest to fell trees they could use as braces. Meanwhile, she explained to others how they would form a line and hand the rubble down it to the outside, switching places frequently so those in the front were always fresh and protected as much as possible from the ghosts.

Once the first tree trunks arrived and some warriors became busy breaking them with their hands into manageable slabs to be used as braces, others carrying them into the tunnels, Hemlock left the area quietly, without being noticed, by backing away until she was out of their sight. She knew this forest intimately from having been here and investigated them thoroughly the nights she waited for news of Valada. She also remembered it well from when she had been Sapiens and she and her brother had played here centuries ago. There was a very direct route to the city through the forest that she remembered and she found that path with no trouble and made her way along it.

Once the enormous gates came into view, Hemlock hung back in the safety of the trees and waited. Soon the gates opened a little and a lone figure emerged. Behind him, the gates closed quickly and she heard them being barred from within.

He made his way slowly but directly towards where Hemlock waited.

When he was close enough, she hissed at him, "Why are you moving like a slug? Hurry up!"

Head bowed, body in submissive posture, Rivard picked up his pace.

"I called you hours ago. What took you so long to fly from the stronghold?" she snarled. Before he could answer, she said, "And the vampirii nearly made it into the city because you took so long in there. Why?"

His body shook in fear and he disgusted her.

To divert her from insisting he tell her why he took so long to obey her mental orders, he answered the second question only. "The Sapiens King was well hidden and I had to wait until he agreed to meet me in a secure location. He had to be assured I wasn't a spy."

"Obviously you passed the information. Did you tell him what I wanted in exchange?"

"Yes, Mistress."

"And did he send any message?"

Rivard hesitated. "No, Mistress. He only received the information, said nothing, then dismissed me."

So, she thought, the Sapiens King may or may not have destroyed Serene; she had no way of knowing now. Frustrated, she snapped, "Then what took you so long to come out?"

He hesitated again and she said, "Answer me, stupid slave, or I will whip you to death and then bring you back for more, you useless moron!"

"I only stopped to visit my home one last time."

Hemlock balled a fist that connected to his face, sending him flying and crashing hard against a birch. She heard a snap, knowing that something in his body had broken but she didn't care. "Get up, you pathetic swine!" she snarled. "Get back with the others and keep out of my sight until I summon you, filth!"

Rivard dragged himself to a standing position and limped off, holding his arm, his lower lip split open on one side.

She could not wait for the day when his usefulness would end and she would chain him in the sunlight and lie in her bed letting his screams of agony infiltrate her dreams!

Hemlock knew another entrance to the city which the vampirii were not aware of, but she and her brother were. It was a place they had played as children and she felt certain he had entered by this route.

This had once been a well, drilled deep into the mountain to catch an artesian stream that had dried up over a century before they were even born. She slid through the shadows and found a rock face that was jagged enough to offer footholds which took her to the hidden opening at the bottom of this abandoned well three quarters of the way up the mountain. The well walls were rock, the roots and foliage around them overgrown, but someone had been here recently and there were openings among the roots. She climbed until she reached the top, checking that she had not been seen before she lifted herself to ground level inside the Sapiens city.

Her destination was close by and she hurried to the location where she knew she would find Wolfsbane.

Chapter Thirty-Seven

Valada and Belladonna rounded a wide curve in the mountain and finally reached the end of it.

"Where are we going, new daughter?"

Valada called over her shoulder, "We're almost there, Mother. Be patient."

She knew the mountain had a hidden entrance somewhere on this side. She had discovered it as a girl. She just had to find it, what looked like a seam and not what it was, and she used the hand of her strong arm to feel along the cold rock face as she slowed.

Finally, her hand slipped into a wide crack that would not have been noticed if she did not know what she was looking for. One side overlapped the other and even from a few feet away, no one could tell this was a cave opening.

When Belladonna reached her, she looked at this opening with surprise on her face. "Well hidden," she said.

"I'm going in," Valada said.

"No! Absolutely not! You aren't well yet. And your broken arm isn't strong enough. I'll go."

"You can't withstand the ghosts."

"And you cannot face our enemy and survive."

"Neither of you will enter!" It was Moarte and both of them turned to look at him.

His anger was directed at his mother and he was about to verbally lash out at her when Valada said to him, "Moarte, this entrance is not known to any but me, I'm sure of it. It will lead us to an area where the warriors live, and I believe Serene might be there. My father told her that if she proved herself, he would give her to a warrior."

"Why didn't you tell me this before?"

"Because I only remembered his words today. And it didn't occur to me to mention this entrance before because I know it doesn't lead to the throne room and that's where we wanted to go when you and I came here together."

"Come!" he said, perturbed. "I will escort you both to the clearing and you will return to the stronghold."

"But Serene is in there! I know it. I can feel it!"

His sigh was one of frustration. "Wife, your *feelings* are irrelevant. If Sapiens warriors are in there, they'll kill us if we try to enter. I'll return with troops."

"You can't."

"Of course I can!"

"You don't understand. The seam is extremely narrow. You're too tall and there's no room to stoop. Both of you," she said, glancing from Moarte to his mother and back. "There are no vampirii warriors who can fit. Only someone my size can."

"Then it's not a route we will use," Moarte said, grasping her good arm.

"Moarte, please—"

"Stop, Wife! Obey me! We are at war and this silliness is distracting."

She yanked her arm away from him with a furious look and then, faster than he could imagine her moving, she slipped into the seam in the mountain wall.

He leapt to the crack and reached in but she was already beyond his grasp. "Come back! Now!"

"My son, let her go," Belladonna said, touching his arm, and he spun on her, his eyes violently red, and hissed, "How dare you disobey your King! You have put my wife in danger! I should imprison you!"

Belladonna blinked once but she did not react as he'd expected.

"I am your mother," she said.

"Then act like it! Be on my side!"

"I *am* on your side. And Moarte, I witnessed many of your childhood tantrums, so you may as well calm yourself and listen to me because what I have to tell you will help you with this battle and if you were not so stubborn and headstrong as was your father, we would not be standing here now but you would have utilized the information you need to beat the Sapiens King!"

It was all Moarte could do to keep from striking her. He trembled with rage. A sound from the seam came through like a whisper. "I've found them!"

Valada had come back with information but when Moarte looked into the darkness in the seam, he could see her too far in and he knew that she intentionally waited so far inside the fissure as to be beyond his grasp. She wasn't coming out, nor coming close enough for him to reach in and pull her out and now he was thoroughly annoyed with her.

Because she whispered, he suspected warriors were close and he kept his voice low. He tried to sound reasonable to entice her closer. "Come back, Wife. Bring this information to me. We will rescue her, I promise you."

"I know Serene is here with the warriors. I'm going to find her and bring her out."

"No!" he hissed, losing it, "Come back!"

But she was gone again, and he could do nothing but wait here for her to return, knowing that he should be with his warriors. Knowing that she was putting herself in grave danger.

His mother, always the mind reader, said, "I'll go in your place to the troops. Stay here and wait. She'll find Serene and bring her here and they will both need protection."

He could not speak he was so angry, but he managed to nod ascent and Belladonna turned and headed back on her own and he was just as glad because he didn't think he could be in her presence without doing her harm.

Moarte stood close to the seam, his ear pressed against the narrow gap in the rock. Even with his acute vampir hearing, he did not detect movement or voices. He was angry and frustrated and extremely worried about his wife's safety. But he was helpless and could do nothing but wait, and that did not suit his temperament at all.

Chapter Thirty-Eight

Before she saw or heard the vampirii, Belladonna sensed them. They were busy, clearly, and as she neared, a number of the vampirii turned in her direction.

"Dowager!" Nightshade said. "We were not expecting you. I thought it was Hemlock."

"And where is Hemlock?"

"We don't know. We've been busy digging out the tunnel to rescue vampirii."

Belladonna realized in an instant that the explosion they'd heard had collapsed the tunnel and that vampirii must have been in there and were now trapped.

"Would Hemlock be within?" she asked.

"No. She was in charge of our mission and once it was underway, she disappeared. I assumed she was reporting to our King."

"Hardly. I just left him on the other side of the mountain."

"What's he doing there?"

Belladonna had no intention of minimizing Moarte in the eyes of his warriors who would expect his attention in this situation to be first with them, not his wife. "He's investigating a new way into the mountain that he discovered. He'll return presently. But tell me, what of your progress?"

Just then, Columbine emerged from the tunnel, her body smudged with grey dust. She approached wobbling slightly, clearly a little disoriented, with a slight nod to Belladonna, as was the vampirii custom with their King's mother.

"Have you found vampirii alive?" Belladonna asked the young warrior she had always liked.

"Yes, Dowager. We are on the verge of freeing the first of them."

Suddenly they heard raised voices in the tunnel then a cry that sounded positive and moments later the first of the trapped vampirii emerged from the opening. He was covered with the thick grey dust, far more than Columbine, so that he looked unreal. His movements were stilted, as if something in his body might be broken and Belladonna hoped it was not bones in his wings. Better a limb or two which would heal relatively quickly.

Vampirii circled him and guided him to a log they had set up where the victims of this cave-in could rest and be treated if need be. He told his story as they all listened, his words slurred as he struggled for mental clarity.

"It was as we began the journey upward, no more than fifty or sixty ahead of me, both vampirii and Sapiens slaves. We heard the rumble but the ghosts were loud and I paid little attention and I doubt the others did either—the voices of the ghosts are strong. The rocks crashed down on us suddenly, from above, and the sides. There was no chance to escape by going forward—I saw the boulders tumbling down the incline fast and I believe all ahead of me are trapped. On instinct, I began to turn to retreat but rock fell behind me as well and I didn't have time to get out of the tunnel. While I lay encased in rubble, the voices grew loud and I thought I would lose my mind. The ghosts did this!" All of the vampirii within earshot paused.

He looked stunned, as if he had suffered brain damage. His eyes were glazed and horror filled them.

Belladonna watched as more vampirii emerged, looking and acting just the same, and she knew that while the physical trauma had been horrendous it was as nothing compared to the ghostly voices. Vampirii were strong, and recovered from most wounds quickly. What she observed in them now was severe disorientation that spoke of mental trauma.

And then the first two Sapiens slaves were carried out and a hush fell over the vampirii. The Sapiens had not fared well. They might not have been troubled by ghosts but their bodies were battered almost beyond recognition by the rocks and unless a miracle occurred, they would all be found in the same condition—dead.

Belladonna stayed with the troops on behalf of her son, but also because she cared about the vampirii and wanted them to know that. But while she spoke with them and encouraged them to continue this arduous task of removing the mountain that had collapsed into the tunnel, she also wondered where Hemlock had gone.

Hemlock was beyond unpredictable. And given what Belladonna now knew about what she had done to Portia, and the lies she told about Valada, this disappearance suggested something sinister.

She regretted not telling Moarte about Hemlock but he had been so enraged that at one point she could barely speak. He would forgive all—at least she hoped he would—especially if Valada found Serene and brought her out of the seam in the mountain and they were both safe. *If* Valada found Serene. Just because she discovered the Sapiens warriors' den, that did not mean Serene was there with them, despite what the Sapiens King had decreed. And the warriors might have abandoned that den and taken Serene with them. But worse, the young Sapiens girl might be dead.

Belladonna knew how desperate Valada was to save her, for both altruistic reasons and also for the girl's skills as a healer.

Suddenly she noticed Rivard limping into the general turmoil of rescue and wondered how he'd gotten here. Presumably Hemlock had called him, but why? He bled from the lip and was holding an arm. Something had happened to him and she wanted to know what.

But just then two more shell-shocked vampirii emerged from the tunnel and what appeared to be a lifeless Sapiens was brought out behind them and then someone cried, "One is alive!"

Belladonna went to the still-breathing Sapiens slave. The frail girl— the one who had begged to be left behind in the last raid—still breathed.

"We found her beneath a warrior. It's all that saved her."

Belladonna examined the girl, whose eyes looked dazed and whose breath came laboriously. "Bring her here, by the stream," she said, scanning the ground for plants, wishing she had a specific herb or two at her disposal, like comfrey, wondering if this girl would live, worrying she would not.

The mourning period for these dead Sapiens would be long and deep for the vampirii. She just hoped that neither Serene nor Valada would be counted among the departed.

CHAPTER THIRTY-NINE

Valada's slight form moved through the almost impossibly narrow crevice of the mountain with great difficulty, and at points she had to bring her body parts along separately: a leg maneuvered so that it was not coming through with her hips, her shoulders flattened as much as possible. Her arm that had been broken needed extra care.

She did not remember this passage being such a problem when she was a child. Even though she was still slender and petite, and her recovery had taken more flesh off her bones, these passageways were proving arduous and her movements agonizingly slow.

She heard Sapiens warriors and imagined they had largely escaped the smoke and were clustered on this side of the mountain, struggling to protect themselves until they could get back through the tunnels. Even from here she could smell the sweet smoke. Likely they had not been able to get out through any of the tunnels that led to the city or the other mountains and retreated here because it was relatively safe and also because a bit of air filtered in from the outside through crevices in the rock like the one she was trying to squeeze through.

They coughed and complained, the sounds echoing around the high-ceilinged cavern, and she heard one say, "We should cover our mouths and noses and make a run for it."

"Too much smoke!" another declared.

"I say, put out that torch! There's not enough air in here as it stands!"

"Then we're in darkness."

"We will be anyway, when the torch burns out."

She had finally reached a place where she could make out a little of this chamber. Most of them must be huddled by the dim light of a torch that she could not see, the source of the illumination far enough away that it kept the opening of the fissure in darkness. There were three warriors in sight, but likely many more out of her view, what sounded like several dozen.

Directly before her lay Serene, on her back, seemingly unconscious, but Valada didn't detect bruising on her face or body, though there wasn't enough light to be sure.

The girl was not five feet away, close enough that Valada could squeeze out of the fissure, take a couple of steps, grab her, and pull her inside, out of their reach. But a Sapiens warrior sat on the other side of Serene and there were two beyond him she could see and although the three faced partially away from Serene, their backs to her, looking towards the area she could not see, they were very close and would react too quickly for Valada to rescue the girl now. And if they captured her, they would use her not only as a shield but also as a bargaining chip with the vampirii and Valada couldn't let that happen.

There was nothing to do but wait. She hoped they wouldn't move on because then she'd have to follow and as much as she understood this crevice in the mountain, there were tunnels on this side she did not know and she might never find her way out. But more, even this far from the lighted chamber she could hear the ghosts in her head calling, their voices far away but recognizable.

She tried to think thoughts they could hear, telling them she would help them, but not now. And please, give her some peace until she rescued Serene! But the voices did not dim.

To distract herself, she thought about Moarte and how furious he'd gotten. Clearly, he did not take well to his authority being challenged. That was no different than her father, and in many ways like her when she had been Princess here in the Sapiens Kingdom. Yet, couldn't he see that she had something important to tell him or she would not have risked coming here in her weakened condition? He refused to listen and she hadn't had time to argue with him, sensing that he was about to physically force her back to the clearing.

Also, she could see that his mother was a bit cowed by his rage, and that worried her because Belladonna was usually fearless. Valada had been startled herself by the strength of the emotion coming from him, so much so that she couldn't find a way to interject the information she had gleaned about Hemlock.

Her intuition had assured her that if Serene still lived, and if she was still in this mountain, she would be here, in the only pocket inside that was available to survivors who had not made it back to the city or into the bowels of the other mountains. It was worth the risk to check it out. She fit into this opening, and Serene, who was smaller even than Valada, could as well, so the possibility of any vampir warriors being able to enter the fissure was almost nil. The big risk was angering Moarte, but now that she'd found Serene, that would mitigate his wrath. And besides, by now Belladonna would have told him about Hemlock.

Her newly-healed arm ached, and she grew tired of standing, but she could easily let the narrow opening hold her up because it jutted out and pressed so close to her diaphragm that she could use it as a sort of shelf to rest her upper body on.

The waiting seemed interminable, as if she'd been here for hours, and the ghosts did not let up. She knew Moarte would be impatient, afraid for her, but she hadn't had time to tell him how safe this was. The only unsafe part was rescuing Serene.

Suddenly, the chamber went black.

"What?" someone shouted, and the others joined in, their voices bouncing around the cavern and it sounded to Valada like a hundred voices at once.

"Just the torch," another gasped over the din, then suffered a coughing fit.

"We need light," a third yelled, his voice a bit fearful.

"Afraid of the darkness?" a snide voice chided.

"We've got another female in our midst!"

And Valada tensed for a second until she heard several laugh, and then a few coughed.

Then a voice that Valada recognized as belonging to the warrior who had dragged her and Serene before her father said, "The darkness hides us and allows more air in here. We need to breathe the freshest air until the smoke clears, then we can get out."

"Unless the vampirii keep the fire's going."

"They can't. They have to retreat in daylight."

"But not the Sapiens traitors with them."

"The tunnel collapse will keep them busy and probably killed all the Sapiens traitors!" the familiar voice said, and Valada suddenly realized what the explosion was and she worried who might be trapped. But she also wondered how these warriors, so far from the other side of the mountain, knew about the tunnel.

"Our King made a good decision, that one, exploding the tunnel," one said.

"How did he know the vampirii were using the tunnel to the city?"

"He's got a vampir spy," someone said. And another laughed.

"I'm surprised the vampirii could enter that tunnel."

"Not easily. But it's not long, and close to the outer wall, so maybe the ghosts aren't so loud in their undead ears."

There was general laughter and a lot of coughing, letting Valada know that their lungs suffered from the smoke and she feared Serene's did as well.

Valada wondered who had 'helped' her father, and why. Something else that Moarte needed to know. Instinct told her she must act soon, and be quick once she did.

While they continued to grouse about darkness and smoke and discuss what food they would eat, who they would fuck, and how and when they'd get out of here, and in general the vampirii and what they would like to do to them, Valada waited impatiently, her arm aching, their voices and the voices of the ghosts echoing, and she was so uncomfortable that she wanted to scream. But she needed to wait here and she also needed to be certain that they wouldn't light another torch. Someone suggested that but the voice she recognized, who was clearly in charge, answered, "No. Leave it out until we breathe better. We can light one when enough time has passed that we know it's daylight. That's our best chance of escaping."

"How will we know the sun's up?"

"Check your watch!" someone called and others laughed.

"Without light?"

More laughter, some of which turned into coughing and spitting sounds.

The familiar voice said, "We know it was about four hours until dawn when the explosion occurred. We've been here for one hour, maybe more. I think we can estimate the time with plenty of accuracy."

Good! she thought. They'll remain here and in darkness for a while. But the urgency to act gnawed at her. That and the ghostly voices with their demands. She struggled to think clearly and logically.

Serene was very close to the crevice, but there had been those three Sapiens on her other side and any noise Valada made moving into the chamber and dragging Serene out would definitely be noticed.

Battling the ghost voices, she struggled to think of how she could deal with this. Essentially she needed to get these warriors diverted so that their attention was elsewhere.

Slowly, carefully and quietly, she moved her body parts through this particularly narrow section so she was at the edge of the split in the rock. She took a step into the cavern and heard pebbles that form the bottom of tunnels and chambers within mountains crunch underfoot.

"What was that?" someone shouted, his voice stressed.

"Calm down, Thorsden. You whine like a girl."

"Well, I heard something."

"A rat, most likely."

Someone else snorted, but then they were all silent. "A ghost," said a voice very close trying to sound eerie, and she knew it was a warrior on the other side of Serene.

"Don't be stupid! They don't talk to us, unless you turned vampir and we didn't know about it!"

"He's too fat to be a vampir," another said, and that brought a lot of laughs and guffaws and coughing, all of which disguised her movements towards Serene.

"Quiet!" That was the one who said he heard something, and Valada held her breath in the silence. Finally, the one with the known voice said in a tone that confirmed that he was in charge, "Rest. You'll need all the strength you can get when we make a run for it out of here."

"What about the girl?"

"I say we leave her. She's dead weight," said another.

The familiar voice said, "Our King wants her kept alive. He has plans for her."

More than ever, Valada knew she had to rescue Serene. Whatever *plans* her father entertained would not bode well for the girl, or the vampirii.

She crouched down and carefully and silently gently touched the pebbles on the floor, picking them up one by one and placing them in the hand of the arm that had broken and was only healed enough for this passive activity. She made sure the little stones would not clack together. Soon she had about two dozen and she stood quietly, waiting.

She stayed still as a statue, making sure not to move or turn. She didn't want to alert them to her presence, but she also didn't want to lose track of both the cave opening behind her and Serene who must now be just a step before her in this pitch darkness.

The ghosts were loud here and she struggled to stay focused on the task. Why they screamed at her when she was only partially vampir, she did not know. She sent questions to them by her thoughts, but they didn't respond.

Finally, when she heard deep breathing and even a snore or two, she picked one pebble out of her hand and threw it far across the chamber to her right. It pinged against the wall. The snoring stopped. She threw another. Another ping.

"What was that?"

"I told you, a rat."

Valada took aim and threw another pebble in the direction of the voice.

"Hey!"

His yell woke the others.

"Fuck, you woke me up! What's the matter with you?"

"What are you yelling for?"

"I felt something! Who did that?"

"Nobody. You're paranoid. Go back to sleep!"

And before they could, she gathered all the pebbles into her good hand and sent a shower of them into the small group of Sapiens. Some hit a human mark and produced yelling, others the cave wall.

A general pandemonium ensued with shouts, curses, coughing, movement that made enough noise that Valada took one more step then crouched down, arms extended, and her hands touched Serene's clothing. She grabbed the fabric with her good hand and pulled the girl directly backwards quickly as she moved that way, now half standing, until finally her back hit the cave wall.

Valada reached around behind her but the opening wasn't there! The noise echoing in the cavern and the ghosts in her head disoriented her. She held Serene in her strongest arm and used the hand of her weaker arm to feel along the wall in one direction then the other until her fingers slid into the opening, a foot or so to her left.

The Sapiens were still yelling and someone said, "I'm lighting the touch!"

Quickly she lifted both Serene and herself to standing and clutched the back of the comatose girl's dress with one hand, keeping her mostly upright.

She had to get herself in first and moving past the tightest area was tricky, but she finally managed, pulling Serene in after her with her good arm. The girl was thinner and shorter and Valada got her through the opening much easier, but not before fire lit the chamber.

Loud voices echoed and one yelled, "Hey, look!" Clearly he had spotted Serene's feet, the last of her pulled into the fissure.

"Get her!" and voices rushed towards the opening.

Valada moved as quickly as she could through the tight space. The voices were close to the opening now and while she knew they couldn't enter, they could reach in and unless she got far enough, Serene would be in danger of being snagged and pulled back out.

Light shone in the opening and she scrambled to drag the girl behind her but could only use one hand in this narrow area and even if she could have used two, she only had one strong arm, and she couldn't turn her body, or her head to look back.

"Reach in and get her!" someone called, and Valada heard a sound in the crevice as if someone was struggling to enter.

She was just about at the first curve and knew that once they rounded it, they would be safe. She squeezed herself through another narrow passage scraping her face and arms and had Serene almost through when she felt resistance; whoever had managed to get their arm inside the crack in the wall had hold of Serene.

"Got her!"

"What's pulling her?"

"Not what, who? Has to be a vampir!"

"They can't be in here. The ghosts."

"Fuck the ghosts!"

"Who cares! Just pull her back!"

The resistance turned into a force that dragged Serene half a foot the other way. Valada didn't know what to do. She could barely hold onto the girl with one hand which was cramping anyway.

Suddenly for no reason she would have been able to explain, she opened her mouth and let out a sound that imitated the voices of the ghosts in her head. It was as if the ghosts were screaming through her. The otherworldly quality of her voice wafted as she turned her head as much as the tunnel would allow towards Serene and the sound moved around the girl and into the chamber like a mist. It caused the one holding her to loosen his grip as he cried, "What's that!"

Valada sent another wail towards him, louder this time, and others in the chamber said, "Wait a minute! Is she dead?"

"That's not a human voice!"

"It's vampirii!"

"No, it's ghosts! I told you!"

"She's a ghost!"

Valada felt a notch less resistance as the one holding Serene clearly felt intimidated. With all her strength, she yanked on Serene's shirt and the girl moved forward sharply and within another second Valada had her around the corner and to safety.

Adrenalin rushed through her and she gasped, her body slick with sweat, her brain in turmoil. She inched along, moving as fast as she could, dragging behind her the heavy weight of the comatose girl Even though she knew they were safe now, she wanted out of this claustrophobic realm, away from the warriors, away from the ghosts; she wanted them both safe.

Behind, the Sapiens were yelling and cursing and she was glad when finally their voices and the voices of the ghosts dimmed as she saw or thought she saw grey light ahead that she moved steadily towards.

Finally, the dim light of fading night became a reality, distinct from the blackness of this crevice, and she managed to reach the opening to the outside.

Moarte was right there, his face a mask of worry and fury, but to forestall any confrontation, she panted, "I have her! Help me!"

She squeezed through the seam, still gripping Serene, but barely. Moarte took over, pulling the girl outside.

Valada, scratched and bruised anew by the rocks, collapsed onto the ground and Moarte lay Serene—also scratched—beside her, checking the girl's pulse, opening her eyelids.

"She's unconscious," Valada gasped, feeling exhaustion overwhelm her. That had been an ordeal, both physically and mentally. Her body was not as strong as it should be yet, her recently-healed arm hurt quite a bit, and the ghosts had left her disoriented.

Moarte bent low and inhaled. "There's smoke all over her. I think she's inhaled it." He opened her mouth and sniffed again. "Her lungs are full of smoke."

Valada propped herself up and bent over the girl. "Let me."

She pinched Serene's nose and blew air into the girl's mouth, doing this until there was some sense of the chest rising and falling on its own. "She needs more than I can do," Valada said, gasping for air herself, her body weak, and Moarte nodded.

He picked Serene up in his arms asking his wife, "Can you walk?"

"Yes." She was exhausted and it was a long way back to the place where the vampirii waited, but she could do it; she had to.

Moarte had already started the trek back, at a pace far faster than she could manage, and she lagged behind, holding onto trees and the mountain to keep her trembling body upright. Twice he turned and waited for her until she'd nearly caught up. But finally, he flung Serene over his shoulder and grabbed Valada about the waist to carry her too.

"Moarte, I can walk!" she protested, but he ignored her. And in fact she was glad to not have to walk. Her energy was spent and she felt near collapse.

CHAPTER FORTY

Hemlock made her way to one of the old abandoned cemeteries at the outskirts of the Sapiens city, this one an acre of land eroded by the elements that was gradually falling over the side of the mountain. It was the spot where brother and sister had played as mortal children. She knew she would find her brother here, waiting in vain for Serene. It was also the place where he'd first encountered the Sapiens girl when the vampirii had raided this city several years ago.

"She was bringing flowers to her mother's grave," Wolfsbane had told Hemlock, his face full of wonder. "She knew the raid was taking place but told me outright, 'I loved my mother. If I am to never visit her grave again, then today I'll honor her for the last time, but honor her I will, despite the vampirii and despite the Sapiens law.' Can you imagine such love and devotion?"

Hemlock thought him a sentimental idiot then and now. He'd been captivated by the girl's beauty, he said, but more so by her spirit. "She wasn't afraid of me," he told Hemlock, his voice awed.

She remembered sneering in her simpleton brother's face just before she said, "Don't be an imbecile! Sapiens are always afraid of us, as they should be. This girl is playing with you."

"No, she's honest. Real," he said, unable as always to see the truth about this as he had been blinded to almost everything since they were born. They were twins by birth only, and nothing more, and Hemlock could hardly believe they had shared the same womb.

She had been particularly annoyed with him over this Sapiens slave, so much so that she'd taken Serene herself, just to break her will, but the arrogant Sapiens had stared at her with hate-filled eyes and Hemlock had beaten her until blood ran down her back and the girl was forced to her knees. But still, she would not submit. Little did Hemlock realize that this act would precipitate her dolt of a brother selecting this slave as his lover so that Hemlock couldn't easily get at her again. And then he announced he intended to try to impregnate her and marry her! What a fool Wolfsbane was!

She had always wondered why Moarte trusted Wolfsbane. Why was *he* the second and not *her*? Her battle skills were as honed, if not more so. She was as fearless as him, far more audacious, the mark of a true warrior. Now she knew why. They were cut from the same cloth, her brother and her King. Weak males too easily swayed by females, and Sapiens females at that! She intended to change this situation.

She found Wolfsbane sitting on a tombstone at the head of the grave of Serene's mother in this overgrown and neglected bone yard, staring out at the mountains to the West, his back to the rusted and collapsed cemetery gates.

"Your melancholia has made you incautious," she said as she approached him. "Anyone could have snuck up on you."

"I'm not asleep, Sister. I can sense the energy of both Sapiens and vampirii. I knew it was you."

She stepped in front of him. "Our King requires your return. We must depart. The night fades fast."

"Go without me," he said. "I'll find shelter here among the Sapiens dead. I need to wait for Serene's return."

How pathetic! she thought. *And if I can help it, Brother, you will never see her again!* Hemlock was not above subterfuge when it suited her purposes. "Then I have good news for you, Brother. Your Sapiens lover has been found."

"What?" Instantly, his energy lightened perceptively. He jumped to his feet and Hemlock could barely keep the glee from her voice.

"Serene has been found," Hemlock said again.

"Is she all right?"

"She's alive and waiting for you. Come. We must go now."

Before she could move, Wolfsbane did the unthinkable in the world of *vampirii*; he grabbed her and pulled her to him. "Thank you, thank you, Sister! You have brought me the best news!"

She could not tolerate this physical closeness, which was an affront, and barely could restrain herself from ripping out his throat. Her skin crawled. Vampirii did *not* touch vampirii, other than in the sex act or blood drinking. Such an action was considered a threat and she struggled to not slash his carotid. She could not remember the last time they had embraced and it might have been centuries ago when they were still Sapiens. She shoved him back roughly and said again, "Come. Time grows short."

They walked to the back of the cemetery where the soil was gradually slipping off the mountain, pulling stones, statues and even the small crypts with it, leaving behind graves half opened, coffins unearthed, bodily remains exposed. Hemlock waited for him to leap into the air, enormous dark wings unfurled, then she joined him. They could not get through the hidden tunnel, which she doubted the warriors had completely unblocked; this was the quickest way to rejoin the vampirii. After all that had happened, she did not expect there would be Sapiens available to fire on them, especially from this corner of the city.

They reached the warriors who were bringing dead Sapiens out of the tunnel and Hemlock could see that several vampirii were covered with grey soot and had presumably been buried there until recently.

She was startled to find Belladonna in their midst and gave a quick nod towards the Dowager who answered with a cold face that said the King's mother knew something.

"Where is she?" Wolfsbane said by way of greeting to the others.

"Who?" Columbine asked.

"Serene. Where is she?"

"She's not here," Belladonna said.

"What?" He spun to face Hemlock.

Suddenly Nightshade yelled out, "Our King! He needs help!"

Columbine and Nightshade both rushed to Moarte who carried Valada and Serene. He let the former slip down to the ground and the latter he pulled from his shoulder and laid gently on the grass. Wolfsbane was beside the girl in an instant.

Belladonna rushed to Valada, who brushed her away, saying, "I'm alright, Mother. Please, see to Serene."

Without waiting for questions, Moarte knelt beside Wolfsbane and told him, "I believe she's inhaled smoke."

"We must get her home as quickly as possible," Belladonna said. "I have herbs there and can treat her. But not here."

"I'll take her now!" Wolfsbane said.

"The sun is about to rise," Moarte reminded them both.

"I can fly fast. I'll get her home," and Wolfsbane began to gather Serene in his arms.

Moarte blocked him. "There no time to return to the stronghold. We can make it as far as the Southern-most mountain top tonight, no further. Carry her there and my mother will do the best she can. Tomorrow we will all reach safety and Serene will be treated. Have faith, my friend, that she will survive."

Belladonna said to her son, "If Wolfsbane can make it to the fortress tonight, so can I. I cannot treat her in the forest. If we leave right now, we should arrive just as the sun rises?"

It was a question, and Moarte did not hesitate. "Alright. Take her and fly fast and hard. We will make the journey part way as the troops are too exhausted for an arduous flight tonight. We'll join you next sunset."

"Thank you, my King," Wolfsbane said, and he already had Serene in his arms and was taking flight, Belladonna behind him.

Hemlock decided to go as well. She had to keep an eye on this situation. She started to unfurl her wings when Moarte said, "Hemlock!" and she was forced to halt. "I need you here to organize the vampirii."

Before she could manufacture a reason why she should go, he had turned and was asking Nightshade and Columbine, "Have all vampirii been rescued from the tunnel."

"Yes, my King," Columbine said.

"And most of the Sapiens," Nightshade added. "There may be four more we haven't found yet; their presence is unaccounted for. They must be dead; we can't sense them."

"Their bodies will remain here for now. We have little time to find shelter from the sun. Each of you will carry a Sapiens, the living first—most are waiting in the middle clearing. Then the dead Sapiens. If need be, the strongest will carry two dead Sapiens. Those who are exhausted will fly alone. We do not have much time." He turned to Hemlock. "Get them moving quickly. Nightshade and Columbine, aid in this organization."

While Nightshade and Columbine jumped to action and vampirii began to take flight, Hemlock watched Moarte walk to Valada, who sat hunched over on the ground, clearly weakened. Without a word, he bent and picked her up, unfurled his wings and ascended.

Hemlock was stunned by this turn of events. The Sapiens King had betrayed her and kept the girl Serene alive! This was not good. If she recovered, she might tell what she knew, although they had an agreement. But what worried her more was the sharp look Belladonna had given her, one that said '*I know what you have done!*'

She took a moment to mentally tune into Rivard and sensed him on the other side of the crowd of vampirii. Even from this distance she intuited that all was not right. Maybe he didn't convey Hemlock's demands because it was his sister. Could he have betrayed her? It was unlikely—she had a strong hold on his spirit and his mind and she knew he was terrified of her physically—but it was not impossible. More, she suspected him of having regrets. She would knock that out of him, but not here or now.

There was no time to deal with or worry about anything. Serene had looked unconscious and with luck she would stay that way until Hemlock arrived back at the stronghold. As to Belladonna, she would wait to see what transpired there.

She turned and began shouting orders and the vampirii still lingering jumped to action. Within a minute she had the last of them in flight, and she joined them.

Chapter Forty-One

The vampirii camped with the Sapiens in a large grotto at the top of the mountain closest to the vampirii stronghold, less than an hour from their fortress home by air. It was one of the few areas inside any of the four mountains with no ghostly voices, mainly because this enormous niche was open to the outside, like a band shell.

During the flight, Moarte said nothing to her, and Valada could feel the tension in his body. She clung to him, barely holding on, her limbs trembling from exhaustion, partially from the ordeal in the crevice but mostly from what she had endured as a prisoner in the Sapiens dungeon from which she had not yet fully recovered.

At the mountain's apex, she was surprised to find this concave gouge in the rock, small to her eyes, given the number of vampirii and Sapiens who would spend the day here.

Moarte alit on a mesa nearby and carried her across what was a natural stone bridge. Some vampirii acting as a reserve force had stayed here, and other vampirii and Sapiens were just arriving, more and more every second, and soon the entrance was crowded.

Some of the Sapiens slaves Valada recognized followed Moarte into the concave opening that did not go very far into the mountain. He laid her down, then left her to their care.

She felt hurt and knew he was angry with her. She had thought that finding Serene would nullify that anger, but apparently it did not.

The Sapiens women were kind to her, giving her water, and a little food, finding cloth for a pillow, and generally treating her well, but she was unhappy. She did not want to be at odds with her husband. She loved him and his coldness wounded her. Maybe this would pass. It had to.

Valada heard crying and wailing and asked one of the Sapiens what was happening. "My Queen, the warriors are bringing the Sapiens dead, leaving them outside on the plateau. They were trapped in the tunnel and died when it collapsed. They were our friends, our family. We're grieving for them."

She was surprised by this. Sapiens, to her knowledge, did not grieve, or at least not audibly or publically. It was more than a custom in her father's city, it was the law. The dead were quickly interred within an hour of their demise, the family expected to go about their business as usual. That she had, at the age of fifteen, quite suddenly experienced grief and mourned her mother was exceptional—or so she thought at the time. When her father saw this expression of grief, he flew into a rage, screaming at her for over an hour, berating her, telling her he would have been happy if she died with her mother, until finally she collapsed in despair. Then he punished her by locking her in her room. This incident was one she only just remembered now, and it left her emotionally roiling.

Valada watched the warriors enter and the Sapiens opened a path so that the vampirii could get to the back of this shell, the darkest part of the narrow niche. Moarte went with his warriors and she noticed Hemlock walking by his side. The treacherous vampir snapped her head around and gave Valada a look full of meaning, then moved closer to Moarte. Valada felt a dual stab in her chest of both jealousy and fury that this vile creature had gotten away with murder and was also ingratiating herself with Moarte. Belladonna must not have told him what this evil vampir had done. Valada vowed to tell her husband about Portia the first chance she got.

The Sapiens formed a kind of human fence at the edge of the shell, a barrier between the many hundreds of vampirii and whatever light might filter into the niche. She knew the entrance faced north, so the sun would neither rise nor set and blaze into this opening. But still, as the sky lightened, she knew that light would hurt the vampirii and hoped they were hidden deep enough.

All throughout the day the Sapiens cried, moaning and wailing softly, and Valada was astonished at this display. She asked one of the slave girls, "How can it be that there is mourning for the dead? You all came from the city and you know this was outlawed."

"You're right, my Queen, we were all raised as Sapiens under King Zador. And none of us were permitted to mourn the loss of loved ones. This caused us much pain, not being able to mourn those dear to us. But we've discovered that this grief is a natural process for us and since we've been rescued by the vampirii, we've come to find our natural inclinations, and mourning is one of them. It's in our nature as Sapiens."

Rescued by the vampirii! Valada had never thought of it this way, but the girl was right. Being with the vampirii made them more human. It was her father that had kept them from their true selves.

Her father. He seemed to be the source of so much evil and so much pain. She could see now that not just she but all Sapiens had been enslaved by him, victims of patriarchal tyranny. And yet, he still lived. No matter what she or the vampirii did, they could not kill the Sapiens King. This situation seemed unreal to her. And more than unjust. He was like some menacing, omnipotent, preternatural being. Untouchable. Just like the ghosts.

CHAPTER FORTY-TWO

As sunlight sank below the horizon, the vampirii stirred.
Valada noticed that Hemlock was in charge of the warriors and had them organized, many with a live Sapiens in tow. They exited the cave's giant mouth quickly and immediately flew into the night air back towards the fortress.

Despite her hatred of Hemlock, Valada instantly recognized the skills this vampir possessed involving both organization and command. It made her realize that Hemlock was far more dangerous than she had initially suspected.

Moarte and Hemlock were the last vampirii to leave the inner sanctum and Valada the last Sapiens. She heard him say, "Send warriors back for the dead."

"Yes, my King." Hemlock then strode out of the cave without a glance at Valada and was soon flying after the others.

Valada and Moarte were now alone in the grotto.

He came to her and waved a hand for her to stand. She had some trouble getting up. He held out a hand, which she took, and pulled her to her feet, instantly letting go of her hand. He turned and moved towards the cave opening, expecting her to follow.

"Moarte, we need to talk."

"I must return to the stronghold. The warriors need me."

"*I* need you too."

He said nothing but when he had reached the entrance of the cave he turned and crossed his arms over his chest, his face utterly still, his pale eyes cold. She had only moved part way towards him and stopped, about to tell him about Hemlock's betrayal.

Before she could speak, he said, "If you prefer to remain here, I'll have Hemlock return for you."

"I'll come with you," she said, moving quickly to him, fearing the idea of being alone with Hemlock almost as much as she feared his icy rejection.

She put her arms around his neck and without looking at her he took off and she wrapped her legs around him as well, as she knew was required. She felt that his body was much stronger now than when they'd flown to the clearing to draw out her father. She also felt she was very weak.

He did not glance at her through the flight. When they arrived at the fortress, he alit on their balcony. The second she let go of him, he moved into the room and towards the door.

"Moarte, please. I need to speak with you!"

He ignored her and left the room, the door slamming behind him, and Valada felt distraught.

She wandered the chamber, not able to decide what to do. She was upset and knew that Moarte was furious with her for disobeying his orders. But she had found Serene; shouldn't that count in her favor?

Serene. She wondered how the girl was doing and left the room, stopping one of the Sapiens slaves in a corridor to ask where the girl had been taken.

Serene was in a chamber adjacent to Belladonna's quarters, and that relieved Valada. At least the girl was protected, and she knew she had to be protected from Hemlock. If only Moarte would listen!

Hurrying to Belladonna's rooms, she saw few vampirii en route and fewer Sapiens. It was as if the inhabitants of the fortress had vanished and she didn't know what to make of that.

She knocked on Belladonna's door and her mother-in-law called, "Enter."

When she saw that it was Valada, she smiled. "Come in, Daughter. I could use your help. Sit down."

Her mother-in-law had her sit and hold a large mortar on a low table while she stood above and crushed herbs in it with a pestle. Clearly she didn't need Valada's help to do this but it was a way of making her feel needed. Valada knew she must look as wretched as she felt.

"Serene has inhaled quite a bit of smoke, and her lungs are saturated with particles. But I have something that will help."

"Will she be alright?"

"I believe so. I placed drops of an herbal infusion under her tongue when we arrived last night. She's strong, and has a will to live. And Wolfsbane is with her and has been from since the sun rose to the sunset and still. He slept through the day, of course, by her side. Even unconscious, the girl will know he's there and that he loves her."

Hearing this made Valada happy for them but sad for herself. She and Moarte were so at odds now. "What about Hemlock. Has she been in the room?"

Belladonna's face turned hard and she stopped mixing for a moment. "I have a guard at the door who I trust and no others are permitted to enter but for you and Moarte. And Rivard, but he has not been to see his sister. I assume Hemlock has forbidden it."

"I'm so worried about Serene's safety. I haven't been able to talk with Moarte."

"Nor I," Belladonna said. She paused in her work again. "What's troubling you, Valada?"

Valada sighed heavily. "Moarte is angry with me."

"With me also. He'll get over it."

"I don't think so. He won't talk with me. At all."

Belladonna took a seat next to her and Valada let her fears out. "He's being cold. As if he no longer loves me. He won't even look at me. I can't get him to spend a minute with me so I can tell him about Hemlock." She stopped and stared down at her hands then up at her mother-in-law. "I rescued Serene. Shouldn't he be happy about that and whatever he's angry about, shouldn't he forgive me?"

Belladonna placed a cool hand over Valada's warm one. "My son, your husband, is a proud vampir. He took on much responsibility when young, and it was I who forced it upon him. I could have ruled but I knew he would be the best leader for the vampirii, which is why I stepped aside. Vampirii are not given to working as a collective and I knew I could not inspire them, but he could, despite his unusual birth. He's had to struggle to learn much over a short time, and to deal with rebellion." Her lips formed that inscrutable smile. "I realize that for you two hundred and fifty years seems an eternity, but for vampirii it's similar to one year to Sapiens. In any event, he's learned a lot and is more confident now. By challenging his authority, you eroded his confidence."

"Me? Eroded his confidence? How?"

"We both did. By not following his orders."

Valada shook her head. "I understand we didn't follow orders, but there was a greater purpose and if he would only listen, he'd know that."

"And he will listen. Eventually. But first you must regain his trust."

"Mother, this is wrong! I should not have to do this! He should accept that my intentions, *our* intentions were good and honorable. And that the end justified the means. He should listen so he can find that out."

"Perhaps he should. But what he should do and what he does do are frequently at odds until he can come to a balance again. You must help him come to that balance."

Valada sat quietly. Belladonna stood and continued crushing seeds and leaves. When she was done, she took the bowl from Valada's hands and poured the contents into a clear liquid with the fragrance of licorice, then closed the container tightly so that she could shake it.

While she did, Valada struggled with her emotions and they burst out of her as if she were dialoging with herself. "Moarte is being unfair. He is! What have I done? You and I arrived at the clearing when he told us to stay at the stronghold. Is that so terrible? No, it's not. Then, when he told us to return, I led you to the secret seam in the cave wall because my instincts were driving me. We disobeyed him again, but was it so horrible? I found Serene and rescued her. Wasn't that one of the two missions of the vampirii? One of the big reasons for venturing into Sapiens territory?" She stopped then blurted out, "Shouldn't he be presenting us both with a medal?"

Belladonna formed that smile again, which Valada wished she understood better. "Perhaps, but do not dress for the ceremony yet." She picked up the container and an eyedropper and said, "Come. I must tend to Serene."

Belladonna led her through a door that opened to another chamber. Wolfsbane was in the room sitting on one side of the bed holding Serene's hand, looking worn and worried. Moarte was also in the room.

Valada hurried to Serene's other side, touching the girl's pale arm and even paler face.

Belladonna came to the small table beside the bed and Valada made room for her.

While her mother-in-law opened the container she said, "Wolfsbane, bring her to a seated position."

He slipped his arms behind Serene and lifted her up until she was braced against the wall and Valada placed the pillow behind her.

"She hasn't woken," Wolfsbane said, his voice low and vulnerable.

"No matter," Belladonna said. "She'll swallow in small amounts. The herbs will clean her lungs."

Wolfsbane looked relieved that help was coming. "Thank you, Dowager," he said, "for any treatment you can provide."

Belladonna nodded then took the eyedropper she had brought with her and sucked in a small amount of the liquid she had prepared.

"Tilt her head back."

Wolfsbane did, and Belladonna opened the girl's lips and squeezed a bit of the liquid into her mouth. The natural instinct to swallow took over and none of the brew came back out of her mouth.

Belladonna repeated this several times and while Valada watched, she was very aware of Moarte standing at the foot of the bed. She was afraid to look at him but forced her head to turn. His eyes were on Serene and what his mother was doing and while he obviously knew that Valada was staring at him, he refused to return her gaze. His features were tense.

She decided to go to him, but at that thought he said, "Wolfsbane, I will find you later for an update. The ceremony will begin soon and the others need comfort."

And with that he left the room quickly, leaving Valada slack-jawed.

She felt stunned, as if he had slapped her physically. He was ignoring her intentionally and this left her hurt, angry and frightened. She didn't know what this could mean, or where it might lead. She wanted to talk with Belladonna about this more but her mother-in-law would be busy here for some time and, too, Wolfsbane was in the room.

Always perceptive, Belladonna said, "Valada, the ceremony for the dead is about to begin in the courtyard, and you will want to be there by Moarte's side. We will take care of Serene."

"Alright," she said, and turned to leave.

Belladonna's words stopped her at the door. "When the ceremony is over, come to see me. It's important."

"I will," she promised.

Valada got to the courtyard, startled to find dozens of Sapiens corpses lying in a pile together in the middle of the lawn. Surrounding them she saw what must be a thousand vampirii and hundreds of Sapiens, those who had been closest to the deceased hovering near their bodies now. Around the dead, the undead and living beings had created circles, circles within circles, the dead Sapiens enclosed. It was an impressive sight.

Moarte was not there but she knelt at the arm of a throne which had been brought out for him and placed at the top of the steps, taking her position by his feet, as she usually did. Or used to, in the brief time she had been Queen when she was not too injured to fulfill her role.

Within minutes, the massive doors opened and through them came Moarte with Hemlock right behind. Again, that stab of jealousy and fury hit Valada. She had to find a way to tell Moarte about this vile and deceitful vampir and what she had done! This couldn't go on!

Hemlock took the place Wolfsbane usually occupied, at the bottom of the steps. The place of the second. Moarte came and sat on the throne, again without even a glance at Valada, which made her feel invisible and abandoned.

Curiously, she did not see Rivard in the crowd, causing her to worry about him.

She realized that an intense quiet had descended. The air became still. She glanced around. The Sapiens had bowed heads, the vampirii were all looking up at the moon, throats bared. It was so silent that soon she could detect the rustle of leaves, branches whipped in the breeze, and swallows crying overhead in the dark night sky.

Suddenly, the silence was broken. At first she was not aware of the sound because it started low, a kind of hum that became apparent to her at some point and by then she realized it must have been going on for quite some time.

The hum built and she could not tell if it was coming from the vampirii or the Sapiens or both and then she heard it from right behind her as Moarte's voice joined in and the sound swelled.

Quickly the sound grew in volume. She experienced it as a vibration rippling through her body, thousands of voices, joined together to create an auditory emotion—sadness. That's the only way she could identify it. And in an instant she knew it for what it was: Grief. *This is what grief feels like!* She remembered feeling this when she was fifteen, when she had grieved for her mother. A hot tear leaked from her eye and slid down her cheek.

No one said a word but at some point one of the vampirii and one of the Sapiens each brought a torch and she watched fascinated and horrified as the clothing of the dead was lit and the bodies became a funeral pyre.

The Sapiens began to wail, some crying loudly, others screaming, falling to their knees, holding themselves, holding one another, and Valada was stunned by these actions which she had never seen before.

This touched her in a deep and basic way and she found herself sobbing along with the other Sapiens while the vampirii stood around them like sentinels protecting them in their time of vulnerability.

Suddenly, she watched vampirii from the outer rim take to the air. She stared in awe as their dark wings spread and one by one they took flight, chaotically at first, but eventually flying in a circular formation. They created levels, a wide circle, a narrower one above that, and another, narrower, above that one, and so on, forming a long funnel to the sky. They flew above the dead, their momentum creating a vortex that brought the grey smoke of the burning bodies up and through the funnel as if directing it towards the heavens.

As she watched the smoke go up the funnel it changed color, from grey to white, and she thought she saw it take the shape of bodies, but that could not be! She blinked, struggling to clear her vision. But each time, like clouds forming pictures, the smoke from the pyre drifting through the funnel looked to her like bodies, one after the other, ascending.

This went on for a long time under the nearly moonless sky, and Valada found herself deeply touched by this ceremony, aware that what Blander had told her was true, the vampirii were guiding the passage, moving the souls away from the earth.

The bodies were still burning but when the funnel deconstructed, Moarte stood, indicating the ceremony was over. He walked quickly to the heavy doors, leaving without glancing at her. Again.

She knew she was probably expected to follow him and would have, but she had agreed to see Belladonna.

While Hemlock instructed the vampirii on the disposal of the ashes and bones that remained, Valada made it appear as if she was following Moarte, for the sake of the vampirii and Sapiens in the courtyard, but also to let Hemlock know she was still Queen and this was *her* husband, although Valada realized she did that more for herself because she felt so destabilized about the relationship.

Once inside, she detoured to Belladonna's chamber and knocked on the door.

"Enter."

Valada closed the door and leaned against it.

"All did not go well?" Belladonna asked.

"The ceremony went well." Valada paused. "Moarte ignored me."

Belladonna nodded.

"Hemlock has replaced Wolfsbane as second."

"Temporarily."

"She's insinuating herself."

Belladonna, who was seated on a couch, patted the cushion next to her.

"I should go to be with Moarte. It's expected of me."

Her mother-in-law said. "Sit with me for a minute."

"I have to tell him about Hemlock."

"Do you not think that allowing Serene to tell this makes the most sense? She was there, you were not."

"But she's unconscious—"

"For now. She will wake."

"But he needs to know right away!"

"Do you feel this is the right time?"

"Yes. He'll see what a monster Hemlock is and that will show him he was wrong and he'll realize I was right about finding Serene quickly and it won't matter that I didn't follow his orders."

"I would think your priority would be to win his trust first."

"That's why I want to tell him this!"

"And do you think he will listen to you now, with this great gulf between the two of you?"

Valada's fear escalated. She was afraid that if she stayed here too long, Moarte would be elsewhere. Or with Hemlock.

As if reading her thoughts, Belladonna said, "He'll wait for you. Sit for a moment."

Valada sighed but went to the couch and sat nervously. Immediately, Belladonna took one of Valada's hands and held it between both of hers. The cool hands added to Valada's unease. "I just want everything to be right!" she blurted. "I want things back the way they were."

"We cannot reverse time. All we can do is move into the future and the future will be different than the past."

Valada paused and suddenly said, "I'm frightened! I don't think he loves me anymore," and tears leaked from her eyes.

"Child, listen to me." Belladonna stroked her hair. "You are so young. Valada, think about this: You're the one he needs to trust most, the one who matters most to him, and you have wounded his pride. A ruler needs pride to lead. Without pride, the warriors will not follow him, they will not have faith in his decisions. And you have shattered that pride and stripped away his confidence."

Valada opened her mouth to speak, to again argue her case, but then closed her mouth.

"You cannot repair this easily but the mistrust *can* be altered. To do that you must be willing to admit that you were wrong."

"But, I wasn't!"

Belladonna smiled. "You are Sapiens—"

"Half Sapiens."

"You cannot know the soul of a vampir. It is nothing like what you imagine and you cannot understand and you will not grasp this knowledge fully until you turn. But trust me: right now, you must be vulnerable. If you want to repair the damage, you must dissect the situation and only address part of it now, the rest another time. You must acknowledge that he was right to order you and you were wrong to disobey his orders. The only way to do that is to submit yourself to his will and obey him and for now forego your desire to prove yourself right."

Valada shook her head. "This is how it was before, when he mesmerized me."

"Not at all. You had no free will then. Now you do. If you can bring yourself to understand that you owe him not just love and loyalty but obedience that comes about through allegiance, you will melt his heart. You who of all of us here must trust him the most. Can you hear what I'm saying?"

Valada thought about it for long moments. "I think so. I'm not sure. How do you know this will melt him?"

"I am vampir but I was Sapiens once. I know."

Belladonna stood and dropped Valada's hand. "Go to your husband. Beg his forgiveness. And mean it. He will forgive you if your heart is true. If it is, he'll feel that. If it is not, he will feel that too, in which case, don't bother because you'll just make everything worse."

Valada stood slowly. She wanted to hug her mother-in-law. No, she needed to be hugged, to feel the reassurance. But Belladonna said, again with that uncanny perception, "Another time. Right now, your first duty is to your husband."

Valada left the chamber in turmoil. She did not understand any of this. Why did she have to admit that she was wrong when she was not? It made no sense. And yet she trusted Belladonna to know what was the right thing to do. And in a small way she did understand pride and leadership because she had been a Princess, High-born, even though she'd had little power.

She reached their room and was afraid to enter, fearful of what she would find. But she had to go in and face him or this would continue, and that she could not bear.

She opened the door unprepared for what she saw: Hemlock and Moarte were talking on the balcony, standing very close together.

She felt cut to the bone. Every part of her wanted to flee this new and deep injury. But they had both seen her and to retreat because of Hemlock would have been more humiliation than she could live with.

She walked to the fireplace and lay some twigs and branches onto the grate with trembling hands, occupying herself until they were finished. The fire blazed high before their conversation, which she could not understand because they spoke the vampirii tongue, ended.

As Hemlock left the room, she switched to their mutual language, clearly for Valada's benefit. "Thank you, my King. It has been a great pleasure to be in your company so frequently and to hear your thoughts as well as to obey your wishes."

And those words alone set Valada's heart pounding. Hemlock obviously used them to worm her way further into Moarte's affections and also to hurt Valada. What a hideous creature! She wanted to rush to Moarte to tell him all the terrible things Hemlock had done but remembered her conversation with Belladonna—this was not the right time, he would not listen, and the truth coming from Serene would be more powerful. And most importantly, there were wounds to heal first.

Valada stood and turned, hoping to find Moarte watching her, but he was not, and that, too, filled her with dread. He was still on the balcony, arms folded, staring out at the mountains, the great barrier between the land of the vampirii and that of the Sapiens. She went and stood behind him, afraid to speak, afraid not to. But she had to say something!

"Moarte?" she said.

He did not turn or move or in any way acknowledge that she had spoken, and that made her more nervous.

She wanted to say she was sorry but the words running through her mind sounded insincere, and inadequate, especially if she said them to his back. If he would look at her, maybe she could apologize with feeling. Maybe the words would have meaning for both of them.

She touched his arm and he spun around so fast, the fury in his eyes crimson-sharpened, that she gasped at this blazing fire directed her way.

Before she could utter a word he said in the coldest voice she could imagine, "How dare you?" The icy violence imbedded in those words left her unable to speak. His eyes built rapidly to scorching red, leaving her frightened and mute.

His next words were spoken slowly and evenly and he articulated clearly and that combination said he was controlling himself and that added to her terror. "You are my wife. You owe me respect and I demand it. And more, I am your King. And you *will* obey your King! When I give an order I expect it to be obeyed by all, including you! You have no special privileges!"

Her throat was dry. She felt so intimidated she couldn't speak, but he seemed to have no trouble talking.

"Any other in my Kingdom who disobeyed me would at best be relegated to my courtyard to be whipped publically and at worse I would tear out his or her throat."

"Moarte, I—"

"Silence!"

She could only tremble before this hurricane-like force that threatened to rip her away from the earth and tear her apart with furious winds. The terror she felt caused tears to leak from her eyes that she could not stop, but they had no effect on him.

"All that may excuse you, *if* you can be excused, is that you are ignorant of our ways. My mother is not, and she will be punished for her disobedience."

He glared at her at this close range and she could barely meet his enraged eyes the color of blood, but she did not have the courage to look away. All she could do was cry, racked with sobs. And despite his warning to be quiet, she whispered, "I'm so sorry I disobeyed you! Please, Husband, my King, please forgive me."

Did the fire in his eyes dim a little, or did she imagine it?

They stood for a long time staring at one another, her body trembling in fear and grief and helplessness, her tears endless. She was terrified that she had lost him forever.

After a long time of strained silence but for her sobbing he said in an even voice, "Go inside."

She turned immediately, went into the room and stood by the fireplace, hugging herself, watching him, trying to get herself under control. He stayed on the balcony, leaving her agitated from anxiety.

Finally, as the night was finishing, he closed the thick curtains and snuffed candles until only the light from the fireplace illuminated the room. Then he lay down on the bed.

Valada didn't know if she was supposed to go to him or not. Her heart and head were crammed with worries that led to inner conflict, leaving her confused and unsure of her ground. But finally she went to the bed they shared and lay down beside him, turning towards him before she lost her nerve.

He lay like the dead, unmoving, rigid. The sun must have been less than an hour from rising so she knew he was not sleeping. She wasn't clear about what to do or if she should do anything but instinctively she felt she shouldn't speak. But suddenly she remember something Serene had said to her: *Your husband needs you.* Oddly, those words gave her courage and strength and calmed her.

She began to touch him gently, his face, his hair, his lips, his chest, her fingers at first tentative but her confidence building as she caressed his cool skin. He did not respond but he did not rebuff her. And while she caressed him, she felt sexual heat rising within her, and startled by this, she let the sensations drive her actions. Soon she had moved aside the metallic skirt he wore, hooking the points of the hem to the belt. Her fingers stroked his penis and testicles, arousing him, which aroused her more, and she bent to suck and lick him.

Still, he did not stir. His eyes were open and he stared at the ceiling.

She pulled off her dress and when she was naked straddled his body, easing his hardness into her moist warmth, feeling pierced by his firmness, sighing at this.

She moved slowly up and down, nearly withdrawing, sliding back onto him, aware of her own heat rising to peaks that built higher. She experienced her actions as a form of worship, a submission of sorts, a giving of herself so that he might take what she offered—her passion—as an homage to his position as both her spouse and her sovereign.

Suddenly, he grasped her waist with both hands and flipped her over and she gasped at such an aggressive action, but the heat inside her loved this, wanted it, and her arms went around his neck in a loving way, her legs clamping his waist.

His lips forced hers apart and his tongue took possession of her mouth. He fucked her fast and hard, relentlessly massaging the sensitive folds within her, leaving her breathless, completely and utterly controlled by him, stoking her fire, building her to orgasm quickly.

She moaned then cried out as her body was rocked by rippling sensation. But even as her passion subsided, he did not stop thrusting.

Over the remainder of the night he fucked her continuously and she orgasmed four times. With each, her vagina spasmed more sharply than the previous time, as if she needed him more and more to fill a deep longing. He only released inside her the last time, his final thrust fierce and at that moment when they came together the distance between them vanished and animosity dissolved. In that moment, instinctively, Valada bared her throat to him and he pierced her and took her blood as was his right, and she gave it freely, as was her right.

She had gone out of her mind and into her throbbing body and was left with tingling skin and cells quivering with sensation. She felt sated. By allowing him to control her she was cleared out and had become crystal clean, sharp, pure. He had driven her to the edge, again and again. She had never experience such power, power that left her trembling in reverence, teetering on a precipice that she fell over. The submitting vaporized her fear and left her completely open to him, and very much alive.

Finally, night ended and he lay on his back, she curled against him, feeling as close as she had felt apart from him only an hour before. He held her tightly in his arms and she whispered in his ear as he drifted into vampir sleep how she loved his strength, his power, his intelligence, his beauty. She whispered over and over that she adored him and said, because she meant it, "Moarte, you are my husband and my King. I will always honor you and obey you. I promise."

She had never felt so soft and yielding. So empowered. Loving and loved.

CHAPTER FORTY-THREE

They awoke simultaneously as the sun set. Her warm skin pressed against his brought him erect. He understood the body readily, slightly less so the mind and emotions less than that, and her body spoke to him. He knelt between her legs and lifted her ankles to his shoulders and took her that way because he wanted to be inside her and at the same time see her yielding to him, to feel again that she belonged to him and was part of him.

He could not believe how much he wanted her. He felt lenient now. She was Sapiens, young, only recently with him, and he could get beyond her mistake because she had not known what he expected of her. But now she did and it would be different. He believed her because her body told him she acquiesced to him, and because he was not a monster. He would both forgive her and forget about this.

He loved the warmth inside her, how her arms encircled him in such a needy yet passionate way, the hot, slick fleshy folds that caressed his firmness letting him feel both cherished and mighty. And she could take his strength which made him love her more.

As he released into her she orgasmed and he smiled because she called his name again, her voice soft, wanting, loving. Endearing.

They lay entwined touching, kissing, still not speaking words, only speaking the language of love. Interrupted when an insistent knocking came at the door, followed by his mother's voice calling him, bringing him to awareness that he was still angry with her.

He stood and said a bit gruffly, "Enter," and as she burst into the room, her face altered his mood and made him immediately ask, "What's wrong?"

"It's Serene."

"What?" Valada asked, jumping out of bed, already grabbing her dress.

"She's dead."

They paused a heartbeat that felt like an eternity. Then, Moarte rushed after Belladonna and Valada was right behind him.

As they hurried through the fortress, he asked, "What happened?"

And Valada said quickly, "I thought she was recovering! You said she would recover!"

"I don't know," Belladonna answered, her voice distraught. "The herbs were having the desired effect. I saw that. Wolfsbane saw it. She had moments of consciousness and lucidity last night, although she was extremely weak, and we spoke several times. I told Wolfsbane to go rest for the day so that he would be fresh tonight. I expected her to open her eyes this evening and be completely coherent and much stronger. When I checked on her at sunset, she appeared to be sleeping, but when I touched her and tried to put the drops into her mouth, I felt the coldness of her skin and realized that she was gone."

They entered the chamber to find Wolfsbane on the bed on his knees, cradling Serene's pale body in his arms, rocking, his low, keening wails heartbreaking.

Valada burst into tears and Belladonna hurried to the bed but there was nothing she could do.

The door had been left open and almost immediately Hemlock appeared, with Nightshade and Columbine behind her. The guard refused them admittance but Moarte said, "Let them enter."

Belladonna was not happy to have them here but she could not challenge her son before them. And really, what did it matter now. The girl was dead and she felt responsible. And she could not understand what had happened.

Suddenly, she heard, "It's you. I *know* it's you!" It was Valada's voice, full of venom, and Belladonna looked up from the bedside where she knelt to see Valada's face and body posture matching her voice.

Valada glared at Hemlock, who stood without expression on her face, as was the vampiric way.

"I do not understand you," Hemlock said evenly.

"Yes you do! You're responsible for this."

Hemlock lips turned down in disdain. "Hardly. I have not touched the girl. She belongs to my brother."

"You are a liar!"

Moarte, who had been watching passively, suddenly tensed and said, "Valada, that's enough."

Valada turned to her husband. "You're taking her side!"

"There are no sides," he said evenly. "Serene was injured from the smoke. She has died. It is tragic, but no one here is to blame."

Suddenly Valada turned back towards Hemlock. "Why don't you tell my husband of your deception!"

Hemlock's face assumed a look of confusion and Valada did not give her a chance to speak. "You came here and told Moarte I was dead when you knew I was alive, imprisoned but still living."

"How was I to know the facts?" Hemlock said, shrugging her shoulders. She glanced at Moarte. "I only had the information given to me by the Sapiens slave."

"Given by Portia, who you murdered!" Valada yelled.

"I have no idea what she's talking about," Hemlock said to Moarte. "Why would I want to kill a mere slave who was to keep bringing information for you, our King?"

"Then where is she?"

"How should I know? Likely she wanted to stay in the Sapiens city."

"No! You changed her then drained her to weakness then ripped out her heart, leaving her in a clearing so that she would not tell the truth."

"How do you know this?" Moarte asked.

"Rivard told me and your mother. It's what I've been trying to tell you if only you would have listened!"

The look on Moarte's face shifted and Belladonna did not miss this nor his body armoring. Valada, wittingly or unwittingly, had challenged him again, this time before Hemlock, Nightshade, Columbine and Wolfsbane. Even the guard at the open door, who was avidly listening to all this. The girl was on dangerous ground and Belladonna did not know what to do to help her.

Still, she tried to catch Valada's eye, to warn her to back off this confrontation. Already it had deteriorated, and Belladonna made a gesture to get Valada's attention, but the girl would not be swayed.

"Rivard is given to fanciful expressions of untruths," Hemlock said casually, again to Moarte, ignoring Valada.

"Because you mistreat him! He fears you!" Valada snapped.

Hemlock laughed easily. "All Sapiens fear vampirii. It is the natural order of things. Sapiens are our inferiors and should respect us." Clearly she was implying that Valada was disrespecting Moarte, and Belladonna had to do something.

"If I may offer a suggestion," she said, standing. Moarte turned to his mother, his face declaring that he was in no mood for suggestions, especially from her, so she hurried on. "Bring Rivard here. Let us ask him to repeat what he said."

"I have no problem with this," Hemlock said readily. And before anything more could happen, she turned and told the guard at the door to send for Rivard.

But Valada could not wait. Belladonna could see she was at a pitch, about to explode.

She turned to her husband and said, "Give him to me! You said you could do this, take Rivard from her. Do it now! It's the only way he'll speak the truth."

Again, she had boxed him into a corner before others, and Belladonna could feel the tension coming off Moarte.

Before he could respond, Hemlock turned to him and said, "My King, I have no loyalty to my vampir slave, and frankly, I find him troublesome and useless. If your wife desires him in some manner, I am happy to part with Rivard. It would relieve me of a burden. I give him freely to her."

Implying that Valada desired Rivard at all was an affront to Moarte but the blame was not on Hemlock, who had broached this skillfully, but on Valada, on whom this insinuation rested.

Just then Rivard appeared in the doorway, appearing haggard and frightened, so dark under the eyes and hollow-cheeked that he resembled a walking corpse. The body of this young vampir who had only recently been a Sapiens male in his prime, was now bent over like an old man's, his wounds and bruises apparent to all, his face and arms full of scabs and the stripes of barely-closed whip lacerations. He trembled uncontrollably from fear and starvation.

Hemlock turned to him. "I have given you to King Moarte's wife. You no longer belong to me."

Every vampir in the room knew this to be impossible. The tie between the one who brings over and the one brought over could never be severed but through death. Rivard might belong to Valada now, but he could still be controlled by Hemlock.

Valada had been told this but Moarte's mother knew the girl did not understand the extent to which it was reality.

Valada turned to him and said, "Repeat what you told Belladonna and me the other night."

Rivard could not look up. He was silent so long, Belladonna thought that Valada might shake him. Suddenly, Moarte's voice boomed, "Speak! I command it!"

Rivard looked up at the King but en route he did not glance at Valada, only Hemlock, and the terror in his eyes spoke volumes.

"I do not recall what I said, King Moarte. I have a faulty memory. Hemlock has punished me many times for this."

Valada looked shocked. "You told us what Serene told you. About Portia. And Hemlock. Repeat it now!"

He wouldn't look at her. His eyes focused on the floor. "I am sorry, my Queen. Perhaps I was inventing stories to gain favor with you."

Belladonna glanced at Hemlock and their eyes met. The sparkle in them said she knew she had won. There was nothing more that could be done. But Valada did not know that, and she did not stop.

She spun and faced Hemlock and screamed petulantly, "I *know* you murdered Portia and deliberately told Moarte I was dead. I *know* you are responsible for Serene's death."

Hemlock wisely did not respond to these allegations but turned to Moarte and said, "Sire, your wife is upset by this Sapiens' death. But please understand, I have not been in this room. Ask your mother, for she barred all but a few, including me. The guard at the door will confirm this. And in fact last night—other than the time I was with you in your chamber—and this night were spent with Nightshade and Columbine."

"It is true, my lord," Nightshade said. "We three have stayed with the warriors upon our return."

"Liar!" Valada screamed at Hemlock. "You are a murderer of two Sapiens and—"

"Enough, Valada!" Moarte said sternly.

"—you fawn over my husband, trying to steal his affections—"

"Stop! I will not tell you again!"

"—and I know you are a tra—"

Moarte slapped her and she fell back against the wall, hitting it hard, sliding to the floor. The silence in the room rang like a bell.

Belladonna stood. She did not know what she could do but she must do something.

Slowly and unsteadily Valada got to her feet, bracing herself against the wall, holding a hand to her cheek, tasting the blood where her nose bled to her lips. When she glanced up she saw every pair of vampir eyes in the room on fire, staring at her blood. It was impossible for them to not be drawn to this.

She looked around the room slowly, her eyes focusing as she did, staring at each face, finally stopping at Moarte's, her eyes savage as she said in a voice laced with bitterness, "Yes, you are vampirii, the undead, and you care about blood. More than anything. More than you care about the truth!"

She raced out of the room and a second later Hemlock looked at Rivard and said, "Well, go! You belong to her now!"

While they were all focused on the finale to this drama, Belladonna had moved through the door to her chamber, quietly closed it after her, then rushed to the hallway door and snagged Valada as she passed, dragging her inside the room even as the girl fought her.

Rivard was close behind but Belladonna slammed the door in his face.

"Leave me alone!" Valada yelled, her eyes wild, her emotions spinning out of control in a myriad of directions.

Belladonna shoved her into a chair and when she tried to get up pushed her back again. They did this four times before Valada finally looked up at her mother-in-law and said with hostility, "What do you want?"

Belladonna sat across from her and only stared at her.

"What?" Valada asked sharply.

"This is not good."

"Why didn't you support me in there, tell Moarte what you know? Take my side?"

"Because you were digging a deep grave for yourself and I did not wish to be buried in it with you. Once again, you have taken the wrong approach."

Valada tried to stand again and Belladonna shoved her back. "Listen to me, Daughter, because you have little time. Your husband is about to divorce you."

That made Valada pause, a look of shock on her face, but then she said sounding puerile, "I don't care! We are not meant to be together. If he cannot hear the truth, then I can't love him anyway."

"Stupid and stubborn Sapiens!" her mother-in-law said, and Valada started to rise but Belladonna held a finger in front of her face saying wordlessly 'don't try it'. "This time, you have not only challenged him but embarrassed him not just before his mother but in front of vampirii. Do you realize that besides Hemlock—"

"I hate her!"

"—Wolfsbane, Nightshade and Columbine were in the room and the guard at the door. And Rivard, who you cannot count on. You humiliated Moarte and still have not proven that what Rivard said is fact. You are in a very bad position."

This got through to Valada and her shoulders slumped. She looked at her mother-in-law. "He hit me."

"And you are lucky he did because it stopped you from what you were about to say."

Valada looked started. "How can you condone that?"

"If you had accused Hemlock of treason without proof—"

Valada opened her mouth but Belladonna spoke over her anticipated objection, "—which you cannot provide—but do let me know if you have proof of this—Moarte would have had no choice but to hold an immediate trial. Treason is one of the two worst crimes among the vampirii, the other being murdering one of our own. The trial would have taken place tonight, and the outcome is you would be found guilty of falsely accusing a vampir of treason and you would be put to death. And not by Moarte's hand, but by the hand of the one you accused—Hemlock."

Valada was stunned to silence.

"Valada, I would have instructed you about our laws had I the slightest notion that you might act so rashly and break them so frequently. But I did not. And you did. If you had given me a clue you were hell-bent on being a lunatic, I could have at least signaled you in that room; for instance, a hand over the heart to alert you that you were on the right track, or one on the head to indicate you were going off the rails. But no, you did not trust me enough to come to me for help. And now, while you've saved yourself from death—unless Hemlock brings a formal complaint, which she may—I don't believe this can be reversed."

Valada sat in silence for a time, her head bowed, the impact of what had happened in the other room slowly sinking in, along with the ramifications. Finally she said quietly, "Rivard did not lie to us."

"No, I don't believe he did."

"Then why wouldn't he tell Moarte the truth? He no longer belongs to Hemlock, she has little control over him."

"This is again where you do not understand the vampirii at all, it seems. It's the blood bond. Hemlock still controls him. She doesn't need physical torture when she can torture him mentally and does, and will continue to do so. He's only freed from future wounds to his flesh, which are the least painful wounds in many ways."

Valada thought for a minute. "She knew he wouldn't repeat what he told us. That's why she called him into the room so quickly and gave him to me so readily."

Belladonna nodded.

"She had an answer for everything, and remained calm while I went to pieces. I played right into her hands!"

Another nod.

Valada looked crestfallen. It was beginning to dawn on her that she had allowed herself to be used by Hemlock to bring about a desired result. Now she had accused Hemlock, who was the epitome of reason, resulting in the treacherous vampir appearing quite sane while Valada had presented herself as a crazy Sapiens making accusations she could not prove. Worse, she had both challenged her husband's rule—again—and humiliated him before his warriors, and likely he would not forgive her this time and would, as Belladonna indicated, divorce her. And she could not prove the truth.

"I have a suspicion," Belladonna said, "that Serene was murdered."

Valada looked up. "Hemlock said she was not in the room. She has an alibi being with Nightshade and Columbine. And with Moarte," she said bitterly. "And your guard at the door, who is not her slave but is loyal to you, I'm sure he'll testify that she didn't enter the room."

"I do not believe she killed Serene. At least not directly."

This got Valada's attention. "What do you mean?"

"I smelled almonds near Serene's lips last night as I gave her the last dose of herbs. It was very late, the weight of the sun was pressing on me, and I thought nothing much of it until I caught the scent again just now in the room. The jar of herbs I left by the bed smells of almonds, and I did not use almonds in the mixture, only some anise which smells of licorice."

Valada shook her head. "I don't understand. Are almonds harmful?

"Not generally. But bitter almonds contain prussic acid which can be easily refined to produce cyanide which is lethal. I believe cyanide was slipped into the elixir I made and which I gave to Serene late last night, inadvertently killing her."

Valada looked horrified. "You're saying that someone poisoned her. But the only people that you allowed admittance were Moarte and me, Wolfsbane and yourself, and none of us would do that."

"And Rivard."

"Rivard," Valada said.

"I will ask the guard if Rivard came to the room to visit his sister, but I think we know that he did."

"If he did this, it was because Hemlock ordered him to and he is too weak to challenge her. Too weak to *not* kill his sister!"

Belladonna nodded. "You are correct."

"There's another thing," Valada said, "and I must tell you now because something may happen to me and perhaps one day Moarte will want to hear the truth."

Belladonna felt saddened hearing this but knew the girl was being realistic. Things had gone very wrong tonight and Moarte would likely decide to divorce her and he would not change his mind. She knew he was already contemplating this because he had to. If he did not divorce Valada, the vampirii would not follow him, it was as simple as that. And there was likely nothing that Valada could do now to make this right.

"When I was in the crevice, I heard the Sapiens warriors talking about my father being very clever to have caused the tunnel to collapse that the vampirii were using to enter the Sapiens city. One of them wondered how he knew the vampirii would come that way, and another said he had help. A spy. A vampir. I believe that was Hemlock."

"You could be correct. And if so, she has endangered all of us and will do so again. This is treasonous and Moarte needs to know about it but I fear he will not listen for some time, and he will not listen to you at all."

"Hopefully he will learn this before he marries Hemlock."

This grim thought left them both sad and Belladonna said quietly, "I spoke with Serene last night. I told her you were hoping to heal and conceive again. She felt very positively that her recipe could heal you and told me the ingredients, the quantity of each, how to prepare them, and the dosage and she suggested I mix this right away so you could start on the road to recovery sooner, before she had fully healed. She loved you."

Valada's eyes filled with tears. "Yes, I know she loved me. And I loved her. But, Mother, it is too late."

Belladonna said, "Yes. I believe it is. Until Moarte has proof of these things—"

"Yes, he requires proof. But it's too late for another reason. I'm already with child. I conceived last night. I felt it."

Belladonna looked stricken at the horrible timing of everything and Valada thought that she might cry and wondered if vampirii could cry. Valada reached out and took her cool hand.

Finally her mother-in-law said, "This is now a tragedy of a greater proportion."

They sat in silence for some time, both contemplating the grimness of fate, when the thoughts of one suddenly diverged. Valada leapt to her feet, shedding her grief and misery and reviving her fury and her will to fight back. "Mother, it's not over yet. I will get proof!"

"How?"

"Trust me. And don't give up hope. I haven't."

She hurried to the door, opened it and found Rivard waiting outside, looking forlorn, broken of body and spirit.

"Come," she said to him, her voice tight with anger she was keeping in check. "I need your wings. And Rivard, remember, you owe me your allegiance now."

Belladonna watched them hurry down the hall, hoping against hope that her sweet daughter-in-law had a valid idea, because the way it stood, Moarte had little choice. And what Valada did not know was that once he divorced her—an extremely rare occurrence in the realm of the vampirii—she would become part of the Sapiens slave pool. And Belladonna knew without a doubt that the first vampir to claim Valada, the new Sapiens slave, would be Hemlock.

Chapter Forty-Four

Moarte felt ripped apart inside. His loyalties were severely divided, leaving him fragmented with no solid ground on which to stand.

Valada, he thought, *must be insane.* There could be no other explanation for it. She had made wild accusations against Hemlock, with nothing offered to back up what she said. Hemlock showed no signs of guilt. Rivard looked shattered, but his sister had died, and in truth, Hemlock did not treat him well. Still, that was between the two of them, not his business. Certainly not important now.

He did not want to think about divorce but knew there was no other direction to go in. Six vampirii had heard this encounter. His authority had been directly challenged, again, but this time before a wider audience, and that threatened his rule. His ability to lead the vampirii was, he knew, even now in question. Most of those who had been here would be telling others what they had witnessed. He could not continue like this. He had to divorce Valada. That, or kill her, or send her back to the Sapiens King which was the same as killing her.

He had given orders to Hemlock, Nightshade and Columbine, and dismissed the guard at the door, thanking him for his service. But before she left, he asked Hemlock to wait and spoke with her in the hallway in private. "I regret what you have gone through tonight. It is undeserved."

"My King, it's not your fault. Your wife is upset, as you well know, a Sapiens tendency."

"She had no right to accuse you."

Hemlock looked down, her shoulders expressing she was slightly pained, but then she boldly stared into Moarte's eyes and said, "My King, I know that I can force this issue with a complaint, but I will not do that. You, too, have suffered because of this. There is no point adding turmoil to your life, which I perceive as difficult enough. As far as I am concerned, this did not happen."

Moarte was more than relieved because he knew if she insisted, he would have to hold a trial tonight, even though he managed to stop Valada from fully verbalizing the accusation that would get her killed.

"Hemlock, you are a kind and understanding female. I do not believe you have received all that you deserve, but I intend to alter that situation in the future. Your position in my eyes has risen dramatically over the last while, and I'm grateful to have you by my side."

She looked a little shy to him, yet still held his gaze. "My King, if there is anything I can do to help you, anything at all of a political or military or even a personal nature, please, do not hesitate to ask. I am here for you. By your side. I always have been."

"Thank you," he said, aware of a strange clash of emotions he felt towards her at this moment.

He stepped back into the room and immediately noticed that his mother had disappeared, which was just as well, although he wanted to question her but not right now. He felt numbed from the shock of how all that had been wonderful when he had awoken just a few short hours before, was now gone forever.

Only he and Wolfsbane remained with Serene's dead body. Moarte stood silently for a long time watching this heart-breaking scene. "My friend," he finally said, "I am so sorry you were subjected to all of this in your time of mourning."

Wolfsbane looked up and nodded, then his tormented eyes travelled down to Serene's sweet, pallid face again, lovelier in death in some ways because she was at peace now. "She is so beautiful. I spent many nights apart from her dreaming only of her and our future together until I slept. And now I will still dream only of her, but without a future."

Moarte closed his eyes as a wave of grief hit him and he knew it was only partly for Wolfsbane and his loss. Moarte's loss was as great. He had lost Valada forever.

The door leading to Belladonna's chamber opened and his mother came in. She glanced at Wolfsbane and then at Moarte.

"Be strong, Wolfsbane," Moarte said, about to leave the room so that he didn't have to deal with Belladonna right now.

Before he could even turn, she said, "Moarte, I have something to tell Wolfsbane which you may want to hear."

He did not want to hear anything she had to say, but at this point

thought, why not? How could this night turn much worse? He hoped
she would not bring up the accusations and said, "I do not wish to cover
ground we've already traversed tonight."

"This is something new," she said.

She walked to the bed and picked up the bottle of herbs she had been
feeding Serene, opened it, and held it for Wolfsbane to smell, then carried
it to Moarte and did the same.

"Why are we doing this?" he asked his mother.

"What do you both smell."

"Almonds," the two males said almost in unison.

"And this is significant how?" Moarte asked.

"I did not use almonds, bitter or otherwise, in my mixture. This
ingredient was added later, I believe late last night. Bitter almonds contain
cyanide and if you smell Serene's lips you will detect this same almond
smell. While cyanide will disorient a vampir and bring on symptoms of
poisoning, they are temporary. For a Sapiens, cyanide is lethal. She was
poisoned."

Moarte was startled. "Are you certain?" he asked, not wanting yet
more unproven accusations flying around.

"I am certain. Someone tampered with this mixture last night. The
guard was here during the dark hours and slept outside the door. He
would only permit both of you, Valada, myself and Rivard in here. I
checked with the guard just now: Rivard came late last night to visit his
sister after Wolfsbane left and before I came to administer her a last dose
of herbs. This was close to sunrise. He stayed only about three minutes."

"You're saying he killed Serene!" Wolfsbane said, jumping to his feet.

"I am. Unless one of us in this room did it, or Valada."

"Where is he?" Wolfsbane's voice turned hard, his body tensed, and
he had already started for the door.

"I do not think you'll find him in the stronghold."

"Where did he go?" Moarte asked.

"I don't know exactly, but Valada wanted him to fly her somewhere."

"What? Why?"

"To get proof that all she said was true so that you would believe her."

This hit Moarte in the heart.

"Tell us again what Rivard told you and Valada," Wolfsbane said,
and Moarte was not sure he could bear to hear all this again, but when
Wolfsbane looked to him, he nodded ascent.

Belladonna repeated what Valada had already conveyed, both earlier here and also included what she had said privately about the comments she overheard when she was rescuing Serene, but adding much more detail to this account. When she finished, Wolfsbane said, "I think I know where she went, and if I have your approval, my King, I will find her, and Rivard, and investigate this proof myself, if your wife has found any."

Moarte, too, had a sense of Valada's destination. "Perhaps I should go," he thought aloud, his mind filled with conflicting worries.

"My son, there have been many questions raised tonight in your Kingdom, many concerns have developed, and it might be best for you to remain here as a symbol of stability for the vampirii. In fact, I would suggest this is a good night to hold court, to show others your strength. The vampirii do not function well leaderless and frankly, there is no one to take your place. If you want to preserve your rule, you must gather the vampirii to you and re-establish yourself as their King, whose reign they can feel confidence in and rely on. "

Moarte knew she was right. He needed to maintain a presence before gossip completely undermined his rule. But he was reluctant to wait here because he felt agitated. If there was proof, he wanted to see it. Now! He hoped there was proof, he hoped Valada could be saved, but he could not let himself travel that path; things had deteriorated to the point where if hope had not died, its imitation of death was remarkably accurate.

"Moarte," Wolfsbane said, "I will do as you yourself would do. Allow me to investigate. I swear to you that if I am able, I will bring both Rivard and Valada back with me along with whatever proof exists of these accusations. And if Rivard has killed Serene and if Hemlock is proven to be a traitor, they will be subjected to vampir judgment."

Finally, reluctant though he was to leave this in Wolfsbane's hands, Moarte nodded his consent.

CHAPTER FORTY-FIVE

As soon as they'd left Belladonna's room, Valada had Rivard fly her to the largest clearing. His body was weak, his wings not yet developed sufficiently for the extra weight, so much so that they were forced to fly low in the sky, and the journey took nearly twice as long as when she had flown with Moarte.

She was furious with Rivard but kept that to herself. However much he had been under Hemlock's control, however much that evil vampir brutalized him, he did not deserve pity. She might be able to forgive him for not confirming what he had told her, but she could *never* forgive him for murdering his sister. And she knew he had. No wonder he looked so wretched! How could he face himself?

Finally, after a flight that lasted close to four hours, so long that she thought she might dehydrate because she didn't want to take the time to bring water, they arrived at the large clearing, a crescent moon's sharp points stabbing the black night sky.

Serene had not told Rivard in which clearing she'd found Portia's body, and there were three. Valada felt it was likely this one, the place where she and Moarte had descended. Where Hemlock was supposed to wait for news. This was the place where she hoped to find Portia's remains.

But Valada had worries. There were three clearings on the vampirii or Sapiens side of the border at the back or side of this mountain. How long would it take her to search this one? And if the body was not here, how many hours, no, *days and nights* might it take to thoroughly search all the clearings and the surrounding woods? And she worried about three more things: She was very close to the Sapiens border, too close; Hemlock may have moved the body, or buried or even burned it; she could not trust Rivard to help her—he still held Hemlock's interests first, not hers.

"Rivard," she told him, "I want you to go fetch me water."

"What should I carry it in, Mistress?"

"Find something in the forest."

"What?"

She sighed. "Use your imagination."

He stood there stooped, looking at her dumbly, as if half his brain had been sucked out. "Go!" she said, pointing in the direction where the stream ran, just wanting him out of range. Whatever she was doing, she knew that Hemlock could likely find out through the mysterious connection she had with his mind. She didn't know if Hemlock could read his mind, and if so, whether or not it could happen without being near him, or at what distance. These were all vampiric skills she had no knowledge of but she didn't want to risk Hemlock finding out where she was and what she was up to, if she could help it.

And now that she knew Rivard had poisoned Serene, she did not want him near her at all, let alone being her slave. She did not know how to renounce ownership of him but it was one of the first things she would find out how to do when she returned to the vampirii stronghold with proof. *If* she could find proof.

Once Rivard was out of sight, Valada did a quick search of the clearing by walking from side to side and looking each way, then taking six steps towards the mountain wall and then walking back the opposite direction, looking at the new ground before her and what she had already seen but a bit more of it. She also checked the woods on the three sides, walking in six feet and scanning both directions, though Serene had said 'clearing' and the girl had tended to be precise.

Valada hoped that she would find the body right away, but, of course, that was not to be.

When she reached the back wall of the mountain, she walked the other way, from the wall outward, the same pattern, in rows, six steps apart.

She finished this and thought she should do the same in the other two clearings. Rivard wasn't back yet and she didn't call him; let him find her.

She made her way through the trees, working towards the second clearing, the mid-size, still within vampir territory, and there walked the same grid-like pattern, with the same result.

The third clearing was just inside the Sapiens border, small but dangerously close to the tunnel where the vampirii and Sapiens had been trapped, where human beings died because of Hemlock's treasonous act. The vampirii warriors had worked from here and the ground was littered with wood that had been chopped by their hands, it appeared, and she imagined they'd used it to brace the tunnel. From what she had seen when she and Serene were carried here by Moarte, the vampirii had been all over this area and she seriously doubted she would find any remains. Still, she walked a grid, much of it over grey earth and debris that had come out of the tunnel. She believed that if there had been a body here, the vampirii, with their sharp eyesight, would have found it, no matter how preoccupied they were.

She didn't like being within the Sapiens border. She had no idea what they were up to now but her father was always up to something, and the fact that they had a spy in Hemlock meant they would have more information than let Valada feel safe. Not that she felt safe anywhere now, and a pang of grief touched her heart. Even if she found the body and could prove some of her allegations, she suspected it was too late for her and Moarte. But she couldn't dwell on that now.

She decided to go back to the first clearing and begin a new search. This time, she would only move a foot from the previous gridline. That would make it a painstakingly slow task, but there was nothing she could do about that. The dim light of the moon didn't help. At least if this search continued into daylight, she'd be able to see much better.

She arrived back in the large clearing to find Rivard standing perfectly still, as if he were listening to something, and this she did not like.

"What are you doing?" she demanded.

He jumped at the sound of her voice and despite being vampir now, he hadn't heard her approach and she knew that meant he was preoccupied and she believed she knew with what and with whom.

"Did you bring water?" she asked, and he looked at her dumbly. "Water," she said again. He shook his head in confusion. "Go back to the stream and bring water."

"What shall I carry it in."

He was more far gone than she'd imagined. "Anything, Rivard," she said. "Use your hands."

The second he was out of sight she recommenced the search, this time starting on the side of the clearing where it would have been most logical for Hemlock to wait, the same side where she and Moarte had entered the forest when they came here together, where she sent Rivard.

She made her mind focus on the most likely scenario as she walked carefully from the rock face with the forest on her right: Portia came from the Sapiens city and would have come down the tunnel, walked around the mountain sticking close to it for safety, until she was near enough to this clearing to enter the forest at an angle, walk a bit, then emerge at the edge of the clearing, where Hemlock waited. This clearing was largest and the best for a vampir to take flight if there was a danger of Sapiens warriors, although, of course, Hemlock may have already given or sold vampir information to the Sapiens King so she might have had immunity from capture. Still, meeting her here was the arrangement Moarte had made and likely Hemlock would have stuck to it so Portia and Serene could find her. At least she hoped this unpredictable and corrupt vampir had more or less held to the plan.

Valada came to the other end of the clearing and took one step only then started back towards the mountain.

Knowing Hemlock as she now saw her, Valada had little trouble imagining her toying with Portia, and that might involve violence before she bit her. From what she had figured out about the process, a vampir had to take blood to the point of death from the Sapiens, then return some, then take that and all remaining blood back. Because the Sapiens had drunk blood that had been cycled through the vampir body, upon complete draining, he or she would awake vampir.

She suspected the transformation from Sapiens to vampir required a complete draining. She had taken blood from Moarte during the marriage ceremony, but she had not been drained and had not turned.

From what Rivard told Belladonna and her, based on what Serene found, Hemlock's puncture marks were still in Portia's throat—she hoped they would still be—and her heart had been removed from her chest. Unless all or any of it disintegrated in the heat of the sun, there should be *something* remaining. Valada just hoped there was, and that it would be enough to validate her accusations.

Back at the rock face she again turned, moved over one step only, and started back.

Hemlock would not have put herself out. Once she drained Portia, she would leave her body. She might have just let it drop, but there was no body or grave a few feet inside the woods beside this clearing on any of the three sides. Maybe she should check the woods further in. More than likely, Hemlock would have stolen Portia's heart and then tossed both it and the body into the clearing to be burned by the sun. Disdain was her style.

Valada turned, took one step, and went back. As she walked back and forth, a sinking feeling escalated. She did not know how long it would take a vampir body to incinerate in sunlight, although supposedly Serene buried it; without tools, it would be a shallow grave. Possibly the evidence was already ash. And what if she couldn't *find* evidence that Portia was murdered? There was no other way to prove that the girl was dead and that this state had come via a vampir. And how could she prove which vampir did it? Hemlock would drum up some excuse or alibi, but Valada didn't think Moarte would buy into it. But then she hadn't thought he would be so open to Hemlock's excuses and be so against Valada's arguments.

Thinking of Moarte upset her. She didn't know if he had turned against her because he didn't believe her, or because she had challenged him, as his mother said. Belladonna felt he hit her to save her from death, but she was not sure she believed that. He had looked furious, but there was no way to know without him telling her what that fury was based one. But even with evidence, he would probably still divorce her—Belladonna had made that clear enough. Valada knew that the relationship likely couldn't be repaired. But a part of her believed that if Moarte had evidence, irrefutable evidence, and he still ignored it, then he really was something alien and so very different than her that they should not be together. But where that left her, she did not know.

She had covered about half the clearing and was tired of walking, but it had to be done. Rivard was nowhere in sight and she thought that was just as well, even if he was in some way alerting Hemlock. She just had to keep going. There was nothing else to do.

Valada wondered about the child within her. She was completely surprised that she had conceived, but as with the first child, she felt it. If Moarte rejected her, she would have to leave. She didn't know vampiric ways but her mother-in-law told her she'd be reduced to the status of slave, and having seen the Sapiens slaves without a vampir protector, she did not want that life for herself or her child. And she would not have the child taken from her under any circumstances!

She could never live with the Sapiens again, at least not as long as her father remained alive. But even if he were dead, how could she live in that world? She would no longer be a princess waiting for the throne. There would be warriors vying for that, and none of them would think twice about forcing her into marriage or, more likely, getting rid of her and her offspring. In so many ways, the Sapiens were more violent, more vicious than the vampirii. But she could do nothing about any of these worries right now. She had to stick to what she was doing—find evidence to incriminate Hemlock—

"Mistress! I have brought water," Rivard said, and Valada was still walking when she turned towards him. And tripped. And nearly fell.

Here, the ground rose into a low mound. She stared at it, instantly recognizing that this elevated earth was the length of a Sapiens body.

She bent down and began digging through the soil, calling, "Rivard, come help me."

He reached her and she looked up into the forlorn face, his hands cupped, water dripping through his fingers, not knowing what to do with the water, like a feeble-minded person.

"Come," she said, indicating he should bend so she could sip the water from his hands. She needed the refreshment.

Then she said, "Help me dig."

He crouched low and began imitating her hands and soon they uncovered a leg, black as the coal in the mountains, and Valada moved to the other end of the mound.

Within a few minutes they had uncovered enough of the body to see the pierced throat, and the hole in the chest where the heart had been.

"It has to be around here somewhere…" Valada said absently while she kept digging. "Help me look."

"What are we looking for Mistress," and she glanced at him, realizing that she hadn't seen him this animated with this much spark of life in his eyes since he had been Sapiens. Was it because they'd found Portia, or was it some mania due to communication with Hemlock? Either way, she wanted help with this task and took a chance and confided in him.

"I want to find her heart, Rivard. That's the proof I need. Help me dig."

It didn't take long to find it, lying not too far from the body, a blackened organ, damaged by the sun, cracked like paper on the outside. Valada knew they couldn't carry the body back, but she could carry the heart and Moarte could send vampirii to bring the rest of the remains.

"Help me recover the body," Valada said to Rivard, and she secretly kept the heart aside without telling him this.

Once there was enough soil and leaves over the body to protect what remained of Portia from another day of sun, Valada turned her long skirt up at the hem, tying knots here and there to form makeshift pouches on either side and while Rivard was looking elsewhere, she discreetly slid the heart into one, retying the knot tighter, securing it for the flight back.

"Come, Rivard. We must return."

She took a few steps and realized he wasn't following her. His eyes were fixed on the sky and she spun around to find Wolfsbane falling from the air smoothly to land not six feet before her. His red-hued eyes were riveted to Rivard.

Valada instantly realized she had to protect Rivard. "No!" she said to Wolfsbane. "We must return with Rivard. He knows things that the King needs to know."

"The King knows what he did to Serene." Wolfsbane's eyes were murderous as he stalked towards Rivard, who cowered. Valada tried to get between them but Wolfsbane shoved her aside.

"I am your Queen. I command you to stop!" she shouted, but he did not until he was inches from Rivard's face.

"You murdered your sister, my lover."

"Nothing can excuse me."

"No. Not even your excuse of my cruel sister and her power over you. You have no right to live and you will not."

Valada tried to jump between them again. She felt the raw violence coming off him. She knew that any second Rivard would be dead.

"Please, Wolfsbane, wait!" she said. "We need to hear what happened. Please. I know Serene would want the truth told and Rivard is the only one who can tell the story." Then she said again, "Please. I need to hear this as do you. And Moarte will want to know. You know all that I'm saying to be true."

Wolfsbane stood like a tightly coiled spring, ready to snap and fly in any and all directions, slashing whatever had the misfortune to be in his path, and Valada felt she had to take the lead. She turned and said, "Rivard, you must know that this time you will die forever. Tell your story. In memory of Serene. It will clear your conscience so that you can meet your end in a manner that shows some honor. You were once honorable. Be that again."

His eyes fixed on hers and she thought she saw something within them that spoke of the hopelessly lost finding a small light to lead them back home.

"I could only do what Hemlock instructed me to do. She and Serene formed a bond. In the dungeon," he said, looking tentatively at Wolfsbane. "You were there. Do you remember? Hemlock blamed me for attacking Queen Valada when she knew it had been Varmik. She did this to hurt Serene because I'm her brother and she loved me, knowing this would wound you as well. But in the dungeon you'll recall Hemlock saying, *I will treat him well, since he is your brother, and since you are almost family and families must stick together.* She was offering to treat me well in exchange for Serene being silent. My sister said, *I know you will treat him well.* She did this for me, so that I would not suffer because of Hemlock's sadism. It was her agreement to keep secret about what Hemlock had done, how she murdered Portia and distorted information she brought back to King Moarte, that Queen Valada was dead. Serene did this for me."

"How do you know this?" Wolfsbane said, his voice hard and laced with skepticism. "You had been almost drained. Nearly dead."

"I know it because I remember it. And also because Hemlock reminded me of it. She used this against me, the knowledge that Serene was no longer able to enforce this agreement with her presence."

Wolfsbane said nothing but Valada could see him contemplating all this.

"She was my sister and she loved me," Rivard said. "She tried to protect me, but of course, she couldn't." His voice broke.

Valada said softly, "Tell us why you murdered her."

Rivard looked horrified. "I could do nothing else. Hemlock commanded it."

"You should have resisted!" Wolfsbane yelled, his patience near the end.

"We need to hear what happened," Valada reminded him.

Rivard looked as if he would cry and once again Valada wondered if vampirii *could* cry. Instead of tears, sorrowful words came from his pale lips. "Hemlock whipped me that night, in the room with Columbine and Nightshade, so she would have an alibi. I could tolerate the physical pain but as I weakened, I could not fight her commands in my mind. Finally, late, just before sleep, she handed me a vial of liquid and told me to visit Serene and if there was medicine there, to empty this into it. If not, to put some on Serene's lips. If I did not comply, she would chain me out in the sun and it would take days for me to die. And she wouldn't let me die, she'd bring me back, and burn me again and again."

"You must have known it was poison," Valada said, and she could see that Wolfsbane was about to destroy Rivard.

"She didn't tell me what it was." He paused. "I suspected."

"Why did you not resist? Or come to me or Belladonna for help?"

"I couldn't resist. You don't know her power. Another, not so weak, maybe, but not me." He paused again and looked wretched. "I betrayed the one person who loved me, who I loved, and now at the hands of the one who loved her most and who she loved most, I hope to find my sister in another life and beg her forgiveness. She will forgive. She was gentle and sweet and kind and—"

"She was, but I am not!"

Valada did not see Wolfsbane's arm move but suddenly it was in Rivard's chest. Rivard's face froze in shock but it did not reflect pain so much as a rapidly growing sense of acceptance of fate.

When Wolfsbane finally yanked his bloody arm out, it was with a war cry that blended fury and pain that filled the night. Rivard's body fell backwards and hit the ground.

In his hand, Wolfsbane clutched a still-beating heart and dug the talons of both hands into it, his long nails piercing the organ, his fingers imbedding deeply.

Valada felt stunned, unable to react, wanting to look away from the grisly sight of Wolfsbane holding the dripping heart to the sky as if offering it to his beloved.

Three sharp claps filled the air and Valada spun around to find Hemlock behind her, viewing the scene with glee in her eyes and her lips twisted cynically downward.

"Brother, you impress me. I didn't think you had it in you. I thought you would forgive him like the weak link you've been since the Sapiens slave became the Master and you became her slave and she took over your existence."

Wolfsbane moved towards Hemlock. "You are the cause of this!" he snapped. "You have always spread chaos and pain around you, since birth."

"Perhaps I was born evil, Brother, but evil wins the night."

"Not this night," Wolfsbane said.

"Oh, I think this and every night. King Moarte is about to divorce his wife and he will be searching for a new wife and a new second. I see you have just killed a vampir, and one that belonged to the Queen, and you as well as I know the penalty for that—death. This," and she gestured towards Valada, "will be banished or killed or perhaps just relegated to the status of slave, and I am not adverse to taking her. There is no evidence that I have done wrong. I see nothing to stand in my way now."

Wolfsbane hesitated, and Valada's heart sank. If what Hemlock said was so, she had removed all the obstacles in her path on the route to acquiring power. Wolfsbane's fate was sealed. Valada's fate also.

"The King will hear of this!" Valada said bravely.

And Hemlock laughed. "Yes, I am sure that he will listen to you and believe you above me. Me, who will soon be Queen and then, when Moarte is gone, ruler."

Valada shook her head, unable to speak. She could not believe how this could come to pass but it all sounded so smooth, so reasonable. "Moarte will believe Wolfsbane."

"Ah, but my brother is honorable. His first duty is to admit that he killed Rivard, and he will not deny it. In fact, he cannot deny it; it is not in his nature and frankly, I can insist that he swear on the memory of Serene."

"You betrayed us!" Wolfsbane said, and both Hemlock and Valada knew he referred to treason.

"Only a means to an end. I couldn't take the chance that Serene would be found. Unfortunately, she was."

"So you conspired with our enemy and sacrificed vampirii? You are despicable!"

"No vampirii died. Only slaves. The King will be eager to believe Rivard acted on his own. Rivard and the Sapiens warriors set a charge in the tunnel."

"You killed Serene!" Valada said. "Admit it if you dare!"

"I have nothing to lose by admitting it. No one will believe you, the guard saw only Rivard enter the room and he is no more. My brother will be executed the moment he returns to the stronghold. His Sapiens slave had to die."

"To keep her from telling what she knew. And you had agreed to treat Rivard well if she kept quiet."

Hemlock sneered. "I have no intention of ever abiding by an agreement with a Sapiens."

"What has made you so evil?" Valada asked.

Hemlock walked to her brother and took Rivard's heart from his grasp. While Valada watched, the vampir turned the organ over and over, thick blood dripping between her fingers. Suddenly she bit into the organ, letting blood drip down her chin, her tongue lapping at it, her eyes scarlet and insane as the ecstasy of power took her over.

Then, just as suddenly, her face distorted. Her breathing became labored and she seemed disoriented. She dropped the heart and her skin paled beyond its normal color, her eyes paling as well, her breathing growing irregular. She seemed confused. Her balance was gone and she stumbled and fell to the ground, her body twisting in spasms that spoke of seizure.

"What's happening?" Valada wanted to know.

"Just my sister receiving a taste of her own medicine," Wolfsbane said. "Cyanide imbedded in the heart. I made sure it was on my hands, under my nails. It's why I took Rivard's heart and did not drain him; I wanted to make sure the heart was poisoned. I knew Hemlock would have used him to find you. She would come here and I felt her arrive. And she would be greedy enough to want to taste his heart."

"You poisoned her. As she poisoned Serene."

"But it's not enough," he said, bending over Hemlock, who still convulsed, but Valada could see the symptoms were already subsiding. "What would be a lethal dose for a mortal will not be so for a vampir. There are only two ways to ensure that she does not rise from the dead."

With unbelievable strength, and despite Hemlock fighting back, he tore her head from her body. Blood spurted from the neck, coating him, coating the grass. Then he plunged his hand into her chest and ripped out her heart.

Valada was paralyzed with horror. This, she realized, was the mortal nightmare. The vampir, unfettered and unleashed, and she could only stare in a kind of ghastly awe.

Finally, Wolfsbane stood, staring at the heart as if mesmerized by it, like a madman, as if it were a red jewel. Or some prize or trophy he had won. He looked insane to Valada and she felt nervous. He had just killed two vampirii. And she was still here, with him, alive.

He turned to her, his eyes blazing red and clearly crazed, but said calmly, "Come, my Queen. I will return you to the stronghold and you will reign beside your husband."

He bent to pick up Rivard's heart and held one in each hand, then looked at her again, waiting, and finally repeated, "Come."

She felt afraid but had no choice. She went to him and put her arms around his neck and he took flight immediately, still holding the bloody hearts of his sister, and Rivard, the unfortunate slave.

Valada clung to him, aware throughout the flight that something in Wolfsbane had died. He had gone from being level-headed and emotionally even-keeled to having lost his way completely. She remembered what Belladonna had told her about the most severe vampiric crimes and knew he had signed his own death warrant. She imagined that the loss of Serene had put him over the edge and that these acts were only the tip of a monstrous iceberg which had encased him in a terrible grief. He evoked her pity. She must find a way to save him because he had just saved her and she owed him a huge debt. She knew he would readily admit to what the vampirii considered crimes punishable by death and there might not be time for him to repeat all that Hemlock had said to them.

The flight back was much shorter, less than two hours, and she talked to him as they flew, her voice in his ear, telling him what she saw happen in the clearing, reminding him of what Rivard said, what Hemlock said, and what Hemlock did. She repeated all this over and over, but he did not respond. She wanted him to understand what she would tell Moarte. "You must confirm what I say, Wolfsbane. There has been too much denial and not only my reputation is at stake. My marriage is, my very life, and especially the life in my belly of Moarte's child that I have just recently conceived. All of this depends on you."

Maybe it was the knowledge of the child that brought him back if only briefly from whatever place within that he had retreated to, but finally he nodded.

The moon still hung in the sky when they arrived at the fortress and entered through the massive doors to find the throne room crowded with vampirii. Moarte sat tensely on the throne, and Belladonna, looking worried, sat by his side.

Wolfsbane walked to the front of the room as if he were in a trance, his demeanor so strange that all the vampirii in the chamber stopped talking to watch him. He was covered in blood and he carried something in each of his hands but Moarte wasn't certain what until he came closer, and then the bloody red hearts were obvious.

He waited for Wolfsbane to speak, aware that Valada had followed him in and stood next to him looking pale, tense, and frightened.

Belladonna, though, could not wait. "What is that you carry, Wolfsbane?"

"Hemlock's heart and the heart of Rivard," Wolfsbane said. "I murdered both of them."

The hush that had fallen over the room split into sound as everyone spoke at once. Moarte was just as glad because he needed a moment to try to gather his thoughts and control his emerging feelings.

Wolfsbane looked as if he'd lost his mind and Valada looked terrorized. He didn't know exactly what to do but felt he had to control this situation and raised a hand, saying "Silence!" his voice booming over the din.

The vampirii fell silent and he said right away, "All vampirii and Sapiens will leave the throne room now but for my war council."

Slowly the vampirii and Sapiens left the hall until only those Moarte had chosen remained, including Valada.

When he felt the chamber was secure, Moarte said, "Tell me what happened, Wolfsbane."

"I found Rivard and murdered him. My sister appeared, and I murdered her as well. I brought their hearts as proof of my actions." He lifted his blood-coated arms as if his bloody hands and the red vital organs he held were a gift.

"Then I now must convene a trial. The charge is murder of vampirii, one the slave of Queen Valada, the other a warrior and member of this council. The council will weigh the evidence against you and render a verdict and I will pass judgment. The trial will now commence. Vampir justice is swift."

After a brief pause, Belladonna said, "The circumstances are mysterious. Wolfsbane, would you care to enlighten us?"

"No," Wolfsbane said.

That caused murmuring among the war council.

Valada opened her mouth to speak and Moarte saw a movement out of the corner of his eye that Belladonna made, touching her head, and Valada closed her mouth and said nothing.

"Wolfsbane, you are charged with murder. Can you not relate what occurred? Perhaps it will mitigate your acts," Moarte asked, hoping against hope that his second could explain this.

"No, my King, I cannot."

Moarte sighed, knowing that the council could do nothing but find Wolfsbane guilty of the crimes to which he had confessed. Crimes that would see him executed before the next sunrise.

It burdened his spirit with a great heaviness. He realized he should not have let Wolfsbane go after Valada and Rivard, and yet again had gone against his instincts. His second had too much at stake, his emotions were too volatile. And now it had come to tragedy and Moarte felt responsible. Wolfsbane would die tonight because of his King's error in judgment.

Another mistake! He had made so many of late. Could he not do anything as it should be done? Even if the vampirii did not yet question his rule, *he* questioned it. Perhaps he was not fit to rule.

Moarte was compelled to go through the motions of instructing the council to consider what had occurred, the confession of the accused, Wolfsbane's past and his exemplary existence and service to the vampirii to this point in time, the circumstances surrounding these actions, the cause of these actions—which Moarte insinuated was due to an emotional upheaval brought about by Serene's death. And finally he said, "Before the council retires to render a verdict, are there any here who can speak of these crimes, or who can speak on behalf of Wolfsbane?"

He was not surprised when Valada said, "I will speak of the circumstances," and Moarte felt torn.

"Be concise," is all he could say to her, "and stick to the subject." Again, he saw a movement by Belladonna. This time, her hand went to her heart. He did not know what that meant but Valada smiled briefly at his mother and then her eyes turned to his. "I will be as brief and direct as possible, my King." And he was impressed by her level-headedness, but wary that it would dissipate into unbridled emotion and he sat tensely worried and waiting for her to condemn herself by her presentation.

He wanted to do something but there was nothing he *could* do. The next trial would be hers. And his next official act would be divorce. But he said, "Proceed."

She turned towards the war council who stood near the throne and took moments to look into each of the eleven pairs of eyes. "I know that most of you do not know me. Or rather, you know me as the daughter of my father, the demonic Sapiens King Zador, and now the wife of Moarte, King of the vampirii. My time in your realm has been very brief. I do not yet understand your ways and I realize that I have breached vampirii etiquette and as well have made some serious mistakes, all of which I deeply regret. I beg your pardon if I have inadvertently offended any of you, or the vampirii nation. I say all this because I want you to know that despite my failures, my intentions have been honorable and what I am about to tell you is the truth, and I beg that you bear with me as I relate these events."

Moarte glanced at the eyes of his warriors. He saw skepticism in some, but most showed an openness he would not have expected. Even Columbine and Nightshade, who had been in the room and heard Valada's outburst against Hemlock, seemed willing to listen.

"One of my biggest mistakes was not trusting my husband."

She turned towards Moarte and he was startled to hear this confession before his war council. Vampirii did not display emotions in this way or make public statements. And yet, a quick glance around the room showed him vampirii eyes that did not rebel at this expression. He hoped their reactions were not simply taking what she said for their amusement.

From the corner of his eye he again saw his mother make a gesture towards her heart and he turned to look at Belladonna but she was looking at Valada.

"My husband, my King, I do not know if it is in your heart to forgive me for this lack of trust. I should have told you all I knew in private and trusted that you would deal with it in an honorable way. I was afraid. That is not an excuse, just a statement."

Before he could say or do anything—although he had no idea what he might say or do—she turned back to the vampirii and began telling them things that had happened. "As you all know, Hemlock returned here with news that I was dead when, in fact, I was a prisoner in my father's dungeon. This information was passed to Hemlock by the Sapiens slave Portia, who was sent on this mission by Serene. Portia never returned to the vampirii stronghold nor to the Sapiens city. Tonight I found her body. The throat shows the mark of the vampir and her heart had been torn from her chest."

A murmur filled the vast space until Moarte held up a hand. When the silence took hold, she continued.

"Her body was left by her murderer in the sun to burn, then covered with leaves and some dirt by Serene, who found her and, had Serene not been captured by my father and had she not died here tonight, she would have told this story herself. Serene did tell Rivard of the murder of Portia and the misinformation conveyed to King Moarte about my death. He told Belladonna and me. This is how I knew where to look for Portia's body. Wolfsbane came to find me and heard Rivard say all this tonight and he also saw Portia's body in the clearing and can verify what I have just told you."

She turned to Wolfsbane who stood directly across the room from her looking shell-shocked but said in a monotone, "Yes, I heard all this and saw the body."

Valada continued. For the sake of the vampirii who were not in the room when Serene was found dead, she explained how Hemlock had given Rivard to her and why, and also what Rivard had told both her and Belladonna. She said it was why she went to find proof of her accusations against Hemlock. "I knew King Moarte needed proof. Wolfsbane knew that Rivard was controlled by Hemlock still and that she would know where I went. He found Rivard and me in the clearing with Portia's body. Rivard confessed everything to him, including how and why he murdered Serene, by Hemlock's orders. Wolfsbane can verify this."

Once again, he said, "Yes. Rivard's confession is as Queen Valada described."

Valada then told the vampirii what she had overheard the Sapiens warriors saying in the cave. The members of the war council began to mutter and Moarte had to silence them again. "Continue," he told Valada.

She repeated what Rivard confirmed before Wolfsbane, how Hemlock had sent him to tell the Sapiens King of the vampirii invasion plan through the tunnel that led to the city. Valada then repeated everything that Rivard said Serene had told him.

Wolfsbane verified this to the now deadly-silent room.

And finally, Valada told them, "Wolfsbane killed him, but Rivard no longer belonged to me."

She glanced at Belladonna and Moarte saw her again signal to the heart. "I had already renounced him as my slave and declared that he no longer belonged to me. He had been sent to murder his sister, my friend, Wolfsbane's lover, with cyanide, as I imagine you have all learned by now was the cause of Serene's death. Wolfsbane did not murder the slave of your Queen. He took the life of a traitor, a murderer and a victim of Hemlock's brutality. Wolfsbane enacted vampir justice by killing the one who had killed Serene, who meant so much to him."

She turned to Wolfsbane, who could only nod. His eyes were so haunted that Moarte was stunned.

Finally, Valada got to Hemlock. "She came just as Rivard was killed. She mocked Wolfsbane and called him weak. Through his questions, she admitted to all that I have told you."

She turned and Wolfsbane said, "Yes."

"She confessed to directing the treasonous act in the tunnel, and the murder of Serene. She declared that Wolfsbane would be charged with killing Rivard, put to death, and she would be named Moarte's second. Then she said that Moarte would divorce me and she would marry him, and I would be nothing but a slave. But she wouldn't let it get that far because I would not make it back to the stronghold tonight alive, and my body would never be found and Wolfsbane could do nothing about it. She saw the heart of Rivard in his hand and demanded it be given to her and snatched it from Wolfsbane's grasp. She bit into Rivard's heart as she had Portia's then looked at me saying mine would be the next she tasted. She was about to attack me and Wolfsbane protected me."

"How do we know that it was she who bit into the heart of the slave girl Portia?" Nightshade asked.

Valada reached to the hem of her skirt and pulled out a blackened object and held it up. "This is Portia's heart. And if you will compare the teeth marks to those in Rivard's heart, you will see that they belong to the same vampir. Hemlock's body, the body of Rivard, and the shallow grave containing the body of Portia are all in the first, the largest clearing at the back of the mountain, within vampirii territory, where we left them. If you examine them, you will see their condition confirms what I have told you. If you examine Hemlock's teeth, you will see that they match the bite marks in both hearts and in Portia's neck."

"Nightshade," Moarte said, "assign three swift vampirii to go to the clearing immediately and bring these bodies back."

Immediately Nightshade left the chamber and Moarte said, "We will await his return before proceeding. In the meantime, let us examine the three hearts. Wolfsbane!"

Wolfsbane brought the hearts to Moarte, who came down from the throne to take Rivard's heart while Columbine, who had gathered around her King with the other members of the council, took the other heart which had belonged to Hemlock. Moarte held out his hand towards

Valada without glancing at her and his fingers waved her towards him. She came to him and deposited Portia's scorched heart into his free hand and only then did his eyes meet hers briefly and he felt forced by the confusion swirling within him to look away.

As he examined the bitten hearts, the other vampirii in the room drew even closer, commenting on the similarity of the teeth marks. "We all know she had a larger left incisor than the right," someone said about Hemlock, and the marks seemed to verify that it was Hemlock who had bitten into both the heart of Rivard and that of Portia.

When Nightshade returned, he said, "It is done, my King. There are warriors en route now. We should have the bodies here well before sunrise." Then he, too, examined the physical evidence.

Belladonna had moved to Valada and was talking with her, which Moarte noticed.

Finally, he had seen enough and needed time to think. He announced to his council, "I will leave this evidence with you to examine further, should you wish to. I do not see the need to imprison Wolfsbane. He came here of his own volition and confessed readily. I do not anticipate him vanishing. And you may wish to speak with him."

There was a general approval of this decision.

"We will reconvene when the bodies arrive and are examined by all of us. Then you can weigh the evidence for your verdict."

With that, he left the chamber quickly.

"Go with him!" Belladonna encouraged her, but Valada felt worried. Her mother-in-law placed a hand to her own heart again, as she had during much of proceedings, and said, "This is the right moment. You must feel that."

Valada did. She heeded this signal and the advice, to align with what was in her heart, despite her fear, and immediately followed Moarte.

She caught sight of him headed through the public gardens and from a distance watched him unlock the gate to his private garden. He entered but did not relock the gate.

He would, of course, know that she followed him—his vampir sense would have picked up on her presence. She took the unlocked gate as an invitation.

Valada stepped into the enormous garden and was immediately astonished by the cultivated beauty surrounding her. She knew he came here to think and to rest his mind and spirit when he was especially troubled and a lush world like this was the perfect environment for meditation. Everywhere were flowers of all types, roses of the deepest red they were almost black, and climbing along one stone wall a verdant ivy. The ground was a carpet of tulips in a variety of colors, white night bloomers and deep blue and brilliant purple impatiens bordering it all. Everywhere she saw a profusion of color, shape and size in this enormous green space and the air was dense with an intoxicating mixture of perfumes. She could only imagine how it looked here under a full moon. And how it must comfort him.

She realized that he had to be the gardener who created this exotic and lush realm. No one was allowed into this garden but Moarte. That she should be here made her feel like an invader, an alien, and she was suddenly both confused and nervous, wondering if perhaps the unlocked gate hadn't been an invitation after all. The last thing she wanted to do was breach yet another one of his barriers.

A maze composed of a ten foot hedge took up the middle of the vast garden and she saw Moarte enter it and hurried to follow him in.

Instantly, she was surrounded by this high green wall of briars, the pebbled passageway only wide enough for one, and she was alone. She came to a fork and did not know which direction he went in but took a chance on the left, soon reaching another fork. This happened again and again and as time passed, she became disoriented and frightened that she might not find him, and might not find her way out.

She must have travelled the maze for over an hour and felt exhausted and more and more worried that she was trapped in here. Maybe he led her here for this purpose, a kind of imprisonment!

And then, mysteriously, when she turned a corner Valada found herself in what must be the center of the maze. The hedges were far apart, the space between them forming a square, with a black stone bench in the middle, images of Nephilim carved into the marble legs.

She sat on the bench and waited, feeling the mild air brush her skin, the heavy scent of flowers fill her nostrils. The slivered moon in the black night sky offered only a small comfort within the darkness of this maze, but it was enough.

The voice came from behind her so suddenly she jolted. "Was there truth to anything you said?"

Hearing his voice thrilled her. But she was worried. She didn't know where things stood with Moarte, and in his mind she might no longer be his wife. And why did he ask her *this* question? As if he believed she was a liar.

She took a moment to calm herself so that she wouldn't react too emotionally. "Yes, my King, all of it."

"You denounced Rivard?"

"In my mind, yes. I didn't speak the words because I wasn't sure of vampiric protocol. But I had separated myself from him. He murdered Serene, whether or not he was being controlled, and I couldn't tolerate the sight of him. I had him go into the forest to hunt for water as I searched the clearing. Still, I knew Hemlock would probably find me through him."

"And was Hemlock about to attack you?"

Here she paused, a flash of memory came of how calm Hemlock had been in Serene's room. Moarte might not believe that she could be as vile as Valada knew that vampir to be. He had not seen Hemlock as anything but calm and reasonable.

She turned to face him, staring up at his beautiful face that completely hid what he felt, like a pale mask with no expression, and she wondered why he felt he had to hide from her. This left her less sure of herself, but still she tried to speak the truth as she knew it, and from her heart, and wanted to phrase this carefully.

"Hemlock gloated over her power. As she bit into Rivard's heart, she stared at me the entire time. I could see that she already envisioned murdering me and hiding my remains. She had a long term plan and that was to marry you then eventually murder you and rule the vampirii. She admitted that as well and Wolfsbane can verify it. I didn't have a chance to tell the council, but I will."

"There is no need for the council to know this unless it becomes important. I do not think it will be."

She knew he was probably protecting himself. If they heard this they would wonder why he had not seen this in Hemlock and that would create another chink in his armor. Holding his position must be extremely difficult and for the first time she was realizing just how difficult.

Moarte came and sat beside her and she felt the tension of confusion in him. She wanted to reach out and touch him but instinctively knew that was the wrong thing to do right now. Instead, she told him, "Moarte, Wolfsbane had no choice but to kill her. She wanted him dead, and me dead, and eventually you dead so that she could take control of the vampirii. Her desire for power drove her to betray the vampirii. He was protecting you as much as me and himself. And his loyalty to the vampirii is impeccable."

"I know Wolfsbane's loyalties!" he snapped. "It's your loyalty I am not convinced of."

She felt angry. After all that she had been through, securing evidence at the risk of her life, knowing that Hemlock would find her through Rivard and likely kill her, after crafting the details of what occurred in such a way as to put Wolfsbane, who she knew Moarte loved, into the best light possible so that there was a chance he might be spared, here was yet another condemnation from him. And she refused, no matter the consequences, to live with this.

"Moarte, I did not trust you, as I confessed to all in that room. But you haven't trusted me, either. I, too, have in my heart what's best for the vampirii. And for you. My loyalties are *here*, and if you can't believe that and accept me and love me and take me as an equal instead of an inferior or an imposter or liar...a Sapiens...divorce might be the only answer. It's not what I want, especially now that I carry our second child within me."

He looked startled.

"One of the reasons I was so desperate to find Serene was that she had a remedy she had used on other women who had been victims of sexual violence and had suffered injuries like mine to their bodies. A remedy that would heal me inside and allow me to conceive again."

Moarte thought for a moment then looked at her. "Serene was not conscious in your presence; you didn't have time for this medicine."

"No, I did not. I conceived last night, the night before she was found dead."

He was silent, staring at her, no doubt remembering that night, as she did.

"Belladonna told me that in Serene's moments of awareness on her last night of existence, she offered the recipe for my healing. And, Moarte, I need it now to heal myself so that I do not lose this child as well. I did not know that your mother had the recipe until after...after what happened in the death room tonight. You impregnated me last night. I felt it, and was excited and frightened and terrified that I'm too damaged to carry this baby to its birth. I feared I'd lose this child too. I'm not making excuses for myself, but I do believe that my emotional state effected my approach tonight. I felt threatened that Hemlock would take you from me when I need you most. Not that I expect you to care about my emotions."

He turned his head sharply. "That is a wrong thing to say to your husband!"

"Then tell me, as you're telling me now, what's right and what's wrong. I've been alone all my life, never available or open to binding to another because of my evil father who betrayed me from birth and destroyed my mother before my eyes. I can learn vampir ways, Moarte. I want to be by your side. Help me. Take me into your confidence. Be *with* me, not *opposite* me. Let me walk beside you not in your footsteps. I can help you rule."

He paused, thinking for long moments, responding only to what she said last. "Our custom is one ruler."

"As is the Sapiens custom. But customs can change. And a ruler with a strong confidant is in a much better position. I know you have your mother, but even she has told me that you need to trust me more, and I must trust you above all others."

He turned away from her. "I'm not certain I'm worthy of trust. I may no longer be the best leader for the vampirii."

She was shocked to hear him say this. And at the same time aware of the delicacy of this confession of his lack of confidence.

Valada took a breath and remembered to speak with her heart. "You're a good leader, one who cares deeply about the welfare of the vampirii."

"I do care deeply and yet my decisions are not always correct. Caring is not enough to lead."

Again, she kept her tone even and her heart open. "No one's decisions are always right, not even a King's."

She stared at his profile as he stared straight ahead. "Moarte, we both need to take a chance on happiness."

He said nothing and she was quiet as well, sitting in the pleasant air of the garden, surrounded, hidden together within the maze, and time passed.

Suddenly he looked up and she followed his gaze, seeing nothing in the dark sky, hearing nothing, but apparently he did. "They have returned," he said, standing.

She felt things were unresolved between them and at first stayed seated, but when he started through the maze, she knew she had to follow or be lost here and not find her way out.

Once they were back in the throne room, Moarte seated as before, she noticed that the space beside him was empty and Belladonna stood in discussion with the council members.

Valada waited in the same place she had before, at the bottom of the steps, to the side. She looked up at Moarte but could not read him.

In the middle of the floor before the steps to the throne lay three bodies, one burnt black without a heart, one with the heart gouged out, one missing both the heart and head, the parts lying beside the bodies.

The war council was examining and discussing the evidence. Wolfsbane stood to the side as he had before, deflated, his gaze haunted.

Valada felt an urge to convey the last piece of information which she had forgotten to tell them in the hopes that it might sway them, but knew that she had to respect Moarte's wish, and understood why. And the council was distracted anyway, talking in low voices, in the language of the vampirii, which she still did not understand. She would have to wait for them to come to a conclusion.

Valada glanced at Moarte's face and it seemed even more like a stone mask than in the garden, no readable expression. She did not know whether to feel hopeful or hopeless about anything.

It seemed hours before the council broke from their circle. It was Columbine who finally spoke on behalf of the others.

"King Moarte, we have reached a verdict for the crimes of which Wolfsbane is accused, to which he confessed."

"It is?" Moarte said, and Valada could feel his tension.

"For the murder of Rivard, we do not attribute blame to him. He acted correctly, taking the life of this traitor to the vampirii who was no longer the slave of the Queen."

"I accept this verdict," Moarte said.

Valada was relieved but she could tell Moarte was not. The greater crime was still to be determined.

"For the crime of killing Hemlock, we have found Wolfsbane guilty with extenuating circumstances. We have determined that he may have forestalled the murder of Queen Valada. Also, Hemlock admitted to treason, for which the penalty is death, though normally that is up to the council to decide. It was a difficult decision but we have found that the mitigating circumstances leave us feeling compassionate towards Wolfsbane, whom we all know to be honorable and just. Your council is unanimously erring on the side of leniency and leaves the decision of punishment up to you, our King."

Moarte said evenly, "Columbine, council members, you have performed a great service tonight, and on behalf of the vampirii nation, I thank you. That you have weighed in such a balanced manner the history of Wolfsbane and the painful and troubling circumstances surrounding the murder of Hemlock speaks well of your abilities and I am honored to have you as my council members. You have reinforced my decision in your individual selection."

He stood and called, "Wolfsbane, come."

Wolfsbane, as if waking from sleep, approached the throne and knelt before Moarte, his head back, exposing his throat.

"The council has left your future in my hands. You have been an excellent second, one I have trusted, who has never let me down. I, like the council, believe you acted in a way that may not have been the best approach, but one which saved both the Queen and also punished a traitor. But, I also believe that you acted in revenge, which resulted in the death of two vampirii. Still, I see your suffering. You have been traumatized by what has occurred. It would be indecent to punish you for what amounts to an honorable act for the most part, and therefore I am superseding the immutable law of the vampirii which requires that any vampir accused of murdering another of our kind who is found guilty of that crime must be sentenced to death. If we cannot offer mercy to one of our own who has acted honorably against a vampir who has acted despicably, then we are no better than the Sapiens believe us to be. I therefore grant you, Wolfsbane, clemency for this crime and order that you undergo treatment with Belladonna to regain your strength and wisdom and to allow you time to both reflect and to revive your hope for the future in order that you may once again join the council and serve the vampirii."

There was a general murmur of agreement from the council. Moarte turned to them now. "There is another law which must be enacted tonight."

Valada felt her heart freeze. Moarte was about to divorce her! Her arms went around her middle as if to protect herself, but there was no protection against what was to come.

"Columbine, you will now function as my second, Nightshade my third. I am creating a new position on the council so that when Wolfsbane returns to us whole, he will assume the role of war strategist, a skill for which he is particularly adept. Our fight with the Sapiens King is far from over."

More murmurs of agreement from the vampirii and they gradually gathered around Wolfsbane to offer him support. Valada had the sense that this was new territory for them but they were adapting.

"And finally," he said, and her breath caught in her throat. "We must mourn Serene. While she was not vampir, she was in spirit one of our own and the beloved of one of us. There are three dead before me tonight as well. We will hold four services, these three, and Serene. The spirits of the four should not intermingle for a variety of reasons that I believe you all understand. Therefore, we will enact the rites four separate times. Our realm will be in mourning for many nights but this is appropriate. Much has occurred and there is much change we must absorb."

Suddenly, Moarte looked at Valada and motioned with his fingers, his long nails waving that she should come to him.

She walked up the steps like a prisoner going to her execution, terrified of what was about to happen. Perhaps she should kneel and bare her throat for his fangs. Probably that would not matter to him at this point; nothing would help. Her destiny was about to unfold.

Before she could do anything, he gestured towards the chair to his right.

In a daze, she went and sat beside him. He stared ahead, his face an emotionless mask, but she understood the symbolism of this seating position. He was trying to tell her in the only way he could that he wanted her with him, as his friend, his confidant, his wife, the mother of his child.

The stress she had been under for so long swelled within her and tears filled her eyes, washing down her cheeks, and she bent over and buried her face in her hands, sobbing quietly.

Moarte did not look at her. He was busy talking with Columbine and Nightshade, but he reached out and placed his hand on her head, expressing this unusual intimacy before the vampirii, letting her know that he was aware of her.

Dawn was about to arrive, solidifying the changes that had unearthed this realm. The bodies were carried outside to the courtyard for ceremonies tomorrow night. The vampirii were ready to leave the throne room, only awaiting their King's departure.

Eventually Moarte stood. "Come, Wife!" he said, and started towards the side exit. Partway there, he stopped. And waited for her to join him, to walk beside him. And she did.

ABOUT THE AUTHOR

Award-winning author Nancy Kilpatrick has published 18 novels, over 220 short stories, 7 collections of her stories, and has edited 15 anthologies, including *Nevermore! Tales of Murder, Mystery & the Macabre*, a finalist for both a Bram Stoker Award and an Aurora Award, and winner of the Paris Book Festival's Best Anthology of the Year Award. Her work has been translated into six languages. Recent original short works are included in: *Nightmare's Realm*; *Black Wings 6*; *Black Wings 5*; *Searchers After Horror*; *The Darke Phantastique*; *Zombie Apocalypse: Endgame!*; *Blood Sisters: Vampire Stories by Women*; *The Madness of Cthulhu 2*; *Innsmouth Nightmares*; and *Stone Skin Bestiary*. Two new graphic novels are: *Nancy Kilpatrick's Vampyre Theater* and her story "Heart of Stone" in *Tales From the Acker-Mansion*.

Friend her on facebook.com/nancy.kilpatrick.31
Follow her on twitter.com/nancykwriter
Check out her websites: nancykilpatrick.com

Curious about other Crossroad Press books?
Stop by our site:
http://store.crossroadpress.com
We offer quality writing
in digital, audio, and print formats.

Enter the code FIRSTBOOK
to get 20% off your first order from our store!
Stop by today!